THE FIRST AND LAST SUMMER

E5

RUTH SABERTON

RS

To dear Valerie
Thank you for sharing the real life La Colina with me.

Published by Millington

CHAPTER 1

KAT - NOW

It was the temperature that hit Kat first; the kiss of warmth which always greeted new arrivals when they stepped from the plane into Mallorcan sunshine. Even though it was still early morning, heat rose from the tarmac and the air shimmered with a promise of more to come. The percussion of the airport filled her with anticipation, a symphony of activity from the drone of planes taxiing, the thump of landings, the whine of trucks snaking along to collect luggage, and the rumble of buses lumbering from the terminal to meet dazed arrivals. Above all this was the musical cadence of a foreign language. Spanish. Her mother tongue. Music to her ears.

Kat blinked as she stepped out onto the mobile stairs. Almost as shocking as the sudden blaze of sunshine was the realisation that her body and her head were not in sync. She no longer moved as she expected to, and now she stood swaying like a sapling in a gale. Frailty was a frustration she would never become accustomed to, and she was certain nobody ever did. The *me* who dwelt within her, the one who inhabited that deep-down place where she was purely herself, was still twenty-one: dark-haired, rebellious and strong.

Kat sighed. What ever happened to the lively girl who'd first landed here, when disco ruled the pop charts and people looked at one another rather than at their phones? The girl who had thought nothing of rickety steps and had walked to the terminal with a heavy rucksack slung over her narrow shoulders. The girl who had hitched a ride to a sleepy fishing town surrounded by mountains and olive groves, with narrow streets, whitewashed buildings and bougainvillea spilling over stone walls, and with no more to guide her than an address scribbled on an envelope?

Where was that girl? When had she vanished? Kat hadn't noticed her slip away until it was far too late. She had returned recently to berate her older self for being cautious and boring, and she was here now, urging Kat to give the stairs a go rather than wait for the promised assistance. *Independent to the last, that's me,* thought Kat with a surge of pride. And if she tripped and toppled down, it probably would be the last thing she did. Death by aeroplane steps. What a way to go! Darling David would die laughing.

Or he would if he were still alive. Oh dear. It was still a shock to remember that he wasn't here. Time to try those steps. How hard could it be?

"Señora Beauchamp! Be careful! We'll assist you."

An air stewardess materialised at Kat's side. She laid a French-manicured hand on Kat's arm as she did her best to stop a silly old biddy from throwing herself head first down the steps.

Although Kat longed to say she was perfectly capable, she knew this would not be true. It had been enough of an effort to walk through the aeroplane from her seat to the door unaccompanied, and at Gatwick she had been driven to the plane on a special cart complete with flashing light and beeper. People had scattered and Duty-Free whizzed by in a blur. It would have been fun if it had been a choice. Since the annoying episode with her heart, Kat's choices seemed to narrow daily.

So she admitted defeat and stood back while all the other passengers disembarked. She picked her battles more wisely the days, but the twenty-one-year-old version of her was seriously unimpressed with this surrender.

Pipe down, Kat told her sternly. *One foot in the wrong place and we'll have a broken hip. How much would you like to spend the next two months in Palma Hospital? No pool there.*

Twenty-one-year-old Kat did not like the sound of this at all. She had packed a new crocheted bikini and bright red nail varnish that would have outraged her mother (*Katalina! ¡Madre de Dios! Only harlots paint their toenails red!)* She had backed off, though not without sulking.

Kat smiled at the stewardess: "Thank you, my dear. That's very kind of you."

"Oh, not at all! Sunshine Air is the airline that cares!" the stewardess trilled.

Deep inside, twenty-one-year-old Kat rolled her eyes.

Then she was helped slowly, and rather ceremoniously, out of the aeroplane and down the steps to where a young man was waiting at the foot with a wheelchair and a cheery "*¡Hola!*"

He was very handsome. Twenty-one-year-old Kat was very impressed by his sloe-dark eyes, slightly too long raven hair, and muscles clearly visible beneath his tight white Sunshine Air T-shirt. Her elderly counterpart was simply glad he had the strength to push her all the way to the bus and, once they'd arrived at the terminal, through the busy arrivals area.

Thank goodness she still held an EU passport and could bypass the long queues. The noise and bustle were overwhelming, and she felt quite dizzy. When had Palma's airport grown so big? It was as though she'd blinked and missed the change. The world was moving on without her, it seemed. She couldn't keep up.

Kat felt this way a lot lately. Change was coming to her, too. It had crept up on her like a game of grandmother's footsteps, and it was too late now to stop it. She was older and times were changing. Her life was changing, too, which was why she had returned to Mallorca for one last summer.

Outside the airport terminal, which had quadrupled in size since her first visit all those years ago, José was waiting for her with the Mercedes. The roof of the faithful car was lowered, as Kat always insisted it was on her arrival, and the blue paint gleamed as brightly as the day it rolled out of the factory. But it was a shock to see that José's hair, what remained of it, was as white as the clouds hugging the mountaintops beyond the streets of Palma.

When had he grown old? Kat wondered, with a jolt. It seemed like only yesterday that he and Jenny had applied for the housekeeping role at Casa la Colina. They had been a young couple, full of excitement, and utterly thrilled when David hired them, but now they were nearing retirement age, if not already past it, and her beloved husband was gone. It would be four years this autumn – four years which felt like one hundred and four without him.

Grief was etched into the landscape of Kat's life these days. It was an ingested loss lodged deep in her very soul, and she felt close to tears, for David should be here now, dressed in his favourite linen suit, the one he always wore travelling to La Colina, and calling greetings to José while cutting a path through the crowded concourse with his wheelie trolley like a fedora-hatted Moses. Loss ambushed her anew, and for a moment Kat could not speak.

"Señora Beauchamp! *¡Hola!* Welcome home!"

José was out of the car – more slowly than usual, she noticed with a pang – and he hurried to help her out of the wheelchair. A rapid-fire exchange in Spanish followed between Kat's long-time handyman and the handsome wheelchair attendant, who was insisting he was owed a big tip for escorting the old English lady so far.

Kat was amused. So much for Sunshine Air's caring ethos! She was also tickled, as always, when a local assumed she was a typical wealthy Brit whose Spanish extended only as far as asking for the bill or requesting directions to the loo. She still laughed on remembering how David had once asked a bartender for two toilets, mixing up the words for 'toilet' and 'beer'. The bartender and Kat had been in stitches. No wonder she had always done all the speaking here. It was no hardship, since Spanish was Kat's second language, courtesy of her mother. Kat's full name was Katalina Innes de Morales Brown, quite a mouthful for a five-year-old, so Kat Brown she had become.

And later, much later, Kat Beauchamp.

"José, just give the man a tip," she said sharply in Spanish. "Ten euros should cover it."

It was gratifying to see the surprise on the young man's face, closely followed by horror as he realised she had understood all his insults about having to wheel this old English lady so far. But Kat let it go. Her twenty-one-year-old self might have relished a fight, but the older version was more than happy to be relaxed. This dear boy probably hated his job and was tired of watching British people buy up all the property on his beautiful island. Kat sympathised. Besides, she was tired from the flight, and only wanted to be on her terrace watching sailing boats head out to sea as she sipped a glass of ice-cold wine. Where did confrontation really get you? The moral high ground was a lonely old place.

With the luggage stowed, José helped Kat ease into the passenger seat. She pulled her sunglasses from the glove box. Faithful old friends, they were big Chanels given for a special occasion, now lost in the fog of memory. She had a vivid memory flash of wearing them while David hunched over the wheel of this very car, guiding it round a hairpin bend near Sant Elm. She had laughed at something, before shrieking as he swerved to avoid a man with a donkey and almost drove them off the road and into thin air. Shaken, they had gone into the small town and recovered at a waterfront restaurant. David had ordered a large glass of Albariño, and Kat had driven home.

Funny, the things she could remember. That must have been over fifteen years ago, but it felt like yesterday. Sometimes she could barely remember what she'd had for breakfast. The mind was a strange thing. More and more, she found herself falling through crevices in time. What if one day she could not claw her way back?

"You look deep in thought, Señora," José remarked, finally sliding the gear stick into fourth as they hit the main road out of the city. The engine and Kat heaved a sigh of relief.

José was a more cautious driver than David. Her husband would have been flooring it out of Palma, weaving through traffic like he was at Brands Hatch, taking exception to anyone who honked, and cutting up all and sundry. He would have been home in under half an hour, unlike José, who pootled along in the slow lane.

Probably metaphorical, Kat thought. There was another man who had once driven fast along this road, but in a bumpy old truck. Her head resting against the soft linen of his shirt, she had breathed him in and wanted that ride to last forever. Of course it could not. Nothing ever did.

She smiled at José: "I was just thinking that there aren't many donkeys on the roads these days."

"No indeed, Señora. It is very busy now. Because … *porque* …"

He frowned, searching for the English required to continue, so Kat switched to Spanish as nonchalantly as changing hats, and they chatted easily all the way to Puerto Andratx, catching up on each other's news and swapping stories of their respective families. José and Jenny's children had played with hers. Now those children had children of their own, almost impossible to believe.

How was she a grandmother? She did not feel any different from the girl who had first stumbled, blinking, into the sunshine at Palma Airport all those years ago. Where had the time gone? And why had she not appreciated the humdrum more? Known the beauty in the everyday? Kat wished she had paused to savour each second, instead of always rushing forward to the next milestone. If only she could go back and tell her younger self to slow down. To relish being young and not be in such a rush to hurtle through her life.

The road swung south, and as the land peeled away to the sea Kat spotted the first outlying indications she was close to Andratx: a large supermarket, a sprawling garden centre, a towering billboard advertising a waterpark. Then came the houses. So many houses. When she had first arrived here, the town was small and none of these buildings existed. The roads were quiet. The hillsides still bare. Tourism was in its infancy, and Andratx little more than a sleepy town in the hills, its ancient church watching over the narrow streets and the port below as it had done for centuries.

By force of habit, she looked up into the hills, searching for Clara's *finca*. The glass cube that had replaced it decades ago glinted in the late morning sun, bright as a migraine and with edges as sharp as the blade Clara had used to slice the haunch of Serrano ham which swung from a beam in her kitchen. Kat ached for what had been, but accepted that Clara would have approved of the modern design. Maybe it was not the building itself, though, that Kat missed, but the people they had been. Young. Hopeful. Dreaming. Thinking only of parties and kisses. They had had no idea of the pain to come. Of the losses.

But that unawareness was youth's gift, was it not?

Another memory surfaced: an ink-dark night: moonlight like chalky thumbprints on the sea, guitar music, lips that tasted of limoncello, her hands on his face pulling him closer …

She blinked, and the image dissolved. There was only sun and road and traffic. The past was long gone, but it underlay everything, and had made Kat Beauchamp the woman she'd become.

"The island's very different now," José was saying as he navigated a roundabout, cutting up a Jeep as he switched lanes. "There's a lot of unrest about tourism and holiday homes, Señora. People are angry. There is no well-paid work. They cannot afford houses, and their children must leave the island. Ours did. I do not know where it will end."

Kat nodded. It was the same everywhere, but she understood the frustration people felt. Was she part of the problem, with her second home and half-life here? Probably, but she loved this place and La Colina was part of her. Besides, she was half-Spanish, if not Mallorcan, and the island was her home too. Kat accepted that change was inevitable, and she knew it was coming for her and for La Colina. It had to. Although that made her sad, Kat understood that the old must make way for the new. This was how life had always been. There were beginnings and endings, not all of which were wanted or happy, and in her life Kat had seen plenty of these. An ending was to be the focus of this stay for this summer at La Colina, one of more than she could count, would be a first in a way. It would be her first *last* summer.

José was busy describing how the island had changed since the 1970s, when Kat had first visited. As he talked, she let her thoughts drift, blinking several times to distinguish the present from the past. Time was peculiar; ebbing, flowing, accelerating, dragging. If José slowed the car just a little more, and if she squinted, Kat was sure she would see her younger self on that scooter, long black curls tangling in the wind, bare legs sun-kissed, arms around a lean boy in front of her, her cheek resting on his back. The place between angel wings of shoulder blades that smelt of lemons and rosemary and him. Oh, so much of delicious *him*.

Over six decades later, her pulse still kicked and her blood fizzed when she recalled how it had felt to be that girl. What a gift to be young and carefree and utterly, gloriously, totally in love, with no idea of what lay ahead. What would she say to that girl now? she wondered. What advice would she give her younger self?

Stay away from scooters, she thought sadly. *You'll fall from one, and it'll break your heart.*

But twenty-one-year-old Kat would not have listened to such sage advice. She had followed her heart and chosen adventure, as young people will. Kat had no regrets, but she wished she could spare that girl the pain that had followed her first summer in Mallorca.

Now José was talking about Jenny, his wife. Her health was not so good. Her knees were painful, and she was struggling with the housework. She had done her best to prepare the house, but he wanted Kat to understand things might not be quite as she remembered. Not as *perfecto*. There might be some dust. Not all the rooms were made up …

Kat reached out to touch his arm and halt the flow of worries. She and José straddled a curious line – more than employee and employer, yet not quite friends. The Mallorcan couple had been unobtrusive wallpaper for decades of holidays. They had facilitated parties, fresh croissants, blue pools and clean linen. They had cared for the house while she was away, and loved it as dearly as she did. They had witnessed the triumphs, joys and sadnesses of Kat's life, but she had been on the periphery of theirs. They knew her friends, could remember who liked black coffee or who always made a fuss if the newspaper was not on the table at breakfast, but she knew nothing of their social circles. They were as familiar with La Colina as she was – perhaps more so, for they spent every day there – but she had never stepped foot inside their apartment in the back streets of the old town. Their lives were interwoven with hers yet separate. When she left for good, life on the island would continue for them. Maybe as though she had never been?

"… and Jenny struggles with all the steps to the tower room," José continued, still worried. "She was relieved when you requested the garden room, Señora."

Kat sighed. Jenny was not alone with this struggle. Kat adored her bedroom in the old guard tower. It boasted an almost three hundred-and sixty-degree view across the blue sea to the island of Dragonera, then sweeping over the port and up into the hills and cloud-scarved mountains. It was her very own princess's room. The restoration had taken years – and too much money, David had often sighed; but it had been worth every penny, for it was their private kingdom and a peaceful place to retreat when parties, guests, children and teenagers became overwhelming.

The tower bedroom was reached by a steep flight of open-slatted wooden stairs, polished to neck-breaking perfection and with nothing to save someone who tripped from plummeting to their doom. Kat had not thought twice about this when she was in her thirties, but once the grandchildren had arrived she saw danger everywhere, so David had quickly attached a heavy blue rope to the wall and secured the open landing with a glass balustrade. Then in later years he had struggled to climb the stairs. On her last visit, Kat had hauled herself up with sheer willpower, only to fret over managing the descent without falling.

This time she'd admitted defeat and opted to sleep in the garden room. Once the old kitchen of the original house, it boasted original beams and walls with deeply recessed windows. It was on the level, adjacent to the new sitting area, and possessed French doors which opened out into the garden, a splash away from the pool and with a breathtaking view out to sea.

From the garden room Kat could, were she so inclined, use her field glasses to spy onto the houses and apartments clustered on the other side of the port, buildings which had mushroomed from the pine-spiked hillside without her noticing – and which had caused David to huff at the change. He had hated La Colina being overlooked, but Kat quite enjoyed it. She liked to imagine the lives going on behind the walls, and invented stories about who might live there. Sometimes she had to remind herself it was all in her imagination, just as she did when she caught herself weaving narratives about the superyachts which wallowed outside the port, laden with helicopters, jet skis and goodness only knew what. How dear Clara would have laughed at such ostentation. She would no doubt have wangled an invite for one of the glamorous parties, holding court as she smoked theatrically and telling mesmerising stories before falling into bed with the billionaire owner, then leaving him broken-hearted.

There I go again, thought Kat, *making up stories.* The younger version of her had loved doing that, too, and now she was older Kat found she spent more and more time daydreaming. She dreamed of her first summer here, of swimming naked, dancing at fiestas, limoncello kisses, sitting on the terrace at Clara's, dining with David at their favourite fish restaurant in the back streets ... Where was the harm in daydreaming, apart from the shocking moment when you jolted awake and remembered the present? That abrupt slam into reality never grew any less painful. It seemed a high price to pay for a few minutes' escape.

Now, the hillside across the water from La Colina – bare pink-and-orange rock and sage gorse when she had first stood outside the ruin of this house and gasped at the view – was peppered with development. One apartment block resembled an Inca temple, a similarity Kat always thought apt, since its holidaying occupants worshipped the sun and the steps ran blood-red with its setting rays.

Whenever she ventured from the garden room and strolled to the end of the terrace, Kat could lean on the balustrade and peer down at the butter-yellow mansion a dizzying drop below. This house had starred in *The Crown* as the home where Dodi wooed Diana, Princess of Wales. All make-believe of course (if Diana had ever visited Andratx, Kat and David would certainly have noticed), but she'd loved seeing a glimpse of the house on the small screen, and knew that the extravagant display of garden lights which danced in the inky water was not put on for the cameras. If she lay in bed with the doors open to the garden she could hear the waves, smell the mimosa-scented air and listen to the strains of chatter and music from the yachts moored in the bay.

Yes, the garden room was a beautiful room. Kat felt privileged to stay there, and it was where so much had started – but oh, how she longed to be tucked away in her tower with David. She ached with the knowledge that those nights in his arms would never come again.

"Señora? You *did* want the garden room?" José was worried. Sometimes he got a little confused, or so Jenny had confided to Kat.

A sudden realisation hit Kat: caring for La Colina was a lot to ask of them, for they were ageing too. Although they were devoted to La Colina they were slowly peeling away from the house towards their retirement. Kat had noticed in May that the garden was less crisp, the paint on the shutters was flaking and dust bunnies were gathering in unseen corners. The couple were trying hard, but it was a struggle; they were ready to move on, too.

Soon, Kat would have to tell José of her decision, but not yet. First, a holiday. A swan song of sunny days, apricot-ribboned sunsets and dreams of the past. Before speaking to them, she would find help for this summer. Maybe she could place an ad on the board in the supermarket? Was this still how young people found jobs? Maybe they used Facebook. Or Tik Tok – whatever *that* was all about. Kat didn't use the 'Devil's Diary', as David had always called Facebook, but her children did. The grandchildren were even worse, constantly glued to their screens.

Perhaps it would be better to ask José and Jenny to put feelers out; they knew a lot of people. Kat was just about to suggest this when José slowed the car and the town came into view. The thought slipped away. She must have seen this reveal a thousand times, but it always took her breath. The deep V of the valley. The houses dotting the apricot-and-sage hillsides, some sharp and modern, others weathered and whitewashed. Best of all was the first glimpse of the sea, cupped by the valley and harlequined with diamonds. This was all beautiful, but Kat's eyes were trained on a smudge of orange set high on the far hillside. Even with dimming sight, she recognised it immediately.

Casa la Colina. Her Eden. Her heart-home. The place where she had found love.

Her tears rose. How lucky and blessed she was.

"Home, Señora," José said gently, following her gaze. "You're home at last."

"Yes," said Kat softly. "I am."

And though the tears she blinked away were happy ones, they were bittersweet too, because Kat knew, as much as she was coming home, this would be the very last summer she would describe La Colina that way.

CHAPTER 2

KAT - NOW

There were few things better in life, Kat thought, than sitting at the big yellow table on the terrace in the shade of the sail umbrella, in the quiet of the morning. It was a simple pleasure, if one her younger self would have scoffed at, wanting to be having some kind of adventure instead.

You feel differently at this age, Kat told her. *You'll understand one day.*

It was nice to sit quietly on the terrace, just a short walk from her garden room, where she'd spent a very good night listening to the waves, and drifting off to the quiet strains of jazz floating up from a yacht moored below. Now it was a perfect June morning. Although it was only 9:30, the sun was already bright in a cloudless sky, the same sapphire blue as the stone in her engagement ring, and there was no wind. The pool below gleamed in the sunshine with scarcely a ripple. It seemed to drop over the edge of the hillside into the sea itself, as though if you dived in you could swim into a whole world of possibilities.

How Kat wished she could. She had packed her swimming costume and sunhat, but sitting on the steps with her feet in the cold water was probably as far as she'd get to a swim these days.

What a waste, twenty-one-year-old her would have said, rolling her eyes. *Aren't these properties wasted on old people?*

Yes, they are, Kat agreed, *but you'll understand one day. We don't really have time to enjoy them when we're young because we're too busy working.*

"Who are you talking to, Señora?"

Jenny had stepped out from the shade of the kitchen and onto the terrace. Her hair, once as dark as onyx, was streaked with grey, and as she balanced a tray laden with fruit salad and a coffee pot she moved more cautiously than Kat could ever recall.

"Just thinking aloud," Kat replied. Jenny probably thought she was going gaga. And maybe she was, for she found herself talking to the younger version of herself far more frequently these days. Perhaps it was being here, in the place where it had all begun, or maybe it was because so many of her friends had drifted away, relocating to be closer to family, or had taken that final voyage to the place where she could not follow.

It was lonely to be one of those who stayed the longest. Nobody ever told you that.

Of course she had her children, but Aimée and Mia were busy with their own lives and their own families. Kat didn't want to be a bother and keep phoning them every day, even when the chasm of loneliness split her in two. She never tried talking to David, probably because she knew that if there had been any way her beloved husband could have reached her he would have done so by now. She might as well talk to the wall, like Shirley Valentine. At least twenty-one-year-old Kat was still present. And she talked back.

"Did you sleep well?" Jenny asked as she set the bowl of fruit salad on the table.

Kat's heart sank a little. She knew how hard Jenny had worked to prepare the food; grapes, melons, strawberries, blueberries and pineapple all popping with colour, freshly sourced from the local market and diced by hand. Jenny had even fetched the croissants, driving up to La Colina in time to lay out breakfast just as she had done for over thirty years. Kat had the appetite of a bird these days, and a bird with a very small appetite at that, but she hated the idea of taking yet another task away from Jenny.

Instead of refusing, she said nothing as Jenny spooned a portion into a dish and stood back proudly. "There, Señora. Enjoy."

"*Gracias.*"

Kat bent to the fruit salad while Jenny watched her with the intensity of a mother monitoring a toddler in a highchair. "It's good, yes? You make sure you eat it. It's very good for you. Lots of vitamins. Good for your heart. You have taken your tablets?"

Oh Lord, Kat thought, they were worried about her. José and Jenny thought she was fading, or going into a decline or something. They weren't too far wrong, but it wasn't anything food could cure.

"Of course," she fibbed. The tablets were such an utter faff. She'd get round to them later.

She picked at her fruit and sipped her coffee, gazing out across the water. It was busy today. The sailing school was out, a shock of sails stretching from the port entrance to the rocks at the far end. Jet skis zipped up and down with frilled wakes spreading out behind them. A fishing boat was returning, seagull confetti raining down upon it. And in the distance, she spotted the whale-like hump of a super yacht setting course for another sun-drenched location. Heaven on earth.

Down by the pool, José was weeding, one hand pressed into the small of his back as he crouched down to tug up grasses and stray chamomile between the paving stones. The sun beat down and his wide-brimmed hat shaded his face, but she could tell from the way he moved that he was grimacing. The weeding seemed to be progressing with the speed of glaciation.

It was time to do something. The previous evening, she'd drifted through the empty house like a ghost, looking at photographs, reliving memories, and staring up the staircase as though the promised land lay beyond and she was Moses, fated never to reach it. Though her eyes weren't what they once were, Kat could see the house was slipping away from them all. Dust coated picture frames. Bathrooms were not as sparkling as in the past. Some of the pool cushions had become mildewed. It wasn't Jenny or José's fault. Kat appreciated that the work La Colina demanded was just too much. This summer, she was going to make sure they had help.

Kat pushed her plate away, and the spoon clattered against the bright yellow ceramic table, painted with blue and green and orange flowers. Another memory clicked into place: David, spotting the table in the dusty window of an antique shop in Palma and falling in love with it. They'd had the devil of a job to move it, and it had taken both of them, together with José, Jenny and several strapping young men from the town to lift it into place on the upper terrace. The scene of many dinner parties and lazy breakfasts, the table would stay here with the house. Who would want to move it? And it would look ridiculous back in the UK. No, Kat thought. This dear old friend belonged here, just as much as the pink geraniums, brash marigolds and lizards who darted out for the croissant crumbs she scattered.

"I think I want to go into the town this morning," she told Jenny. "Would I be able to catch a ride down with you?"

"Of course, Señora." Jenny paused. "Is there is anything you need? We can fetch it."

"I just fancied sitting in one of the restaurants with a coffee and watching the world go by," said Kat.

A coffee? younger Kat exclaimed. *What about a beer?*

Okay, maybe a glass of wine, Kat acquiesced. Her younger self could offer sensible suggestions. And what could be better than sitting in the shade of a harbourside restaurant and sipping wine so cold the glass ran with condensation, while the town paraded past?

Arrangements made, Kat spent a pleasant hour sitting at the edge of the pool with her feet in the water, reading the latest Elly Griffiths. She'd grown fond of Dr Ruth Galloway and feared the end of the book, which was the last in the series. The characters had become friends, keeping her company through the long, achingly lonely small hours when David's absence was unbearable. Ruth's saltmarsh and its mysteries had been a perfect escape. *Thank you, Elly.*

"You should write your own books, Mum," Aimée had said. The girls had grown up loving her stories, especially the ones about her misspent youth on Mallorca. But Kat never told them everything. Not even David knew it all. Some things a woman kept secret. He had guessed, of course – he'd been there to pick up the broken pieces – but a part of Kat's heart had always kept a quiet space for the dark-eyed boy with the slow smile and gentle touch. She feared that if she spoke his name too often he would vanish for good. After a lifetime of holding him close, Kat didn't think she could bear that.

The memory was precious to her. It was integral to the person she had become. She was afraid that if she released it her whole world would crumble. That was why Kat had always resisted social media. She had ignored the temptation to Google his name and find out what had happened to him. She hoped he was happy, wherever he was, and she hoped he was healthy. How strange to think he would be in his eighties now! In her mind, he was still twenty-two, lithe and beautiful with his butterscotch tan and dark eyes. He was an unselfconscious Adonis with a quiet magic about him and a laugh that made her own heart rise. He had been so beautiful it had almost hurt to look at him. She had no photograph to remind her, but Kat didn't need one; he was forever young and vivid in her dreams.

They had been so young. They had made the choices and mistakes that youngsters do when the world is black and white, and emotions run high. He had broken her heart into a thousand shards, but she had never hated him for that. Kat wished him only well. Sometimes she thought she caught sight of him: in the back streets of Andratx, in the turn of a head, in a white shirt tucked into dark trousers, in the fall of dark hair over darker eyes, in the plaintive chords of a guitar drifting from a window. But it was never him. Of course it wasn't, for he was no more that boy than she was that girl.

If he saw me now, this old woman, would he even recognise the girl he used to know?

"Señora, are you ready?"

José was juggling the car keys in his hand. He'd stopped weeding a while back, and now wore smart clothes, ready to chauffeur her to town. Jenny had cleared away breakfast, prepped lunch, and checked the fridge twice to make sure Kat would have everything she might need until they returned the following morning.

"I'm sorry. I must have nodded off," said Kat, feeling a flush of embarrassment. How long had she sat gazing into the water as if it were a crystal ball and she could spin dreams of the past?

"You're on holiday, Señora. You relax," José said. "It is good to see you resting."

"I can rest when I'm dead," said Kat darkly.

It was something twenty-one-year-old her might have said, and something her daughters hated. "Don't say that, Mum," they would groan. "It's morbid."

"It's realistic," Kat would reply.

José looked shocked by her remark, and Kat felt bad for worrying him further. The last thing she needed was her helpers feeling they had to be on suicide watch.

"British humour," she explained quickly. "Yes, it's lovely to rest."

José drove slowly down the steep winding road into Port Andratx. Kat had pride of place in the front seat of the car while Jenny sat in the back, leaning forward and giving her husband instructions and advice on how to drive a stretch of road he'd navigated every day for over thirty years. It was these rhythms of marital life Kat missed the most: the in-jokes, the familiar bickering, the well-worn grooves of a long love. Funny how you didn't notice them until they were gone.

"Just drop me by the fishing boats," she said once José had navigated double parking and a Range Rover driving the wrong way up a one-way street. She had a fondness for this part of town, the part that was still resisting gentrification and development. There was an honesty to it, a realness in the tang of rotting fish, nets piled high and trawls strewn across the elegant boulevard with no concern for tourists in their designer shoes who might trip on a coil of rope. It felt like taking a trip back in time to when Andratx was a sleepy fishing town, with no idea that the tourism boom was about to transform it forever. None of them had known, back in the 1970s, what lay ahead. Maybe it was just as well.

José duly dropped her off, and Kat walked slowly, stopping to catch her breath whenever her breathing grew laboured. She settled at a restaurant overlooking the harbour where the owners of the hire boats vied for trade. Young Kat would have been admiring the boys in board shorts and tight white T-shirts, mirrored shades pushed up into dark hair and all swagger and suntans. These days her older counterpart was more than content to sip coffee in the shade and picture the girl she had once been, in a floppy hat, flared jeans and crocheted halter top, basket swinging from her arm, sauntering by with not a clue in the world that her life was about to change forever.

There are moments in life that everything hinges upon. A word. A glance. A spontaneous decision to turn left instead of right. A moment that sets you on a path so different from the one you were on. As she watched the ghost of her younger self toss her hair and decide to head into the back streets to a fiesta, Kat knew everything that followed had stemmed from that unconscious decision. It was why she was here now.

"Señora, can I get you another coffee? A glass of wine?"

A waiter stood at her elbow – young, of course, for they were all young now. He was ready to assist, and all deference. It fascinated Kat how people responded to you once you reached a certain age and once you wore the signifiers of wealth: a good watch, a well-cut dress, a discreet but expensive handbag. Hospitality workers were trained to spot them.

She smiled. "No, thank you. Just the bill, *por favor*."

It would have been too easy to while away another hour or two with a bottle of something cold and sharp. But Kat had learned soon after David's death that solace wasn't found in the bottom of a glass. Blissful oblivion maybe, but when it wore off his absence only came back sharper than before. It was better to stay clear-headed. Easier. It was too painful to face the dawning of the truth day after day.

Bill paid, she walked slowly up a sloping side street which led towards the shops. The street was quiet; it was still early, and the restaurants had yet to fill since the tourists were on the beach or in their pools. Once this would have been siesta time. Shops would pull shutters down and the whole town would catch its breath. Kat missed those slower days; everyone hurried so much now and were always at the mercy of phones and iwatches. There was never a time to pause or just be, to watch stripes of sunlight move slowly across a tiled floor, and she thought life was poorer for it.

Kat meandered through the narrow streets, pausing to admire the bright garments hung enticingly outside the shops. The colours popped against white walls; hot pink, burnt sienna, lime green, sky blue. There were floaty dresses, tasselled scarves, towering platform sandals – the kind of beach fashion that only worked on holiday. She had wardrobes full of the stuff. Funny, too, how cheesecloth, flares, platforms and wicker baskets had all come back into fashion. It was oddly circular. And that felt right.

She paused for breath outside the fish restaurant that had been David's favourite. They had shared many a paella and bottle of Rioja at the shady corner table by the shutters or enjoyed raucous meals with friends. Now it was closed until the dinner service. She stood beneath the green awning, dreaming of the parties, the music and the laughter – until something made her look up and gasp.

It was him. He was here. Tall and strong, he was carrying

two heavy bags of shopping for the girl at his side, who looked up at him with a face like a flower turned to the sun. Her long black hair brushed the small of her back, and her orange tie-dyed skirt trailed the dusty pavement. They were utterly lost in one another as they paused at the vegetable shop, choosing the ingredients for a salad they would eat in the shade of a ruined *finca* in the hills: ripe tomatoes that popped seeds into their mouths and spilled juice down their chins, and crisp lettuce that bore no relation to the limp, salad-cream-smothered leaves eaten in England. The meal was a lifetime ago, but she could still taste it, and feel his lips when he kissed away the juice trickles on her collarbone …

Look! It's us! cried twenty-one-year-old Kat.

But it wasn't real. She wasn't there, and neither was he. Nor was the little fruit and vegetable shop they had visited. That had become an upmarket estate agency, selling properties worth dizzying sums. It was the sort of outfit where the realtors would salivate at the chance to market La Colina, and Kat almost heard the theme from *Jaws* when she looked at it.

She knew her daughters thought that La Colina should be sold. It was expensive, isolated, and difficult for her to manage. Travelling out was becoming harder too, and Brexit had made staying out there difficult for anyone who didn't hold the right passport.

"Mum, I've looked on Rightmove Spain," Aimée had said only the previous week. "Houses like yours are going for €3 million! That would buy you a lovely place near to us. And it's so hard for you to get out there, especially with your heart problems. I worry so much after you were in hospital. We all do."

Guilt needled her. Kat loved her daughters and grandchildren dearly. Was she being selfish to hold onto the property this long? To worry them? Aimée was referring to the angina attack Kat had suffered from recently, but she had enough pills to sink a ship now, and felt right as rain. The biggest issue was remembering to take them all, something she had done religiously for David but couldn't be bothered to do for herself. She must be more disciplined.

As for selling? It wasn't as though there hadn't been interest in La Colina; estate agents often left cards in the mailbox outside. José said one of the biggest developers on the island had called only the week before, asking if it was true that La Colina was coming onto the market.

"Señor López personally telephoned last week, Señora," José had said, troubled. "I told him La Colina wasn't for sale and said next door is, but he only wanted this house. No other."

Kat had heard of Tomás López. He was a big player in Mallorca and indeed in Spain, a multi-millionaire developer whose sugar-cube glass villas already colonised parts of the hillside. One had stamped all over Clara's pretty *finca*. He built stylish marina apartments and millionaires' homes. No surprise he had his eye on La Colina. Eight acres of hillside was ripe for exploitation, and after the erection of the 'Inca temple' opposite, David had blued what savings remained on buying the parcel of steep scrub land that was directly below the house.

"We don't want someone hollowing out the hillside and doing the same here," he had said. "It would be terrible. What about the wildlife? The plants? The goats?"

"You hate the goats," Kat had reminded him. David had spent a fortune trying to fence them out. They leapt into the garden, devoured every plant in sight, and on one memorable occasion chowed down on a pair of his Prada sunglasses.

"I don't hate them," David had protested. "I just don't want them in the garden. I'd much rather have them on our hill than a load of flats."

Kat had teased him about being a nimby, and he'd admitted he was guilty as charged. One of the things she'd loved most about her husband was his honesty, as well as his kindness, his generosity and his endless capacity to make her smile even through her tears.

Oh yes, he'd always been good at that.

It was funny, Kat thought now, as she gathered her breath outside the closed restaurant and prepared to continue her walk through town, funny how the things you value most as you age, are kindness, honesty, friendship, laughter. Oh yes, laughter. That mattered more than anything. Sometimes only laughter could heal anger or dry tears.

When you were young, it was all about attraction: a racing pulse, the feel of muscle beneath sun-warmed skin, a thigh pressing against yours. Who was to say that a youthful love would have gone the distance if it hadn't been cut short?

You're wrong, pointed out her younger self. *You never saw the man he became. You just knew the boy. You had the first kiss, but the woman who has his last? She'll be the one who truly knows him. You're judging a memory.*

Kat nodded. It was true. Their time had been and gone years before. She pushed the memories away and continued her stroll.

The supermarket was tucked behind the main street, elegant shops and galleries replaced abruptly by functional apartments draped with washing and adorned with plastic garden furniture. It faced a scrubby car park edged with tired metal fencing and tufted with grass growing between heaps of hardcore or poking through heat-cracked concrete, and chained shopping trolleys huddled together like old ladies at a rainy bus stop. Every so often a car pulled in or out, idling impatiently while the boot was heaped with brown paper bags and the owner fiddled with returning the trolley.

From the outside, the supermarket looked small and unimpressive, but Kat knew better. Inside it was a treasure trove: cured meats and nutty cheeses, wines lined like jewels in their racks, and fruits so glossy they looked lacquered. She and David had loved coming here. He would go up and down the aisles like an explorer, and she often teased him that the highlight of his holiday wasn't the beach, the sunshine or even her company. It was the grocery shop.

"If only you found Sainsbury's this enticing," she'd sigh.

Today, though, Kat wasn't here to stock up. She was on a mission, for surely there would be a noticeboard. Every local shop had one, and she'd brought with her the little advert she'd written out the night before, carefully copied in her best handwriting onto stiff cream card.

WANTED

A daily help for six days a week

Light household tasks, basic gardening, some assistance with meals, and occasional driving.

June–September.

Good rates, and accommodation available

For more information please contact Mrs. K Beauchamp, La Colina.

(Mobile number below)

KAT HAD DELIBERATELY USED her mobile number; she didn't want the house phone ringing and startling Jenny. The last thing she wanted was for her dear housekeeper to feel she was being replaced. Jenny had been loyal and kind for decades, but it was clear that the house, the gardens and the endless small tasks were simply too much for two ageing hands, and Kat's own were no help.

The vague plan was to find someone friendly, capable and tactful. Once she'd found the right person, she'd gently explain to Jenny that it was just extra support: someone to do the upstairs rooms and some of the trickier chores.

Kat reached into her pocket, her fingers brushing over the crisp edge of the card. She was just about to enter the shop when the door burst open and a young woman staggered out. Her arms were laden with paper bags, overstuffed and stretched to breaking point, and she was hurrying. In her haste she didn't see the uneven kerb, and she caught her sandal. As though in slow motion, Kat watched her lurch forward, bags tearing, knees buckling and shopping spilling across the dusty ground.

Without a moment's thought for her heart, for her age or her own unsteady knees, Kat hurried over.

"Careful, dear!" she called, crossing the space between them, arms out.

The young woman hit the ground with a soft gasp. Oranges bounced and rolled away. A bunch of coriander trailed behind her like seaweed. A bottle of olive oil rolled in a wide arc and settled by Kat's sandal.

The young woman was trying to right herself, brushing grit from her palms and pushing strawberry blonde hair from her flushed face.

"I'm so clumsy."

"You're certainly not," Kat said firmly, crouching with more speed than sense and ignoring the protest from her knees. "You tripped. Happens to all of us."

She began scooping up runaway oranges and plopping them back into a now slightly crumpled bag.

The young woman's hands trembled slightly as she gathered the rest. "I didn't see the kerb. I wasn't looking."

"As long as there's no real harm done. Just bruised fruit and pride."

The girl smiled then, a real smile, her eyes crinkling at the corners. She had a smudge of dust on her cheek and an air about her, something familiar. Something grounded and quietly capable. She looked to be in her late twenties, maybe thirty, with green eyes and hair the colour of Tabasco sauce. There was a smudge of blue ink across the back of her hand, and a set of keys looped on her finger with a cork keyring bearing the legend 'Casa del Mar'. Her hands were shaking so much it was quite hard for Kat to read the print.

"Thank you for helping me," she said. "You didn't have to. You're out of breath now."

Kat was indeed puffing. She pressed her hand against her breastbone. "I'm fine. Bit too old to go diving across pavements, but no harm done."

"I'm Lily," the young woman filled in, offering her hand. "Lily Martin."

Kat took it. "Katalina. But everyone calls me Kat. Or Señora Beauchamp if they're being terribly formal."

"Oh! You're Spanish!"

"My mother is. I was born in Fulham. Far less exotic."

Lily laughed. "Pinner for me. Far worse. Neither the town nor the country. Well, thank you, Señora Kat. I'd better get back. I've been way longer than I was supposed to be. No rest for the wicked."

Kat studied at her a moment longer. Lily's voice was light, but the words contained an underlying weariness, and sadness shadowed her smile.

Without overthinking, simply trusting her gut, Kat reached

into her bag and pulled out the advert. "I don't suppose you're looking for a summer job?"

"I'm already au pairing for the season," sighed Lily.

Kat nodded at the keys. "Casa del Mar. That's by the yacht club, yes?" It was one of the sugar cubes, as she recalled. There were stacks of them set around a pool. Kat had once attended a party there, aeons ago when friends of theirs had owned it. But she had no idea who owned it now; Andratx had grown so large she no longer knew anyone.

"Yes," said Lily. "Not that I've been to the yacht club. Samantha – that's the woman I work for – goes there a lot, but I have the children most of the time."

I bet you do, thought Kat. She'd met many Samanthas. "We should go there for a coffee. It's lovely," she said mildly.

Lily looked horrified. "Sam wouldn't like that. She doesn't like staff mixing with her social circle. And anyway, I've got to get back. I've been longer than I said I would. I'm supposed to be taking Tarquin and Jocasta to tennis."

The under-eye shadows and nervous energy were starting to make sense.

"Well," Kat said, still offering the card, "I might have something not quite as demanding. If you want a change of scene."

Lily glanced at the card, then up at Kat. "La Colina. The big house on the hill with the tower?"

"That's the one."

"Wow. My godmother, Clara, often spoke about it. She lived here in the seventies."

Kat's world started to spin and whirl. Was she having one of her heart episode – or did Lily just say her godmother was Clara, one of Kat's dearest friends? It was very likely, for Clara had always collected people: artists, lovers, friends and latterly a veritable army of godchildren who, she often laughingly said, bankrupted her at Christmas and had no hope of receiving any religious instruction from her.

"Clara Schneider?"

"Yes. Did you know her?" Lily's beautiful green eyes were wide.

Kat thought for a moment. How to explain Clara? Her dear, dear friend. Her mentor. Keeper of secrets. The only person who had been there for her when … but no, Kat wouldn't visit that dark place now. Better to remember Clara as the queen of Casa Cielo Azul, all flowing kaftans and ice-blonde hair and wild parties, than to revisit what had followed that first summer here.

"We were good friends," was all she said.

"Wow. That's a mad coincidence."

Kat smiled. "Or not? Clara would call it Fate and say we were meant to meet. Serendipity."

Lily nodded thoughtfully. "I'm afraid I don't remember her very well, but that does sound like what I know of her. She used to read tarot cards for my grandmother."

And she made it all up, thought Kat fondly, for she had seen this too. How Clara had loved the theatrical! Or maybe she'd had more psychic ability than they had all given her credit for?

This chance meeting was so very peculiar it felt predestined, and she could almost hear Clara's throaty laugh of joy.

The past was never far away here. That was another reason Kat loved this place so much.

Lily glanced down at the card in her hand, and then back at Kat. She seemed to relax, and Kat knew that Clara's name had thawed her, the association rendering her somebody to listen to rather than a random old biddy outside the supermarket handing out job offers.

"I'd love to know more about her life here," said Lily. "She died when I was very young, but I've never forgotten her. She seemed larger than life to me back then, and so very colourful."

"That was Clara," agreed Kat, who missed her old friend every day. For a woman she had seen only sporadically, Clara Schneider had left a huge absence when she died. "She was larger than life and way ahead of her time. She was an utter force of nature."

Lily nodded. "I remember that she seemed to fill the house when she visited."

"Even La Colina wasn't big enough to contain her personality," smiled Kat, thinking of all the parties she and David had thrown when Clara held court or misbehaved with somebody unsuitable and caused a scandal. Life had never been dull when Clara was about, and it was less sparkly without her, that was for sure.

How peculiar that this young woman who'd literally fallen at Kat's feet was Clara's goddaughter. Or maybe not peculiar at all? Perhaps her old friend was only a shimmer away and meddling to bring them together, as much a bringer together of people in death as she had been in life? Kat liked this thought a lot. Lily Wilson was meant to come to La Colina, she felt certain of it. There's a greater pattern; we just can't always see it.

"I've often wondered what the view must be like from your house," Lily was saying, turning the card over and over in her hand.

Kat smiled. So had she once, and looking had changed everything.

"Come and visit. You might like what you see. You have my number now. At the very least, come and chat about Clara."

"Thank you," said Lily. "I'd like that."

And just like that, something shifted. A thread pulled gently. A compass setting a new course. A little hello from a much-missed friend. A chance meeting. A moment of kindness that, as Kat knew these things could, might lead to something wonderful.

Kat smiled as she turned away. The future was quietly opening a door, and she couldn't help but think her old friend was holding it open. She hoped with all her heart that Lily Wilson would step through.

CHAPTER 3

LILY - NOW

Samantha was sunbathing by the pool when Lily arrived back at Casa del Mar. The French windows to the terrace were wide open, letting all the air conditioning out. A trail of wet footprints skittered across the tiles. Lily had mopped these before going to the *supermercado* and cleaned the kitchen until every surface gleamed. But now the place looked as though an explosion had happened, with Coco Pops littering every surface, sun-creamy prints smeared on the door handles, and lakes of milk souring on the floor and countertops.

Lily's heart sank. The joy of bumping into the kind lady who'd known her godmother evaporated in nanoseconds. She'd known that leaving Tarquin and Jocasta with their mother was asking for trouble. Samantha Monroe was not used to looking after her own children – or herself. At home she had a nanny, revolving short-lived au pairs, a housekeeper, a gardener and goodness knows who else to run around and pick up the slack. Here in Andratx, she only had Lily, who was meant to be a part-time au pair but had somehow become cook, cleaner, counsellor, Deliveroo and whipping boy all rolled into one.

Lily's knees stung from the fall outside the shop, and her arms ached from lugging the heavy groceries all the way back from town. For the first time since the fall, she felt close to tears. Everything was too much. What she longed for more than anything was a kind word and a hug, followed by a cup of tea and a biscuit and a sit-down in the cool while the groceries were put away and the mess cleared up.

That wasn't going to happen. It was the housekeeper's day off and, without Raquel, Lily had more hope of being swept away by a handsome billionaire who had sailed into the marina on his superyacht looking for love than she did of tea and sympathy.

She really must stop reading trashy romances, thought Lily sadly. Everyone knew real life didn't work that way. *She* knew it didn't. In real life handsome princes invariably turned into frogs, and knights in shining armour turned out to be, as her best friend Hannah always said, tossers in tinfoil. Hannah was going to be in Andratx tonight, crewing on a yacht that was mooring here for one night before heading off to Ibiza and beyond, and Lily couldn't wait to see her. Hannah had a gift for making her laugh and putting a positive spin on events, and heaven only knew Lily could do with that today. They were meeting at Tim's Bar in the port, a fun waterside place where locals and tourists mingled happily, Malibu was practically measured in pints, and the live music set toes tapping all over town. Lily had been looking forward to this reunion ever since Hannah had emailed with her itinerary.

She'd have to wear a long dress to cover her skinned knees, she thought as she dumped the shopping on the kitchen island and made her way out to the pool area. She frowned. There was no sign of Tarquin or Jocasta here, which was either alarming or a relief (she couldn't decide which), but their mother was laid out on a sun lounger without a care in the world. Clad in the tiniest bikini, which barely covered anything, Samantha Monroe was working very hard on topping up her tan.

"Wherever have you been, Lily?" she snapped, without even raising her enormous shades. "The children have been absolute hell. I'm exhausted."

"I went to the port."

"Traipse into town in your own time in the future, next time. I should dock your wages."

"You asked me yesterday to go early this morning to fetch fresh salad for lunch. Your friends are coming," Lily reminded her, mentally counting to ten. She'd been up since six preparing the linguine with lemon and prawns, and sported the grated knuckles and eye bags to prove it.

Samantha flapped a languid, red-taloned hand. "Oh yes, I probably should have said – I've changed my plans since then. The girls and I are going out to Puerto Portals instead. We're probably going to stay for the afternoon, do some shopping and maybe get some tapas in the evening. Lily, darling, would you mind keeping an eye on the children for me?"

Lily did mind. She wanted to see Hannah and she hadn't had a day off in over three weeks. Every time she was due to have her agreed evening off, or her mythical entire Sunday, Samantha's plans magically changed, and Lily was required to look after the children or drive them to one of their many activities in a giant Range Rover that might scream its price tag but was utterly unsuited to the narrow, traffic-lined side streets of Andratx.

Samantha's husband, a marshmallow-waisted banker called Toby, only managed to get out to their villa every couple of weeks, so Samantha was on her own for most of the summer, spending his money and drinking her way through his wine cellar. She often complained about his lack of attention and said she felt very hard done by – but not nearly as loudly as she complained when Toby arrived and spoiled all her fun. He was bumptious, red-faced and the cliché of every city boy Lily had ever met, but he was Samantha's husband, and Lily sometimes felt a bit sorry for him because he never seemed able to do anything right.

Not that Lily said this out loud. All her private thoughts were confided to the diary which she had kept religiously since she was fifteen. If she did ever dare talk to Toby, Samantha went spare and glared daggers. 'Do we have a spare towel?' was apparently code for 'Let's have sex in the hot tub', and heaven forbid he might thank Lily for anything. Samantha was exceedingly jealous, and convinced every other woman was looking to steal her wealthy husband. It really wasn't the case. Even if Lily's heart wasn't in pieces and Toby Monroe wasn't married, he was still the antithesis of her ideal man, so she'd never want to get to know him any better; but having been on the sharp end of Samantha's tongue many times, and not wanting to lose her job, Lily had learned the hard way that it was easier not to talk much to Toby or indeed to anyone at Casa del Mar. Thank goodness for her diary and WhatsApp exchanges with Hannah.

"I'm going out this evening," Lily said nervously.

"Go out tomorrow instead," Samantha yawned. "Simples."

"My friend's only here tonight. The yacht she's crewing on is in port. I told you about her. My godmother was her great-aunt."

Samantha's botoxed brow attempted to frown but remained a taut billiard ball. "I can't be expected to remember the details of your social life, Lily. I'm a very busy woman."

After six weeks, Lily was rarely surprised by her employer,

but Samantha's lack of self-awareness was breathtaking. Yes, her life was busy – but she wasn't out saving the whales or fighting for world peace. She was lunching in expensive restaurants with other twig-thin women with tortoiseshell hair, big sunnies and expensive sandals, or having a trolley dash through Palma's designer stores.

When Lily had been interviewed as an au pair, Samantha had wanted to know all her credentials, which was understandable, Lily had thought at the time, since she was employing a stranger to look after her precious children. Samantha had pored over Lily's CV for ages, as though negotiating a trade deal with Donald Trump. Once satisfied with Lily's English degree (2:1 from Leeds) she hadn't asked anything about her time at the Blackwood Estate agency (just as well, Lily hadn't wanted to explain that CV gap) but instead had been far more interested to learn that Lily's godmother once lived in the hills above the port.

"That's an expensive area," Toby had said sagely, chins nodding in agreement.

Lily didn't know much about Clara Schneider's Mallorcan life. It was long ago, back in the seventies when her own granny was a girl, and all she knew was that their paths had crossed much later when Clara settled in England and opened an art school. Clara had become a family friend and was close to Lily's own mother. She'd loved hearing Clara's long-ago stories of sun-drenched terraces, swimming naked in coves, and dancing until her feet were sore at fiestas; for a child growing up in the bland suburbs, these tales had seemed as fantastical as anything Scheherazade might spin.

It was the jewel-bright memory fragments of Clara's stories that had drawn Lily to Andratx when life had gone a little pear-shaped – that, and the thought of sunshine and an escape. She remembered her godmother with fondness, for although Clara had died when Lily was a child, she had taught Lily many things; how to work with clay, how to look at colour and light, how to find the beauty in the everyday, and how to make the best of anything. Lily never knew why Clara had left the island; she had seemed to adore her bohemian life there, but Lily had learned from her that life had many seasons, and if you didn't accept change, you withered and became mired in the past.

"You must always keep moving," Clara would say in a voice still rich with the cadence of the Alps and chalets, and which suggested slow-moving rivers guarded by fairytale castles. "Like this wheel, you see? When it stops spinning – *pah*! The pot loses its beautiful form and is no more than a useless lump of clay. Movement and change are life."

As a child, Lily had loved visiting Clara's studio. She'd loved playing with Clara's great-niece, Hannah, and the girls had adored looking at the feather boas, rusting bird cages and strange wire sculptures that might look like junk but were in fact, as Clara explained, art. Lily loved the bright colours, the scarves and the garden with its rambling vine – and even now the faintest notes of ylang ylang sent her tumbling down the years and back to the small house in Pinner, sitting on a lap and with her hands plunged into clammy clay as the wheel span and a pot grew into life.

Movement was life. To stand still was to become a useless lump of clay. Remembering these words, and egged on by the adventurous Hannah, Lily had packed her bag and booked a ticket to Palma. A sunny bus ride later, she was wandering through the streets of Port Andratx looking for the budget hotel she had booked for a few nights. Already in love with the place, she had no plans beyond finding a job for the summer. Her life and her heart might be in tatters, and her parents perplexed at why a girl with a good education would want to leave 'a secure and well-paid job', but time here would be healing. Mallorca had been special to Clara, and as soon as Lily first glimpsed the old town standing sentinel over the blue and white of the port, her heart had lifted.

It was just a shame that finding an employer had been tricky. Several false starts, and too many wandering hands when she waited tables, had led Lily to answer the Monroes' advert for a live-in au pair who spoke English. Her tenuous link to one of the town's more exclusive areas had seemed to clinch the deal.

"Clara left years ago," Lily had said, when the Monroes stared at her expectantly. "I think the house was sold in the seventies."

"That's one of the most expensive areas, almost as expensive as here," Samantha was keen to boast, which, looking back, should have been a warning sign. "If she'd held onto it, she would have sold the plot for a fortune. Four? Five"

"López would pay at least four," agreed Toby. "He charged enough for this, but I got him down to two point six."

Lily had stared at them blankly. *Two point something what?*

"Million," Toby provided, kindly, on seeing her expression.

Lily blinked. She'd no idea what Clara's *finca* had sold for. She had never seen it. The Clara she had known lived in Pinner and had taught her grandmother at an evening class. The two women had become friends, their families had become entwined over the years, and when Clara eventually moved back to Germany she had been dearly missed. Millions had never come into it.

Now, as Samantha pointed out how lucky Lily was to have the Monroes as employers, these memories whirled through Lily's mind. She knew her evening with Hannah was slipping away; Samantha always got her way and Lily needed her job. Credit card bills didn't care much for broken hearts or missed nights out, and Lily was working hard to get herself sorted. She couldn't afford to upset Samantha, no matter how difficult or selfish the woman was, or how bitterly disappointed she felt.

"... so you can catch your friend another time," Samantha concluded. "Please don't be difficult. I'm very flexible with your working hours, as you know."

Lily did know. Samantha was indeed exceedingly flexible with hours, flexing them in her direction and to her advantage. So Lily mentally bade farewell to an evening out with an old friend, and to a few precious hours of being a person rather than a cross between Cinderella, a referee and Super Nanny.

She exhaled wearily and agreed to sacrifice her night off. Again. "Where are the children?" she asked.

Samantha shifted slightly on the sun lounger, one razor-sharp hip bone jutting up as she leaned onto her left elbow. "Oh, I don't know. They were here just now, I'm sure. See what happens when you go out and don't come back in time? It's absolute chaos. You'd better go find out where they are and hope that they're in one piece."

Lily opened her mouth and closed it again. She knew from bitter experience that whatever went wrong was going to be her fault. She simply had to button it and take the money. Goodness, it was hard.

Leaving Samantha basking in the sunshine, Lily walked to the edge of the pool and braced herself. Casa del Mar had been built with architecture at the forefront of the designer's mind, not the safety of small children. The house was full of hard surfaces and sharp edges and trendy glass staircases that simply shouted out for broken arms or bashed-in heads. Everything was marble. Everything was glass. Everything was high and expensive.

The pool was no exception: a deep blue square, the deep end of which was nine feet. It was the centrepiece of three achingly trendy glass buildings, and for some unknown reason the shallow end was in the middle. Samantha vaguely thought the architect was going to put a fountain there, but something had changed his mind. In any case, the pool was an au pair's nightmare, because any children who wanted to splash in the water tended to hurl themselves towards the middle and hope they landed there, or could doggy paddle to safety. Neither Tarquin nor Jocasta were great swimmers. If they missed their landing site or didn't wear armbands, the consequences were going to be dire.

Lily peered over the edge, slightly nauseated at the thought of what could be in there. To her great relief, the pool was clear and cool and empty. All she saw was the glitter of blue tiles sprinkled with sparkles.

The children hadn't drowned. Anything else was surely a bonus.

Letting herself into the kitchen, which was cooling down now that she had closed the French windows, Lily followed a trail of Coco Pops, footprints, swimming trunks and toys. The television den had the blinds down and Nickelodeon playing at full volume. There was no sign of the children here. Ditto the laundry room, the bedrooms, the formal sitting room – and even, God forbid, Samantha's bedroom. Where were they?

Taking her life in her hands, Lily even ventured out onto the flat roof, which was only accessible through a tiny hatch and was a place she had found quite by accident when Raquel showed her a spot where the staff hid from Samantha.

"Come, you come now, yes?" Raquel had said when Lily first arrived. Not yet understanding the importance of this reveal, Lily had followed her and watched in admiration as a woman in her early sixties shimmied up a ladder, squeezed through a tiny hatch, and then crawled across a narrow gutter before stepping onto the flat roof of the furthest sugar cube.

"This my place," said Raquel proudly. "Now yours too. It quiet."

Lily had looked around, and her breath caught at the view. Samantha and Toby's villa was slightly uphill from the yacht club, a location important to Toby because he liked to show off his boat to anyone who would look at it, even though he hadn't a clue how to sail the thing. As far as Lily could gather it was a very expensive floating drinks platform.

From this vantage point, Lily admired a picture-perfect vista of clean blue sea, sparkling white boats, and the timeless elegance of the old town across the harbour, all cradled by the high hills with the beautiful tower house at the farthest end, which always captured her imagination. Beyond all this was only the wide-open water and the sleeping dragon island that watched over the bay. From this secret rooftop you could still hear the bustle of the marina, the chink of coffee cups, and the rise and fall of voices, as well as the chug of the forklift and whine of the winch, but you were in Andratx not of it. And best of all, Samantha had no idea this place existed.

It was now Lily's sanctuary. She would often squeeze through to it, and either stand alone or in companionable silence with Raquel. Had the children seen her escape up here to catch a few moments to herself? To cry, to write long messages to her ex that she then deleted, or stalk him on Facebook and hate herself? Lily didn't think so, and a quick check showed her fears were misplaced.

Tarquin and Jocasta were clever children. Tarquin was as whip-thin as his mother and sharp as lemon juice in grazed fingers. Jocasta was more lumpy and solid like her father, but possessed a level of cunning Lily hadn't seen before in a small child and thought quite alarming.

The only place left to check was her own bedroom, but Lily felt certain the children wouldn't be in there. They weren't allowed – not that that would stop them, because they did pretty much anything they wanted to, with Samantha's blessing as long as she was left in peace. Surely Lily's room held no interest. It was small and narrow and didn't even have a view, unless you counted the service area between Villa del Mar and the equally ostentatious villa next door. If you liked views of dustbins, mops and last year's barbecue, it ticked all the boxes.

The room had very little apart from a double bed, a wardrobe, and a small shower en suite. She often wondered what it must be like to be Samantha, with her palatial bedroom, massive balcony overlooking the harbour, king-size bed and a bathroom that would have put a top-class London hotel to shame, but failed; her imagination simply wasn't that good.

She opened the door and gasped. Her room was ravaged, and Jocasta was reading her diary while Tarquin was parading around in a bikini and sunhat.

"I'm you!" he shouted when he spotted Lily. "Look at this big bikini! It would fit a hippo!"

The violation of her space made Lily feel as though she'd been slapped. "What are you doing in my bedroom?"

"It's *not* your bedroom," said Jocasta imperiously, lolling on Lily's bed. "It's our parents' bedroom, and that means it's ours too. Nothing here is yours."

Their lack of respect for her privacy was shocking. Lily knew these weren't bad children – sometimes they could be quite sweet – normally when they wanted something – but they had been left to run wild and were never disciplined. Whenever they did something wrong Samantha's only answer was to take offence that anyone was criticising her offspring.

She seemed to take this as a personal affront, and rather than punish them, would give them treats. Even when they did something that their mother couldn't ignore – for example, when they poured paint into the swimming pool – Samantha's only answer was to say that she would punish them by removing a treat, only to forget later on.

"I don't understand why he did it. All I ever did was love him," read Jocasta mockingly. "Oh, that's so, so sad."

Lily couldn't take another second. "Out! Out of here right *now*!" she shouted. She had never raised her voice at the children before, and they looked shocked.

"I said OUT!" she roared, stepping forward. "NOW!"

Jocasta and Tarquin, naughty but not stupid, realised they'd gone too far and fled. Moments later, Lily heard them on the veranda, sobbing to their mum about how Lily had been shouting at them and had been mean.

Lily blinked back tears as she picked up her diary. It had been her confidant during a really hard time when she hadn't spoken to anyone. She placed it in her suitcase and, as quickly as she could, flung her clothes inside before diving into her tiny shower room and sweeping all her toiletries from the shelf. It was quite sad how very little she possessed and how quickly she could be out of this place she'd devoted six weeks of her life to.

She swallowed the sense of regret and reminded herself that she deserved better.

As she pushed her hands into the pocket of her shorts, she felt the sharp edge of the thick card that had been handed to her earlier by the lady she'd met when she'd tumbled outside the supermarket.

A card which advertised a job working for her godmother's friend. It was like a sign.

Lily had been rushing to get back to the house because she

knew the children were unsupervised, and had fallen in her haste. Her first thought hadn't been whether she was hurt, but that she was stupid and clumsy, all the things her ex used to say about her. She was also worried that Samantha would be furious that the fruit was smashed or the olive oil spilled. She would be in trouble.

But Katalina Beauchamp had been kind. She hadn't been at all concerned about anything other than whether Lily was all right. How long had it been since somebody had been that kind to her? Far too long, Lily thought sadly.

Sometimes self-esteem was worn away by attrition, like pebbles on the beach. The blow from her ex had been huge, but it was the little chips over the years before and afterwards, people like Samantha or the other women Lily had babysat and cleaned for, that wore away at her soul. But Kat, a wealthy woman no doubt, had seen beyond grazed knees and awkwardness. She had seen Lily as a person.

And she had offered a lifeline.

Lily hadn't been thinking about leaving. She certainly wouldn't have run out on her responsibilities until a new au pair was in situ, but this utter disrespect for her as a person was a step too far. She couldn't overlook it or forget it.

Her fingers closed on the cardboard and her pulse slowed. Once she had stopped shaking, she dragged her case down the polished concrete stairs and placed it by the front door.

Samantha was waiting in the kitchen.

"What have you done to my children? They're distraught. What have you said to them? Honestly, you are absolutely the limit. Why the agency keeps sending me useless girls, I don't understand. You're lucky I don't just sack you."

Lily took a deep breath. There are moments in life you know you will savour, and this was one of them.

"You don't need to sack me, Samantha," she said calmly. "Because I'm quitting. Right now. Enjoy your lunch."

And without another word, she turned on her heel, walked away from the open-mouthed Samantha into the hall, lifted the handle of her suitcase and wheeled it out into the sunshine and freedom.

She raised her face to the light and looked across the marina and the wide harbour mouth to the far side of Andratx. There, high up in the hills, was the faintest smudge of terracotta and the brown blur of a tower. Windows twinkled in the sunlight as though they were laughing and smiling at her, beckoning her forwards.

Lily stepped through the villa's gates, out onto the pavement and into freedom. Towing the case, she rumbled down to the marina, where she found a table at the café and ordered a *café con leche*. Gin would have been better, but that was a slippery slope.

While the coffee cooled and the conversation ebbed and flowed around her in a gentle tide of mingled tongues, her heart rate slowed to match the town's pace. Lily withdrew the card from her pocket and laid it on the table, smoothing it with her hands and smiling at the way events had clicked into place.

It was time to call Katalina Beauchamp's number.

CHAPTER 4

LILY - NOW

"Do you like your room?" Kat asked.

Lily's new employer was seated at a yolk-yellow table, blissfully shaded beneath a square sail umbrella, on the highest of La Colina's terraces.

Lily laughed out loud. She couldn't imagine anyone not liking the room that would be hers while she worked at La Colina – unless they had a hankering for bins and mops, adored the growl of aircon units almost as much as they hated sweeping vistas of ocean, sage hillside speckled with villas, and sun-warmed gardens with a sparkling infinity pool.

"This can't be meant for me!" Lily had exclaimed when Kat's housekeeper, Jenny, threw open the door to a gorgeous room.

"Yes. Is yours."

Wide-eyed, Lily had stepped into a large room with huge French doors swathed in white drifts of fine floaty nets and boasting breathtaking views of Andratx. She blinked as her eyes adjusted from the cool of stone walls and tiled floors to the bright light, but the room remained unchanged. A king-size bed covered in snowy white linen barely filled a third of the space. In a daze, Lily followed her guide who proudly showed off the fitted closets complete with white towelling bathrobe, gleaming mahogany floors (Señor and Señora had them restored, *¡muy caras!*), and the heavy brocade curtains, before flinging open a heavy door to reveal a cavernous ensuite with a bath and double walk-in shower. Best of all was the balcony beyond the French doors; running the length of the room it had its own table with a large sunshade and panoramic views. Lily could see right across the water to Samantha's villa which, from the lofty heights of La Colina, seemed small and hemmed in.

"*La vista es muy bonita*," said Jenny proudly.

Lily could only nod, taken aback by the understated luxury and the simplicity of class and beauty which had no need to boast. Did she dare to imagine herself here? Brushing her hair in front of the huge oval mirror set into the large dressing table? Or pushing aside the heavy brocade curtains to step onto the balcony, lean her arms on the wrought-iron balustrade and drink in the town peeling away below, edged by the vast blue sea peppered with sailing boats and yachts, and above it all the bright sky with wisps of cloud trying their best to climb the hilltops. Or watching the stars peep out and the lights of the town began to bead the hillsides and dance in the darkening water?

It was the best room she had ever been lucky enough to sleep in – not just in a hotel, but anywhere. And now it was where she was going to work. She turned to Jenny, confused. Maybe there was a language issue?

"This isn't my room, surely?"

"You no like? You wish another? It not clean?" Jenny said with a frown. She was standing by a bookcase filled with holiday reads popular over a decade ago, Katie Price's hot pink novels, chicklit and Beckham's biography, and was running her fingers over the top. Holding up a hand covered in dust, Jenny started to explain something very fast and in Spanish, with much gesticulating and pointing. Lily was worried Jenny thought she was criticising the cleanliness of this beautiful room. A-level Spanish was good enough for buying food or getting about, but Lily was far from fluent and hoped she hadn't upset the housekeeper already. That wouldn't bode well.

"It's perfect," she said quickly. "*El dormitorio es muy bonito.* But surely it isn't a room for staff?"

Jenny halted mid-flow. "Ah! *¡Ya entiendo!* You think too good for you?"

Lily felt a hot wash of shame. Jenny was right. She did think this. "It's not what I'm used to. The people I have worked for … they wouldn't give a room like this to a helper."

Jenny nodded slowly, and Lily knew she understood, had met many Samanthas who employed people like her and her husband, or bossed them about in shops and restaurants.

"Señora is a very unusual lady. She is very kind and so thoughtful. She thinks I do not know she has hired you because I cannot keep up with the work. I know she is trying to help me." Her brown eyes narrowed. "Some people might take advantage of her kindness, but José and me, we make sure that doesn't happen."

The warning was clear, but rather than feeling unnerved, Lily was comforted by the knowledge that Kat Beauchamp inspired love and loyalty. This spoke volumes, and any misgivings Lily might have had about throwing her lot in with a stranger met by chance outside the supermarket vanished. In their place was a huge surge of gratitude to whatever stroke of Fate had caused their paths to cross. Thank goodness she had decided to act on her gut instinct and call the number on that piece of card ...

The taxi ride to La Colina had passed in a blur of shock. Lily had made the phone call to Kat, and the older woman had sounded delighted, insisting she come straight away. Lily had finished her drink, then hailed a taxi.

Once in the air-conditioned VW she sat back into the leather seat and gathered her thoughts as she was driven through the bustling streets which edged the waterfront. The taxi crawled past the pretty restaurants with their umbrellas and sun terraces, before threading its way through the narrow back streets and beginning the steep climb out into the hills.

This was one of Lily's favourite parts of town, although she hadn't been here in a while, being so busy. When she had a rare day off, she loved to swim off the rocks opposite the old hotel which, long closed and with its terrace bereft of diners and chinking glasses, slumbered behind nailed-up shutters and dreaming of its glory days. The path to the small cove below was shaded by ancient pine trees, and she would scrabble down the worn steps, slipping on dried pine needles and clinging to what was left of the rickety handrail. Then she would bob in the water and gaze at the boats and let her thoughts drift with the clouds, thinking how lucky she was to be there and not thinking about the mess she had made of her life.

The road into the hills was steep. By the time the taxi reached the top, all pedestrians had given up on the incline, and the wide streets, lined with bougainvillea-frilled villas with gateways revealing portrait squares of deep blue, were empty. There were no tourists with their peeling noses and sunburnt limbs up here, and the Fiats and Peugeots were usurped by Range Rovers and Mercedes. What had once been empty hillside and rough farmland had become the Beverly

Hills of Andratx, and the driver was happily providing Lily with an unrequested running commentary.

"This house *aqui!* It belongs to a very wealthy film director," he said, pointing to a dazzling metal and glass construction. "That one belongs to a politician. He comes now and again. *Mucha securidad.* That one below? It was in *The Crown.*"

Lily nodded and murmured appropriate sounds, but her attention was fixed on the house they were approaching.

"That's the one," she said. Her heart was racing, and she was nervous. La Colina might only be a mile so away from town, but it felt as though she was entering another realm altogether.

"La Colina," the driver confirmed. "That is a beautiful house. Original. You see the old lookout tower built into it? *¿La torre?* It's centuries old. The low roof with the shade, that's very Mallorquín."

He parked the car and retrieved Lily's case from the boot while she stepped out into the glare of the afternoon sunlight. There was little shade here, and heat ricocheted off the pavements, sizzling against her bare skin and headache-inducing. Lily put on her sunglasses and looked up at the fortress-like wall that surrounded La Colina. It felt like its own little kingdom. She wondered how she would get in.

She rolled her suitcase along the weed-strewn pavement until she reached a castle-like door made of dark, gleaming wood and studded with brass. Nervous, she pressed the buzzer just as the door swung inward and Kat Beauchamp appeared in the opening, beaming.

"Welcome, my dear. Come in. Welcome to La Colina."

Kat led Lily through a terraced garden filled with brightly coloured flowers in pots. At one time, she explained, they'd grown vegetables, but no one had time to plant them now. Lily noticed that some beds were overgrown, and weeds were sprouting between the tiles. Several of the steps they ascended were cracked, the topiary was as ragged as her own cuticles, and a split garden hose was abandoned in slack loops in the middle of a lawn. But none of this detracted from the beauty of the house or the view, which was spectacular. How did anyone get anything done in a place like this? You'd lose hours just watching the world go by.

Kat appeared breathless after the short walk. When they reached the pool, she crumpled into a wicker chair beneath a large umbrella and groaned, saying that if her husband was still alive she would give him a piece of her mind for designing a garden with so many steps.

"It was all well and good in our thirties," she sighed. "Now just walking from the gate to the house feels like climbing Everest."

She motioned for Lily to take the seat beside her. They were soon joined by a couple in their late sixties. Kat introduced them as José and Jenny, her housekeeper couple, and sang their praises. They seemed a little wary of Lily, which she had expected since from her earlier conversation with Kat she'd learned that they were likely to be unnerved by someone new arriving.

Kat had described them as wonderful, part of the family, but – like her, she'd laughed wryly – they were getting older and finding it all too much. That was why she needed Lily at La Colina: someone who could handle the heavier tasks and help with shopping, polishing, pulling weeds. Even driving her about, Kat had added. There were so many places she wanted to see before––

She had stopped abruptly, and Lily hadn't pressed her. Instead, she had let Kat describe the Mercedes convertible and how it had been her late husband's very late mid-life crisis.

Once Jenny had poured them all iced water and José had

been persuaded to sit down, Kat had explained that Lily was here to help them, not replace them. She would answer to the couple and assist them in whatever they thought would help make life easier.

"And she can keep me out of trouble," Kat had laughed. "If I want to hit the town or drink cocktails until the small hours, Lily can be my chaperone and stop me running off with some old lothario who's after my house!"

This had made everyone laugh and, like the ice in the jug, José and Jenny had visibly thawed. Lily felt reassured that just as Kat promised, they would soon become staunch allies, and she could see that they were relieved to have some of their pressures lifted.

Since Kat struggled with stairs, saying that on this visit she was grounded, Jenny had given Lily a tour of the house. With its old Mallorquín charm, stone walls, tiled floors, archways and dark rafters, La Colina stole Lily's heart at hello. In contrast, Samantha's elegant villa was a showpiece designed to flaunt Toby's wealth. It was stylish, yet cold. Empty and soulless, designed to intimidate rather than embrace and include. Lily hadn't realised how ill at ease she had been there until she stepped into La Colina and felt a weight slip from her shoulders.

Kat Beauchamp had been so welcoming to a stranger, so keen to give her a chance, to trust her so readily. She was offering more than a job; she was offering an opportunity to belong, to be part of a new family, to heal. It was the kindest thing anyone had ever done for Lily. It was a rescue. An intervention. One she felt her godmother had staged.

Lily knew already she would be loyal to Kat, just as she knew the older woman had recognised something in her that needed help. She had a feeling they would become friends.

She smiled at Kat and said she loved the room, grateful and

dazed, and excited about what this new chapter would hold. Then Kat poured her a glass of wine and turned to her with a smile.

"So," she said, "That's the work stuff over and done with. Now, let me tell you a little about your godmother …"

With those words she swept Lily away from the present and back into the seventies, when La Colina had been filled with guests. Kat described Clara's wonderful fashions, the parties she had thrown at her house in the hills, and the long lazy lunches they had shared when Clara lived in England. With each story she told, Lily felt a new thread stitch her closer to Kat Beauchamp and into life at La Colina, and by the time the sun was starting to slip towards the sea she felt as though she had always been there.

It felt to Lily as though she had come home.

CHAPTER 5

LILY - NOW

Evening was falling as Lily slipped out through La Colina's heavy wooden door. From this vantage point, she watched the warm night settle gently over the port below, like the finest cashmere shawl draping the shoulders of a beautiful woman. Above, the first stars played peek-a-boo with a small smile of moon.

This had been one of Lily's favourite times of day: a rare moment to catch her breath (usually on the flat-roof hiding place) before bracing herself for the next battle of feeding and bathing Tarquin and Jocasta, and persuading them to go to bed. Samantha would vanish into her bedroom, emerging only once the fray was over to berate Lily about the state of the house, then depart in a cloud of Dior, draped in her latest designer dress, for drinks or a party. It had been a rare treat for Lily to be out herself, free to see the night fall over the port without being pelted by baked beans and insults.

But now, as she followed the steep road into down to the town, she watched the sky shift from salmon pink to apricot, gold, turquoise and mauve. By the time she reached the first bar on the waterfront, the light was a deep, hazy blue, and the first restaurant lanterns were flickering on. Their shimmering reflections wobbled drunkenly in the petrol-blue water, as though staggering over the marina to join the jewels spilled from fairy lights strung on yachts. Cigarette smoke drifted on the soft breeze, stirring half-forgotten memories of teenage summer nights and beer gardens, and filling Lily's heart with wistfulness for times long lost. From one of the waterfront terraces, the plaintive chords of a guitar plucked at heart-strings, and she wished it were possible to capture this achingly beautiful moment. She would do her best to describe it in her diary, but felt sure she would fall short.

The walk downhill had passed in a daze. Lily wasn't sure whether it was drinking wine in the afternoon that made her feel so languid and relaxed, or the relief of no longer being bullied by Samantha. Her whole day had taken on a surreal aspect, and if it wasn't for the sting of grazed knees and the slap of her sandals on dusty pavement, she might have thought she'd dreamed the whole episode. How awful that would be! Lily shuddered at the thought of waking to find herself back at Casa del Mar.

In the port, busy now as tourists arrived to eat and the wealthy cruised past in convertible Range Rovers and the odd growly Ferrari, Lily paused to catch her breath outside a small restaurant where diners chattered over plates of tapas and large glasses of Rioja. Beyond the roped-off edge of the terrace, fishing boats were returning home. In the marina, expensive vessels were moored for the evening, halyards clinking gently in the warm breeze.

Lily took a moment to drink it all in. Until now, she'd been so frenetically busy she hadn't had the chance to appreciate where she was. At Samantha's there had been no time to contemplate the view or mull over existential matters like the fleeting beauty of time and one's place within it. At Casa del Mar, she'd been lucky if she'd had time to go to the loo or throw together a sandwich. Life at La Colina would still be busy – she could already see there was much to do, from tackling the weeds sprouting across the terrace to deep-cleaning the parts of the house Jenny's fading eyesight had missed – but it would be a different kind of busy. She was looking forward to getting involved with it all.

At La Colina that afternoon, she had spent a very happy hour sitting by the pool with her feet in the water, face tilted to the sunshine as she watched the busy traffic of boats and jet skis zipping in and out of the harbour far below. A gigantic superyacht, more a floating hotel than a boat, had crawled into the outer harbour like a creature from mythology, to moor for the night. While Lily flicked glistening water into the air and wriggled her toes in the pool's cool depths, she watched the crew scurry around with lines and lower the tender so the pampered occupants could be ferried into Andratx for shopping and drinks.

She liked to imagine who might be on such ships. Jeff Bezos was rumoured to have visited Mallorca recently, and it wasn't unheard of for celebrities like George Clooney to sail in for a night or two. Imagine if she bumped into him – her mum would pop!

A smaller boat glided by to moor within the marina. With sails now neatly furled and ropes coiled, it looked like the sort of yacht Hannah would be crewing on, and Lily gave it a wave just in case. She knew how amused Hannah would be to think she was up here in the garden of this beautiful house, watching the goings-on below like one of the rich and famous. She could hardly wait to tell her friend what had happened today.

Once the sun started to make her pale skin feel a little too warm and her nose was turning pink, Lily retreated from the poolside to the coolness of the house. Fetching some iced water from the kitchen, she spent another hour beneath the sun umbrella on her balcony, writing in her diary and watching the world go by. It was impossible not to write here; everywhere she looked, there were stories.

Lily loved to write, and as a child had harboured secret dreams of becoming an author, dreams that Clara had encouraged. But teachers telling her this was unrealistic, coupled with a lack of self-esteem and the busyness of earning a living, had put paid to those hopes. But she still loved the alchemy of seeing her thoughts appear on the page, and marvelled at how they crystallised in a way that seemed quite magical. It made her happy to scribble her thoughts down, and although she wasn't quite Samuel Pepys, neither was she Bridget Jones. Sometimes Lily sketched, too, and if she had time, added colour with brush pens. Her journal was her friend and her escape, and this was why Jocasta's violation had been the final straw.

A succession of notebooks contained the thoughts and hopes of a lifetime, and her latest was the recipient of her first impressions of La Colina. Once she'd finished writing, Lily scanned her words and was surprised to find that rather than simply recording facts, she had started to paint word pictures through vivid imagery. Her entry flowed with rich descriptions of the house: from the cascades of scarlet bougainvillea to the sea-green ivy scrambling over the walls and reaching to the tower, to the quicksilver lizards flashing across the tiles of her balcony. This place was already working its magic on her creativity. Writing in the shade of the old tower, Lily felt like a princess with her kingdom laid out before her. Her rescue by Kat certainly had the makings of a fairy tale, which cast

Samantha as either an ugly sister or a wicked witch! That thought made Lily smile.

Diary entry written, she took a shower in the ensuite and marvelled at the jets, which needled her skin and made it sing. This was as far removed from the sluggish trickle of her old shower as the small rowing boats were from the massive superyachts. There was a selection of shower gels and moisturisers too, and Lily scrubbed until her skin tingled, then moisturised from head to toe and wrapped herself in the snowy bathrobe before padding to the dressing table.

She felt as though she had scrubbed off her old self and become something new. Looking in the mirror, she was surprised to see the bright-eyed girl gazing back. Her skin glowed with sunshine, freckles dusted her nose, and the weariness that had shadowed her eyes for so long had lifted. Even her hair had decided to fall in soft waves as it dried naturally. It was amazing what an afternoon of rest and sunshine could do for a girl.

She dressed quickly in a simple green sundress that covered her scraped knees and fell in gentle folds to just above her ankles. Feeling inspired, Lily painted her toenails scarlet, then pushed her feet into her trusty old Doc Marten sandals, a fun statement juxtaposition of the utilitarian with the pretty summer dress and, best of all, perfect for walking and wonderfully comfortable. A quick slick of lip gloss, a sweep of mascara, followed by a squirt of Mademoiselle, and she was ready to go.

Lily collected her door key from the place Kat had mentioned, grabbed her wicker bag with her purse, and let herself out of the house. She couldn't remember feeling so contented and relaxed in all her time on the island.

Hannah was sitting at a table overlooking the waterfront in

Tim's Bar, a favourite place for food and socialising. It boasted a prime position by the water, and although it was only 6:30 pm, the place was already crowded. Lily spotted her friend at once. There was no mistaking Hannah. Her tall, lithe body, strong and toned from hauling sails and winding winches, was showcased to perfection in strappy top and buttock-skinning hotpants. Her glossy blonde hair was swept into a high ponytail which displayed her swanlike neck and butterscotch-smooth shoulders perfectly. Hannah Cooper turned heads wherever she went, yet always seemed oblivious to her own beauty. Even now, among the groomed women of Andratx with their designer clothes and expensively styled hair, she stole every glance.

If Hannah hadn't been such a kind-hearted and down-to-earth girl, Lily would probably have been intimidated by her. But they had been friends since primary school – one tall and looking like a supermodel, the other short with ginger hair and *not* looking like a supermodel – and Lily's heart soared to see her.

"There you are!" Hannah's face broke into a wide smile. "Come on over and grab a seat!"

Lily wove her way through the crowded restaurant, doing her best not to take out diners or plates with her large wicker bag.

"You look amazing," said Hannah. "Okay. Who is he?"

Lily laughed. "I've had a shower and an afternoon off. That's all."

Hannah arched an eyebrow. "Is that what they call it nowadays? Come on, spill."

"Honestly! I promise, if there was a man, I'd tell you. But you know I'm sworn off men forever."

"Just because *he who shall not be named* was a knob end doesn't mean they all are." Hannah raised her glass and winked. "The best way of getting over one man is getting under another."

The gorgeous Hannah had never had her heart broken in her life. She was far more likely to be the one doing the heart-shattering. She loved being free, and refused to be tied down – unless for fun, as she liked to quip. Although she envied her friend, Lily couldn't imagine being like Hannah; when she gave her heart to somebody, she gave it one hundred per cent. To flit from one gorgeous hunk to another like a butterfly would have broken her.

"I'm sworn off for life," she insisted, sliding into a seat and helping herself to wine.

"Let's see if I can change your mind. We're on the waterfront, and some of Mallorca's richest and most eligible bachelors are out and about. All you need to do is pick one."

Lily reached for the menu. "I'm more interested in picking the next bottle of wine. How does Fishes on Bicycles grab you?"

"I can take a hint," said Hannah. "But you're missing out. You're gorgeous, Lil. Don't let Tosser Face stop you finding somebody lovely. Now, pass me that menu and I'll say no more. I'm starving. It was a long sail over."

The conversation shifted from men to food as the girls ordered a bottle of crisp white wine and some dishes to share: grilled prawns, *padrón* peppers, calamari and a basket of warm bread with aïoli. Their laughter bubbled easily as they swapped news and stories, the familiar ease between them untouched by time or distance.

"So, what's the plan now you've escaped?" Hannah asked, tearing a piece of bread and dipping it into the aïoli. "Stay at this new place for the season, and then what? You *were* heading to Geneva with the Evil Queen after the summer, weren't you?"

Lily shuddered. Samantha had made noises about hiring her permanently.

"I'm going to see how it works out at La Colina. The place is special. I can't believe that Clara knew it and was friends with Kat." She paused, searching for the right words. "It feels like it was meant to be."

Hannah gazed across the water toward the hills. In the darkness, lights shimmered like dreams. One of those was La Colina. Maybe Kat was at the yellow table on the terrace with the supper Jenny had prepared, citronella candles fragrancing the air, and remembering times when she had dined there with the smiley-faced man from her photos.

"Maybe it was?" said Hannah. "Or it could be that Clara knew everyone wherever she went. It was a nightmare going to the High Street with her. It took hours to get anywhere because everyone wanted to chat."

Lily took a *padrón* pepper, salt crystals dancing across her taste buds as the soft flesh melted. "Whatever the reason, it feels heaven-sent, Han. I'll make it beautiful and drive Kat wherever she wants to go. Write a bit. Sleep. Garden. Just take some time for me, you know? I feel lucky right now."

Hannah raised her glass. "You deserve all the luck in the world. Here's to a perfect summer. Clara would be proud."

The harbour shimmered, lanterns glowed on tables, and the sea carried the low thump of music from one of the yachts moored just beyond the marina wall. Lily felt sure everything was possible, and this was going to be a perfect summer.

As they finished the last of their prawns and debated pudding, two young men strolled up with the casual confidence of those who never hear the word No. Both were good-looking in a polished, careless way with identikit sun-kissed skin, cream chinos, floral shirts with sleeves rolled to tanned elbows, and designer shades pushed up into artfully tousled hair. One was dark-haired, sharp angles and cheekbones, with a cheeky grin hinting at danger. The other was blond, broader, a rugby type who looked at his peak and was likely to run to fat. He reminded Lily unpleasantly of Toby Monroe, right down to his Rolex, which caught the light as he leaned a forearm on their table.

"Evening, girls," he said, flashing a smile. "You look like you might enjoy a little excitement."

"Do we?" Hannah asked, amused.

Lily glared at him. She hated pushy men masquerading as charming. And 'girls'? Hadn't he heard of #metoo?

The dark-haired companion leaned on the back of her chair with easy confidence. The scent of Sauvage hit Lily and she fought to keep the lid shut on the chest of memories.

"You're here," he said, "but you could be out there." He nodded toward the darkening water. "See that Princess by the pontoon? That's Nauti Lady. Our boat. Not the biggest – but hosting the best party tonight."

Hannah looked disappointed. "Oh. I thought you were going to say you owned *Athena*. Now that's a boat."

"I wish," he admitted, looking crushed. "She belongs to Tomás López."

"You know, the property guy," added his blond sidekick.

Lily didn't, but Hannah, who had been crewing in the Med for years, nodded knowingly.

"Who is he?" Lily asked Hannah.

"I'm sure you've come across him," she responded, unimpressed. "He's bought half of northern Mallorca and turned it into gated villas and infinity pools. Marries a new model every five years and pays off the old ones with Louis Vuitton bags. Probably sold Psycho Sam her villa."

It rang a bell.

The two young men exchanged glances. Used to yachts

doing the heavy lifting, they were wrong-footed by the girls' reaction.

"We're heading out to Nauti in an hour," the dark-haired one said, flashing a toothy grin. "She isn't quite on López's level, but we've got live music, proper cocktails and a chef."

Hannah considered it. "That sounds fun."

"You should come," he said, his gaze lingering on Hannah. "Both of you."

Lily shook her head. "Thanks, but I'm calling it a night. I start a new job tomorrow."

Hannah glanced sideways at her. Lily knew her best friend was willing her to loosen up, live a little, get over Harrison by ... *urgh. No thank you.*

"Just for a bit? Could be fun, Lils."

Lily shook her head again. "You go and have fun. I'll catch you on the next pass."

"I might join you guys later once we've finished dinner," Hannah said, flicking her ponytail and shrugging nonchalantly. The young men seemed pleased by this and moved on, buoyed by youth and testosterone.

Hannah watched them go and sighed. "You know, you don't have to swear off fun just because one man turned out to be an arse."

Lily looked away, her eyes on the glittering water. "It wasn't just that."

"I know."

And she did. Hannah had been there when Lily's world imploded. She witnessed the betrayal, the humiliation, the public mess. Lily had walked out of the office with her head held high – but her life was in tatters. She hadn't just lost a relationship; she'd lost her career, her confidence and the shape of her future.

"I don't want to be that girl," Lily said quietly.

"What girl?"

"The one who believes every word and wakes up with nothing."

"You're not that girl. You never were. They're not Harrison, Lils. Just two guys wanting some summer fun. You might enjoy yourself."

Lily smiled, but her mind was made up. She'd been an idiot once. It wouldn't happen twice.

After sharing tiramisu and sinking a couple of limoncellos, they split the bill and left Tim's. Saturday night in the port was busy, and they linked arms as they strolled through the crowds past pop-up markets with racks of floaty kaftans and cheap sparkly flip-flops. Once at the pontoon, they hugged goodbye.

"Call me next time you're here?" Lily said, voice catching.

"You bet," Hannah replied, hugging her back. "Maybe I'll visit you at La Colina? See how the other half live. If I don't run off with Mr Rolex tonight!"

Lily watched her stride away, with the easy confidence of someone who expects life to roll out a red carpet. A pang of envy twisted inside her; Hannah made life look so easy. She always had. Perhaps she took after her great-aunt? She'd have to ask Kat.

As Hannah hopped into the tender with the dark-haired guy, Lily waved. She wasn't angry that Hannah chose to party, or envious. She was just done with men, and the pair who interrupted their meal had reminded Lily too much of her ex: brash, confident and effortlessly charming. Harrison hadn't just broken her heart. He'd unravelled her until even the things she loved – her job, her social life, even her journal writing – felt unbearable. She'd spent too long stitching herself back together, piece by careful piece, to ever fall for someone like that again. Hannah, with innate beauty and confidence, would be fine.

But Lily wasn't Hannah. She couldn't risk being hurt again.

From across the water, the sounds of the party rose: distant music, laughter, the faint thud of bass. Lily wandered slowly along the waterfront, feeling like a party pooper, the quiet happiness of earlier a distant memory. The town had transformed into a catwalk: slender young women in impossibly tiny dresses, long-legged and wobbly as Bambi, accompanied by portly men in crisp linen shirts, loafers without socks, all wearing watches costing more than most cars. Stalls sold jewellery and overpriced sarongs. Artists sketched portraits. Small dogs trotted behind women in designer heels. It was all colour and spectacle and summer gloss.

She watched the parade and tried to memorise it for later, the thin women with shiny hair and bored expressions, old men with leathery skin and ballooning stomachs clutching hands of girls young enough to be their daughters or even granddaughters. Lily's spirits rose. It was Mallorca in peak season. She was lucky to be here, and no matter how painful the past she was grateful it had led her here.

Then, just as her spirits lifted, she tripped. A careless misstep on a coil of rope half-hidden in shadows. As her foot caught, she pitched forward with a gasp, only for a strong hand to steady her just in time.

"Careful," said a calm voice. "These ropes are like traps for unwary tourists."

She blinked up, winded, to see concerned dark eyes beneath a shock of tousled black hair. The speaker's face was all clean lines and symmetry. It the kind of handsome that makes the brain trip, too, and his smile was warm and kind rather than predatory.

"Thank you for saving me from the second fall of the day," Lily said.

"A second fall?"

"I tripped on the kerb outside the Aprop supermarket. I was carrying too much shopping." She blushed, aware she was talking too much.

"Anyway," she said, suddenly shy. "I'm Lily. Lily Wilson."

"I'm Rafe Cruz," he said with a smile. "One minute. These lines are lethal."

He crouched to tidy the ropes, tutting, and within moments the spaghetti tangle became neat coils. Lily was impressed.

"Do you work with boats?" she asked.

"I love to be on the water. It's freedom."

"It must be wonderful," Lily agreed, thinking of boats setting course for the horizon. She had been in Mallorca almost a month, but had yet to venture out. Samantha and Toby hadn't invited her, choosing instead to entertain friends and leave her to placate their children.

"It is," he said simply. "Out there you can be yourself. Nothing matters but the wind, the sails, the water."

He sounded wistful. It was lucky he worked with boats, Lily thought, although she supposed wealthy boat owners were much like Samantha and had all the fun while their staff enjoyed the water vicariously. Rafe probably spent all day polishing some captain of industry's powerboat and swabbing decks. Lily had no idea what swabbing was, but imagined a lot of it went on.

"Well, thank you," she said finally. "You saved me from another fall."

"I'll take a coffee as repayment," he said easily. "There's a place in the back streets by the fish restaurant. Best mochas."

Lily didn't know why she said yes. Something about him, the easy confidence without arrogance, and the magic of the warm evening made her accept.

"Sounds good."

"*Bueno*," said Rafe. "Thought I'd have to trip you up again otherwise."

She liked the teasing tone. He didn't take himself seriously. Rafe steered her away from the noisy main street to the quiet back alleys where light spilled from balconies with people sitting watching the world go by, and the air was heavy with the rich scent of garlic and tomatoes. They sat at a quiet café with lights strung overhead. Guitar music drifted from across the street, and they chatted easily over coffee. Rafe spoke perfect English, though unmistakably threaded with Spanish.

"So how did you really know I wasn't a local?" Lily asked, sipping coffee.

He tilted his head. "The hair. Like sunrise. And your shoes."

"My shoes?"

"They're *muy* ugly!"

Lily was affronted on the behalf of her DMs. "How dare you?"

"Apologies!" He pressed the heel of his hand to his heart. "Sensible then. No Mallorcan girl would choose sensible shoes."

She laughed. "Actually, my mum hates them. She says I should wear pretty sandals with heels."

Rafe looked concerned. "Not if you trip in those. We'd be talking at least a broken ankle before you reached the end of town."

It was nice to drink coffee and make a friend. Rafe didn't push or flirt; he just talked about the sea and the summer tourist chaos, and made her laugh with tales of strange requests from rich people on boats. In return Lily told him about Samantha's demands, and was pleased to find them funny now she had escaped.

Coffees finished, Rafe walked Lily to the taxi rank and waited until she was inside.

"Thanks again," she said.

Rafe smiled. "*Nada*. Try to stay upright tomorrow."

The door closed. The cab pulled away and Lily didn't look back. She knew she'd never see him again. But as the taxi climbed the dark road to La Colina, she found herself smiling, for her life was changing.

Quietly, slowly and wonderfully changing.

CHAPTER 6

KAT - NOW

Kat sat on the terrace with a glass of wine, the cool stem resting between her fingers as she absently swirled liquid the colour of the sun she had watched sinking into the sea. Above the town, the sky deepened to blue velvet, and strings of lights twinkled on the waterfront like fallen stars. The soft chirrup of cicadas filled the warm air, and far below, beyond La Colina's boundary fence, waves sighed as they broke on the rocks. From the town, music – languid, sensual and unmistakably Spanish – spilled from a bar, and somewhere a dog barked.

These sounds were timeless; they had changed so little since she had first sat here, open-mouthed at the view. Kat could almost believe the past decades were little more than a strange dream and, if she closed her eyes, she could leap to her feet and head out for the night as she had done hundreds, if not thousands, of times before.

Oh, to be young again, she thought wistfully, glimpsing Lily closing the garden gate before turning downhill toward the port. How marvellous to be full of energy, heading out for tapas and dancing and flirting. Better still, how wonderful not to long to collapse into bed once night fell. For as much as she loved the idea of a night in town watching fashionable people parade and dance, Kat suspected the noise and sheer energy of Andratx's nightlife would quickly become exhausting. She also knew sitting alone in a restaurant made David's absence ache like a phantom limb; she would inevitably find herself turning to tell him something, only to be winded by loss all over again.

No, she decided as she sipped her wine and watched a yacht glide into the harbour, better to stay at home with her memories and a comfy chair rather than spoil the fun for others. She did have vague plans to visit the town for an early supper and take day trips to a few other locations on the island that held meaning, hence employing Lily to drive her about rather than forcing José to do it. She would frame these excursions as sightseeing, but in truth these would be farewell visits, for this summer at La Colina would be her last. It was the end of a season of her life, and although leaving would feel like ripping away a part of herself, Kat accepted that the time to sell up had come.

Her eyes might not be as sharp as when she had first visited La Colina, but they saw how the place, like her, was fading away, and far from what it had been in its prime. Paint was peeling, tiles slipping, plaster crumbling and weeds sprouting between paving stones. Ivy crawled over the walls, and the oleander trees, once shaped into perfect umbrellas, sprawled shade and dropped leaves across the mossy lawn. The stonework of the far walls was crumbling, large slabs occasionally plummeting into the goat-nibbled wastes below, and the once-regimented lavender and rosemary beds were now wild, if romantic, drifts. Yes, the garden was dreadfully overgrown despite José's best efforts.

Inside the house was no better. Cracks marred the paintwork, window frames rotted, and in corners of seldom-used rooms dark mould crawled across skirting boards and bloomed behind furniture. The garden room bore the unmistakable odour of damp. Maintaining La Colina as it deserved required both energy and a large pot of money, and Kat was realistic enough to know she didn't possess enough of either.

It was time to let her beloved home go. The questions were, who deserved it and who would do it justice? Selling La Colina wouldn't be hard. Rarely did a week pass without a real estate agent's leaflet dropping through the letterbox or a hopeful approach by a property developer.

Oh, but it was hard when she didn't feel as though she was growing old, not really. Her knees complained when she bent to deadhead the geraniums, and she sometimes forgot names (though not faces) – but inside, where it counted, Kat was still the girl who'd first arrived on the island with nothing but a rucksack and a vague idea that she needed more from life. That had been over half a century ago, and this house had been a ruin then. No one had seen its potential except her and . . .

Unbidden, she was overwhelmed by a vivid image of strong arms pulling her against a lean body. Smouldering dark eyes gazed into hers. Lips brushed her temple before straying to her neck, tracing the line of her collarbone. Silken fire kisses made her melt and pool like the Mahón cheese in the wicker basket he had carried, abandoned in the full glare of the Mallorca sun as their kisses grew in intensity. There was the scent of crushed thyme and grass as they tumbled on the picnic rug, food forgotten, then only his skin on hers and the blue of the sky above . . .

No. Kat wouldn't think about that. She had trained herself not to, locking those memories away for a lifetime. She would not amble down memory lane now. David might have died, but she had loved him for a lifetime – and loved him far too much to dwell, even for a second, on another. No matter how she had first found La Colina, it had become their home, the place where the family they made had spent so many happy summers.

Her beloved husband had always known why it meant so much to Kat and had understood. Of course he had. David had been there when she was broken, and had been a shoulder to cry on, and eventually his friendship had helped heal her shattered heart. A quiet love, with the depths of a still deep pool, their romance might not have sprung from the white-hot burn of instant attraction, but it was deep and true, the solid foundation upon which a life and marriage were built. A youthful passion, no matter how seared upon her soul, was nothing in comparison.

And in the end, La Colina would outlast them all.

Kat glanced across the terrace toward the tall arched windows and soft stone walls, still sun-warmed and gently crumbling in places. The fallen petals of the bougainvillea she'd planted so long ago were scattered like confetti across the tiled walkways, and the lemon trees in their azure pots dreamed of burgeoning fruit. Every corner of the place carried the ghosts of laughter and long, wine-fuelled evenings with David attempting to play his old guitar under the stars, and their children racing through the olive trees like wild things before diving into the pool with piercing shrieks. Clara laughing and smoking. So many memories.

Which was, of course, the problem. It was hard to say goodbye.

"You're a sentimental old fool," she muttered, taking another sip of her drink. "Take the money and move on. López wants this place."

López had written three times and was most persistent. His letters were polite and oddly personal, as though they shared a past, which they most certainly did not, since he must have been young enough to be Kat's son. He wrote about his plans with a sort of reverence, and always signed off the same way, too: 'I understand your hesitation, Señora Beauchamp, but I see something here that is special and only wish to protect it. Perhaps we should talk.'

Not bloody likely, thought Kat. She'd met him once, years ago, at a gallery opening in Palma with his second or maybe third wife, and he had hardly given her the time of day because he hadn't wanted anything from her then. Now that he wanted her house he was willing to pretend an elderly English woman was worth his attention. Kat knew he would pay her a good price, but she couldn't bear the thought of La Colina being demolished. Was it too much to hope that somebody with a big heart as well as a big wallet might make her an offer?

In the early eighties, when Andratx was still relatively undiscovered, nobody could have dreamed a derelict property so inconveniently high up in the hills might one day be worth a fortune. For Kat and David, buying La Colina had never been about making money. It had been their passion project, but Kat wasn't naïve; she knew the equity tied up in La Colina would mean proper care if she ever needed it, and would provide a safety net for her children (though God knew they were too proud to ask). Selling the house would mean she could stop worrying, finally, about paying for the upkeep of a property thousands of miles away from home. David had bought it with the money his parents had left him, and always said that although he might not earn a fortune as an academic, La Colina was their pension and would keep them in their old age.

Her throat tightened. How unfair it was that David had never got to enjoy his much-looked-forward-to retirement. The cancer had been quick and cruel; there was scarcely time to absorb what was happening before he was gone, leaving his family reeling with shock and grief. Later, much later, it had hurt dreadfully to acknowledge that David would never see another sunset from the terrace or enjoy the fruits of his investment.

Maybe, Kat thought as she made her way to the kitchen for a top-up, Fate had been kind by sparing David the pain of having to admit he was struggling to travel to Mallorca and the worry of affording the maintenance on the house. He hadn't been forced to confront the dreadful spectre of selling it and letting Jenny and José go. He didn't need to weigh up what was best, or feel his stomach turn at the idea of bulldozers roaring and glass cubes replacing hand-painted tiles and ancient beams. He would not see diggers ripping up the old pine tree where the owls nested and where the girls had made a tree house. Tomás López might insist his vision for La Colina was *muy simpático*, but Kat didn't trust him an inch.

What did López really want? Why this house? Why *her* house?

Kat poured herself another glass of wine and carried it back out to her yellow table. She wasn't done thinking yet, and she was not ready to sign anything until she had made peace with the past. Some houses, like some memories, didn't like to be let go of. There was no rush; she could enjoy the summer here and take her time before deciding what to do. Now she had Lily to help, the immediate pressure was off José and Jenny, and Kat could consider her options carefully.

Lily Wilson was a godsend. Their meeting was meant to be. Clara must have had a hand in it somehow.

Kat sipped her drink and, as twilight bloomed across the bay, her mind wandered to her old friend and the years that had slipped away since they had first met here. The past was never far away. It wouldn't leave her alone. But maybe, just maybe, the future held some surprises too.

CHAPTER 7

KAT - THEN

It was the golden summer of 1970. Port Andratx was drunk on sunshine and sangria, ragged around the edges and far from the luxury destination it would become, but after the rain and unrelenting greyness of the UK, it was heaven to Katalina Brown.

Though she worked long hours in the small, whitewashed guesthouse overlooking the port, earning a fraction of what she had in Oxford, Kat didn't mind one bit, for she was in love with Mallorca. In return for her board and a little spending money, she was spending the summer improving her Spanish, ostensibly preparing to apply for bilingual secretary jobs back in the UK, but in fact having fun once the sun went down and partying while the town's lights burned in the darkness.

Cleaning rooms, making beds, folding towels, and ferrying trays of strong coffee and fresh bread to mismatched tables felt like a privilege when glorious sunshine trickled onto the vine-woven veranda. The guesthouse owners, Maria and Francisco, worked her hard, but they were kind, and Kat liked them. They seemed to like her too, and she knew they appreciated how easily she settled the increasing number of English visitors. Many of these struggled with the language and food, but relaxed when they found a friendly Londoner working at the guesthouse.

"You look Spanish!"

That exclamation was the soundtrack to Kat's new life in Mallorca. With her long dark hair, golden suntan and fluent Spanish (though her Mallorquín was faltering), locals and visitors often mistook her for a native.

"My mother's Spanish," she would explain patiently each time. "I grew up in Oxford."

That always ended the conversation. Visitors were thrilled to be able to ask for familiar food, and rarely wanted to know more beyond ordering chips or a roast dinner. Kat never elaborated on why her maternal grandparents had fled Spain in the 1930s. People on holiday didn't want tales of war and persecution, and since Mallorca had been a Nationalist stronghold, she didn't speak of how deeply the Civil War had scarred her family. Her maternal grandparents never returned to their homeland, and her mother had no interest in visiting Catalonia. Carmen Brown had become a proud Londoner, even though she clung to her Catholic faith and claimed to dream in Spanish.

Kat was proud of her heritage, and relished this chance to embrace it. This summer spent in Mallorca was an escape from the confines of home and a chance to explore another culture. She wanted more than secretarial college, a safe job and an engagement ring. She wanted to experience another way of living. Kat wanted more from life than the ordinary. She longed for adventure and passion, but something told her these would not appear above the hammering keys of an Olivetti Lettera.

Kat had enjoyed her course at the Ox and Cow, her

college's affectionate nickname, but she was certain life held more than typing and being home by half five for tea. Soon, she would need to find a full-time job. Her mother wanted her to work as a bilingual secretary, confident that Kat would excel, and convinced she'd meet a 'nice young man' that way, always sighing whenever Kat's friends got engaged or married. Kat wasn't on the shelf, but Carmen Brown was convinced her daughter was firmly bolted onto it and gathering dust.

"You're such a pretty girl," she would wail. "You could have your pick of the boys!"

Kat's standard response was an eye roll. She wasn't interested in any of the boys she knew. She'd had her fair share of attention and a few kisses, but nobody had set her heart racing. She was beginning to wonder if she was the problem.

"And jobs," Carmen would continue. "You're top of the class, *querida*! You could work anywhere."

"I don't know what I want to do," Kat would begin, only for her mother to tut and express despair in rapid Spanish, the language she always chose to express extremes of emotion. Carmen didn't understand her daughter's yearning for a fulfilling career. To her, a job was just something to fill the hours before a husband and children arrived. And why not? It had worked for her; a few months filing in an office, then marriage to her boss. Job done.

Kat was sure her parents were happy. Eddie Brown adored his fiery wife, and Carmen loved fussing over him. Their pebble-dashed semi in Cowley was their world. Eddie enjoyed pottering in the garden while Carmen presided over the house, polishing, vacuuming and dusting her Royal Doulton collection. It was understandable they wanted the same security and contentment for their only daughter, and Kat felt guilty for failing to follow their plans.

She wasn't sure why she wanted more. Maybe she took after her Spanish family, who hadn't settled for the status quo and had fought for their convictions. She knew her uncles had died for what they believed, in ways so horrible nobody spoke of them, and her grandfather used to hiss and then spit whenever he heard General Franco's name. Kat knew she was fighting in her own way by dragging her heels with job applications, mostly from fear of being penned in by a nine-to-five. She dreaded the claustrophobia of closing doors and irreversible courses. There had to be more than typing and getting married. Everything inside her said so. She just had to discover what it was and how to get it.

Kat had been beyond grateful when Dr David Beauchamp, a shy young don teaching Modern Foreign Languages and whose notes she typed for pocket money, hadn't argued when she declined his offer to be departmental secretary. To her surprise, he asked what she *did* want to do, then listened without trying to change her mind, and didn't insist he knew best.

He had nodded sympathetically when Kat explained shyly that she wanted to see more of the world, experience other ways of life, and maybe even use her languages. When she was done, he suggested she contact a friend of his in Mallorca.

"Clara Schneider knows everyone," he said, peering at Kat from behind wire-framed glasses that twinkled almost as brightly as his green eyes. "She was at the Ruskin for a while in sixty-eight, as part of a German exchange. She's great fun, throws wonderful parties. All the chaps were a little in love with her, and she left a trail of broken hearts when she left."

David, clearly more interested in Cervantes than señoras, blushed as he said this. Kat was intrigued. Had this *fräulein* broken his heart? Was he still a little in love with her? Kat longed to know but didn't press; she simply took Clara's address and wrote to enquire about summer work in Andratx. Weeks later, an airmail letter plopped onto the welcome mat, addressed to Kat in exuberant violet cursive.

If David says you're good, you must be, Clara wrote in swirling ink. *He never exaggerates or gives false praise. The most honest man I know. So sweet and earnest. I have a contact whose cousins run a guesthouse in Port Andratx, and they'd appreciate someone who can translate for English visitors. And wait at table! I'll recommend you.*

Clara was as good as her word. A few weeks later, Kat was in Mallorca working at the Can Estella guesthouse. She had yet to meet Clara, who was away in Germany, but looked forward to visiting her house, Casa Cielo Azul, when she returned. Set high in the hills above the old town, it was known as *the* place for parties and gatherings, as was often said with a shake of the head or eye roll. *Alternative* and *hippy* were also adjectives flung Clara's way, but rather than putting Kat off, they only piqued her curiosity.

She imagined glamorous parties peopled by Mick Jagger and Marianne Faithful types, deep conversations stretching into the small hours, the sweet smell of joints and patchouli lacing the air while she sat on the veranda watching the sun peek over the distant sea line.

Clara Schneider represented adventure. She was educated, well-travelled and independent, qualities Kat admired. Clara sounded like a modern woman with a career and freedom, the person Kat longed to become, even if she felt a little overawed. It was very reassuring that David Beauchamp, who was kind and sweetly old-fashioned, held Clara in esteem. Kat trusted his judgement, as did her parents, so she had flown to Mallorca to an unknown job with strangers and hadn't been disappointed. The guesthouse owners, Maria and Francisco, were honest and kind. Kat loved the house with its slices of sea views and rosemary-studded terraces. Though always busy, she adored her new life. Her skin was always warm from the sun and her fingers scented with cleaning products, and although by nightfall she was exhausted, she felt utterly right in a way she never had before.

She felt she belonged here.

Mallorca was her place. What was not to love? The coves were quiet, the hillsides a bare mass of cream rock, sage scrub and wind-gnarled olive trees. The people were friendly and welcoming. The sun smiled down, soft breezes filled the air with a rosemary aroma, and clouds drifted dreamily over the slumbering mountains, as if mustering for the first scene of a fairytale.

Andratx was the kind of place you stumbled across once in a lifetime, if you were lucky. Nestled in the jagged folds of Mallorca's western coast, it was a secret small town known for centuries only to the sea. At the foot of steep hills, it was a huddle of terracotta rooftops and whitewashed walls peppered with sun-faded shutters in endless shades of azure and sage. By day, the town snoozed in the sunshine, watched over by mountains and the benevolent gaze of Santa Maria Church. By night, lights twinkled and guitar music floated on the soft breeze.

Here, the days sauntered rather than marched. Time stood still, and even though travel to the island was increasing, little had changed in Andratx. Kat knew that if she wandered down narrow side streets, she'd find old men in flat caps sitting outside, smoking hand-rolled cigarettes and playing dice as their grandfathers once had. Children darted through market stalls, laughing and playing chase while mothers called and scolded. Bees hummed in bougainvillea foam spilling over ancient walls. At lunchtime, the clink of glasses rose from the bars on street corners, and the air was rich with garlic.

Artists were drawn to the port. Each morning painters set up their easels, squinting against sunlight to capture light spangles on azure water. Canvases lolled against stone walls bright with sun and sea. Sketchbooks lay open on warm steps, pages curling around summer scenes. The light was special here, and Maria told Kat the town even made heartache seem beautiful. Kat had never had her heart broken, but when she set breakfast tables and glanced at the view, she felt sure Maria was right.

One of Kat's jobs was visiting the market to fetch fresh vegetables, fruit and crusty oven-warm bread. As she strolled along the quayside, a wicker basket swinging from her arm, she admired tied-up boats and inhaled the stench of diesel and fish. She was already sure that for the rest of her life, these smells would send her hurtling back to this time and place. The fishing port was a little rough around the edges, and unfashionable compared to other parts of the island, but Kat thought it had heart. It was real, and it felt as if nothing had changed here for centuries.

Some evenings Maria sent Kat to the quay to buy the pick of the day's catch. While the sun sank into the sea, turning it molten gold and spilling reds and pinks across the sky like ink seeping into blotting paper, Kat would wait for the boats to come in. The fish was so fresh it was almost swimming, but Kat enjoyed haggling for a good price almost as much as eating the sardines Maria grilled with sea salt and rosemary. It wasn't fancy fare, but it was honest. Kat loved her new diet of fish, vegetables and golden olive oil. Her skin glowed, she was fit from all the walking, and her sun-kissed skin was the colour of butterscotch ice cream. She was ready for something wonderful, and adventure was poised to happen here. Kat felt sure of it.

It was a Friday, her day off, and she had spent the afternoon at the cove the locals favoured, dipping in and out of the water in her new red crocheted bikini and basking on the rocks, her face shaded by a huge floppy hat as she read Lorca and felt very sophisticated. It was lovely to have time to herself to enjoy the town and to relax. She'd been in Andratx almost three weeks, but this was only her second full day off. It felt quite indulgent to loll about with nothing to do but swim, eat a picnic of crusty bread and gooey cheese, and bite into sun-warmed peaches so juicy that her chin and hands were soon so covered she had no choice but to dive back into the water to wash it away. Heaven.

As the sun began to slither into the sea and the sky turned the ballet-slipper pink, Kat knew it was time to head into town where she was meeting Annika, a glamorous Swedish girl she had chatted to in the market. They had arranged to meet for drinks and tapas before exploring a small festival that was taking place. Annika had promised she'd come after finishing her shift at the hotel where she was a receptionist.

Kat ducked behind an outcrop of rocks and changed into a dress she'd picked up in the market when she first arrived. Made of thin cotton, printed with wildflowers, and already faded from sunshine and washing, it was floaty and pretty, and made her feel the same way. She slipped her feet into sandals of plaited leather and tugged a brush through her hair, which was curly from the sea-swimming and tumbled down her back in wild waves. She wore little make-up here, having learned it soon melted in the heat, but she pulled a compact mirror from her bag and smudged just a little kohl along her lashes and dabbed a touch of colour to her lips. She had bought a small bottle of patchouli oil from the market, which she dabbed onto her wrists like perfume. The sweet smell mingled with the heat and the peach juice on her skin, and was far more exotic than her usual Charlie.

She felt ready for adventure. A rare, unsupervised escape from check-ins, market lists, and awkward translations between British tourists and Mallorcan fruit sellers. She didn't want to waste it at the guesthouse. Kat wanted to live a little, and where better than this beautiful town?

She climbed the steps hewn from rock which led from the cove to the street and wandered through the narrow streets of Andratx, her beaded bag swinging from her hand. White-washed walls glowed in the light of the setting sun. Bougainvillea tumbled from balconies. Someone was playing a guitar behind a shuttered window. The port was readying itself for the night, and her stomach twisted with delicious anticipation. Magic was in the air – Kat could feel it.

She found the bar Annika had mentioned, a small place by the water that served cheap drinks and played 'Santana' on repeat, and the waiter brought her some sangria and tapas while she waited for her friend. Kat nibbled olives and sipped her drink as slowly as she could, but Annika never came. After an hour, Kat realised she wasn't going to. She was on her own.

She could have gone back to the guesthouse and plumped for an early night, but the evening was warm and too full of possibility to go to bed, so she stayed at her table by the water, her sandals dangling from her feet, enjoying the soothing sensation of cool air between her red-tipped toes. Boats bobbed gently against their moorings. Lights from the yachts cast silver streaks across the sea. The waiter returned, his manner suggesting the table should be vacated, and so she asked for her bill, deciding to explore the town as it came to life.

The lights came on one by one, strung across the narrow streets like Christmas decorations. Paper lanterns flickered in the breeze, casting soft shadows across the sun-worn stone. Somewhere, a transistor radio crackled into life and spilled

'Santana' into the air. The streets were filling. Young men in flared trousers smoked by the church steps while old women positioned themselves in folding chairs, eyes sharp beneath their lace mantillas, waiting for the festival to start. Street vendors hawked their wares. Kat bought a paper cone of *almendras tostadas* and munched happily as she followed the sounds of music and laughter.

Turning into a wide side street she joined a crowd of young people who were dancing and singing. She stood at the edge watching girls in full skirts spin while boys clapped and called to them, stamping their feet and then joining in. Soon her toes were tapping to a wild rhythm that made her blood sing.

The music rose and fell, the shouts and calls softened by laughter. Someone was playing the *tamborí*, and above it a flute piped out a haunting melody that made Kat want to smile and cry at the same time. It was wonderful, and she clapped in time to the music but shook her head when the dancers beckoned to her. For now, she was happy to watch.

Then she heard it; a thin wail rising above the music. High-pitched and filled with fear, the cry rang with distress and she turned to see a little boy, no more than five, pushing against a tide of legs and baskets and careless knees. He was sobbing, and his words came tumbling out in such a rush that Kat caught only fragments of what he was trying to say.

She frowned. Something about *placeta*? Certainly something about *mama*, which was easy to understand in any language.

She knelt quickly, ignoring the bite of cobbles through her thin skirt. "*Hola, cariño. ¿Estás bien?*" she asked, her Spanish careful and coaxing.

The boy looked at her, hiccupped, and mumbled something again in rapid Spanish.

Kat blinked. Not quite Spanish. This was Mallorquín. It was akin to Catalan, her maternal grandfather's tongue, and it made her think of him. Kat's own Mallorquín was improving daily, but not enough to reassure a crying child. Did he say his mother had a boat? Was on a boat?

"It's all right," she said softly, trying anyway. "*No pasa nada*. We'll find her. I promise."

The child's lower lip wobbled, and he clutched a ragged teddy bear to his chest like a talisman. His eyes brimmed with tears, and he looked ready to howl again. He wanted his mummy, and although Kat scanned the crowd frantically, she didn't spot a worried-looking mother. She rose to her feet and held out her hand, feeling helpless.

"*Eh, petit, no pateixis*." The voice was warm, assured, and just behind her.

Kat turned, and found herself looking up at a boy. No, not a boy but a young man. He was tall and lean, maybe twenty-one or twenty-two, and was dressed in a white linen shirt undone to show a tanned chest and beaded necklace. The sleeves rolled up to the forearms and the snowy fabric loosely tucked into flared jeans in softest powder-blue denim jeans slung low on narrow hips. His feet were in deck shoes, as though he was a nautical Jim Morrison. His long dark hair was slightly dishevelled as though he'd run a hand through it too many times, but his Mallorquín was fluent, and after her own rough attempts it was like hearing music returning to its correct key.

The man crouched beside the little boy, his presence effortless and calming. The child turned instinctively toward him, still crying but quieter now, the serrated edges of panic blunting into trust. The man spoke gently, and the little boy pointed with his teddy bear, muttering between heart-wrenching hiccups. The man nodded and replied, something about taking him there and boats. Kat's ears, still growing used to the local variation of her own language, realised she had misheard.

"I think his mother was down by the boats," the man said softly. He spoke English with a musical accent that brought to mind beaches and flamenco and dark soft nights.

Kat sat back on her heels. She was doing her best not to stare, but some people exuded star quality and yet were oblivious to it. This young man was the kind you looked at not once, not twice, but three times to make sure you weren't imagining things. Then she pulled herself together. Jim Morrison wanted an answer.

"He was trying to say where he saw his mum," she said. "I caught the word for 'water', but not the rest." She had swapped to Spanish without thinking.

"You were close," he said, smiling at her changing tongue too. "Very close."

His accent was light, a soft lilt that made everything sound more intimate. Together, they stood up and the child took their hands without hesitation. The man led them through the thinning crowd, away from the music and chatter, into a quiet side street that still held the heat of the day, and which led to the waterfront. A woman came running towards them, her face taut with fear.

"Miquel!" she cried.

The child tugged from their grasp and ran towards her. His bear tumbled to the cobbles. "Mama!"

The woman scooped him into her arms, kissing him and scolding him, and thanking God, the saints, and the holy virgin. When she saw the young man and Kat, who had retrieved the teddy bear from the road, her words came fast and grateful, each one falling from her lips as fast as her tears. As Kat's ear tuned into the nuances of the language, filled with sepia-tinted memories of her grandparents, she thought she understood what the mother was telling them: Miquel had wandered off while his parents were talking to a friend, one of the fishermen. When she'd turned around there was no sight of him, and she had been so frightened. She pressed her hand to her heart and thanked then both, adding that when they had their own little ones, God willing, they would understand.

"Oh!" Kat said, flustered and her cheeks warm. "We're not …"

The Mallorcan Jim Morrison placed his hand on her forearm, a touch which said they didn't need to correct this poor lady, who was still shaking. His fingers were firm and cool against her skin. He smelt delicious, of lemons and bergamot. The way his eyes crinkled and slight lift of his mouth suggested Kat needn't be embarrassed, for the misunderstanding didn't matter. For some reason this made her feel as giddy as if she had downed ten glasses of sangria.

He replied to the mother in a warm and kind way, reassuring her that this was no trouble and that he was glad, they were both glad, to have helped. He wasn't showing off or expecting thanks, Kat noticed. He was genuinely glad to have assisted. She felt a warmth towards him that took her by surprise.

When Miquel and his mother departed and they were alone, Kat felt awkward. She was too aware of his hand still on her arm, of the racing of her heart, and her proximity to him. She stepped away and pushed her hair behind her ears. "Thank you," she said. "You were so kind."

"So were you. Most people would've just walked past. Everyone was having too much fun to even see him apart from you."

She shrugged, blushing.

"No," he insisted. "It's true. You are kind, señorita. Kind and beautiful. That is a rare thing."

Something in her chest fluttered. Was he teasing? Perhaps his true meaning was lost in translation? Or was he being sincere? Kat had never been called beautiful before, and knew she wasn't, but she held this compliment close. She was even more struck that he mentioned kindness first. Kat had long thought kindness was an overlooked quality.

"Thank you," she said.

"¡*Nada*! I'm Pablo. Pablo García."

Not Jim, then. Kat wanted to tell Pablo what she had been calling him, but wasn't sure it would translate. She smiled instead and when he smiled back she decided he was nothing like Jim Morrison at all. He was far more handsome, and exuded warmth rather than angst.

"Katalina Brown," she said. "Everyone calls me Kat."

"Katalina." On his lips her name sounded exotic and beautiful, which was exactly how the warmth in Pablo's eyes made her feel. "That suits you."

They stood smiling shyly at one another, and it seemed to Kat as though the whole town held its breath and the revelry around them quietened. Pablo looked as though he was about to ask her something – for her address, she found herself hoping, already knowing she didn't want these few moments to be the sum of their acquaintance. *Please ask!* How Kat wished she could be a feminist and ask him first. She felt sure this was what Clara Schneider would do.

Then a black car pulled up with a blast of a horn and the moment to speak was lost. Pablo inhaled sharply and raised a hand to the driver. He turned back to Kat with a regretful expression.

"I have to go."

The car was sleek, expensive, and out of place on the

cobbled street. The back window was down just far enough for Kat to see a woman sitting inside. She was dressed in black with her hair drawn back from a beautifully made-up face. Pearls nestled against her throat and glowed from earlobes. She was watching them through narrowed eyes.

"Pablo. Ara."

Pablo's posture changed. Not dramatically, but enough to tell Kat he understood he was being summoned. It was clear to them both that he had no say in the matter.

"I think you're wanted," she said.

Pablo nodded. The corner of his mouth lifted in a regretful smile. "I have to go, Katalina."

"Of course."

He lingered. The moment stretched.

"You do speak beautifully," Pablo told Kat gently. "Even when you don't know all the words."

And then he walked away and opened the car door. As he disappeared inside Kat thought it was as though he had been spirited away, back to the other world he had appeared from. She watched the tail lights vanish into the night, her paper cone of almonds forgotten in her hand, and the music fading behind her and suddenly too far away to reach. Kat no longer had the heart for festivals and dancing. She wanted to be alone to relive this encounter.

She sighed wistfully and began the slow walk up to the guesthouse, no longer thinking of pinching sandals or her heavy bag, but of a beautiful boy called Pablo who thought she was kind and beautiful and who had liked her voice.

A boy she would probably never see again and who already seemed like a dream.

CHAPTER 8

KAT - THEN

After that night, Kat found herself looking for Pablo García everywhere she went. She took different routes in and out of the town, hoping to catch sight of him, and on more than one occasion altered her way back from the market so she could retrace the steps she had taken that night. Yet no matter how hard she looked, or how many times her heart lifted at the sight of a dark-haired young man in soft denim jeans and a linen shirt, it was never Pablo. It was as though she had imagined him.

After too many disappointments to count, Kat concluded he had been on holiday and returned home to the mainland. She resigned herself to reality; the chances were that she would never see him again. Pablo had probably forgotten all about their encounter. Kat knew she ought to do the same; they had shared a moment in time, nothing more significant, and although his words had been flattering, she mustn't read anything deeper into them.

Unfortunately, this was proving easier said than done, because Kat's thoughts persisted in drifting to Pablo. *Don't fool yourself*, she would scold herself sharply as she yanked her focus back to slicing bread or pegging out washing. There was no greater meaning in their unexpected meeting. No machinations of Fate had brought them together, nor any celestial alignment, even though it had felt as though there had been a magical connection between them. She was imagining there had been an instant accord which had made her feel as though she had known Pablo forever.

Kat was furious with herself for replaying their meeting over and over. She knew better than this! There was no such thing as a soulmate. Love at first sight was the stuff of fairy tales, not real life – something her mother often said when she complained that her daughter was too fussy. There had been no magic with Pablo, and the sangria she had enjoyed while waiting for Annika had made her relaxed and fanciful. That was all.

These were logical arguments, but they didn't stop her daydreaming. Kat had never been the sort of girl who read Mills & Boon novels or spent her days fantasising about wedding dresses (although, if anyone really wanted to know, something floral and floaty by Laura Ashley with bell sleeves and a floppy hat would have done nicely). But now her thoughts kept drifting back to the dark-eyed stranger with the slow, sweet smile and gentle way with children.

If she were to imagine falling in love, Kat grudgingly supposed it might be with someone like Pablo. Already, she suspected his face would become permanently superimposed on any romantic hero she imagined from now on.

It was for the best that Pablo remained no more than a lovely memory. Kat had no desire to spend her time nursing a broken heart or worrying about whether someone liked her or was going to cool off. She had seen too many of her friends waste entire evenings waiting by the phone or trying to invent some sort of logic behind why the object of their affections hadn't been in touch. The truth was usually unpalatable, and Kat had often helped concoct kinder excuses: perhaps he had been called away, couldn't make it to the club or had met with a terrible accident and was in hospital.

Kat had been hard-pressed not to tell anyone about her encounter with Pablo. Said out loud, it didn't sound particularly significant. She had found a lost child, a young man had spoken to him in soft Mallorquín, and they had returned the child to his mother. Then the young man had left. This sparing version of events didn't come anywhere close to conveying the Cinderella magic of having Pablo whisked away, if not in a pumpkin carriage, then certainly in its modern, sleek Mercedes equivalent. Kat wasn't entirely convinced the elegant woman with the icy stare had been a fairy godmother, either. More like a wicked witch, swooping in to snatch him away! She had half-expected to see a deck shoe left behind on the cobblestones and to be instructed to try it on every handsome young man on the island. The thought made her laugh despairingly.

Kat had one real friend on the island: a girl her own age called Lina. Lina's family owned the bakery in town and had lived in Port Andratx for generations. They knew everyone and everything, and Lina's mother, Señora Perez, a large lady with eyes like bright currants and a shelf of a bosom on which her small gold crucifix rested, could always be relied on as a source of local gossip. There was no need to wait for the papers to be driven in from Palma when she knew all the news, or at least the parts of it involving who had said what or upset somebody. Lina was a younger version of her mother, and Kat knew that if anyone could tell her more about Pablo it was her.

It had become part of Kat's routine to rise at first light and walk into town to buy the groceries with a wicker basket swinging in her hand. She loved this part of the day, when the air was still cool, the clouds hung over the mountains, and the sea was the colour of milk. The town was coming alive as the locals made the most of the sun still being low by going about their work. Kat would choose vegetables and fruit, buy fresh eggs so Maria could make her delicious aïoli, and wedges of Mahón cheese. The last stop was always the bakery, where Lina's family sold pastries sweetened with olive oil and almonds, crusty bread and beautiful flaky croissants which melted in the mouth. Only the thought of her crocheted red bikini stopped Kat from devouring an entire baguette slathered with thick, yellow butter when she arrived back at the guesthouse. She was not surprised that Lina and her mother were so curvaceous. It would be impossible to be surrounded by such treats and not succumb to temptation.

Over the past few weeks, Kat had got to know Lina, who often served behind the counter while her parents were tending the ovens. The girls had started chatting, and shared a passion for Bowie, albeit one Lina kept low-key, saying her parents didn't approve since they were traditional and, like many of the locals, viewed newcomers and foreign culture with deep suspicion.

The girls had met for coffee, and on the rare occasion when their time off coincided, had swum in the cove and basked on the beach. Lina was gossipy and great fun, a girl who knew her mind. She was 'courting', as she sweetly put it, one of the young fishermen, and already planning the five children they would have together.

Lina's family were devout Catholics, and her mother, although probably only in her forties, dressed like a woman several decades older, always in black, often fingering her rosary beads or making her way to Mass. Though they were civil and polite, Kat knew the Perez parents didn't approve of English girls in red crochet bikinis and bell-bottom jeans, or subversive music. When Kat had once mentioned Clara Schneider, Lina pulled a face and said her parents believed that the German woman with the big house on the hill lived an immoral lifestyle.

"So, you won't be going to any parties with me, then?" Kat joked.

But Lina hadn't laughed. "No," she had said simply. "My parents would not allow it."

Kat had friends at home with strict parents. This never stopped them from attending discos or parties, although a fair amount of fibbing and subterfuge was usually involved. She knew suggesting pretending to be going elsewhere would shock Lina and maybe even offend her, so she was resigned to going alone when – or if – she was invited to Clara's house.

Cultural differences aside, the girls had become friends. Lina showed Kat where to buy the best leather belts or flowing cheesecloth sundresses, and in return Kat gifted her make-up, which Lina experimented with secretly. She said her boyfriend, Esteban, found it slightly shocking, but had also said the kohl made her eyes even darker and as beguiling as a shaman's. Kat very much doubted Esteban had said it quite like that; he was a boy of few words, and when he did talk it was mostly about his catch. More likely Lina had picked up the phrase from one of her romance novels and attributed it to him after he'd said she looked nice.

It was early morning, the sun-flushed sky the colour of strawberry milkshake and the petrol-blue sea as smooth as glass. The forecast had predicted a heatwave, so Kat had set out earlier than usual. Even at this hour, the day shimmered with heat, and Kat now understood the appeal of siestas. As she set off down the road, her basket over her arm, she could already feel the sun's warmth through the soles of her sandals.

The bakery was open, as it always was, and Lina and her mother were already busy behind the counter. Spotting Kat, Lina smiled warmly and waved. "*¡Hola!* The usual?"

Kat placed her basket on the counter. "*Por favor.*"

Señora Perez asked after Francisco and Maria (some kind of cousins, apparently, although Lina joked that everyone in town was some kind of cousin), then nodded in the direction of the basket.

"Hurry up, Lina. We do have other customers. Serve Katalina while I check the ovens."

While Lina selected the loaves and pastries, she chatted away about Esteban and his plans for buying a boat of his own so they could afford to marry. She had saved up enough for the wedding, she said, and wanted to visit Palma to look for fabric for her dress. Maybe Kat would like to join her? The cathedral was beautiful, and the shops even more so, to her way of thinking.

Sometimes Kat envied Lina. She had a plan – working in the bakery, living in Andratx, raising a brood of children – and seemed perfectly content. It must be peaceful not to always be striving and constantly scanning the horizon for what lay just beyond. Why couldn't she do the same?

While Lina wrapped up the bread and selected croissants, Kat inhaled the delicious aroma. Her mouth was watering, and when Lina offered her an almond croissant, she didn't say no.

"I shouldn't eat too many of these," she said through a mouthful of sweet, flaky pastry. "I'll be too fat soon for my swimming costume."

Lina snorted. "You are so tiny! You need to eat more."

"You sound like my mother," Kat said with a grin. "She'd feed me all day long if she could."

"Mine too," sighed her friend. She studied Kat thoughtfully. "Do you miss your family?"

Kat considered the question. Did she?

"I suppose I do," she said after a moment. "In an abstract sort of way, because everything here feels so new and exciting. Oxford, by comparison, seems very grey and dull. Like another life, and very far away. It's as though I'm another person here."

Just yesterday, she had received a letter from David, full of news and college gossip, and asking if she had seen Clara Schneider yet. He was planning to visit in September, he said. Clara had promised they would walk in the hills, and he was keen to see the cathedral again before flying on to Madrid. Perhaps he and Kat could meet up. It would be lovely to share some tapas – if she had time, of course. He understood she might be far too busy.

It was the third letter he had written, and Kat felt guilty for not having replied to any of them. She made a mental note to do so that afternoon during siesta time. David was sweet, and it was thanks to him that she was here, so the least she could do was write back. It might even help jog Clara's memory; after all, Kat hadn't made it up to Casa Cielo Azul yet.

"They're only a few hours away. Seems silly to miss them," Kat added.

"I think you're very brave," Lina said. "I couldn't bear to be away from here and my family. I think I'd be so homesick I wouldn't be able to eat a thing – which tells you something!"

Kat was itching to ask her about Pablo, but Lina's mother had returned and was listening in. So Kat waited for a few moments until she was deep in conversation with another customer about the scandalous woman who had worn a scarlet scarf to church, then seized her chance.

"I met a really interesting person the other day," she said casually.

Lina's eyes lit up. "Do you mean a boy?"

Kat felt her cheeks warm, and not from the ovens. "Well … yes. A young man, really."

Lina's eyes were saucers. "Who?"

"That's the problem," Kat said. "I don't know anything about him. I was hoping you might be able to help."

She explained how she had met Pablo, how he had helped soothe the lost child and find his mother. She didn't bother describing how he looked like a Greek god. She didn't need to.

Lina clapped her hands.

"You're in love with him! Love at first sight!"

"Don't be silly. I only met him for five minutes. I haven't seen him since and probably never will again."

"But you've been looking for him."

Kat couldn't deny it. "But I don't even know if he lives here. I haven't come across him again." She lowered her voice, just in case – Señora Perez had ears like a bat. "I was hoping you might know who he is. He said his name was Pablo García. He got into a very smart black car."

Lina's eyes widened. "Pablo de la Vega García?"

Spanish surnames were complicated, often including maternal names. Kat nodded. It made sense to simplify. "I guess so. Do you know of him?"

"*Sí*. I know who Pablo de la Vega García is. His parents own a beautiful house near Sant Elm."

Kat stared at her friend. She couldn't believe it had been this easy. Sant Elm was the next town along the coast. It was pretty, and a popular spot for swimming and eating tapas. She could easily catch a bus there or even walk, provided she set off when it was cool.

"He's local?"

Lina nodded slowly, but her expression was troubled. "In a way. His family own a holiday house above the town. A beautiful place. They're very wealthy. He's the only child. The heir to everything. He's very, very rich."

Kat was speechless. The sleek car aside, Pablo had seemed modest, and had dressed like an artist or a student.

"They're old money. His father is Don Álvaro de la Vega. You've probably seen him in the town or at church? Grey hair, always in a suit, even in the heat. Looks like he's judging the whole world."

Kat's stomach gave a little lurch. She hadn't seen him, but he sounded terrifying.

"They're not from around here," Lina continued, selecting a baguette and placing it in a paper bag with unnecessary precision. "They come from Madrid. High-up people. Very important. Very powerful. Pablo's father ..." She swallowed nervously. "He's close to the government."

"Franco's government?"

Lina nodded once, eyes scanning the shop to make sure her mother was still occupied. "*Sí*. He is old Falange. Very respected, very proud. He believes in tradition. Catholic values. Discipline. Control. He doesn't like foreigners. Especially not British ones."

"Charming," Kat muttered. She thought of her family and her sweet grandparents, who had suffered so terribly during Franco's rise to power. She didn't like the sound of Don Álvaro at all.

Lina glanced at her, her voice dropping further. "Kat, you must be careful. You are not Catholic. You are not Spanish. You are not suitable."

Kat was offended. "Good to know what people here *really* think of me."

"I'm sorry." Lina was genuinely pained. "But you must

understand, Kat. Men like Pablo's father live by different rules. They don't see us as people who matter. They are not like the rest of us."

Pablo wasn't like that, Kat thought, with a flash of anger that surprised her. He was kind and gentle, and he saw the little boy, Miquel, as somebody who mattered. He saw her as somebody who mattered, too. She knew he did.

Lina was still trying to explain. "His mother, Doña Mercedes, looks like a movie star but has a heart of stone. She would never allow it. They have already chosen someone for Pablo. A girl from Madrid. Old family. Very Catholic. Very quiet."

"But does he want that? It's the 1970s, Lina!"

"It doesn't matter, Kat. This is not England. It's not London. Here …" Lina shrugged as she struggled to explain. "Here, love comes second to duty. To reputation. Family is everything."

Kat looked away and out the bakery window, where the sunlight bounced off the terracotta rooftops. A skinny cat stalked across cobbles. A fishing boat unloaded the night's catch. Life here hadn't changed for generations, and the warm pastry-scented air was suddenly tainted with the bitter scent of her friend's warning.

"It is dangerous to be involved with such people," Lina warned quietly. "You could be hurt. Or blamed."

"Blamed for what, exactly?"

"Whatever might follow."

"Because I'm half-English? Because I wear a bikini? Listen to Bowie? Read banned books?"

"Because you're free, Kat. You don't live in fear of them. And people like Pablo's parents, they hate that more than anything."

Kat fell quiet for this made perfect sense. Then she exhaled slowly. "My grandparents fled Spain during the war, you know. Franco's soldiers shot two of my great-uncles. My third uncle was murdered in Madrid. My mother's never spoken of it, not really – and my grandparents never went back home."

Lina reached for her hand. "Then you understand better than most. These people haven't changed, Kat. Not really. They are waiting. Holding onto what power they have. Franco is old now, but his grip still holds. And families like the de la Vegas don't forget. They don't forgive."

Kat gave a brittle laugh. "And here I was thinking he just had nice eyes."

"He does," Lina said with a wink. "And a nice bum! He's an absolute dish – but don't lose your heart to a boy locked in a golden cage. No matter how handsome he is."

The shop bell jingled and a pair of tourists wandered in, chattering in London accents about the heat and whether croissants were 'authentically Spanish'. Lina's mother, who had just returned with a tray of oven-warm loaves, bustled over to serve them, smiling politely but keeping one ear on her daughter.

Kat picked up her basket, now heavier than before. She felt heavier too, weighed down by the truth. Yet somehow, the truth didn't seem to matter. Pablo existed outside of his parents. He was a young man, not a child. Already, Kat was wondering when she could borrow Francisco's scooter and visit Sant Elm. She wanted to see Pablo again. It made no sense at all, especially after this warning, but there were some things in life that couldn't be reasoned away.

She turned to Lina. "You're probably right. I should forget him."

Lina smiled. "Yes, you probably should, but you won't. Not yet. You're just ..."

"Just?"

"I don't know. In too deep?"

"I only met him for five minutes!"

Lina shrugged. "Sometimes that is all it takes. Just don't follow him too far. Some roads don't have signs back."

As Kat left the shop and turned for home, her friend's warning words echoed in her ears. Was she already walking down a road that would only take her in one direction? The heat rose in shimmering waves, and the sea was beginning to sparkle. Somewhere far off a church bell rang, and the town bustled into life. It was time to get back to work and to put Pablo from her mind.

Kat squared her shoulders and told herself she wasn't going to think about Pablo again, but even with this thought she knew in her heart it was too late.

She was already planning how she might be able to see him again.

CHAPTER 9

KAT - THEN

Her conversation with Lina only made Kat even more curious about Pablo de la Vega García, and more determined not to be put off finding him. It was never pleasant to be told you weren't good enough for somebody, and hard to hear that although she was half-Spanish and *felt* Spanish, the locals didn't see her as Spanish at all.

Not for the first time, Kat had the unsettling sensation that she didn't belong anywhere. She was neither English nor Spanish. With her dark hair and skin that tanned easily, she was seen as foreign in her own country, yet viewed with suspicion in the land of her mother's family. She didn't fit in. Didn't belong.

Perhaps she never would?

Kat knew she ought not to pursue Pablo. She was only here for the summer, after all, and their meeting had been fleeting. It could easily be put aside. She was also acutely aware that just as much as his family would not approve of her, her own mother's family certainly wouldn't approve of a boy linked to a high-ranking official in Franco's government. They would be equally horrified. Perhaps it would be best to leave her daydreams firmly in the realm of imagination?

In which case, she really shouldn't be planning a day trip to Sant Elm …

It was probably a blessing in disguise that the guesthouse was full. For the next few days, Kat was run off her feet and there was little chance of an evening off, never mind an entire day to go gallivanting around the island on a wild-goose chase. Between welcoming guests, cleaning rooms and waiting tables, she barely had time to breathe. She had struggled even to write her usual letter home, and feared it was much shorter than before. She had intended to write back to David and she began a letter, only to put it aside. Kat suspected he was sweet on her – something her mother had pointed out excitedly – and she didn't want to give him false hope. David Beauchamp was a lovely man, but he didn't make her insides squiggle as Pablo did, and neither were all her dreams filled with fleeting images of his face.

Kat had only spoken to her parents a handful of times since she'd arrived on the island. Phone lines in private houses were still rare here, and the guesthouse didn't possess one. So once a week, Kat would queue at the Oficina de Correos to request an international call. It was expensive and she only had a few minutes, but even so it was wonderful to hear her parents' voices. She wished they would venture out to Mallorca for a visit, but her father didn't like the idea of 'abroad', and her mother said she had no desire to visit Spain, even a part of it that considered itself distinct from the mainland.

Kat's most recent call home had been the day before. Her mother had sounded surprised when she said she had wanted to know more about their family's past, and had been unwilling to say anything over the telephone. "You do not know who is listening, *querida*," she'd warned.

Kat realised then how the fear of Franco and his regime was hardwired into her mother. It was a reminder that the same would be true for Pablo's family, though most likely from the opposite political persuasion. If Kat was looking for signs that she ought to leave her fascination with this boy well and truly alone, she was certainly getting them.

It was Thursday afternoon, the same week she had spoken to her mother, and Kat was lying on her bed trying to grab a siesta before the busy evening shift began. The ceiling fan tick-tick-ticked lazily above her head, and sunlight tiger-striped the tiled floor as it trickled through the blinds. A slight headache beat at her temples, and her feet ached from running up and down the stairs with bags followed by a long shift waiting tables at lunch.

Kat was just drifting off when Maria popped her head round the door: "Katalina. Are you awake?"

Even in the half-light, Kat could tell her employer's face was set in an expression of displeasure. She wondered what she had done now. Had the difficult guests in Bedroom 3 complained because they hadn't understood that gazpacho soup was meant to be cold, and taken offence at her explanation? Or had she not swept the terrace thoroughly enough after lunch, once again creating a feast for hungry ants?

"I am," she said, sitting up on one elbow. "Come in."

Maria didn't. She preferred to hover in the hinterland of the door jamb. "You have a visitor. Downstairs. In the parlour."

Her scarved head withdrew, and Kat heard her wooden sandals clacking down the passageway. Even her footsteps sounded affronted. What was up? Who could her visitor be? She didn't know anyone here apart from Lina, and Maria would hardly show the baker's daughter into her best parlour. For one silly moment, her heart soared thinking it must be Pablo. Then it plummeted again, since he had no idea where she worked. How could he find her even if he wanted to? A girl called Katalina would be impossible to trace here.

Now her heart began to race; was there something wrong with her family, necessitating a visit from her father or mother? Maria had certainly looked serious. Perhaps Kat had misread disapproval for worry.

She leapt up from her bed, adrenaline chasing away the last traces of lethargy, splashed water on her face at the washstand, and pulled her hair into a low ponytail. Slipping her feet into flip-flops and grabbing a shawl to cover her spaghetti straps (Maria was big on decency), Kat hurried downstairs.

The parlour was a grand name for the small room at the front of the guesthouse, which was reserved for paying customers but rarely used. It was a claustrophobic space, filled to the seams with fussy furniture draped in lace and macramé. A large mahogany dresser dominated the far end, and the small windows, shrouded in net curtains, were never opened because the frames were old and delicate. An electric fan was often switched on, stirring the air like warm soup, but even so anyone inside felt as though they were being slowly smothered. Kat hoped whoever was calling hadn't passed out.

She opened the door and was surprised to find a woman standing by the window, admiring the latticework. She was tall and bone-thin, dressed from head to toe in a flowing orange pantsuit with bell bottoms almost covering her cork wedge heels. Her slender arms were stacked with bangles, and the room no longer smelt musty but of a rich, exotic perfume. Ice-blonde hair was swept up into an elegant chignon, and a tasselled bag in jewel colours hung from her bony shoulder.

The visitor had her back to the door and the room was

dim, but Kat already thought she might be the most elegant woman she had ever seen. She instantly wished she wasn't wearing plain shorts and a vest.

"This ironwork is exquisite, *ja*?" The stranger turned from the window, offering the question as though she were genuinely interested in Kat's opinion.

Kat hadn't really noticed the window until now, other than wishing she could fling it open and gulp in fresh air like a drowning man, but on looking closely she saw that it was indeed beautiful. Swirls, stars, seashells linked together, and all finely wrought.

"The artist who made this had much talent. Probably he was influenced by the Moors, if not of Moorish heritage himself. So much beauty lost to ignorance and religion."

Kat wasn't sure how to reply, and the woman gathered herself with a small sigh. "Apologies. I find myself lost in such things."

She gave a little shake of her head. Large gold hoops swung and brushed against her pale cheeks. Kat was mesmerised. She wished she had the confidence to wear such jewellery.

The visitor held out her hand. Her ringed fingers were slim yet stained with rainbow hues, the nails short and workmanlike.

"I am Clara Schneider. It is good to meet you, Kat Brown. I'm sorry I wasn't here to welcome you when you arrived on the island."

Of course this was Clara. Kat was not at all surprised that this tall woman, with the grace of a fashion model and the knowledge of a professor, was the lecturer David had been so enthralled by. Now Kat understood why. Clara was mesmerising.

They shook hands, a rather formal gesture which felt to Kat as though they were sealing a pact.

"No need to apologise at all, Mrs Schneider," Kat said. "I'm so grateful to you for finding me the job here."

Clara threw back her head and laughed. "You do not need to thank me! You've no idea how many people wanted to employ a British girl who spoke Spanish. I could have found you a hundred jobs. Maria does not approve of me. She thinks I'm dreadfully wild and bohemian – which is quite true, I assure you – but she also knows I have good judgement, since I employ her cousin and her husband as my housekeepers."

She lowered her voice, so Kat had to lean in. "Nico had been in … how shall we say? A little trouble with the law in the past. Prison, I believe. Not the sort of man everyone would hire. But I take people as I find them, Kat, and I found them honest in saying what he had done, and he was so keen to have a second chance. Doesn't everyone deserve one? If we always hold grudges with the past, refuse to own it and take responsibility? To learn from mistakes?" She shrugged again. "I think my fellow countrymen and I have learned that holding onto judgement doesn't allow anyone to move on or make amends. To become better. You understand?"

Kat did understand. She knew what Clara was saying. The past was still an open wound, as her own family could testify. "I do, Frau Schneider," she said.

Clara's nose wrinkled. "Please, call me Clara. Herr Schneider is long gone – Harvard, I believe – and Frau Schneider sounds like my ex-mother-in-law."

"Of course, Clara."

The name sounded exotic on her lips. Clara Schneider was the most interesting woman Kat had ever met. She couldn't believe they were now on first-name terms.

"That makes life easier. I am German for certain, but not a fan of formality!" laughed Clara. "David speaks highly of you, Kat, and I feel sure we are going to be great friends."

Her eyes, the bright blue of the cool blocks Kat placed in the fridge to chill guest picnics, were sharp. Kat felt sure they missed nothing, and she flushed. Clara knew David had feelings for her.

"David's very kind. I only typed some essays for him and did some freelance work in the languages department after I finished my secretarial training."

Clara waved her hand, bangles chiming. "Yes, and he says you'd be wasted as a secretary. He says many things – not all I will repeat – but he is right about you being a very pretty girl. And I can see you are intelligent. Please forgive me if I sound blunt. You may say it's a German thing. I say it's just my character. Why waste time? I think being here will change your life, Kat, and I like to think that in some small way, I am a part of changing somebody's course. Do I have a God complex? Perhaps!"

She laughed, a deep, throaty sound, and rather husky. Probably from smoking, Kat thought, as she caught the notes of tobacco beneath the perfume. She wasn't sure how to answer Clara, who strung questions and statements together like linguistic beads on an intricate necklace. Her mind was racing.

David thought she was pretty. This was good news in some ways, and not in others. Kat wasn't naïve. She'd seen the admiration in his eyes. But he thought she was too clever to be a secretary? That was interesting. She wondered what he thought she should be doing, then looked at Clara and realised it wasn't David's place to decide.

It was hers.

That was what she needed to do; she needed to work out what she was truly interested in. She knew she liked music, literature and travel, and as she talked to Clara about the latticework and the beautiful inlay on what she'd once thought an ugly dresser, Kat thought perhaps she liked art, too. She loved colour. She wanted to know more about how it worked. When she looked at Clara's outfit, she realised for the first time that colours could clash and still look good. Maybe she liked design?

"I'm having a small gathering at my house on Friday night. I'd love you to come and meet some new people," said Clara, little realising she'd just uttered the magic words Kat had been longing to hear.

"I'd love that," Kat said.

She hoped she'd have the night off. But if Maria was difficult, Kat already knew she'd go anyway and forfeit pay. She wasn't going to miss a visit to Casa Cielo Azul.

"*Wunderbar!* It's a casual thing, so no need to dress up," Clara continued. "Just some friends. They are an interesting bunch, and I think you'll enjoy meeting them. Nothing much happens before nine, so no rush. We'll no doubt go into the small hours."

Invitation issued, Clara Schneider smiled and glanced at the watch on her slender wrist. Cartier, Kat noticed.

"So. I'm teaching a pottery class this afternoon, and I never like to keep anyone waiting."

She stepped forward and, to Kat's surprise, took her chin gently in her cool fingers, tilting her face to the light. "I would love to sculpt you, Katalina. You have exquisite bones. All my artists will be clamouring to have you as their muse. So, pick wisely."

And with that, Clara Schneider departed, calling a farewell to Maria in Mallorquín, while Kat stood dazed in the parlour, feeling the cool imprint of Clara's hands still on her face and reeling from the intensity of the visit and heady perfume.

She couldn't wait for Friday.

CHAPTER 10

KAT - THEN

Kat stood in front of the small mirror propped on her washstand, biting her lip and frowning slightly. Her wardrobe had yielded a jumble of cotton sundresses, faded denim shorts and the odd halter top – practical and cool for certain, but hardly the stuff of elegant soirées. Clara had said it was a 'casual' gathering, but somehow Kat didn't imagine that meant flip-flops and yesterday's vest.

She eventually settled on a dress she had not yet worn, a soft, off-white number made of gauzy cheesecloth with narrow beaded straps and a drawstring waist. It skimmed her figure just enough for her to feel feminine without trying too hard, and when she moved the fabric floated around her knees like seafoam. She had bought it at a market stall in town, drawn to the way the fabric felt cool against her sun-warmed skin, and she had loved how the hem swayed with the breeze. It felt just the right thing to wear to a party filled with creative types.

She tied her hair back loosely with a silk scarf, blue with a pattern of lemons and vines that looked as though it belonged on a bottle of limoncello, and it added a splash of colour to her outfit. A few dark curls slipped free to frame her face, but she left them, liking the impression that she had not tried too hard, even though she had been agonising over what to wear from the second that Clara Schneider had issued her invitation.

For jewellery, she chose only a pair of small gold studs and a narrow bangle she had found at a flea market. She dabbed a little of the perfume she had been given by Lina only that morning – a light, jasmine scent – onto her wrists and collar-bone, and that was that. No heavy make-up. Just a sweep of kohl around her eyes and a touch of lip balm. She wanted to look like herself. Not trying to impress. Not trying to belong. Just being herself.

Lina was almost as excited as Kat, and agog to hear about the famous German artist. That morning she had packed Kat's basket with all the wrong items (only discovered by Kat when she had got back to the guesthouse kitchen and Maria was despairingly asking her where the croissants were and why they had five loaves … Was the Good Lord due to perform a miracle?). Lina had been scolded several times by her mother for not paying attention, and her father had hollered after her when she left the shop to follow Kat outside for a moment.

Lina had pressed a bottle of perfume into Kat's hands. "For good luck!"

"Maria's given me the night off," Kat said. She was still unable to believe this had happened when they were so busy. Clara Schneider had magical powers, that was for sure. Or maybe Maria was simply grateful she had given her cousin's husband a chance of a new start?

"For confidence, then," said Lina, pressing the bottle into Kat's hand. "My grandmother bought it in Madrid, and whenever I wear this I feel as though I am one of those rich women who shop in the city and buy Chanel. There will be some of them at Casa Cielo Azul tonight, for sure. Clara Schneider has some wealthy patrons."

"Like Pablo's parents?" It was awful, this bright flare of hope Kat felt at the mere thought she might see him again.

Lina's dark brows drew together. "Maybe. People like them, anyway. People who judge the rest of us."

Kat recalled the way Pablo's mother had appraised her through narrowed eyes, as though not much liking what she saw.

Lina was right, and Kat loved her friend for trying her best to provide some armour. She tucked the bottle into the pocket of her shorts. "Thank you."

"Remember, you may not be rich, but you are as good as anyone there," said Lina fiercely, hugging her. "Have a wonderful time."

There was a lump in Kat's throat as she hugged her friend back. Then Señor Perez shouted for his daughter yet again, a note of irritation in his voice, and Lina returned to the bakery, calling over her shoulder that the next time Kat came to the bakery she wanted to hear everything about the party.

Now that party was just a walk away.

Slipping on her leather sandals, Kat gave herself one final glance in the mirror. The dress had creased a little in the drawer, and her scarf was probably too bright, but somehow it worked. She looked like a girl who lived on a beautiful Mediterranean island. She might not be polished or wearing couture, but she felt confident and excited. She did not know if Pablo would be there, though of course she hoped so. Kat wanted him to see her like this. Not dressed up like a doll or trying too hard, but looking a little more sophisticated than before.

She followed the dusty path out of town, her sandals crunching softly on the dry earth as the last rays of sun bathed the hillside in molten gold. The air was thick with the hum of cicadas, a constant electric buzz that pulsed like a heartbeat in the background. She passed the old fig tree by the roadside, its heavy fruit scent mingling with wild thyme and the sharp tang of pine, and as she climbed the town slowly fell away beneath her, its terracotta rooftops glowing like embers in the evening light.

Clara's house clung to the hillside for dear life. Ramshackle and sun-bleached, its whitewashed walls were cracked and crumbling in places, ivy curling around the shutters and a tumble of bougainvillea spilling from the terrace. From a distance, it looked like it might tumble down with the slightest whisper of wind, a romantic ramshackle bolthole where an artist could be free to create and express herself.

As Kat climbed higher, the last of the sun gilded the hills like honey poured slowly over stone, melting into the dusty folds of the mountains. Below, the old town of Andratx shimmered in the last of the heat, lights flickering on like fireflies as the evening stole over the island. Kat paused to catch her breath, and could just see the sea beyond the port, a silver mirror to the rising smile of the moon.

As she drew closer to Casa Cielo Azul, tucked in the olive trees like a secret, she could hear music drifting on the breeze: something slow and smoky with a beat that made her heart race. A woman was laughing, and the clink of glasses and low hum of conversation reached her ears like a promise of the good time which lay just ahead.

The house was ancient, its stone walls thick and cool, its blue shutters faded to the perfect Mediterranean sigh of colour. Jasmine curled up the beams of the porch, its scent caught in the breeze and carried like perfume through the courtyard where the party was in full swing. It was the most exotic place Kat had ever seen.

Kat let herself through a listing gate and followed a path which led her around the back of the house, where the land dropped away into a tangle of olive trees and wild fennel. Here, in a natural hollow, fairy lights were strung between twisted branches and sagging fenceposts, glowing softly and creating a sense of enchantment. People were gathered in loose clusters around an old stone pool, its edges chipped and mossy but still managing to dazzle like a film set. Barefoot women in batik dresses danced slowly to the music, heads tilted back. Men with sun-bleached hair and open shirts sipped from glasses of wine and smoked lazily, their laughter echoing in the warm night air.

It was not as polished as Kat had imagined sophisticated parties might be, but better because it was bohemian and possessed a thrown-together vibe the best designers would envy. There were mismatched chairs and battered cushions scattered across the terrace, platters of olives and cheese and torn hunks of bread scattered on tables. Someone had brought an old record player outside, and the music changed, something bluesy and American, maybe Janis Joplin. It suited the place perfectly.

Kat paused at the edge of it all, under a lemon tree, and her heart fluttered like a moth. The lights caught in her scarf and the breeze lifted the hem of her dress. No one looked up, and no one stared. This was not a party of entrances or curated perfection.

She took a breath, stepped down onto the terrace, pulled her shoulders back and smiled. This was what she had dreamed of doing when she had dared to imagine spending the summer on the island. She had longed for a life away from the ordinary, and here it was, waiting for her and beckoning her to step into a whole new world. She had the strongest sensation that her life was about to begin from this moment. It was not a time to be shy.

There was no sign of Clara with the dancers. Kat turned to the house and stepped inside, where Fleetwood Mac drifted from a record player, the vinyl hissing softly under the needle. A peacock-blue silk kaftan fluttered from a nail on the wall. Someone had turned an old pottery wheel into a makeshift wine table, and bottles, half-full, stood among bowls of sun-warmed olives, lemon wedges and tapenade. A large Mallorcan man was piling his plate high, and his voice rang out above the music like a bell as he held court. Other people were draped on chairs or sprawled on beanbags in a huddle of bronzed limbs, long hair and flared jeans. Somebody was smoking hash, which filled the air with its sweet and heady scent.

To her left, a British man in cream trousers and a paisley shirt unbuttoned to his hairy navel was deep in conversation with a French woman, drinking Rioja from the bottle and getting quite animated about metaphor. Two beautiful blonde girls draped in gauzy scarves and barefoot danced with their eyes closed, arms rising like smoke as they swayed to the rhythm.

Clara was here, holding court. She was barefoot too, and her hair fell in a white-gold sheet down her back. She wore a loose linen dress, belted low with a piece of woven leather, and paint still clung to the inside of her elbow. She moved through the gathering kissing cheeks, topping up glasses, and laughing with her whole body. Kat was feeling as though she was watching the party from outside herself. Everyone was so glamorous and at ease.

"You know," someone whispered beside her, a woman in a feather-trimmed shawl and bearing a tray of drinks. "This house is built on an energy line. Like, a ley line." She offered Kat a glass of red wine and added, "That's why everyone ends up here. Why it feels the way it does. It's magical."

Kat did not doubt this. She wanted to see and hear everything. She turned and wandered out onto the terrace where a teenage boy sat on the old stone wall, strumming a battered guitar and watching the party unfold with the intensity of someone who knew he would write about this night for years to come. Kat closed her eyes. She inhaled the scent of jasmine, hash and sun-baked stone, and stepped into the music, letting herself be pulled into the spell.

And then she saw him.

Pablo.

Her breath caught, and her heart seemed to turn a slow somersault because it really was him. After all the days of dreaming and longing, and telling herself she would never see him again, he was here, and he was just as beautiful as she remembered.

Pablo stood just inside the arch of the gateway, under the soft strings of fairy lights. His white shirt was open at the neck, sleeves rolled up, and the long dark curls brushed his broad shoulders. And then he looked right at Kat, and it was like a storm surge in her chest. The same lurch she'd felt when she'd first seen him. The tug of mutual attraction. The quiet sympathy that had flowed between them.

Their meeting replayed in a heartbeat. The little boy's cries. Pablo's soothing. The ease between them. The soft voice that said she was kind and beautiful. Then came the black Mercedes, the sharp voice of his mother, the door swinging open. His glance back at her just before it shut. The longing in his eyes. Her lonely walk home.

And now here he was. Not a memory. Real.

Here.

Pablo smiled delightedly. He waved and crossed the terrace with ease, as though he'd always been expecting to find her here.

"*Hola*, Katalina," he said softly. "You look beautiful."

Kat felt her heart turn over. When Pablo's gaze rested upon her, beautiful was exactly how she felt.

"And kind?" she teased.

"I hope you will be kind," he replied. "Kind enough to let me apologise for leaving so abruptly the other night. It was unforgivably rude."

"It's fine. I could see you were in a hurry."

"I wasn't in a hurry," said Pablo. "My mother, though! She is always impatient. Mama hates to be kept waiting."

Kat understood better than most that Spanish mothers ruled their children with iron fists holding lacy fans.

"It's fine," she said again. "You had kept her waiting long enough."

Pablo looked as though he wanted to say more, but instead he sighed.

"*Sí*. I was sorry to leave, though. I hope you can believe that."

Kat did believe him. She didn't know why, but she trusted Pablo. "I didn't think I'd see you again," she said, her voice lower than usual.

"I hoped I would see you again. I tried to find out where you lived, but finding a girl called Katalina who lives in Andratx is like …" He spread his hands in a gesture of hopelessness.

"Like looking for a needle in a haystack," Kat finished, repeating it in Spanish when he looked puzzled. "It's an English saying. It means impossible to find."

Pablo nodded. "Yes. You were a needle in the biggest

haystack ever. I was starting to despair. You're my Haystack Girl!'

"I found out who you are," Kat said. "Pablo de la Vega García. I know lots about you, and it all sounds very serious."

He laughed softly. "It is. Very serious. My father thinks so, at least."

"And your mother?" she asked.

Pablo looked at Kat. His eyes, as warm as sherry, held hers. "She thinks I should stay away from strange English girls who appear Spanish, but she does not understand that it is too late for that."

He felt the same way. Kat hadn't imagined it. As they sat beside one another on the wall, not touching but so close she could feel the heat of his skin through his shirt, they both knew there was no need to say more. As they watched the lights of the town twinkle like a galaxy, their fingers brushed, hesitantly at first, before their hands deliberately found one another. Neither spoke, afraid to break the fragile magic of that simple, world-changing gesture.

Then Pablo rose and pulled Kat to her feet. Still holding hands, they walked through the olive grove just beyond the house, where lanterns swayed in the branches and behind all was inky dark. The voices behind them faded into murmurs. The two began to talk as they strolled, and the conversation flowed easily. They chatted about music, films, books. Their families. His, unyielding like marble and hewn from old Spain. Hers, a blur of cultures and a tangle of contradictions. Her uncles, who had died too young. Her mother, who never wanted to visit Spain. Her English father, who still called Mallorca 'Majorca' and had no idea what to do with a daughter who wanted to read Lorca and live by the sea.

"I'm staying at the Can Estella guesthouse," she said. "Working there. For the summer."

"Its name suits it better now."

Kat laughed. "I bet you say that to all the girls."

"No," said Pablo, "I don't. I have never said anything like that before, Katalina."

She loved the way he said her name. It sounded ripe and sensual on his lips, a linguistic echo of how the warmth of his hand in hers made her feel.

"You should stay longer," he added. "You belong here."

"You sound sure."

He raised her hand to his lips and brushed it against his mouth. It was a simple gesture and almost chaste, but the most erotic moment of Kat's life. Her skin felt electrified, and she thought she would dissolve with yearning for more.

"I have never been more certain of anything in my life."

They paused to sit on the wall at the far end of the garden. The lights of Andratx shimmered below, and far beyond that the low silver line of the sea gleamed faintly under the moon.

"I've told you all about my family, but you haven't said much about yours. I know they are rich and powerful, but what are they like as people?"

Kat had been honest with Pablo, laying out the history of grandparents who had fought against Franco, the uncles who had been killed under the Spanish ruler's regime, and explaining her mother's refusal to return while the man she still referred to as 'that dictator' was in power. Pablo had listened, voicing sadness and sympathy, but had not responded in kind. He gazed out over the town as though searching for the right words.

"They are complicated."

"All families are."

"Indeed. But to paraphrase Orwell, some are more complicated than others."

She gasped. Franco's regime had imposed strict censorship

on literature, and any material considered politically subversive was banned. Orwell's work would have to be smuggled in and read in secret. Pablo was taking a risk alluding to having read *Animal Farm,* and he was also giving her a very clear message: he did not think like his parents. He thought like her.

"You've read Orwell?"

"I couldn't say. Walls have ears here. Or they certainly do at home."

Kat's heart went out to him. Pablo was subject to pressures she couldn't even begin to understand.

As the party continued, they sat in the darkness and talked themselves inside out. Pablo told her about his life in Madrid: the suffocation of rules, his mother with her high expectations and rigid religious beliefs, his father, Don Álvaro, a man of duty, image and control who wanted his son to follow him into politics and to share his own political persuasion.

"I am not what he planned or wanted his son to be," Pablo confessed, his voice low. "But I pretend sometimes that I am. To keep the peace. To not disappoint him."

Kat looked at him. "And now?"

He met her gaze. "Now I don't want to pretend."

Kat didn't know how long they talked. There was no before or after. Only this: his hand holding hers and her head resting on his shoulder. The scent of jasmine perfume in the breeze. Her bare leg touching his. Eventually the sky behind the mountains began to blush as dawn came soft and slow, and the town blushed palest pink. Even the moon slipped away with the morning star hot on its heels. She realised the noise of the party had ended some time ago.

"You're not going to disappear again, are you?" she asked him.

Pablo squeezed her hand. "Not if you want me to stay."

"I do. So much."

Kat's heart was wide open. She was scared and alive, filled with a terrible sensation that she was out of control and hurtling towards a new future with no means, or desire, of stopping.

The sky was softening to the gentlest gold, the dark edges of night retreating like a tide. Birdsong had begun somewhere in the valley below, the chorus just before the world properly wakes, as nature celebrates surviving through the darkness to a new dawn.

Together, Pablo and Kat watched the breaking of a day that was the start of something very special. Kat could feel Pablo beside her, and sensed he wanted more. She knew she did. She ached to kiss him and feel his mouth brush hers.

And then, slowly, deliberately, he reached for her and drew her towards him. His touch was tentative and gentle, as though he was asking a question with no words. Kat's breath caught, and she turned her face toward him. They were so close their eyelashes were almost touching.

"*¿Está bien?*" he asked softly.

Kat nodded. "*Sí.*"

And then he kissed her.

It wasn't rushed. There was no performance in it, just the tender press of his lips to hers and the warmth of his hand as it cupped her cheek. His kiss tasted of red wine and sunrise. It was slow, sweet, unguarded – and it set Kat aflame.

She realised this was her first real kiss. Those at school dances or walks in English gardens vanished like smoke in sunlight. This kiss ignited all the quiet parts of herself she'd kept folded away. It made her want more. It made her want *everything.* How was it possible that such a simple kiss could become so powerful?

When Pablo pulled back, he stayed close, his forehead

against hers. Kat's eyes stayed shut a moment longer. She didn't want the spell to break.

"That was ..." she began, then stopped, smiling shyly.

Pablo whispered, "*Yo también.*"

They sat there, hand in hand, as the sun finally rose above the mountain and the rest of the world began to wake. The sky was pale gold now, and the hills wore a soft lavender mist. The *finca* behind them murmured with the echoes of laughter and the clatter of crockery. There was a splash from the pool and a peal of laughter. The smell of frying bacon drifted in the air.

"Clara always provides breakfast," Pablo explained. "People are hungry after all the partying."

"You've been to her parties before?"

"A couple of times. A friend of my mother's is a sculptor. Clara invited her. My parents and I came too, but my father didn't approve of the company. Too many artists and intellectuals for his taste, and my mother's too, but I found it interesting. Clara was kind enough to say I'm always welcome when I am on the island. I think she likes to educate people."

"Set them on their path," recalled Kat. This party had set her on a new path, all right. Her head was spinning, and all the things she had fretted about before – her career, or lack of it, the guesthouse, what her parents thought – was as nothing.

Pablo brushed his mouth with his. "She has certainly done that," he murmured.

Neither Kat nor Pablo wanted to return to the aftermath of the party, to drink Bloody Marys and eat *tortilla Española*. They were still under the spell of the magical night, and reluctant to break it. Instead, they quietly made their way to the gate and out onto the steep lane which led back to town.

Kat's sandals hung from her fingers. The path down to the town was warm underfoot, scattered with dry leaves. Pablo walked beside her in silence, their shoulders brushing, and Kat couldn't stop smiling. Pablo glanced at her and smiled too. They were in on a delicious secret.

"I don't want the night to end," he said.

"Me neither."

"You're so different, Katalina."

"Different how?"

"You don't try to impress anyone. You are just yourself. You are so sure of who you are. You were alone at that party, but you didn't mind that. I watched you and I wanted to be with you so much I ached."

Kat looked away. Her heart was doing something strange and swooping. "I was hoping you might come," she admitted.

"I saw only you, the second I arrived," Pablo continued. "You were by the lemon tree. I couldn't believe that I'd found you at last. It was too good to be true."

"It feels like that," she agreed. "Is it too good to be true?"

"No," he said firmly. "It's real."

She nodded and he took her hand again. They walked the rest of the way like that, and the quiet between them was rich with things that didn't need words.

When they reached the street which led to Can Estella, Pablo slowed.

"Can I see you again?"

Kat was thrilled. "Yes. Yes, please."

One side of his mouth rose a little higher than the other, a quirk which melted her heart. He shook his dark curls from his eyes and beamed at her. "That makes me so happy. I have a boat. Not a big one, just something I take out sometimes. There's a little cove near Sant Elm. Nobody goes there. Not tourists. Not many locals either. It's quiet. Secret. Will you come there with me?"

She looked up at him. "When?"

"How about this afternoon," he suggested, dark eyes shining. "We'll take food. We'll swim. Just us. *¿Sí?*"

"*Sí,*" Kat agreed, thinking that she was so glad Maria had given her the day off, muttering that she'd be no use to anyone after staying out all night. "Yes, please."

He bent and kissed her again, this kiss rich with the promise of more. Then he stepped back. "I'll be at the quayside. At noon. Don't be late, Haystack Girl."

Kat laughed. She loved his daft nickname. "I won't."

"And bring your sunhat!" he called. "It's going to be a beautiful day!"

"It already is," said Kat. It was the most beautiful day of her life.

She watched him walk away, tall and lit by the morning sun, and was filled with peace. There would be no games with this man. No wondering whether he liked her. No sitting by the phone or analysing his every word with her friends. Kat didn't need to second-guess Pablo, because she knew he felt the same way she did. She saw with a sudden rush of clarity that this wasn't a silly crush. This wasn't a holiday romance or a summer fling. This was far more. It was the beginning of something huge. It was the start of the rest of her life.

CHAPTER 11

KAT - THEN

The café was tucked into a crooked alley near the church, its faded awning sagging gently in the morning heat. Cicadas rasped in the olive trees, and the scent of strong coffee and warm bread floated from the doorway. It was not a place Kat knew well, but Maria's cousin had called at the guesthouse just after 8 am, bearing a note from Clara:

I did not see much of you last night, little English swallow! You flew away before I could find you. I will catch up with you at Café de l'Alba at eleven. C x

It was a summons. No amount of swirly violet writing could disguise this as a suggestion; Clara was telling Kat to be at the café. There was no hint that Kat might be tired and wish to sleep or be otherwise occupied.

"Why did you not see her last night?" Maria had asked, peering over Kat's shoulder and squinting at the note.

There was no way Kat was telling Maria about Pablo. Floating on air around the guesthouse, she had held the memory of his kisses close to her heart and played them through her mind over and over again. Buzzing with a strange energy and unable to sit still, she had already swept the terrace and helped set the breakfast tables, singing her way through *The Sound of Music* and paying extra attention to 'Sixteen Going on Seventeen'. When Maria arrived with the shopping, Kat had even unpacked it and made coffee.

"There were lots of guests last night," Kat answered. "She was busy talking to them."

Unfortunately for Kat, Maria was the mother of daughters and didn't miss a trick. She snorted. "You were with a boy, I suppose. You have that soppy look on your face, and you keep singing. Now Madame the Artist wants to know all the details."

Clara could ask all she liked, thought Kat. She wasn't telling her a thing. Still, she did feel a little guilty that she had hardly exchanged more than a few words with her hostess. Since there was no way to tell Clara she couldn't make it to the café, Kat had gobbled a croissant and had a quick bath before heading out again.

Knowing she was meeting Pablo again at noon, she wore a long green sundress over a white one-piece swimming costume, rammed a floppy crocheted sunhat onto her curls and pushed her feet into flamingo-pink flip-flops. Sun cream, sunglasses and a towel were stowed in a raffia bag, and she even stopped to make a quick picnic of crusty bread, Parma ham and strong Mahón cheese, peaches and lemonade. Fortunately, Maria was serving breakfasts and couldn't comment, but Francisco, reading the paper at the kitchen table, winked knowingly and wished her a good day off.

When Kat arrived at the café, Clara was already there. She sat at a wrought-iron table under the bougainvillea, a pristine linen shirt knotted at the waist, the creases on her indigo jeans ironed with military precision. Enormous dark glasses hid her eyes. A cigarette curled smoke in the ashtray beside a tiny cup of espresso. She looked like she had stepped out of a French film, effortlessly stylish, a little dangerous and unmistakably European.

"Kat," Clara smiled, rising to kiss her on both cheeks. Her lipstick was red, and the espresso cup bore a scarlet kiss. "You look radiant."

Kat slid into the chair opposite. "Thank you."

Clara signalled the waiter with a flick of her fingers. "Espresso for her. And a pastry, if they're still warm. She's in love."

Kat laughed. "I'm not."

"Nonsense. Don't think your slinking into the dark with that beautiful boy went unnoticed. Ach! I am quite jealous. If only he was a little older!"

"We just talked."

Clara took a drag from her cigarette and waggled thin pencilled brows. "How I miss *talking.*"

Kat grinned, then looked down at her hands, twisting the silver ring on her middle finger. She didn't want to say any more, but it was growing harder by the minute to hold this joy inside. She wanted to jump up and down and tell everyone she had been kissed by Pablo de la Vega García.

Clara studied her a moment longer. "You know, Kat, I think you're wonderful. You remind me of me. A long time ago, of course. You're a lot like me."

"Only less German and sophisticated," Kat pointed out.

Clara's smile was quick and self-deprecating. "Yes. That too. You are a strange mix of both your cultures. Hot-headed and reserved. Passionate and controlled. No wonder that poor boy is smitten."

Kat's heart rose like a hot air balloon to hear that Clara thought Pablo was smitten. She said nothing, drawing on her British genes for reserve and restraint while her Spanish ones longed to shout her news from the rooftops.

The waiter brought the coffee. Clara waited until he was gone before speaking again. "So. Pablo."

Kat's pulse fluttered at the sound of his name. "Yes."

"I saw the way he looked at you last night. The way you looked at him. It's sweet but very dangerous. You should step away while you can."

Kat frowned. She wasn't expecting this. "Are you warning me off?" She was puzzled; Clara Schneider was a free spirit. Pablo had said that several of the men at the party were rumoured to be her lovers, and some of the women too. If she was on a morality crusade, she didn't have a jean-clad leg to stand on.

Clara leaned back in her chair. The bougainvillea above her shifted in the breeze. "I suppose I am. I know boys like Pablo. I've kissed boys like Pablo. I've loved them. They shine like fire, and you think this is real. This will change everything. This is the beginning of something wonderful. Maybe even the rest of my life?"

Kat was jolted. These were the very thoughts chasing around her head. "And doesn't it?" she asked. Clara seemed a woman who had all the answers.

The older woman looked sad. "It changes you. But it doesn't change the world they belong to. It only makes the distance greater, *ja*? In the end, the world they belong to, the one their parents are a part of and that they have been born to inhabit – and to *run* in the case of your Pablo – calls them back. Then you are left behind. A beautiful bird that wanted to soar, left with broken wings."

There was a silence for a moment. Coffee machines hissed. Knives chinked against plates. Kat's pastry sat untouched.

"Take Pablo's parents," Clara went on, her voice gentler now. "They are not people who bend. His father is a man who expects total obedience and respect. His mother is quieter, but no less proud. They have a future in mind for him that was planned before he was born, and you will never be a part of it. They won't understand this, you and him. They'll call it a distraction. A mistake. They will want him to marry a girl whose name fits next to his in the newspaper. Who goes to Mass. Who doesn't work in guesthouses or drink wine under fig trees. A girl who is not from a family that resisted Franco and who privately calls him a dictator. The man whose regime has raised them high."

Kat looked away, feeling uneasy because Clara was voicing her darkest fears. "He isn't like them. He's different."

"I know," agreed Clara. She and blew a perfect smoke ring. "He is a lovely boy. But I have met his parents and, trust me, they rule him with a rod of iron."

"He's twenty-two! He knows his own mind."

"I'm not saying he's not sincere. I'm sure he means every word he says to you. Today. Right now. But he will be pulled back into their world sooner or later. He will. It is as certain as the tide turning. And when it happens you, *Liebling*, will be left on the shore."

Kat swallowed hard. "I don't care."

"Don't you?"

"No. I mean, I would care, but I don't think he's like that at all. Pablo would never do that. I know he wouldn't. You don't know him like I do, Clara."

"My dear, you only met him last night."

"No! We'd met before."

Kat had to make Clara understand. She hadn't known the

German woman long, but she already liked her and valued her judgement. She understood Clara was trying to protect her and was touched. But it was already too late to be protected; Kat knew she was head over heels in love with Pablo de la Vega García.

While Clara lit and smoked another cigarette, Kat described how she and Pablo had first met. She talked about his kindness to the small boy and his quiet determination to find the worried mother. He had even tried to make her feel better about her clumsy Mallorquín.

"I know you think I'm just some silly girl who's going to get hurt, but I'd rather feel everything than feel nothing," she finished. There. Let Clara laugh and think her foolish.

But Clara wasn't laughing. She looked even more concerned. "I don't think that at all. You are far from silly. I just fear you will have your heart broken."

Kat thought a broken heart was a small price to pay for feeling so alive. "I'm not going to pretend it's not real just because it might not last," she declared, raising her chin. "I can't live my life in fear of what might happen. That's not living, is it? That's existing."

Clara stubbed out her cigarette. She reached across the table and squeezed Kat's hand. "You are going to break your heart so beautifully. Oh, to be twenty-one again. You won't listen to me, and why should you? You must make your own choice. Know that whatever happens, I am here. You are always welcome at Casa Cielo Azul. Both of you."

Kat shivered. It felt as though a cloud had passed over the courtyard, but looking up she saw the bright sun was still climbing up the sky. She returned the pressure of Clara's strong fingers.

"Thank you for caring. And for being a friend."

Clara was old and wise enough to know when to back off.

She turned the conversation to the guests who had been at the party, telling Kat how an actress had fallen into the pool and been rescued by one of the local fishermen who attended at all her parties because he was so ridiculously handsome and a lothario. They had sloped away together apparently, and the actress's husband was furious. Clara hoped the *Daily Mail* didn't find out.

Bubbles of gossip rose and fell, but Kat's attention was already drifting toward the harbour, where Pablo would soon be waiting with his boat. She sipped her coffee and nodded at Clara, counting down the minutes until noon. It was wonderful and terrifying that everything in her world had changed from the moment she had first glimpsed Pablo in the busy street.

The boat was a traditional *llaut,* old but charming, Pablo said, and something of a summer project. With cheerful blue paint and sun-bleached wood, it tugged at its moorings as though eager to head off over a sea that sparkled like powdered glass. Pablo had tied a red scarf to the mast, fluttering like a flag and an homage to the sails that would once have powered it, rather than the diesel engine which thrummed away.

As Kat approached, she paused to admire him as he coiled lines. He was stripped to the waist and wearing only jeans as he worked in the full glare of the sun, his curls held back from his face by a red and white bandana. Muscles swelled and contracted beneath tanned skin and, barefooted, he hopped on and off the quay. He was like something from a film or an advertising campaign, and Kat was suddenly nervous, perhaps catching some of Clara's misgivings.

She swallowed her nerves and called a greeting. Her dress clung lightly to her in the heat, and her hair was loose, a little wild from the breeze, but when Pablo glanced up he looked as though he had seen a goddess.

"You came!" His delighted grin was wide as he held out his hand to help her aboard.

"Of course," Kat said. Her heart was beating as if she had run all the way down from the hills.

"Welcome aboard *Brisa,*" he said. "She's old and she's not glamorous, but she's the best boat I know."

"She's the only boat I know," confessed Kat as the deck dipped and lurched beneath her feet.

"Really? You've never been on a boat?"

"Not unless you count a punt," said Kat, and when he looked puzzled, she added, "It's a very flat river boat you propel with a long pole."

"Aha. Like a gondola."

Of course, his family probably visited Venice all the time, looking at art and culture. Kat's family were lucky to make it to the banks of the Isis for an ice cream on a hot day.

"Not much boating goes on for me," she said.

Pablo placed a hand on her shoulder. "Time to change that. Here, sit at the front and make yourself comfortable. I'm going to make sure you enjoy your first voyage from Port Andratx."

"My first? Will there be more?"

Pablo held her gaze and smiled, a slow smile filled with hope, which made her own mouth curl upwards in reply. "I hope this is the first of many."

Leaving Kat to settle down, he shrugged into a T-shirt and slipped his sunglasses on. Lines were pulled in and fenders stowed as they set off slowly, the motor puttering them through the narrow trots between moored fishing boats and yachts with fancy names and polished decks. Pablo stood at the back, steering, while Kat sat on a folded blanket near the bow, legs stretched out and her toes just grazing the warm wood. Already she loved the way the vessel sliced through the water, leaving the noise of the town behind. Dragonera basked in the distance, and beyond that the deep blue of the sea and the horizon. Adventures and possibilities unfurled like the sails of the yachts which shark-finned the water.

Pablo steered the boat with casual ease. Soon they were past the last of the moorings and beyond the confines of the harbour. He opened the engine then, and the little boat leapt up onto the plane, zipping above the waves and heading out and away to the right, passing in moments outlying houses which Kat had never seen before, and which clung to the headland like limpets. She held onto her hat tightly and let the wind whip her hair from her cheeks, whisking away all worries and inhibitions. Oh! This was marvellous.

Once they were past the town, Pablo cut the engine and let the boat drift. The silence was sudden and complete. All Kat could hear was the slap of waves against the hull and the cry of seabirds. After the bustle of the town, it was blissfully peaceful on the water, and she felt the tension slide away. She peered over the side of the boat and gasped; the water was the deepest turquoise she had ever seen. Sunlight turned it clear at the edges, so you could see straight down to the rippled sand and rocks below, with the shadows of darting fish silver threads in aquamarine.

"It's so clear! I can see fish."

Used to the murky green of the British sea, usually glimpsed from Brighton Pier, Kat was enchanted. This was magical!

The boat dipped and rocked as Pablo joined her.

"We're over sand. You can see maybe twenty feet down. Sometimes there are turtles. The marine life here is spectacular." He pointed to the island on their left. "That's why many locals don't want Sa Dragonera to become a tourist spot.

There are big protests whenever anyone suggests developing it."

"It's so beautiful," said Kat. "Is it always this quiet?"

He nodded. "Only locals come here. The yachts head for Sant Elm. There's a hidden cove ahead, behind that point." He pointed at a rocky outcrop. "We'll anchor there. You can swim if you like."

"Can I? Really?"

"I didn't bring you all this way to stay out of the water."

They reached the cove, a hidden inlet carved between two rocky arms of pine-covered hillside. The beach was entirely deserted, and steep cliffs rose behind it like a shield.

"The only way here is by boat," Pablo explained. "And today we seem to be the only people here. We have our very own private cove. Today, this is ours."

"I feel like I'm in heaven," sighed Kat. Oxford and typing and family had never seemed so far away.

She slipped out of her dress and stood on the deck in her white swimsuit. Pablo turned away politely, then pulled off his T-shirt, kicked off his jeans and dived in. Kat followed, shrieking and laughing as she surfaced.

The water was so clear it was like swimming in gin. She could dive down and see the rocks and darting fish, or lie on her back and stare up at the deep blue sky, unblemished by clouds. They swam lazily, floated, and chased each other in slow circles. Eventually they tired, and Pablo climbed onto a rock and pulled her up beside him, both dripping and breathless. They sat side by side and stared out over the water, skin warm and prickly with salt.

"You're very quiet," Pablo said.

"I'm trying to memorise everything so I can never forget it."

Kat had never known that a day could be this perfect. It

made her ache for a loss yet to happen and she wanted to capture this moment to keep it forever.

Pablo reached over and tucked a strand of wet hair behind her ear. "Everything feels perfect with you, Katalina," he murmured.

He kissed her again, and the world seemed to pause around them, waves lapping gently, wind brushing across their skin, the faint cry of a gull circling high above. When the kiss broke, neither of them moved for a long time.

"I never want to go back to Madrid," Pablo said quietly. "I wish I could stay here in Mallorca."

"Then don't. Stay here."

He smiled sadly. "You say that like it's so easy."

She shrugged. "Maybe it is."

"Maybe," he agreed, dropping a kiss onto the nape of her neck and pulling her against him. "Maybe."

They lay back on the rock, side by side, and drowsed in the sun. When the heat became intense, they plunged back into the water, blissfully cool against their hot skin, and swam back to the boat to share the picnic. They ate slowly, with their fingers. Pablo passed Kat olives from the palm of his hand. She tore the bread into rough pieces, smeared on cheese soft from the heat, and fed him a chunk without thinking, then laughed at herself, surprised by her own ease. Pablo pulled curls of Parma ham from waxed paper and lowered them to her lips from his own, kissing her when they reached the middle and forgetting then for a while all thoughts of food. For dessert there were ripe peaches bursting with juice, which they kissed away from their fingers and lips, and even places the juice had not reached. As they lost themselves in one another, Kat knew for certain that this was what happiness felt like.

The sun climbed higher, the boat rocked like a cradle while beneath a turtle swam by, secret and silent. For a few hours, time forgot them. There was no Don Álvaro, no Doña Mercedes, no family names or expectations. No politics. No worried friends. No real lives waiting to be resumed in Madrid and Oxford. There was just salt and sunlight, touch and taste, laughter and love, and the feeling that everything, absolutely everything, was possible.

CHAPTER 12

KAT - THEN

After their magical afternoon on the water, Kat knew there would be no turning back. She could lie awake at night and list every reason why falling for Pablo García was a terrible idea, but it wouldn't make the slightest difference because her heart was already his. She could no more step away from him than she could fly to the moon.

Now she understood why poets penned sonnets, why musicians poured their souls into heart-breaking ballads, and why *Romeo and Juliet* was as relevant today as it had been in the sixteenth century. Kat thought she Pablo were the modern-day equivalent in flared jeans and cheesecloth sundresses. She hoped they would have a happy ending.

After the boat trip they didn't manage to meet up for almost a week, which felt like decades to Kat. Pablo had to accompany his parents to Barcelona, and she was flat out with no time off until the following Monday. She had already used up owed days and a fair chunk of Maria's patience, since she was distracted and dreamy, delivering the wrong food to guests, pouring red wine into glasses meant for white, and forgetting items from the shop.

"What's the *matter* with you?" Maria grumbled when she unpacked the basket and discovered Kat had forgotten to buy eggs. "Your head's in the clouds ever since that party."

She was right. Kat was daydreaming about Pablo and counting down the hours, minutes and seconds until he was back on the island. They had arranged a picnic during siesta at an olive grove on the edge of the old town – a secluded and shady spot, Pablo promised – and close enough to the guest-house that Kat could be back in time for her evening shift. They would only have a couple of hours together, but that was better than waiting until her next full day off.

The grove was a short bus ride beyond the old town, past the last crumbling stone walls and down a narrow trail lined with dusty fennel and wild chamomile. It felt forgotten, the path worn by goats and secret lovers. The heat of the day had begun to swell, and the air smelled of hot earth and rosemary. Kat was glad of her sunhat and the shade of the ancient trees, their trunks time twisted, roots clawing the parched ground. Silver-green leaves fluttered overhead, catching the light like coins tossed into a fountain, and dappling the earth.

When Kat arrived Pablo was already there. He'd spread a striped blanket beneath the trees and arranged their picnic with such care it made Kat melt: a heel of crusty bread, a wedge of Mahón cheese in waxed paper, tomatoes split by the sun, and a bunch of green grapes. A bottle of wine wrapped in brown paper rested in the shade.

Kat was breathless from walking uphill in the sun, her sandals dusty, curls sticking to her neck. She wore yellow sundress, one strap always slipping from a shoulder to reveal tanned skin. She knew it was a dress you wore when you wanted to be kissed but wouldn't dare ask, and she hoped it would make him want her the way he had when they'd lain in the bottom of the boat and lost hours in one another's arms. What if he no longer felt the same? Her stomach dipped at the thought, because Lina had spent most of the week warning her not to fall too hard.

Any doubts Kat had vanished the moment she saw Pablo. Wearing shorts and a white T-shirt, his hair caught back with a strip of leather, he waved and smiled as though she was the only person in the world.

"You're early," she said as he swept her into his arms and spun her around. Her skirt swirled and the shoulder of her dress slipped further, a silent invitation she now knew he would accept.

"I don't want to miss a single second with you," Pablo said, then kissed her, and all was right with the world.

They sat on the blanket in the blissful shade, eating slowly with their fingers, talking and kissing in turns. A bee hovered near the wine. Somewhere in the distance a goat bleated, followed by a shout from a farmer's boy. A church bell rang the hour. Crickets chirruped.

Replete and drowsy, Kat leaned back, resting her head in the crook of her arm. Pablo echoed her posture, and they lay side by side with full bellies and smothered yawns, like an old married couple after Christmas dinner.

"Happy?" he asked.

"Very. It was a lovely picnic. Thank you for organising it."

"My pleasure. I knew you'd like this place. It feels like old Mallorca."

"Did you come here as a child?"

"Never. I found it one day when I was out for a drive. My family stays by the coast. Our house is all manicured gardens, high walls, bright blue pool. It's all neat and ordered. We rarely even eat lunch on the terrace. We certainly don't picnic."

She opened her eyes and studied him. He sounded sad.

"And you?" she said.

Pablo studied her. Kat shivered at the longing in his dark eyes. "Now I don't want to be anywhere else."

She turned towards him. "I feel the same."

"I know."

"How do you know?" she teased. "I thought I was being mysterious and making you work hard."

"Trust me! Carrying this picnic basket and sweet-talking our ancient gardener into lending me his truck is working hard. Now Felipe knows I'm up to something, and I'll have to keep him quiet. I'll probably be made to mow the lawns."

"Heaven forbid a García should mow a lawn!"

He pulled a mock-offended face. "I'll have you know we Garcías can mow as well as anyone."

Kat laughed. "I don't believe it, unless you mean cruising around on a ride-on. Do Mercedes even make those?"

"Right. That's it. I won't be so disrespected. Take it back!"

Pablo lunged to tickle her. Kat giggled, shrieked, and gasped, writhing beneath his hands and loving every second. "All right! I take it back! I surrender!"

"Thank you. Although, for the record, it *is* a ride-on mower."

"I knew it!"

"You already know me too well," he agreed.

Although Pablo had stopped tickling, his hands lingered at her waist. Her skirts were ruched to her knees, and her chest rose and fell as she caught her breath. Kat's heart was hammering, but whether from exertion or anticipation, she couldn't say. When his hands finally fell away, the sharp sting of disappointment surprised her.

They sank back onto the blanket and lay quietly for a while, hands loosely linked and recovering their breath in the dappled shade. Kat felt dreamy as she watched sky-blue patches ebb and flow in a sky tide through the dancing leaves.

"I am so glad I found you, Haystack Girl," Pablo murmured.

The words seemed to hang in the air, caught between the branches and the late-afternoon light. He reached out and brushed his fingers along the curve of her shoulder. Kat's breath caught, and when Pablo leaned in, it was as natural as breathing to arch towards him and meet his kiss.

After that picnic, they saw one another as often as possible, unable to bear being apart for long. It wasn't easy to find the time, for Kat's hours were filled with the guesthouse and Pablo's with family obligations, but they snatched every opportunity they could. He would arrive in the battered old truck belonging to the family's gardener and whisk her away to hidden corners of the island where they could walk hand in hand through the streets of sleepy villages without fear of being recognised.

Some of Kat's happiest moments were spent in the front seat of that old truck with Pablo's hand resting easily on her bare knee as the road wound through pine-covered hills. Guitar music spilled from the radio, mingling with the soft clack of rosary beads swinging from the rear-view mirror and the smell of pipe tobacco-scented leather.

Kat was aware that, like Shakespeare's doomed lovers, they had families divided by politics and marinated in the bitterness of the past. Her mother would be horrified to know that her daughter had fallen for a boy whose father kept a portrait of Franco above the fireplace. The Garcías would be equally aghast to learn their son was involved with a half-English girl connected to the Republicans. So it was easier not to think about it and live in the present.

Any potential difficulties went unspoken. Neither dared to voice them, afraid that naming such obstacles might drag their sun-drenched romance into the cold light of reality. Better to let love flourish in the Mediterranean warmth, ripening through the lazy, golden days that seemed endless. Love would be enough – wasn't that what films and romance novels promised? Kat was head over heels in love with Pablo, and he promised he felt the same, confessing, with a shy sweetness that made her heart squeeze, that he had loved her from the first moment he'd seen her in that crowded street. Clara's response when Kat repeated this was a roll of the eyes, but Kat knew it was true, for had been the same for her.

Kat and Pablo were meant to be together.

As summer stretched on and the guesthouse filled with visitors, Kat grew busier than ever. Her scant free time belonged to Pablo, whose parents were spending the season at their elegant holiday home and trading Madrid's oppressive heat for the sea breezes. His father often flew back to the mainland, leaving Pablo with his mother, and then it was even harder for him to escape.

"Mama finds Mallorca dull," Pablo told Kat with an eye roll. "She prefers the city, so I take her into Palma to shop and lunch. In the afternoons she has a siesta, and I tell her I'm going to go fishing. She's fine with that."

If Doña Mercedes suspected that her son had a lover, she never mentioned it. Pablo was certain his mother knew nothing. Kat hoped he was right, though part of her suspected Mercedes might simply be turning a blind eye until summer ended, expecting her son to fall back in line when autumn came. He had warned Kat about his parents' strict rules and high expectations, and she remembered Clara's gentle caution, back when her friend had thought there had still been a chance to protect her heart.

Lina, ever sensible, was more direct. "I heard he's engaged to a girl in Madrid," she had said over coffee at a small waterside café. "Please, Kat, be careful."

But Kat brushed this warning aside. How could Pablo be engaged to someone else when every kiss, every whispered word, was for her? She felt certain their love was moving towards something deeper. Maybe even marriage? How strange that something she had previously shied away from was suddenly wonderful and to be hoped for!

"That's just gossip," she said.

"Have you asked him?"

Kat hadn't. There was a whole part of Pablo's life she was shut out from. She had never been beyond the high walls of his family's wedding-cake-pretty villa in Sant Elm. She would never be invited to dinner with his parents, never stand beside him at a public event. Their love existed only in vivid, stolen moments when she could slip away from work, or when he could escape his family. They avoided public places, preferring the boat and the hidden olive grove.

But Lina was not a girl who lived in the moment. Her life was carefully planned, hence her engagement to solid, dependable fisherman Esteban and her preparations to take over her parents' bakery. She couldn't fathom Kat's willingness to ignore the question of what next, but she wanted her friend to be happy.

Kat, Lina admitted grudgingly, was glowing. Everyone could see it.

She was right. When Kat caught her own reflection in the age-spotted mirror above the washstand, she had to agree. Her skin seemed lit from within, her eyes sparkled, and she even thought her lips were softer from all the kissing. The sun had toasted her limbs, her hair was thick and lustrous, and she slept deeply every night and woke brimming with energy. It could have been the Mediterranean diet, but Kat knew better. It was love.

Clara had remarked on it too. "You look radiant," she declared as they lunched on her terrace and tucked into calamari fresh from the grill and glistening with lemon juice. "Love suits you, little swallow."

Kat smiled. She couldn't deny it.

"But I hope you're being careful," Clara added, lowering her voice so her housekeeper couldn't hear. "If you need to get anything, you must come and see me. This is still a Catholic country, remember."

"Get what?" Kat asked through a mouthful of food.

Clara leaned forward. "The birth pill. Trust me, it's the best thing that ever happened to women. We can find a doctor here if you need to."

Kat was no longer shocked by Clara's bluntness and laughed. "Fear not. I'm still a good Catholic girl."

A small voice deep inside her was asking if good Catholic girls pressed themselves against sun-tanned chests, surrendered to lingering kisses, and ached for more. Probably not something to ask the priest back at home, if she ever went back.

"But is *he* a good Catholic boy?" Clara shot back, and her blue eyes were serious.

"Of course," Kat replied. And it was true; Pablo had been nothing but a gentleman. Kat knew she should have been relieved but instead, she found herself wondering why he hadn't pressed for more. It was the 1970s now. Women (very rare ones, granted) could be pilots, physicists and surgeons. *Cosmopolitan* insisted they could take charge of their own sexual pleasure, whatever that meant, which sounded very positive to Kat. The nuns at school would have been horrified to know how often Kat dreamed of making love to Pablo somewhere wildly romantic. She supposed this would ideally be after a wedding, which felt suspiciously unfeminist.

"Good," said Clara with some relief. "I'm glad. Because you do realise he's leaving at the end of summer and returning to Madrid? And if the rumours are true, there's a fiancée waiting for him there."

Suddenly the calamari tasted like rubber bands and the lemon juice burned her tongue. Kat pushed her plate away. "I don't want to talk about this, Clara."

Clara nodded, and the subject was dropped, but the conversation haunted Kat for the rest of the day, because she was becoming worried. It was mid-July, and she was meant to return home at the start of September to search for a sensible job. The Garcías would return to Madrid once August's punishing heat had faded and the city became bearable again. He'd told her many times about how beautiful Madrid was in the autumn, its fountains and parks shimmering under golden leaves – but he had made no mention of what came next for them. Maybe nothing, since his parents didn't know about her.

Kat hadn't told her parents about Pablo, either. She didn't know where to begin. The brief weekly phone calls didn't feel like enough, and although she could have written about him in her letters home, she hadn't. Pablo was her secret, and she kept him close to her heart, not wanting to hear their concerns. What if her mother realised who he was? If she found out her daughter was in love with the son of a man who supported Franco, Kat suspected her mother might disown her.

She'd finally written to David Beauchamp, a cheerful letter thanking him once again for suggesting she worked in Mallorca and for introducing her to Clara. She filled three pages with funny anecdotes about guests, and tales of her swims and boat trips (carefully omitting who was doing the sailing) and David wrote back quickly, full of enthusiasm, saying how much he was looking forward to visiting at the end of the summer. His arrival would be a collision of worlds and Kat was worried: would David's presence burst the fragile bubble of her perfect summer?

There were so many things to think about, but she was busy, and it was easier to pack these thorny questions into a box marked 'Later'. For now, she would enjoy her work, her friends, her sun-drenched life and her handsome Spanish love. They had so much to look forward to.

CHAPTER 13

KAT - THEN

At the end of July Kat and Pablo visited the ruined farmhouse known locally as Casa la Colina, Hill House. A smudge on the hillside headland, the remains of its walls sagged beside a ruined guard tower, keeping watch patiently over the port as though waiting for a loved one to return. Kat felt certain this place had been waiting for her to find it. She had fallen in love with the ruin from afar, and tumbled a little more each time she glimpsed it when *Brisa* slipped back into the port.

While Pablo steered the little boat home, Kat would sit cross-legged on the bow, her eyes scanning the apricot-and-sage blur of the headland until she spotted the tower and scarlet splash of remaining roof tiles. Peeking through tangles of pines and olives, she thought it was the Mallorcan equivalent of Sleeping Beauty's castle.

"Pablo, look!" Kat exclaimed the first time she'd spotted the ruin, pointing to the curve of the headland. "There's a house hidden up there."

Pablo shielded his eyes against the glare. "*Sí*. La Colina. It's been derelict since I was a kid. There can't be much left."

"The view must be amazing."

Kat imagined standing on the headland, gazing over the mouth of the port: Sa Dragonera basking in a mosaic of blues, the town pouring over the hills to the right with the distant mountains veiled in mist, and then the sea rolling on forever. You would feel like the queen of the world with such a view, Kat thought. Unlike the identical terraces and streets of her childhood, which hemmed you in and stitched you into a life you never chose, it was a view that promised freedom.

"It must be wonderful," Pablo agreed. "It's a shame it's fallen into such a state. I suppose it's just a bit too far out of town. It's quite a hike up hill."

Kat had longed to visit La Colina, hike or not. She dreamed of restoring it, of living there with Pablo and the ragtag band of children they would have, children with his warm sherry eyes and her dark curls, and brown as berries from the sun and swimming. They would grow fruit and vegetables, spend their days on the water or hiking the hills. How happy they would all be! Who was to say dreams couldn't come true if you wished hard enough?

Though Pablo had spent many summers in Andratx, he knew little about La Colina, only that it had been deserted for as long as he could remember. Kat asked around, pleased her Mallorquín was improving enough to converse with the old women who mended nets outside their houses, muttering darkly about the hills and defeated rebels.

According to Lina's parents, the house hadn't been lived in since before the war, and had belonged to brave rebels like Kat's uncles. Maria and Francisco said that the tower had been built centuries ago to protect the town from pirates. Pirates and rebels! It was so romantic. Clara had heard from her lawyer that the property belonged to an old woman who had gone to live with her son in Barcelona. Whatever the truth, everyone agreed on one thing: Casa la Colina was isolated and inaccessible. Who would want to live all the way up there?

Me, Kat thought. She was itching to see it for herself, and eventually Pablo gave in and agreed to hike up with her. They met at the locals' cove when Kat had an evening off and Pablo's parents were at a function in Palma. Sunlight filtered through the Aleppo pines, zebra-striping the road with light and shadow, and the day's heat pressed through the soles of Kat's sandals. Her hair was soon damp at the nape of her neck, and as she climbed her T-shirt stuck to her back. The road ahead was increasingly steep and rough, and Kat started to wonder if maybe La Colina was too high up after all.

As Port Andratx was still small and you never knew who might be watching, they walked independently up the steep road leading toward the headland. Before long the road abandoned all pretence of being more than a track, and houses became sparse. The further from town the path went the rougher it became, until it narrowed into a winding track encroached upon by undergrowth and shaded by tall pines.

Once they were certain they were alone, Kat and Pablo walked hand in hand, stopping every now and then to sip water and exchange kisses. It felt like a magical adventure as lizards darted from rock to rock and cicadas shrieked from the scrub, protesting the intrusion. Finally, the road levelled slightly, and the old guard tower loomed up, peering at them suspiciously over crumbling walls.

Kat bent double, hands on her knees, recovering her breath. Her feet were blistered from her flimsy sandals, and her head throbbed from the heat. The hot air was soup-like. Was it thinner up here too, high among the wheeling gulls and falcons, or was it excitement making her dizzy?

"Here." Pablo passed her the water bottle. Kat drank deeply, then handed it back. He followed suit then wiped his mouth on the back of his hand. "That road is even steeper than it looks from the sea," he remarked.

Kat no longer cared about the long walk up. Her sore feet and the arduous hike were as nothing as she peered beyond the crumbled boundary wall, and the shell of La Colina appeared like a half-remembered dream. In the sunshine they glowed the warmest apricot, and Kat promised herself that one day she would paint them that exact hue so the house would shine all day.

Tears of happiness filled her eyes. She was home.

"Let's explore," Pablo suggested.

Kat scrambled onto the lowest part of the wall and jumped down into what remained of the garden. She tore through overgrown shrubs and rampant brambles, oblivious to scratches, until she reached what had once been a paved terrace, now cracked and tufted with grass. Bees hummed among rampant lavender, and chamomile crawled over low walls, tracing whispers of pathways. It was enchanted, and with every step Kat fell deeper in love. She longed to restore the garden while keeping this glorious symphony of natural abundance.

The old house, crumbling yet stubbornly upright, looked out over the sea like a sentinel. Sun-bleached shutters were listing or missing. Bougainvillea had scurried up the southern wall, hot pink blooms defiantly bright against pale stone. The roof was mostly gone, leaving a rafter ribcage framing slices of sky like artwork. Tiles clung to parts of the single-storey addition, bold terracotta against the sea beyond.

"It's a wreck," Pablo said, glancing around and shaking his head.

"But so beautiful," Kat whispered. "And it could be beautiful again."

He pulled her to him kissed the top of her head. "You're in love, I think."

She smiled. "Oh yes, Pablo. And I like the house too."

They held each other, high above the port, and with the sea and sky their only witnesses. Inside, the house whispered its forgotten past: bare rooms, rodent-chewed furniture, an iron bedframe in the cobwebby master bedroom, chimneys filled with leaves, remnants of bird nests. Yet touches of life remained: colourful tiles, a rusting range cooker, a hook with the ragged remains of an apron, an oil lamp on a shelf. Dust clung to everything. Sunlight sliced through gaps in the roof, and a mouse scuttled across the kitchen floor.

As they explored the ruin, Kat envisioned it restored: walls freshly plastered, floors polished, rugs strewn across dark wood boards. There would be a bright, cheerful kitchen, terraces full of pots and flowers, a grand rebuilt staircase, hammocks strung between olive trees, deep window seats, dinners on the terrace with friends, strings of lights and candles, children splashing in a sky-blue pool …

She turned to Pablo. "We could fix this. New beams, shutters, walls, floors, kitchen – we could!"

"New everything, you mean."

"Yes. Why not? The bare bones are here; the rest is cosmetic. Imagine living here! It's like a castle."

He slipped his arms around her waist. "You'd live up here?"

"Maybe not alone," she said, glancing at him from beneath her lashes. "Maybe with someone special. A handsome prince, maybe?"

"Or a frog?"

"Let's see!"

She kissed him, and he kissed her back, holding her for a

long, quiet moment. Their first kiss in their forever home, Kat thought hopefully. One day, would she tell their children this story? How her plans had changed! Once she had shied away from marriage and children, but now she wanted those things so badly it hurt. Pablo had changed everything.

The breeze sighed through the broken roof. Outside, the distant shimmer of the sea lay as a liquid line in the fading light. A falcon circled in the high thermals. Pablo's fingers traced the stone wall as though he was grounding himself.

"I would very much like to be that prince," he said quietly.

"You already are," Kat replied.

They returned the following week and many times after, always careful not to be seen together. Felipe's truck had four-wheel drive, so sometimes Pablo collected Kat from the port or rescued her from the hike when she was halfway up. Once he borrowed a scooter. As July sweltered into August, the house felt as though it was theirs. They explored every room, measured walls, and assessed which beams could be salvaged or needed replacing. For Kat, La Colina was more than just stone and tiles. It was a promise. Even if it never became exactly what she imagined, she had already discovered the future she wanted to build with Pablo.

One evening, when the sky was the colour of plums and lightning flickered in the distance, they watched a storm roll in.

"Will you promise me something, Katalina?" Pablo asked.

"Anything. You know that."

He nodded. "*Sí*. Will you promise you'll always come here? Even if I can't."

Kat was alarmed. "What do you mean? Where are you going?"

"Nowhere, I hope – but promise me, Kat? You love this place so much. Promise me that you always will visit, no matter what happens. I would always want to think of you here and happy."

There was a tautness to these words and an urgency that stopped Kat from demanding to know what he might mean or attempting to dredge meaning from him. She loved this place, and she loved Pablo. It was not a hard pledge to make.

"I promise."

Pablo pulled her closer and kissed her hungrily. They had kissed before, slowly, teasingly, like it was a language they were still learning, but this was different. There was an urgency, a hunger between them that had nothing to do with the gathering storm and everything to do with the summer passing too quickly.

Outside, thunder grumbled. Inside the shelter of La Colina's remaining walls Pablo's fingers read her face as though he was trying to memorise it. "I love you, Katalina," he whispered. "So much."

They lay back on an old blanket and he folded his jacket beneath her head. Kat's fingers found the buttons of his shirt and as she undid them his breath caught. Kat, pulled him closer, and her voice was trembling when she whispered, "I love you too."

His fingertips brushed the bare line of her collarbone, and she realised he was holding his breath, as though he hardly dared to breathe. Kat slid her arms around his neck, pulling him down into a kiss that told him there was nothing to be fearful of. No need to hold back.

It was a slow and searching kiss at first, but as their mouths found rhythm, their hands didn't hesitate. Kat felt warm under his weight and alive in a way that made her dizzy. His shirt came unbuttoned beneath her fingers. Her legs curled around his hips as Pablo buried his face in her neck and exhaled like he had been holding on to something too long.

For a moment, there was only breath and heartbeat. Blood was singing and pulses racing. Kat's fingers pressed against the curve of his spine, pulling him closer and closer. She arched into him, and as his body moved instinctively, she knew this was the moment she had been longing for.

And she wanted it more than she had ever wanted anything.

"I can't. We can't. We mustn't."

Abruptly, Pablo pulled away.

Kat reached for him. His whole body was trembling, and so was hers, with longing and need and a thousand other emotions she couldn't describe.

"It's all right. I want this."

He closed his eyes. His jaw was tight. "I can't."

"You can," Kat insisted. "It's all right, Pablo. I want to."

"I want to, as well. But I can't!"

His voice was anguished and suddenly Pablo was on his feet, practically backing away from her.

Kat felt as though she had been doused in ice water. "You don't want *me*, you mean."

The words slipped out before she could stop them. They sprang from a deep well of hurt, and she sat up quickly, wrapping her arms around herself, feeling humiliated.

Did Pablo think she wasn't good enough for him because she wasn't some Spanish girl handpicked by his parents? Was that it? Or did he think she was a slut to go this far and was now disgusted by her? Lina had warned her men thought this way, even though Clara insisted it was right for a woman to want sex too and enjoy it. This was the 1970s, after all. Why shouldn't women have pleasure just as much as men? But maybe to a good Catholic boy, this way of thinking was shocking?

Her eyes prickled with tears. What was the right response?

Until this moment she hadn't stopped to think about any of this; she had simply followed her heart and done what felt natural and right. She had never felt shame with Pablo or been pressured into going any further than she wanted to. Kat only knew she longed to be as close to him as one person could possibly be to another. She had wanted to give him everything, him and only him, and to be rejected cut to her soul.

"Do I disgust you?" she asked. Her voice was tight and choked.

"No! Never! Of course not!"

Pablo knelt beside her, reaching to take Kat in his arms, but she flinched.

"Don't!"

"Katalina! I want you so much it makes my chest hurt. You must know that."

"Then why?" she whispered, tears catching in her throat. "Is it a Catholic thing? Do you think this is a mortal sin?"

Pablo laughed. "I don't believe in any of that. You know I don't."

Kat did know. They had talked at length about what they believed, both being Catholic by birth rather than conviction, and she also knew that Pablo was more experienced than she was, having been in a relationship while at university. Kat was jealous of this unknown ex-girlfriend because she wished she could have been his first love in the same way he would be hers.

"So, what is it?" she asked, trying hard to hold her tears back. Had this unknown girlfriend meant more to him? Was that it? He didn't feel enough desire for Kat. She wasn't special enough to make love to.

Pablo didn't answer right away. Rain had started to fall, soft at first, then louder, drumming on the broken tiles above them.

Then he sighed. "Because I love you."

Kat was confused. "That doesn't make sense. That's not a reason."

"It is," he insisted. "If we do this, I won't be able to stop wanting you. Loving you."

He was anguished in a way she had never seen before. Kat said nothing, but she was frightened.

"Somebody saw us together," he said quietly. "A friend of my mother's saw us in Santa Ponsa and told her. My parents know about us. They are angry."

It was what they had feared. It was why they had been so careful and only let their guard down when away from the port.

"You didn't say anything."

"I didn't want them to spoil today."

She understood. Their time together was precious. "Are your parents going to punish you somehow?"

"My parents think I'm indulging a phase," Pablo said bitterly. "Sowing my wild oats, was how my father viewed it. He clapped me on the shoulder and said I should have fun, but not bring shame to the family."

"Charming," said Kat. Who did the Garcías think they were? *'Franco-loving traitors,'* she heard her grandmother hiss.

Pablo laughed mirthlessly. "Yes, indeed. *Muy* charming! But they are old-fashioned, Kat. This is the way things have always been done in a family. They have a 'suitable' girl in mind for me who comes from Burgos. Her father's in Madrid, close to—"

He stopped. He didn't have to say 'Franco'. The name sat unspoken between them like the bad fairy at a christening.

"Who has arranged marriages now?" Kat cried. It was ridiculous.

He spread his hands. "I know, but modernity doesn't

matter to people like my family. There is tradition and duty and expectation. Dynastic marriage is expected, and I am their only child. You know it all rests on my shoulders. You've always known."

It was true. Kat did. Pablo had always told her this.

"So that's it? I'm just a phase?"

"No," Pablo said fiercely. His eyes were fire bright. "You're the only true thing I've ever had. The best thing in my life. You are everything, Kat, and that's why I cannot risk hurting you. It's why I should never have started this. But God help me, I couldn't stay away from you."

Kat leapt to her feet. Her dress caught on a floorboard nail and the skirt ripped. She didn't care. She grabbed her sandals and her bag.

"Well, you can now. I'm going back."

Summer rain was beating down.

"Don't be ridiculous, Kat. It's pouring."

He was right, but Kat wasn't being ordered about by any of the Garcías.

"Don't tell me what to do."

"I'm not, I never would – but it's three miles back to the guesthouse. You'll get drenched."

"Good. Maybe I'll catch my death of cold and die. Then you can be free to marry your perfect Spanish girl."

Her voice wobbled, but she was determined to walk out of the house with her head held high. She wouldn't look at Pablo or listen to his sensible arguments and protestations of love. If she did, she might fall into that ridiculous hope that he'd come to his senses, forget he was saving himself for some perfect Spanish bride, and take her in his arms. She wanted nothing more than that, but she had some shreds of pride left and was determined to cling to them.

She stormed outside before Pablo could speak, and the rain

hit her like pins. It soaked through her dress in seconds, her hair sticking to her neck, and her thin sandals slithering against the slick terrace. Kat didn't care. Let it rain. Let it pour. Let the whole island flood. Her heart was breaking. She had known this would happen. *Everyone* had known.

She had been a fool to think otherwise.

"Don't think he'll ever choose you over his family. Spanish boys like Pablo don't marry girls like you. They have their fun and leave," Lina often said.

Kat's eyes filled, because Pablo hadn't even wanted to have his fun.

Clara, quieter but no less certain, had shrugged. "Be careful, little swallow. You're playing with fire."

It hadn't felt like fire to Kat. Her love for Pablo García had felt like sun-warmed rock above ice-cold water. It was soft bread, torn and slathered with runny cheese. Olives and ham finger-fed. Peach juice on hot skin kissed away by exploring lips and tongues. It had felt so right. But she was burned all the same.

She stumbled over a root. She caught herself in time and kept walking. One hand clutched her bag, the other was wiping her face, not that it made any difference. Rain and tears were the same now.

"Kat! Kat, stop!"

She didn't, but Pablo's hand caught her elbow, firmly enough to stop her forward march into the storm and pull her around to face him.

"Don't touch me," Kat choked.

"You can't walk back alone in this."

"I can. I am."

"Please, Kat. Just listen to me."

Pablo looked shipwrecked. His dark hair was plastered to his forehead. His denim shirt clung to his chest. His eyelashes were starred with raindrops and his eyes were dark with misery.

"No," Kat said, twisting from his grasp. "You've made your choice. You don't get to chase me down like the hero in some film. You said we couldn't, remember? You said *you* couldn't. You have a perfect fiancée waiting for you. Leave me alone!"

"I didn't mean to hurt you. That was why I didn't want to say anything, I just—" He exhaled sharply. "Loving you scares me."

His pain was so honest, so raw, that Kat's rage was paused. "Why?"

He bowed his head. "Because if I'd made love to you, I will love you even more than I can bear. It'll break me, Kat. It'll kill me. How can I love you *and* honour them? How can I do my duty *and* follow my heart?"

She stared at him. The rain blurred the edges of his face, and a muscle ticked in his cheek. Kat realised Pablo was close to tears. The burden he had been carrying alone was breaking him.

"I already love you more than I can bear," she said sadly. "Not being with you breaks me, Pablo. I ache for you when we're apart and I long for you all the time because you're in my every thought. Being close to you is everything. *You* are everything."

He stared at her as though seeing her for the first time.

"If I am with you I can bear *anything*," Kat told him. "Trust me; my mother will disown me and her expectations of me will be dust, but *I don't care*. Do you hear me? *I don't care.* Nothing matters, except being with you."

Her heartfelt words broke something in Pablo. She had breached the barrier of logic that he'd erected to protect himself. Slowly and tentatively, as though he was a wild creature whose trust she had to win, she stepped towards him.

When she rested her hands on his chest Kat held her breath, almost afraid to scare him away.

"I don't want a world without you in it," he whispered, "but I don't know how to live in one where I can keep you."

"We'll work out how," said Kat. She didn't think she knew how to live in a world where she wasn't with Pablo either. Now her anger was extinguished she felt only sadness for the complications loving her brought to him.

His leaned his forehead against hers. They were drenched and shivering, but oblivious to the weather. They were so close their breath mingled, and their eyelashes brushed.

"We'll work it out somehow," she whispered. "I promise, Pablo. We'll find a way."

He kissed her, a soft kiss which told Kat he was hurting as much as she was, because the world they lived in would never make it easy for them. Being together might cost them too much and the price they paid might be all the joy they found in one another. Kat hoped her kiss told Pablo that she understood the road which lay ahead of them was hard, but not walking it would be harder.

The storm passed and they returned to the town hand in hand but saying little. They knew trouble lay ahead. Pablo's parents would tighten their grip, while Kat's would want her to return home to a sensible job and find security with a nice young man. This perfect summer was already slipping from their grasp, and only a sigh away from becoming the past. Their first and last summer. But they had now, thought Kat. The future she would face when it came, and she already knew she would fight for Pablo and the future they had dreamed of. It was the 1970s, and times were changing.

Why couldn't their parents accept that?

CHAPTER 14

KAT - NOW

It was the sound of the rain that woke her. Insistent and unrelenting, it beat a tattoo on the shutters and snatched her from her dreams.

Kat blinked up at the ceiling of the garden room. Originally the old kitchen, it was whitewashed now, with sturdy new beams and a roof that arched above her, where once only stars had kept watch. She was in a large double bed with plump cushions and snowy linens – but all alone rather than lying on blankets beside a beautiful boy. So much had changed. So many years had passed since that moment, yet the pain of Pablo's words still had the power to snatch her breath.

Silly really. Kat hadn't been that girl for years, and she was quite certain that Pablo de la Vega García, wherever he might be now, was no longer that boy. She probably wouldn't even recognise him. He was long lost to her. This thought made Kat's throat tighten, and a wave of grief threatened to knock her off her feet. How ridiculous, when she had lost Pablo a lifetime ago.

"So much has changed."

She said this aloud, just for the comfort of hearing a voice above the merciless rain on the roof. Rain could be so cosy when you were cuddled up with someone; so lonely when you were alone. She wished there was somebody here she could turn to and say, "Do you remember when?" or even ask if they would like a cup of tea. It was always in these early hours when she woke with a start. This dark time, before the first tentative fingers of daylight caressed the sky, was when Kat found her loneliness hardest to bear. It was easier to dream of the past while she waited for the dawn, and less painful than thinking about the present.

Yes, so much had changed since that long-ago evening, but in some ways so little. If she opened the curtains the view in the darkness would look almost the same as it had then: Dragonera slumbering in inky waters, the lights of the town and the diamond necklace of the bridge, and in the hills beyond the lights of houses. There were subtle changes, though, and like her own reflection the town was the same yet different. Clara's *finca* had once nestled among oleanders and pines but had been knocked down long ago and replaced by a smart modernist cube. Maria and Francisco's guesthouse was now a smart holiday home, and Lina's bakery a smart restaurant. Kat still missed those flaky croissants that melted in the mouth and the crusty bread that smelled so good it was a struggle not to tear into it straight away.

Lina and Esteban no longer lived in Andratx; they had moved to Toledo, where their eldest daughter lived. Kat hadn't seen Lina in years, for their paths had diverged once Lina had married and quickly become a mother. They had written for a while, but once Kat was living back in the UK the letters had petered out. When Kat and David bought Casa la Colina and began to visit Mallorca on a regular basis, Kat had hoped to reconnect with her old friend. They had met up for coffee several times, but struggled to find common ground. Once Kat had become the owner of La Colina, she had sensed a reserve in Lina, and as the years passed and property on the hillside became more desirable the gulf between them had widened.

And then, once Jenny and José were hired Kat had no need to visit the bakery, and the friendship drifted. Kat sometimes felt sad about this, for Lina had been a staunch ally during some of the best and worst times of her life, but age had also taught her that people come into our lives for a reason, a season or a lifetime. Friendship, like love, cannot be forced to remain.

Clara Schneider had remained for a lifetime, and although she had died many years ago Kat still sometimes struggled to stop herself calling her or buying a piece of art Clara might like. It was a friendship that had sustained her. Although Clara sold Casa Cielo Azul and moved to Italy, their friendship endured. Clara had been a mainstay of Kat's life, and a big support during some of the darkest times, as well as the loudest cheerleader of her most wonderful achievements.

It had been such a joy to Kat when Clara moved to England in the 2000s and set up her art school in London. They regularly met up for lunch at Browns to reminisce about the 1970s, when the music was better, the fashion far worse, and the young men divine. During those long gossipy lunches filled with laughter and memories, Kat felt young again, and it was a shock sometimes to catch a glimpse of two older ladies in the glass of the door and realise it was them. It felt as though she had only blinked, and yet time had raced away.

Even when her health was failing fast, Clara's wit and quick tongue were as sharp as ever, and she was still sculpting right into her final weeks. When she died, she bequeathed Kat her Cartier watch, which Kat wore every day, and a huge piece intended for the garden at La Colina, which now had pride of place on the terrace.

"My favourite place," Clara had said with a sigh, her eyes bright with tears. "It makes me happy, Kat, to think that even when I'm dust part of me will remain forever in Mallorca."

But forever was a long time. Kat knew she couldn't remain here forever, no matter how much she loved La Colina, which held so many cherished memories. Those would come with her, as would the sculpture, which she intended to donate to the Tate in St Ives. It would look marvellous there, framed by stark white walls and with the deep blue sea as a backdrop, just as her friend had stipulated. Her daughters could use the money raised by selling La Colina to pay off their mortgages and send their children to good schools, and onwards to university and eventually to buy houses of their own. La Colina would keep the family safe. It was what their father would have thought sensible – and it *was* sensible, just so hard.

Kat would miss this place desperately, and the thought of Tomás López, or another like him, ripping the house down broke her heart. She had dreamed of making it beautiful when she lay in Pablo's arms and gazed up at the sky as they shared dreams and kisses, and she had kept the promises made to this property even if the other vows made here had crumbled like damp-soaked plaster. Passing La Colina to a man like López felt like betraying a dear friend, and although he would pay far more than thirty pieces of silver, Kat felt the transaction was the same.

"Somebody has to buy it, Mum," Aimée had said wearily that morning when Kat repeated these thoughts. "If it isn't him, it'll be somebody else who'll flatten it, no matter what they tell you."

Her daughter was right. Aimée was a pragmatic girl. Kat thought she got this trait from her father. David would have sold, too, and agreed that there was no guarantee the site wouldn't be developed. Kat had once mooted putting in a legal clause on the ownership title that could prevent development for several years, but David pointed out that a wealthy buyer could happily break such a covenant and pay the fine, still netting a huge profit. He was right, as always, and Kat knew her husband would say it was better by far the money was in Kat's pocket than a stranger's.

She groaned. If only David was here to talk all this through with her, and help her make the right decision for La Colina and their family. It was so hard without her beloved sounding board, confidante and best friend. López's latest letter might have been out of sight, but it wasn't out of mind. It was waiting for her like a real estate booby trap, set to blow her world apart. He wanted the property very badly, that was obvious, and it made sense to sell to him, but still Kat hesitated. He was too confident and too certain of himself for her taste, and she baulked at proving his assumption that he could have whatever he wanted simply because he was rich.

She'd known people before who used their wealth to throw their weight about and bully others, but she wasn't going to think about that now. She was wide awake. Perhaps a milky drink would help to settle her. It was pouring down *gatos y perros*, and she would be soaked by the time she crossed the terrace to the porched entrance to the kitchen – but anything was better than lying here wide awake and stewing over past hurts.

Kat sat up, a process that took her some time these days, and hauled herself out of bed. She pushed her feet into sandals and made her way to the French windows. The doors groaned open, and she stepped onto the terrace, raising her face to the bucketing rain which pricked her cheeks like pins. Within minutes Kat was drenched, but she didn't care.

She felt alive.

How funny, she reflected, that the emotions of yesterday could still hurt just as fiercely in memory as they had when lived. Would she have been happy with Pablo if life had worked out differently? They might have lived in this very house, had the children they once dreamed of, and baked bread as Pablo had imagined. But Kat would never know how that life might have looked. She could never wish for it either, because that would mean wishing away the beautiful life she'd made with her beloved David and their wonderful family. But still. It was only human to wonder.

"Mrs Beauchamp! I mean, Kat! You made me jump."

Lily's voice carried across the terrace and above the drumming of rain on tiles. She was sitting at the yellow table beneath the giant parasol, which now served as an umbrella. Kat glanced at the Cartier and saw it was past 1 am. While that might seem late to an old fogey like her, she knew it was early for someone Lily's age. She must have just come home from town.

"Is everything all right?" Lily sounded concerned, and Kat realised she must look a sight, having been walking in the rain and her hair dripping. Lily probably thought she was losing her marbles.

"Just enjoying the storm," Kat called. It was a truth, of sorts.

"Me too," Lily replied. Lightning lit up her face and her eyes were wide and bright. "I feel so alive!"

Kat recalled that long-ago evening when she had stormed away from Pablo. She had certainly felt alive, too. Every nerve ending had been on fire.

"I feel a bit daft," she confessed, once she was beneath the umbrella.

"You're drenched."

"I am, but it reminded me I'm alive … just!"

Lily nodded. “I get that. Why don’t you dry off while I make us a cup of tea?”

Kat hadn’t had someone make tea in the small hours for her since David had died. It was one of the many small losses. Another death, in a way. The end of something so mundane, yet still enough to make her well up.

“That would be wonderful, thank you,” she said, blinking away the tears which spouted too easily these days. “Give me five minutes and I’ll be there.”

“I’ll fetch you a dressing gown,” offered Lily.

Once dried off and wrapped snugly in a white robe (she felt very glad now that David had insisted upon buying good quality ones from El Corte Inglés for their guests), Kat joined Lily in the kitchen, where they sat at the table sipping tea and watching lightning scissor the sky.

“Did you have a good evening?” she asked Lily, though she already knew the answer. There had been a boy involved; she recognised that sparkle in the girl’s eyes.

Lily didn’t bite. “Yes, thank you. It was lovely to see Hannah. She’s great fun.”

“The port’s a wonderful place to meet friends,” agreed Kat, smiling to herself. “I used to have such fun there with my friend Clara. She had a beautiful *finca* in the hills and threw the best parties.”

“Yes. She was my godmother,” Lily reminded her gently.

Kat tapped her forehead with her palm. “Oh, yes. What a lovely coincidence too, it was meant to be. I’m a silly old fool and I forget things these days. Clara was a lovely friend. I also had a friend at the bakery too.” She paused, her throat tightening. “And … a boyfriend.”

“Really?” Lily seemed unflatteringly shocked.

“Yes, really! I wasn’t always this age!” Kat was surprised

she'd mentioned Pablo. She never usually did. Her daughters certainly didn't know about him.

"What was he like?"

Oh, there weren't the words in existence to describe him, thought Kat wistfully. His lean torso, tanned from sun and swimming. His amontillado eyes. The long dark curls that kissed his golden shoulders and in which she loved to wind her fingers when she pulled his mouth to hers. The delicious place between his shoulder blades. The carefree way he sauntered along the quay, unaware that all eyes followed him. How just looking at him turned her blood to lava …

"He had a boat. We used to go on picnics. Wonderful ones. We swam and had lots of fun."

Lily gave her a knowing look, and Kat laughed.

"Yes, all right. We may have kissed, and it was very romantic. I do think it's sad that kissing gets overlooked in later life. It becomes the starter before the main course, bolted down as a prelude to the real deal – but it's just so delicious, isn't it?"

"I think it depends on who you're kissing," sighed Lily. "Mostly frogs in my case."

"A prince is on his way." Kat felt certain of this, because her new helper was simply gorgeous. Princes must be queuing up.

"Hmm," Lily seemed doubtful.

The poor girl's confidence was on the floor, and Kat wondered what daft idiot boy had knocked the stuffing out of such a pocket Venus. *Men.*

"We used to visit this place together when it was just a ruin," she continued, half to herself. "I spotted it from the boat and was desperate to see it. I think I knew then it was destined to be mine."

"Wow," said Lily. "Fate."

"Maybe," said Kat. "Or perhaps I made it happen. I had to make a lot of things happen after my first summer here."

She'd said more than she meant to and turned her attention back to her tea. Lily probably sensed there was more to this story, but she was a sensitive girl and said nothing. Kat appreciated not being pushed. Talking about Pablo de la Vega García was harder than she'd expected it to be.

"I met somebody tonight," Lily blurted.

Kat wasn't surprised. The young woman possessed the unmistakable glow of being the object of romantic attention. Her own feelings for Pablo must have been written all over her face even though she'd thought she was playing it so cool. No wonder Maria and Francisco teased her, and Clara was worried.

"A date?" she ventured. Maybe she had got it wrong, thought Kat, and Lily was swiping and Tindering all over the place. It had all changed these days.

But Lily shook her head. "I met him by accident."

"The best way," said Kat, guessing Lily wanted to talk about him. She looked fit to burst.

While they sipped their tea and listened to the rain, Lily told Kat how she'd tripped over a mooring rope and a boy called Rafe Cruz had helped her. He worked on one of the smaller yet still smart boats, the kind the wealthy and powerful used to float about the Med if they didn't want to bother with the mega yachts which were in effect private hotels on water with helicopter pads and tenders the size of small houses. Talking of these, Kat glanced across the water and sure enough Tomás López's yacht was glowing faintly in the darkness. It was as though he had left it there on purpose, a nautical reminder of his offer to buy La Colina.

"Will you see Rafe again?" she asked, once Lily finished describing how he'd helped her into a taxi. This young man sounded chivalrous. Pablo would've done the same for her. So would David, of course. Her husband had been a perfect gentleman. His quiet kindness was easy to overlook, but his heart was pure gold.

"I don't know," Lily said.

There was a pause. Lily studied the marble tabletop as though it held the answers to the universe.

"I guess the question is, do you *want* to?"

"Part of me would like to, but I'm not sure I'm cut out for relationships."

It was a strange thing to say. Kat frowned. "Whatever makes you think that?"

Lily shrugged. "Things haven't worked out for me in the past. I met someone and I thought everything was good between us. I loved him, Kat, and I trusted him. Which turns out to be a stupid thing to do."

"Loving and trusting somebody is never stupid." Kat was certain of this, although she knew it was something you only truly understood with age.

Lily looked out across the dark water. Her reflection trembled in the glass, and raindrops ran down her mirrored cheeks like tears.

"I was engaged. Harrison was my childhood sweetheart, and we grew up together. Our parents are best friends, and it seemed the natural thing to happen. Everyone was thrilled for us. I always thought we'd grow old together, but I don't think I ever really knew him."

Kat said nothing. She'd learned it was best not to disturb a person in pain. If someone wanted to speak, you simply stayed still and quiet as though they were a wild creature ready to flee at any moment. Besides, Lily didn't want Kat's opinion; she needed someone to listen.

She sat quietly as Lily talked about her childhood sweetheart and explained how they'd got engaged before she went away to university because he wanted reassurance. Lily had been faithful through university while her fiancé stayed in their hometown, and she never questioned whether he had been faithful. He went into the family estate agency business and after graduation she worked there too as a secretary. Lily didn't mind the work, and she did enjoy putting together the sales information and penning descriptions of properties, but her heart was set on being a writer. She loved keeping journals and dreamed of writing a novel, she said shyly, but Harrison was scathing about this and said it was a pipe dream. He would sneer at her English degree, saying she was lucky he had a profitable business and could employ her.

Kat bristled. How dare anyone stamp on another's dreams? She was glad this young man was no longer Lily's fiancé; he sounded controlling and potentially abusive. He didn't deserve her, and she hoped Lily would see this eventually. It took a lot of effort to bite her lip and not say anything. Lily needed to tell her story without Kat chipping in.

She listened as Lily explained how unhappy she had become. As, looking back, she realised there were lots of signs that things were wrong. A changed phone passcode. Urgent whispered phone calls that ended the moment she walked into a room. Business trips to conferences she wasn't invited to. At first these were small and easily explained. Each time, Harrison reassured her or made her feel as though she were imagining things or going mad. Paranoid. Possessive.

Of course, she wasn't any of these things. A month before their wedding, Lily came home from work early with period pain and found her fiancé, who was supposedly out on a viewing, in bed with another girl. This time there was no gaslighting. The harsh truth was undeniable. As it turned out, lots of their mutual friends had known, and even Lily's parents weren't surprised.

"I left my job, of course. The flat was his, so I went back the next day, packed my bags and moved back in with my parents. I was back where I started, only it felt worse than before because now I was older and sadder." She swallowed. "I felt so stupid. The cheated-on girlfriend. The last to know. I think what was worst of all was being turned into a cliché."

"Oh, my dear girl." Kat reached across the table and laid her hand on Lily's in a gesture of solidarity. "I know you'll have heard it a million times, but you had a lucky escape."

"Yes, I know that. Logically at least, although it doesn't always feel that way. I lost my job, and the future I thought I had. I didn't even want to stay in my hometown. Everyone knew. I managed six months, but it was hard, and I was really low. That's when my Hannah suggested a change of scene. And here I am, in Mallorca. Clara's place." She pressed her fingers into the corners of her eyes and smiled sadly. "I can't believe I'm still crying over him after all this time."

"Time doesn't always work the way we think it will," said Kat gently. "And I don't think it's him you're crying for. I think it's the person you used to be, and the chances you missed out on because of him."

"Do you think?" Lily asked. "I don't miss him. In some ways I was relieved when it all happened. He made me feel guilty a lot of the time."

"I certainly do think. He sounds like an utter shit. Clara would have said the same."

Lily stared at her, the way young people always did when someone old swore, and Kat laughed. "Don't look so shocked. I wasn't always this old. I've had heartbreak of my own too. Though nothing quite like yours."

"You mean if it's a competition, I win?"

Kat closed her eyes. She saw the sea, silken blue and the matching sky above. Felt the sun on her skin. Soft lips skimming her neck. Her insides turning to honey as she reached for him.

Pablo.

"I could give you every cliché in the book right now," she said. "Plenty more fish in the sea. What doesn't kill you. Make the most of being young. Yada, yada. But you already know all that. I'm not going to patronise you, my dear. You sound like someone who's already starting to move on. Maybe the young man you met last night will be a part of that?"

Lily sighed. "I probably won't see him again. But he made me feel like there could be more. He saw me. You know?"

"Oh, I know," said Kat softly. "I believe in Fate, though. Maybe you'll see him again next time you're in the port?"

Lily looked thoughtful. "Maybe, but he could have sailed away by now and be anywhere tomorrow. Maybe rescuing another girl. Still, at least I have a lovely memory."

"Cherish it," advised Kat. "One day you'll be my age, and you'll look back at that ex-fiancé and thank him for setting you free. It might have been the key to finding true love."

Lily's eyes, an unusual jade green flecked with amber, widened. "You sound like you know what you're talking about."

"Well, yes," said Kat. "I do. I've been there too."

The rain was easing. The storm had passed. Soon, the mountains would blush pink, just the way Lily's cheeks did when she spoke of this boy, Rafe. No matter what, the sun always rose, Kat thought. That was a comfort. There was always a new day.

"Will you tell me about it?" Lily asked. "Those early days here? When you first met Clara? If you're not too tired?"

Kat didn't need much sleep any more. It was an unfortunate gift of growing old. If she didn't go back to bed now, she could always doze on the terrace later. And there was one age-related benefit – naps were acceptable!

"I don't want to keep you up," she said. "Jenny's a hard taskmaster."

"I couldn't sleep if I tried," Lily replied. "I've had so much coffee, and my brain's whirling. I'm going to work like crazy all morning and impress Jenny. Then if she lets me, I'll sleep in the afternoon. Do people still have siestas?"

"Jenny does. She's old-fashioned, and siestas are written into the job description. They're practically law in this house."

Kat smiled at the memory of a time when whole towns slept the heat of the afternoon away, shutters drawn and streets silent. A pause in the busyness of a day before life bloomed again beneath the rising moon and shy stars.

"Well then," she said, hauling herself up and heading for the kettle, "I'll put this on, make more tea and tell you a story about another girl who once met a boy in a small Mallorcan town …"

CHAPTER 15

LILY - NOW

Lily wouldn't have believed it was possible to get by on so little sleep. She and Kat had talked until 8 am, when Jenny and José arrived, stunned to see the two women sitting in the kitchen drinking tea and watching the sun rise. Jenny shooed Kat back to bed, scolding her as though she were a child, and as Kat caught Lily's eye the corners of her mouth twitched in a silent acknowledgement that she was allowing the older woman to fuss over her.

Promising that she would not reappear until at least 11, Kat vanished into the garden room with strict instructions to rest. Not long afterwards the heavy curtains were drawn and Lily imagined her snuggled into the soft bed, drifting off to a sleep filled with dreams of the past and a dark-eyed lover called Pablo.

How wonderful it was to share these stories of the past! Lily felt touched and privileged to have been taken into Kat's confidence. While Jenny brewed coffee so strong it could lift weights Lily ran upstairs for a shower. As jets of cool water needled away the remnants of tiredness and shocked her awake, she loaded up her sponge with shower gel and relived her own magical encounter.

Rafe had been a revelation. Kind and funny and a gentleman, he hadn't said or done anything to suggest he might find Lily attractive, but she had seen the appreciation flare in his warm sherry eyes. There was an ease about him which was contagious, and she had felt relaxed in his company, soon forgetting that they were strangers and that he was one of the most beautiful men she had ever seen.

He was so handsome it was almost a joke, for surely nobody was that good-looking in real life. Dark curls brushed off his forehead, bone structure worthy of a film star and dark eyes with sable lashes; she knew she had been the envy of all the other girls in the café, who would have loved to sit with him. Lily recalled the way his sculpted muscles shifted and danced beneath the fabric of his T-shirt and shivered at the unbidden image of those arms holding her. His legs were lean, muscular and very brown, and she laughed at herself for admiring male legs like somebody at the court of Henry VIII. Lily had never thought of legs as sexy before, but Rafe's certainly set her pulse racing. Team all this with his wide smile, easy laugh and quirky sense of humour – and there you had it, Lily decided: he was the full package.

What a shame she would never see him again. Just her luck that the first man she had been interested in since Harrison happened to be one presumably far away by now, sailing to another port where no doubt more girls would fall at his deck-shoed feet and require rescuing.

It was alarming how her stomach lurched at this idea. She was being daft, thinking she was special, but it had been one of the most romantic moments of her life. Not that there was a huge amount of competition, since her ex's idea of romance had been to lower the toilet seat, but even so …

She closed her eyes and relived the scene, and although the room was flooded with sunshine her skin was dusted with delicious shivers. It was a moment Lily already knew she would revisit whenever she needed a little magic in her day, or a reminder that there were decent men out there, and she guessed she needed to be content with this. Rafe was no more than a memory now.

By the time she was dressed in shorts and a T-shirt and back in the kitchen, drinking black coffee and looking at the long list of jobs Jenny had allocated for her, Lily was convinced that Rafe was no more than a footnote in this early chapter of her summer in Andratx. It was time to focus on her new job.

She was used to working hard. She wasn't afraid to get her hands dirty, and even though she had been employed as an au pair at Samantha's house, she'd had a lot of cleaning practice there too. Casa del Mar had been a modern study in glass and steel, which looked fantastic but was horribly impractical. It took a lot of scrubbing and polishing to remove smeary starfish handprints from glass and metal, and Lily had been mopping stone floors from morning to night. She had no problem with the idea of doing this work all day long at La Colina, but to her surprise Jenny had other ideas in mind.

"I can mop and clean," she said when Lily asked why these jobs were missing from the list. "What I cannot do is climb up on chairs to dust. See the curtain rails? See the tops of the pictures? The light fittings, *aqui*? They are very dusty. I need you to clean them all."

Lily nodded. She could do this.

"The whole house needs a deep clean," Jenny continued. "It will take many days, but it must be done for when ..." The housekeeper lowered her voice, "Señora sells."

Lily was taken aback. In her mind's eye, Kat was still young and La Colina no more than a shell of a *finca,* a secret lovers' hideaway on a lonely headland. She could not wait to hear what had happened next to Kat and Pablo after their first row. Kat had been on the brink of telling her when Jenny and José arrived. The conversation had ended abruptly, leaving Lily with lots of questions and desperate to know what happened next to the young lovers. She needed to know how Kat came to own this place. Why did she marry another man when she adored Pablo? What happened to divide them? She understood why La Colina meant so much to the older woman; it was where she had fallen in love. She was shocked to think Kat might sell. Why would she want to do that?

"This big house is expensive to run and needs work," Jenny explained when Lily voiced this question. "Her family live in England. That is where her life is, and Señora finds travelling harder now. She is unwell. Her heart. It will not be hard to sell La Colina. Many, many developers want to buy this place. Tomás López is keen, and has made an approach. He's a man who always gets what he wants."

"I saw his boat last night. It was too big for the marina," Lily recalled.

"*Sí,* it is a big, big boat. Señor López is preoccupied with size. I wonder why that might be?"

The two women looked at each other for a moment. Then Jenny winked and they burst out laughing. That easily, Kat's oldest and newest helpers became friends.

"What are you two cackling about?" asked José, who had wandered into the kitchen to fill his water bottle. He held it up to his wife. "Empty already. I need a bigger one."

Jenny and Lily laughed even harder. José rolled his eyes, filled his bottle from the iced-water dispenser and left them to it. He was old enough and wise enough to recognise women's talk.

"Would Señora sell to Tomás López?"

Once the mirth ebbed away, Lily's laughter was superimposed with worry. She hadn't been in Andratx long, but she knew the tycoon's reputation for knocking down old properties and replacing them with extravagant lairs fit for Bond villains. The thought of this beautiful old house being bulldozed made her heart sink; surely Kat couldn't do that to La Colina? Not when her memories and her past were as much a part of the place as the glowing wooden floors and off-white plaster.

Jenny shrugged. "Who knows? It would be a shame to see the house go – but look at the town. It's *muy* different now to when Señora was a girl."

There was not much Lily could say, but she thought it would be more than a shame for La Colina to be demolished; it would be a travesty. For the rest of the morning, while she cleaned and dusted and scrubbed places that had not seen water and soap for many years, Lily wove elaborate fantasies about EuroMillions wins or finding a kind and handsome billionaire to fall in love with her – preferably one without a penchant for bondage and cable ties. All daydreams, of course, but she was already head over heels in love with La Colina, and with its owner too. She couldn't wait to hear more about what had happened next to Kat and Pablo. Knowing how things looked in the present, Lily feared it had not been a happy ending.

When the sun was at its fiercest, José came in from the garden and sat in the shade of the terrace with a cold beer. Lily joined him with a Diet Coke, and they watched over the busy town, doll-sized and so quiet from this vantage point, in companionable silence. Lily was giddy from lack of sleep and pleasantly achy after a morning of hard physical work. Jenny was in the kitchen preparing a simple lunch of salad, with crusty bread which made Lily think of Lina's bakery, and *tortilla Española,* which smelled delicious and made her mouth water.

Jenny plated up portions for the three of them and left Kat's in the fridge for whenever her employer decided to eat. Then Lily, Jenny and José carried their food to the far side of the house and ate in the shade of a large pine tree. It was the one Kat had described seeing from Pablo's boat, a pale green smudge against a terracotta roof, and Lily felt quite emotional thinking about what that tree had witnessed over the years.

This stately old tree had known the woman who owned this house as a young girl. It had watched as she and Pablo climbed the wall and jumped into the garden for the very first time. It had heard them whisper promises of love, and its roots were watered by Kat's tears. It had welcomed a young bride, seen her family grow and seen her dear ones leave. What would it see next? Lily wondered. She hated to think what its fate might be if Tomás López bought this house. Would he appreciate its shade and love its aged wisdom, or chop it down? Gazing across the town at the sparkling homes of the wealthy, so many of which López had built in place of traditional houses, Lily feared she knew the answer.

There was no time to dwell on this. After a brief siesta, which made her feel groggy and hungover, and a quick catch-up in her diary (where Rafe took a starring role) Lily's afternoon was no less busy than her morning. She stripped all the beds and remade them before doing the laundry and pegging washing onto a listing line on a scrubby ledge below the terrace and above the herd of curious goats which clung to the steep hillside. Then she was dispatched into the town on some errands with José, her job to run to the shop while he circled the one-way system slowly to avoid trying to park Kat's enormous convertible Mercedes. Andratx bubbled with tourists and Lily had to shut her eyes as José drove through the narrow, crowded streets. He wouldn't put the roof down or use the aircon without his employer present, so it was with huge relief on many fronts that Lily hopped out of the vehicle. She was off saunas for life after fifteen minutes travelling with José.

She picked up some shopping from the supermarket, thinking how strange it was that it was only a day since she'd fallen over here, yet already her life had changed so much, and visited the small pharmacy on the quayside to collect a prescription for Kat. While she queued, listening to some English visitors talking loudly and very slowly as they explained they needed suncream, Lily glanced outside and across the road to the spot where she had met Rafe. She told herself she wasn't looking to see if he was there but simply admiring the view. And if she felt a little down swell of disappointment not to spot him on a pontoon checking lines, it was only because she wanted to know for sure whether he really was as perfect as her imagination was painting him.

By the early evening Lily was exhausted. Lack of sleep had finally caught up with her and the heat had stolen her last reserves of energy. Her day finished at 5:30, at least according to Jenny, and as she stowed the last of the pool furniture away and made sure any damp towels were in the tumble dryer, Lily looked longingly at the pool. Kat had enjoyed a dip earlier; Lily had watched her bob up and down with a determined breaststroke, but now the pool was unruffled and its surface a poured mirror of sky.

How Lily would love a refreshing dip after her hot and busy day. Of course, she wouldn't dream of asking Kat. She was staff and it was not appropriate, but she thought longingly about how wonderful it would be to float in the cool water while the fishing boats chugged home and the sailing school drifted out towards the horizon. Heaven.

"There you are," said Kat when Lily passed the garden room with her arms full of towels. The older woman was sitting on a rattan chair with a book held loosely in one hand and a glass of rosé in the other. Her long silver hair was pinned up on top of her head with a glittery slide, and she peered at Lily through huge sunglasses. "My goodness, did I leave those wet things there? I'm so sorry. How very idle of me."

"No need to apologise," said Lily, pleasantly surprised. Samantha was given to clicking her fingers as though Lily was a waiter in disguise. "You're on holiday and it's my job."

Kat shook her head. "People picking up after me. My mother would have a fit." She leaned forward and lifted her sunglasses, studying Lily through narrowed eyes. "You look hot and tired."

"That's exactly how I feel," laughed Lily. She stifled a yawn. "My days of staying up all night without sleep the next day are over, I think. If they even began!"

"Rubbish," said Kat. "They are just beginning. Why, when I was your age ..."

She paused and Lily waited for her to finish, but Kat didn't want to say more. Instead, she shook her head and changed direction. "Why don't you have a swim? You look as though you could do with cooling off."

"Are you a mind reader?" Lily asked.

"Nothing so exciting. I've just lived here for a long time. Don't forget, love, I used to do what you're doing. I was always hot and exhausted when I'd finished at the guesthouse, but I could walk to the cove in five minutes and cool off or ask a lovely young man to take me out on his boat to swim. The next best thing to that is probably this pool."

La Colina's pool was the most exquisite in the whole town. It was an infinity pool, which gave the impression that you could swim straight out to Dragonera. Lily imagined swimming to the edge and looking down over the bustling town while cool water caressed her skin and her kicking legs frilled the surface. Heaven on earth.

"Are you sure?" she asked.

"I wouldn't have said so otherwise," Kat said.

Lily was nervous suddenly. She hardly knew Kat Beauchamp, but her experience of Samantha and Toby had taught her that employers could be capricious. She didn't want to do anything that might annoy Kat later and jeopardise her job here.

Kat fixed Lily with a stern look. "And please don't ask me whether or not it's appropriate or come out with some nonsense that you're staff and shouldn't use the pool."

Kat's mind-reading skills were terrifying. Her daughters must get away with nothing.

"My husband would be spinning in his grave, if we hadn't cremated him and scattered his ashes right here, to think the pool was standing empty most of the year. He's probably watching from above and urging you on to enjoy a lovely swim in the pool that he designed." She crossed her arms. "I'll be quite offended on his behalf if you don't."

Apart from not wanting to offend her new employer, Lily was not going to turn down the offer of a swim. She scooted up to her room and pulled out her bikini. It was a cute red and white frilly affair, which Hannah said made her look like a 1950s starlet.

"You lucky cow! I wish I had boobs!" Hannah had cried when Lily nervously tried it on in the changing room. Lily, who was worried the bikini showcased her assets a little too much, had pointed out how much she wished she was skinny and athletic like Hannah.

"You get far too much attention when you have boobs," she sighed. It was easier to cover up in a baggy T-shirt or wear a rash vest over a swimming costume.

"That's the whole point, you muppet!" Hannah said in despair. "If you've got it, flaunt it. Never did Katie Price any harm."

That was debatable, but Lily had seen herself through her friend's eyes at that point: sexy and curvy rather than chubby. She had liked this vision of herself and bought the bikini. She didn't wear it often because she was self-conscious, but there was only Kat here and it would be lovely to work on her tan. Lily scooped her hair up onto the top of her head with a butterfly clip and pushed her feet into flip-flops before running back down to the pool and diving in.

The water was like silk on her hot skin and almost painfully cold for a few seconds. Then it was bliss. She drifted on her back, looking up at the clouds and seagulls so high they must surely need oxygen, before swimming a few lengths. Then she hooked her arms over the edge of the pool, resting her chin in her hands and looking at the town which peeled away to the mountains. Harrison, estate agencies and broken engagements seemed a world away. How had she got so lucky?

Across from her vantage point, the marina was a moving picture of marine traffic. Fishing boats were returning to the port with gulls falling like snow behind them, and jet skis iced the water with lazy circles. Tomás López's large boat was still moored outside the harbour in the deepest water, a leviathan of glass, painfully bright white fibreglass and glowing orange teak. The smart tender was missing and there was no sign of life on board. The important man must be in town or perhaps had even flown away to one of his other properties. A life like that must be surreal, and Lily wondered how much was enough. When did you accrue enough money to satisfy you?

"Lily! Lily!"

Kat was calling her. She sounded excited. "Lily! There's a visitor for you!"

Lost in her thoughts, Lily had been a world away. Several times she thought she had been close to falling asleep as she rested a cheek on the sun-warmed edge of the pool and listened to the chirrup of cicadas.

She splashed around, wondering who this visitor might be. Hannah, she hoped, and not Samantha coming to drag her back thanks to some spurious clause in a contract Lily had no memory of signing.

But Lily was wrong on both counts. As she shielded her eyes against the brightness, she saw that the person with Kat was male.

Male and tall, and so handsome the sight of him made her breath catch.

"*Hola*, Lily," said Rafe.

CHAPTER 16

LILY - NOW

Of all the people to appear while she was in her bikini, it had to be Rafe. What were the chances? Lily splashed to the other side of the pool, acutely aware of just how low-cut her polka-dot top was, and wishing she'd started her Get Beach Body Ready plan before flying to Mallorca.

Rafe looked as comfortable on the terrace of La Colina as he had on the quayside. He wore faded navy board shorts, a long-sleeved white T-shirt, and clean tan deck shoes. His mirrored wraparound shades were pushed into his dark hair. A stainless steel watch gleamed at his wrist, and the air between them carried a pepper-and-lemon note of his cologne.

He didn't look as though he'd climbed the steep path from the harbour at all. He was as fresh as the proverbial daisy, the sort of infuriatingly perfect person Lily, firmly in the *imperfect* camp, could only gape at. She couldn't decide whether to laugh or cry. Secretly she'd wanted to see him again, but the last thing she needed was for him to catch her looking, as her ex so charmingly once put it, like a beached whale.

She forced a smile, praying her horror wasn't written all over her face. "What are you doing here?"

"Oh, just delivering a new yacht for the owner," he said deadpan, then laughed. "I came to find you, of course. Wanted to make sure you hadn't hurt yourself after last night. That was quite a tumble."

"But how did you know where I lived?"

"I put you in the taxi, remember? I flagged the driver down on his return had to buy him several beers to get your address. Apparently, it's against his code of conduct." He bit his bottom lip. "Sorry, that sounds awful when I say it out loud. I sound like a stalker. I promise I'm not."

"That's exactly what a stalker would say," Lily replied with a straight face. He looked so stricken that she broke into laughter. "I don't think you're a stalker. I think ..." She hesitated. "I think you're really kind. I managed to survive my injuries, just about."

"So, the pool is physiotherapy?" he asked lightly. "Very wise."

He turned to take in the view: the port, the sleeping dragon island, the sky melting into evening. Candyfloss-pink clouds were piling on the horizon, and everything below turned apricot and rose. Even Tomás López's angular houses glittered like sugared cubes in the golden light.

"It's amazing, isn't it?" said Lily. She was still calculating how to leave the pool without exposing her stomach and thighs. Kat, inconveniently, hadn't returned with a towel. Lily wasn't sure if she was glad or not.

"Yes," Rafe agreed. "Beautiful." But his eyes weren't on the view.

Lily blushed, no small feat in cold water with an evening breeze skimming her skin, and realised she liked the way he looked at her: as though she were golden, luscious, like some kind of goddess or a ripe peach.

Throwing caution, pride, and dignity aside, she climbed out using the steps. If Venus de Milo could manage grace, so could she.

"Here, let me," Rafe said, jogging to the pagoda. He came back with a thick green towel and wrapped it around her shoulders.

"It gets chilly when the evening breeze picks up," he said. "At sea we welcome it, but after a hot day it can be a shock."

She was about to tell him *he* was the real shock to the system, but he was right: the higher terrace was brisk with cold air. She hovered, unsure if she ought to invite him to sit – after all, this was Kat's home and she was only staff – but Kat solved the problem by arriving with a tray bearing water and two glasses.

"You have a beautiful house, Señora," Rafe said as Kat poured him a drink.

"Thank you," she replied with a warm smile. "It's been a good friend to me."

There was a pause, and Lily realised Kat was waiting for an introduction, though the twinkle in her eyes betrayed recognition.

"I met Rafe last night," Lily explained. "He helped me when I tripped like a clumsy idiot."

"You're not clumsy," Rafe cut in hotly. "Those ropes are a menace. You're not the first to fall and won't be the last. But," he added, softly, "you're the first I've come to check on."

They stared at one another. Lily's voice had deserted her.

"That's very thoughtful," Kat said, coming to the conversational rescue. "Oh dear, I've left something in the oven. I'll leave you two with the view."

"That was tactful," Rafe murmured once she'd gone. "But she didn't have to."

"She's giving us space," Lily said. "To chat."

"Well, you've got most of the property to yourself tonight. Not every employer would be that generous."

"Would yours?" she asked before she could stop herself.

He glanced at the harbour, his expression unreadable. "Nothing like your Señora Beauchamp. I hear she's a special lady."

"Who told you that?"

"Everyone. She's loved here."

"She loves it too. It'll break her heart to leave."

"Is that likely?"

Lily sipped her water. She didn't want to gossip about Kat, but it was hardly a secret.

"Maybe. The house is huge, and she's far from home. Developers have been sniffing around, so she says."

Rafe's brow furrowed. "There's anger about that everywhere in Spain. People don't like change, and I don't blame them. Bulldozing through destroys the soul of a place. Developers should work *with* history, not against it. If it were me, I'd preserve what's here."

"I guess deckhands don't make those decisions," Lily said lightly.

No," he agreed. "They don't."

The air between them shifted. Serious now. Lily pulled the towel tighter. He'd confirmed she was fine, so why was he still here?

"Thank you for checking on me," she said carefully. "I don't want to keep you."

"You're not keeping me. But," his eyes sparkled, "you *will* need to change if you're accepting my invitation tonight.

Unless you're planning to go in that bikini. You'd look incredible, but it might get chilly."

Her heart leapt. He'd come not just to check on her, but to *see* her, again, so soon.

A warning line from *Romeo and Juliet* echoed in her head – violent delights having violent ends – and she shivered. A curse of an English Lit degree: there was always a quote for doom. But this wasn't Shakespeare. This was a lovely, absurdly handsome man asking her out. Hannah's voice in her head kicked her firmly: *Say yes.*

"Only if you want to," Rafe added quickly, suddenly nervous. "You probably have plans. You must have plans …"

"I don't," Lily said, taking pity. "But I'd better check Kat doesn't need me. What did you have in mind?"

His smile was slow and devastating. "There's a local band at Cala Llamp, the next bay. They're brilliant. We'll take a boat, listen from the water. Lots of people do it. Or we can go ashore, grab beers. It'll be fun. Different. I'd love to show you."

The words 'boat' and 'music' painted her imagination with moonlit water, starlit kisses, private swims. *But you don't know him,* whispered a voice.

True. But there was something about him that felt safe, honourable. Kat had told her to trust her instincts. She hadn't done that with her ex, and had paid the price.

"I'd love to," she said simply.

His answering look was almost relief. "It's not kindness, Lily. It's selfish. I want to see you again. I want you to see this place properly."

He gathered the tray and carried it back up to the yellow table, Lily following with the towel clutched around her. Kat was reading, but looked up with a smile.

"It's going to be a beautiful evening. That sky, blue and pink, the calm sea. I wish there were a word for it."

"I think of evenings like this when it's winter back home," said Rafe.

"Where's home?" Lily asked. She'd assumed Mallorca.

He hesitated, then said. "Madrid."

"I've never been. It's on the list."

"It's beautiful. Fountains in the parks, galleries crammed with art. There's a real buzz."

Kat interrupted. "Is that where your family's from?"

Rafe shook his head. "No, Señora. My father's from Zaragoza. My mother was born in Sevilla, though she moved often as a child."

Kat sighed. "I had a friend from Madrid once. Long ago. He said it was beautiful. I always hoped to see it."

"There's still time," Lily said gently.

"You should visit," Rafe agreed.

Kat's voice was quiet. "No. That time's gone." Then she seemed to gather herself and smiled. "Anyway, enough of me wittering on. Lily, you need to go and get changed. And before you ask if you're allowed out this evening, the answer is of course you are. I'm not a slave driver. You've worked very hard, and you finish at half past five. So I can't imagine anything nicer." Kat looked innocent, but Lily knew match-making when she saw it. Kat was living vicariously, remembering her own adventures with Pablo, no doubt.

"In that case, I'd love to," Lily said to Rafe. "It's really kind of you to invite me."

"It's not kind," he said simply. "It's extremely selfish. I just really want your company."

Lily excused herself and left Rafe and Kat chatting companionably about boats and the Andratx coastline. As she hurried up the outside staircase to her balcony room, she heard Rafe talking about the ports he'd visited. His voice was full of happiness. He clearly loved this island, and though she didn't really know him Lily liked what she'd seen so far. More than that, she liked the way he spoke to Kat. Polite, yet with real warmth. Her ex would have been checking his watch by now, sighing, glaring at her for taking too long. Rafe was the opposite. He listened. He gave people time. He was kind.

She showered quickly and pulled on a pair of cut-off denim shorts and a floaty paisley-print top. She didn't bother with much make-up, just a sweep of mascara and tinted balm. Her curly hair went into a ponytail. Her scraped knees didn't matter; Rafe didn't seem like the type to care. Her reflection looked glowing and sparkly-eyed, as though someone had slipped her a free makeover. She smiled at herself, blew a quick kiss, and headed downstairs.

"You look great," Rafe said when she rejoined them on the terrace.

"Take a hoodie in case it gets chilly on the water," Kat fussed.

"It's still about twenty-six degrees," Lily laughed, but she appreciated the concern.

"I have a collection she can choose from, Señora," Rafe promised. "I'll look after her."

Kat regarded him thoughtfully. "Yes. I think you will."

"Phew," Rafe muttered as they stepped through the old wooden gate in the wall. "I feel like I've passed some sort of test."

"You have," Lily laughed. "I've only been working for her less than forty-eight hours, but I can already tell Kat Beauchamp is a force of nature."

"I've heard that," he said.

"Oh? That's town talk too?"

Rafe didn't elaborate. He was too busy unlocking an ancient Land Rover Defender. "Your chariot awaits, my lady."

"Why, thank you." Lily was quietly proud she could hop up into the passenger seat without needing a hand.

"It's basic," Rafe apologised, starting the engine. "But perfect for island life, with all the steep hills and slipways. It's bumpy, though. You might want a chiropractor after this."

"I'll send you my bill," she teased, and he laughed.

"You do that. I am not – what is it you English say – kidding?"

He wasn't. The car was a rattly bone shaker but great fun and unusual. There were plenty of other Land Rovers on the island, although most were glistening Range Rovers or soft-top Evoques, parading along the seafront like designer handbags on wheels. This was clearly not that. Lily liked that it was his. She liked that he didn't care about impressing people with shiny new kit. Her ex had been car-obsessed, and his Mercedes had been his prized possession. At the time, Lily had felt protective, because it meant so much to him and she thought he was vulnerable by needing to impress. Now, with hindsight, she thought it reflected his shallow nature. Rafe didn't need status symbols. He was happy in his own skin, and confident without being cocky.

They drove down into the town. Families were out for dinner, children darting across the road to look at something in the market, tiny dogs trotting at their owners' heels in the cool of the evening. Rafe slowed for all of them, smiling and waving people on. Lily could almost hear her ex's horn blaring and his voice shouting out the window. The contrast made her dizzy.

They crossed the bridge at the far end of town and turned into the marina where the rich and powerful moored their yachts. Samantha and Toby kept their Princess here, and Lily said a quick prayer they wouldn't be around. A confrontation was the last thing she wanted.

Rafe drove straight through, waving at a few locals, and parked at the far end away from the Bentleys and sports cars, among battered trucks and marine engineers' vans. Ropes, chain and tools were scattered about. It was the working end of the marina, and Lily exhaled. No chance of bumping into Samantha here.

Rafe jumped down from the driver's side and sprinted around to open the door and help her out. His hands rested briefly on her waist and Lily felt something spark low in her belly. She wasn't imagining it either, for Rafe drew in a sharp breath and their eyes met. Lily knew he'd felt it too and, flustered, she stepped away quickly and fiddled with her rucksack while Rafe pointed to his boat.

"Your superyacht for tonight."

His boat was a modest tender, owned by a much larger yacht, and fifteen feet long at most. It wasn't glamorous, but when Rafe took her hands and helped her on board, Lily felt like a queen stepping onto a royal yacht.

They set off, and the sun was melting into the sea like an apricot into poured silver. The sky was stained rose-gold. The engine purred beneath them, low and soft, matching the quiet thrum in her chest. Lily felt as though she was inhabiting a dream. She had never done anything like this before. It was so impulsive. Sailing off into the unknown with a boy who made her laugh and who made her feel like she mattered had to be the craziest thing sensible Lily Wilson had ever done.

But she had left sensible Lily behind a long time ago. This new Lily was fun, and embraced life, grabbing new opportunities with both hands. She was in the driving seat of her life now, not the passenger's.

"Hold tight," Rafe said, grinning. "This next bit gets choppy."

Lily braced herself as the boat picked up speed. Her hair

flew in wild tangles, but she didn't care. The wind, the spray, the fizzing excitement, were all part of the adventure.

They rounded the headland and Cala Llamp appeared: a quiet crescent tucked between the cliffs. A few boats had already anchored, bobbing lazily in the water. From the rocks, music drifted: guitar chords and the haunting ache of a Spanish ballad. The scent of barbecue hung in the air.

Rafe cut the engine, and after the roaring the sudden silence was magical.

"I brought supplies," he said, pulling out a wicker basket from under the seat. "Like a proper local. We're way too mean to pay for food out here. Everyone knows they put the prices up for the tourists."

He laid out Manchego, *jamón*, olives, *pan con tomate* and a bottle of Cava on the deck. It was simple food, but Lily thought nothing had ever tasted so good. As they ate, they chatted about their friends and families. Rafe's parents were divorced and had remarried – his father, several times – and he had been brought up by his grandfather. He loved boats, enjoyed poetry, and wasn't thinking much beyond the summer.

"You'll crew until the end of the season?" Lily asked, licking tomato juice from her fingers.

"Yes. I may stay even longer now there is something in Andratx I want to remain for."

Her mouth dried. His meaning was clear.

"How about you, Lily?"

She loved the way he pronounced her name: Lil-ee. On his lips the vowels and consonants were magical.

"I'll stay here as long as Señora Beauchamp does."

"Then we must make sure she stays for a long, long time," said Rafe.

He raised his glass, foaming with the Cava which, shaken

from the trip around the headland, had exploded when uncorked. It had frothed everywhere, and they'd drunk from the bottle as though it were a fountain, laughing at the mess. Rafe said it was not the impression he had hoped for, but Lily thought it was funny and liked him even more for laughing too and not getting upset when his perfect plan was ruined. Harrison would have sulked all evening.

"To La Colina and to Señora Beauchamp."

They clinked glasses. Lily was more than happy to drink to Kat. Falling over in front of her had changed everything.

The music played, voices joined in and stars began to blink into life overhead. Boats drifted in like glowing fireflies. Someone danced on the deck of a nearby yacht, silhouetted against lanterns. Others headed to the beach, but Lily and Rafe were content to lie on the deck, heads pillowed by a collection of hoodies and sweaters, and listen from afar. Neither of them felt the need to socialise.

Lily looked up at the sky. There was a slice of moon which seemed to smile at her, and her heart was full of a strange feeling.

Happiness, she realised. She was happy.

"This doesn't feel real," she whispered.

"It is," Rafe said quietly. "This is real, Lily. I promise."

She turned to him, and in his eyes she saw the flicker of something new. Instead of saying anything, he reached for her hand. His was warm and steady and felt just right.

They lay hand in hand, listening to the music until it ended. Applause rippled across the water and the sky was ink-dark. As other boats switched on their navigation lights, spilling emeralds and rubies into the black water, Rafe rose to his feet and started the engine. Lily trailed a hand over the side as he steered them home.

Halfway back, he stopped the engine. The other boats were

soon out of sight, and they were all alone. Silence fell, velvet-dark and complete, broken only by the soft lap of waves. High on the headland lights twinkled from the houses which clung to the hillside. Somewhere amongst them was La Colina, thought Lily dreamily. No longer standing alone as it had all those years ago when Kat had first seen it, but still guarding the entrance to the port, its faithful tower watching over the people who lived here.

"I'll never forget tonight," Rafe said, his voice low. "Not ever. It was magical."

Lily's breath caught. She knew he meant it. "Me too," she whispered.

As she kissed Rafe under the smile of the moon and the benevolent gaze of La Colina, Lily knew she had utterly fallen for him.

CHAPTER 17

LILY - NOW

Lily had never known happiness could feel like this.

It was a revelation to discover that waking up every day was a joy, each new morning no longer another hurdle to overcome but an adventure waiting to unfold. Everything seemed so much brighter, as though the world had turned its colours up a notch, and even the everyday jobs were approached with a smile. Now Lily understood why poets and musicians were so obsessed with celebrating love, because it went hand in hand with life. It was impossible not to sing from the rooftops when you floated through the day and were so happy your cheeks hurt from smiling.

A great deal of this joy was down to Rafe. Lily couldn't pretend otherwise. He was a wonderful addition to her life, and she was falling for him more and more with every passing day. But it wasn't just because of Rafe that Lily felt so gloriously happy; her joy ran deeper than any one person, and was as much about falling in love with herself and with life as it was with him. Their new relationship was another beautiful layer laid on top of days that already felt rich and fulfilled.

Rafe enhanced her life, but he hadn't become her life, and now Lily realised that this was what a relationship should be like. A relationship shouldn't be needed to complete a person or fix a broken existence; it should enhance what was already whole and be the proverbial icing on the cake. Love was not about needing someone for validation or meaning, but the sparkle on an already vibrant life. And these days her life sparkled like the blue water which glittered and shifted far below La Colina.

Lily was in love with the beautiful villa, too. The view from it never failed to take her breath away, no matter how many times she looked at it. She never tired of gazing outwards from it, and sometimes had to force herself to tear her eyes from the sight of boats bustling in and out of the marina or the activity on the small sickle of beach opposite, to focus on the task in hand. José and Jenny, used to the view after a lifetime of working at La Colina, teased her about staring and being slow, but Lily didn't mind, because their laughter was good-natured. Besides, she loved her work and was happy to take time over it, often continuing well beyond her agreed hours before joining Kat on the terrace for an evening drink.

Lily was every bit as busy as she'd been at Casa del Mar, and many of her jobs were far from glamorous (she spent plenty of time cleaning toilets and scrubbing floors), but here she was appreciated and valued, which made all the difference. The days were long and the work often physically demanding, but the villa was filled with laughter, and she loved the sense of camaraderie and loyalty. Jenny and José had taken her under their wing, and every day was peppered with jokes and smiles.

Jenny's wonderful cooking was also a highlight, and to

combat the extra calories Lily had taken to walking to town and back uphill each morning to fetch the papers and croissants. As well as keeping her fit, this walk meant she was also able to snatch a few moments with Rafe, who began work early and was often on the quayside doing whatever it was he did with his employer's boat.

The beautiful vessel didn't appear to leave port very often, but Lily supposed anyone rich enough to spend hundreds of thousands on what was essentially a toy could afford to waste money. She knew from Hannah's experience that crew like Rafe were kept on standby for whenever the boss decided on a whim to set sail, and she was only glad that he hadn't been ordered to leave for another part of the Med. She would miss him far too much for somebody she hadn't known long.

But feelings don't care about timescales. Lily knew she was falling for Rafe, and she realised she had never been in love before, properly in love, where your every cell yearns for the other person and you count the seconds until you can inhale their scent and feel their skin against yours. Her feelings for Harrison had been a pallid imitation, and Lily wondered why she had stayed so long or shed any tears over him. She felt she'd been so silly – but she realised, too, that she'd had nothing to compare her relationship to, and had mistaken base metal for gold, something she would never do again.

"Who does this sex god crew for?" Hannah asked when Lily had finally managed to schedule a FaceTime call with her best friend. The girls often exchanged messages, and Hannah was thrilled to learn that Lily was 'back in the saddle', as she'd put it – but nothing beat a proper face-to-face chat.

"I'm not sure," Lily admitted. She'd never asked, and Rafe had never volunteered the information. "Somebody rich."

Hannah rolled her eyes. "Yeah. Well, that narrows it down. What kind of boat? Princess? Sunseeker?"

"I'm not sure. It's a big one. He's always doing things to it."

"Lils! You're hopeless. What's it called?"

Lily thought hard. "Spanish for 'dream', I think. Or maybe 'daydream'? Or 'fantasy'?"

"Very helpful, not! Is he the skipper? An engineer? A 'lowly, lowly cook'? Will he save the day? And will you jump out of a cake?"

Hannah was referring to *Under Siege*, an action movie set on a warship where the cook was a Navy SEAL in disguise. Hannah's brothers had been obsessed with the film, and in their teen years the girls had watched it many times.

"Rafe's buff, but he's not Steven Seagal," Lily laughed. "And no, he's not a cook. Just a lowly, lowly deckhand, I should think, although he saved my day when I tripped up."

"Does he live in Andratx? Does he have a house? Where's he from?"

"What is this? One hundred questions?"

"I'm making sure this man is good enough for my friend. No more tossers, Lils. Not on my watch. So, where does this Rafe live? Is he local?"

"He's from Madrid," Lily said, "and he lives on the boat."

"A bunk in crew quarters, then. So where do you guys go to have all that lovely wild sex?"

"Hannah!" Lily blushed the same colour as her hair. "You can't ask me things like that!"

"Don't be such a prude. I'm curious, because I know what *I* do. Maybe I can give you some tips? The heads are horrible, unless you're into that kind of kink! The galley's too cramped. The deck is way too risky, unless that's your thing. But the tender at dead of night is perfect!"

Lily put her hands over her ears. "Not listening! And anyway, none of your business."

She loved Hannah dearly, but what she shared with Rafe

Cruz was special. It was sacred and between them, and to discuss it felt sacrilegious. Rafe was increasingly important to her, and the new bond they shared was precious and beautiful.

"I hope you know what you're doing," Hannah sighed. "I would tell you just to use his body and not fall in love, but I know you won't listen. It's probably too late now."

Lily said nothing, because Hannah was right; it was far too late.

"Anyway, I'll be back in town soon. We need to have some work done on the boat, so I'll be about for a few days. I can meet this paragon and make sure he's good enough."

"I'd love you to meet him," Lily said. She was thrilled her best friend would be in Andratx again, and excited that she would meet Rafe. She smiled at Hannah. "And trust me, he's more than good enough. He's perfect."

Hannah made a cynical quip, which Lily ignored. Rafe Cruz had made her believe in hope. He had shown her that life did contain unexpected joys and second chances. The slow and delighted way he smiled whenever he saw her told Lily that he was equally amazed. There was no imbalance in their feelings, no struggle to assert dominance or need to point-score and win arguments. They simply wanted to be together, just as happy to be chatting on the pontoon, their legs swinging over the green water as they watched the flicker of fish below, as they were to sail away to secret coves to be alone and delight in one another.

They met whenever they could, between the rose bloom of dawn when Lily ventured into the port while it was still cool, or in the lavender hush of dusk when her day was over and he was free. They swam in secluded coves, sipped coffee in waterfront cafés or strolled along the quayside, and the world was always golden when they were together.

Their favourite place was a rocky outcrop just downhill

from La Colina, a rare empty patch of scrubby land where the goats still roamed and the developers were yet to venture. It was close enough to the villa that Lily could be there in minutes, and Rafe was able to abandon his Defender on the side of the road.

To reach it required an undignified hop over a wall followed by a scramble down a hillside thick with rosemary and stunted olive trees, but the view and the seclusion were worth the effort. The sequinned sea and the shush of waves were their only companions. It was their own Eden. Sometimes she brought thermal mugs of strong coffee and Rafe would produce a paper bag with *churros* which they shared, their fingers brushing lightly through the sugar dust as they watched the world turn.

"I don't think I've ever met anyone like you," Rafe had told her one evening as they shared the *churros* and watched the sunset.

"Because I'm greedy and constantly covered in crumbs?" Lily teased, brushing her dress where the flakes clung.

He laughed. "No. Because you see all this." He gestured at the bay and the sleeping dragon island. "You manage to see me too, and you still stay."

Lily ached to hear this note of sadness in his voice. She had no idea who or what had hurt Rafe, but someone had clearly damaged him, and he often alluded to feeling as though nobody had really seen beneath the surface until now. They saw the face, he said. The sailing. The smile. The deck shoes. They saw the marine cliché. But did they know he loved poetry? Always cried at *Titanic*? That he loved his grandfather and feared nothing more in the world than losing him?

Lily had pieced his story together, and knew Rafe was the child of warring parents, both remarried and busy with new partners and families. She glimpsed the sadness beneath his smiles, and this note of melancholy was one of the things she found herself drawn to. The cracks Rafe tried to hide, and the vulnerability beneath the good looks and smiles, had melted her heart. She wanted to take the pain away. Wanted him to have a place and a family of his own. Wanted him never to feel sad or afraid, and to know he would never be alone again.

She knew she was in deep.

In the evening Lily would sometimes walk into the port, and they would wander through the streets hand in hand, past the smart yachts, fishing boats and lamp-lit terraces of seafood restaurants. Rafe's hand, calloused and warm, fitted perfectly around hers, and she loved this simple, innocent connection. Sometimes they would share some tapas. Other times they would watch the stars sprinkle like salt across the indigo tablecloth sky and listen to the waves lap the sides of the boats. Rafe would hold her close, and she would rest her head against his chest and hear his heartbeat, steady and sure, and know hers matched.

"Do you ever think about the future?" she asked him one night as they sat in his car outside La Colina, reluctant to say goodnight and hating to be parted. The question had risen in her throat like a tide.

He was quiet for a moment. Then he nodded. "Yes. Lately, I think about it a lot."

"With me?" The words were out before she could stop them. She couldn't hide how she felt – and, Lily realised, she didn't want to. She wanted only honesty between them.

His fingers brushed her cheek. "*Sí.* You make me want things I didn't think I could have. Things I don't deserve, Lily."

And she didn't know what to say to that, except to press a kiss onto his lips. Rafe said strange things at times. It was the language barrier, of course, for why on earth would he not deserve a future with her? It made no sense. There was a future for them, Lily was certain of this, and she was slowly allowing herself to imagine it. That he wanted this too made her glow all over as though she was lit from inside.

Rafe made Lily happy, but he was not the only part of her life in Andratx that she was falling for, as there was Kat too. Kat Beauchamp was more than an employer. She was kind and warm, and possessed a wonderfully dry sense of humour. Lily loved spending time with her and hearing her talk about the villa and how she and her husband had restored it. Though work kept Lily too busy for long chats, she treasured the moments gleaned from hectic days for a glass of rosé and a story. Kat didn't treat Lily like the hired help, but like a friend. She made Lily feel seen, valued and, most importantly, welcome. Lily understood why Jenny and José were so devoted to her, and she wondered, and worried, what they might do if Kat decided to sell La Colina. The house and its owners were a huge part of their life.

Life at La Colina was a world away from the lonely drudgery at Samantha's villa. The pay wasn't any better, but there were a thousand other ways Lily felt rewarded: her beautiful room, access to the pool after a long, hot day, and the freedom to invite friends over on her nights off, something she was hoping to do when Hannah arrived. At La Colina she was treated with respect rather than barely tolerated and worked to the bone. She sometimes caught her reflection and hardly recognised herself: tanned, glowing, eyes bright with joy.

Lily was happy. Truly, radiantly happy. She hoped it would last, but as the summer days melted into one another she worried that she was living in a beautiful dream. As her mother said, all good things had to come to an end.

CHAPTER 18

KAT - NOW

The lemons had ripened late this year.

Kat wondered what this meant. Perhaps it was that the fruit, like her, was clinging on to life here for as long as possible and equally reluctant to admit its summer would soon be over and the year turning inevitably towards a new season? Were they making the most of the views from La Colina's gardens before Tomás López, or another like him, ripped them out and tossed them away?

He had written again, another letter offering even more money, and Kat had read his latest with a howl of despair, knowing that her daughters would think she was mad to refuse. She looked at the trees and knew they were as deeply rooted here as she was. They were a part of this place. To be torn from the soil would kill them.

It wouldn't kill Kat to leave La Colina, but it would be a death of a kind. One life over. Gone for good. A season of her life that would never return. Kat's memories, both good and bad, were planted here alongside the trees, the bright hibiscus and the rosemary. She could still see them all, those dear long-lost faces of the past if she only squinted a little against the light. Tired eyesight, sunshine and tears would blur and dance until …

– oh! There they were! Darling David was sitting at the stone table on the lower terrace reading the paper, Panama hat tipped over his eyes, and nose as pink as the FT in his hands, Clara smoking beside him, and effortlessly chic in a large hat and Chanel glasses, while a young José picked the lemons and passed them to Jenny. Pablo was here too, just at the edge of the terrace, a sun-kissed angel with the sunlight gilding his curls like a nimbus. Everything about him was beautiful, and every line of his body was poetry. His cheekbones were as sharp as the lemons in Jenny's basket, and his mouth was made for kisses. Forever young and forever lost to her – but while she owned La Colina Kat still had a little piece of him, and she felt sure that Pablo, wherever he was now, kept a sliver of her close to his heart.

It was hard these days not to read meaning into so much, thought Kat. She couldn't help but infuse every moment with significance. There was symbolism everywhere she looked, and melancholy tinged even the happiest memories. David had planted those trees, and the two of them had picked the fruit themselves, delighted with the first few sunshine-yellow offerings and declaring that no lemon had ever tasted so good. He'd sliced them into gin and tonics, always poured with famously generous measures, while she grated the zests into seafood linguine or squeezed the juice over calamari bought fresh from the port. Their children had fished slices out from glasses and sucked them, noses screwed up at the bitterness and shrieking as they spat pips at one another.

Such happy times here. Sad ones too, but even these were overlaid with joy. How she would miss this place and the life she had led and so carelessly taken for granted, assuming nothing would ever change. If she had known how fast those golden years would tear by, would she have paused to savour them? Worried less about her body? The first grey hairs? The silly irritations of married life, the who did what and the ebb and flow of marital life? Kat felt sure she would have done so.

There she was over by the pool, her fifty-something self, swathed in a jade kaftan to hide a belly she felt ashamed of and worrying about whether David had loaded the dishwasher. Should she heave herself up from the chair? she wondered. Give herself a stern pep talk? Something along the lines of *you're still young, you silly woman, and you have everything! Throw the newspaper in the pool and drag him upstairs for a siesta! And lose that ridiculous robe. You're gorgeous!*

The chink of china tugged Kat from her daydreams. Lily was crossing the terrace, barefoot and wincing at the heat of the sun-warmed tiles as she balanced a tray of glasses with the unselfconscious grace of youth. She was humming a tune in Spanish, the latest summer hit that slipped into the ear and stayed there for a season, and which would forever conjure this point in time for her, as Fleetwood Mac did for Kat.

It was late afternoon, and the sea was glassy with the heat that lay over Europe like a duvet this very hot summer. The air shimmered and cicadas droned from the undergrowth; Kat thought that even they sounded listless. She was glad to be beneath the shade of the large sun umbrella and catch what breath of sea breeze there was. Even the pool was warm. Her book lay in her lap, untouched for an hour, for turning the pages felt too much of an effort.

Lily set the tray down. "You look like a queen sitting there," she said, smiling. "Very regal, and watching over her realm."

"I'm only regal because I'm too hot to move," Kat said. She flapped her hand to waft some air over her hot skin. "I'm tempted to head inside and hide in the air conditioning, but it seems such a waste. I'll miss the sunshine when I'm home."

"Maybe a cold drink will help." Lily poured water into a long glass and passed it to Kat. The ice rattled against the glass. Kat's gaze drifted to Lily's face. Yes, there it was, the tell-tale softness. The glowing and unguarded expression she knew only too well. This was a girl in love. Full of hope and dreams. Shimmering with longing. She'd been that girl once. And suddenly it almost hurt Kat to look at Lily.

Lily poured herself a drink and sat down. "Do you mind if I invite some people over for supper tomorrow?"

"Wonderful!" Clara clapped her hands, bracelets jangling.

"Who?" David was frowning over his paper. "We'll need more wine if there's more than five, darling."

"Can we stay up?" squealed the children.

Kat blinked, and the past vanished, David and Clara returning to that summer country where there were always parties and wine and newspapers, while her sweet little girls suddenly transformed into middle-aged mothers.

"Only if you're happy, though," Lily said quickly when Kat didn't reply. "I wouldn't want to impose."

Kat blinked. "Of course. Who did you have in mind?"

"My best friend, Hannah. Clara's great-niece. She crews, and her boat is in the port for a few days. Han's great fun; you'll love her, Kat."

Kat nodded. "I'm sure I will. I wonder if she looks like Clara?"

"Was Clara blonde, slim and beautiful?"

"Oh yes," sighed Kat. "She was gorgeous."

"Then very alike," said Lily. "And I'd like to invite Rafe too."

Rafe. The handsome young man who had visited and whose name was spoken by Lily at least twenty times an hour and was entirely responsible for her smiles and singing.

Young. Handsome. Spanish. Loved to sail. A gentleman. A small bell chimed in Kat's mind, but she ignored it. Old age was making her see things that didn't exist.

"Ah," she said with a wink. "The young man who came here that day. The one who works on a boat."

Lily lit up like the restaurants at dusk. "He's lovely, Kat. Funny and kind. He loves poetry, too. I might even let him read some of my bits."

"My goodness, he must be special," said Kat, watching how Lily's cheeks flushed as she spoke. So much feeling on show. Young love didn't guard itself or hold back. She remembered that feeling so well. That kind of passion threw itself in at the deep end without thought of drowning. She'd been lucky. A lifebelt had been thrown to her, and a wonderful one too – but not everyone was as blessed. How Kat hoped Lily wouldn't need one.

"We've been seeing a lot of each other," Lily admitted.

Kat hid a smile, because she already knew this. One of the curses of old age, along with living in sniper alley and aching joints, was not sleeping well, and as she lay awake in the garden room she often heard Lily letting herself in through the gate late at night. It hadn't gone unnoticed, either, that Jenny no longer needed to collect the papers and croissants each morning.

Kat didn't need to ask Lily if Rafe Cruz was special. She saw it in the way the young woman constantly drifted into a dream world and how her gaze often flickered to the port as though searching for him.

Kat took another sip of her iced water. "Does he make you happy?"

"Yes," Lily said without hesitation. "He really does, and I think it's the same for him. That's all that really matters, isn't it?"

She looked so hopeful, so full of youthful optimism, that Kat nodded even though her chest felt pulled as tight as one of her old granny's corsets. "It should be. Sometimes it even is."

Lily tilted her head. "That sounds a bit like a warning."

"I only mean that love's the easy part," Kat said, trying hard to recover her youthful self, that girl who had read Lorca, swum naked in the cobalt water of the cove below this very spot, and loved a boy with amontillado eyes. "What comes next? Well, that's the hard bit in my experience, but ignore me, love. I'm being old and daft."

"Is this because of Pablo?"

"I suppose it must be," Kat admitted. "You know how our story ended, since I married somebody else."

Lily lay her hand on Kat's. The difference in their skin jolted Kat. When had hers become so thin and bruised?

"This is different. Nobody arranges marriages these days or worries about tradition more than happiness. Not young modern people, anyway."

Kat feared Lily was wrong, but said nothing.

"You never told me what happened next. After the storm, when you argued," Lily added.

"No," Kat agreed. "I didn't."

It was painful to talk about what had followed. How and why this was possible a lifetime on, Kat had no idea. The terrace blurred. The lemon trees melted at the edges and the heat shimmer intensified as the past pressed in. It was more than memory now. It was sensation. It was real.

Pablo's hand holding hers. A candle stuffed in the neck of a squat bottle, light dancing in the glassless window. A hallowed hush between kisses. His voice whispering to her that this was all he ever wanted. She was all he wanted.

Kat closed her eyes. Deprived of that one sense, she felt that the sea sounded closer. *Then* bled into *now*. For a flicker of time's candle, she was back in the ruin of La Colina with the taste of him on her lips. Her skin was young and unlined, and her racing heart bright with hope. She let herself drift and although Lily was speaking Kat didn't hear, for she was asleep and far away from the ache in her hip and the grey of her hair. She was still here, but it was the here of a lifetime of summers ago, and the day that changed everything. The day she had always done her best to never think about. A day so beautiful that it had become the most exquisite pain to recall it.

And a day which had tumbled into the night when Kat's life had changed forever.

CHAPTER 19

KAT - THEN

It was late afternoon, and the dog days of summer. Kat had arranged to meet Pablo where the fishing boats moored up, and she spotted him straight away, perched on some crab pots and skipping stones across the water. He threw one with such force that it almost hit a boat, and she knew at once that something was wrong.

"What's up?" She perched beside him, her nose wrinkling at the smell. The pots were scratchy against her bare skin, and she wished she'd worn her long dress rather than shorts.

Pablo's face was shadowed by his curls. His head was bowed. "My father's summoned me back. He wants me in Madrid by the end of the week."

Kat didn't speak. She couldn't. Pablo had explained enough times the demanding standards his father had, and the crushing weight of the expectations laid on him, the only son. He had never pretended it was any different.

Reality settled on them like the seaweed on the coiled trawler nets. Impossible to pick out. Meshed in. She glanced out to sea, past the entrance to the marina and then to the horizon. The glittering sunlight trail suggested that escape lay beyond, a life filled with endless and unlimited possibilities, but it was a mirage. An illusion. Suddenly everything around her was closing in, measured and finite.

She swallowed. "And you'll go to Madrid?"

"My father's not the sort of man you say No to."

Kat understood. She had encountered Don de la Vega García a few weeks earlier, when she had least expected to. It had been market day, and she had been dispatched by Maria to buy the freshest produce. The town was alive with noise and colour: strings of peppers, great haunches of cured meats glistening with salt and studded with cloves, silver-scaled fish – vivid scenery accompanied by a backing track of shouting vendors and shrill-voiced haggling women. Kat was filling her basket with tomatoes, plump and red as love hearts, when the same black car Pablo had hopped into all those weeks ago, in that strange grey-hued time before they were one another's, rolled slowly by. Black and gleaming, too sleek and clean for the dusty road, it drew up beside the church.

She paused, tomatoes tumbling from her hands, as a uniformed chauffeur hopped out. Kat studied him closely. This man appeared faintly military and, in his mirrored sunglasses, rather sinister. Recalling her family's recent history, she couldn't help shivering.

The chauffeur opened the car door and stood aside respectfully as a tall man uncoiled himself from the air-conditioned depths. He was immaculately dressed in a dark suit despite the heat, and mirrored shades lent him, too, a sinister and alien air. Cufflinks glinted in the sun, and the watch on his left wrist dazzled when it caught the light. A thick mane of iron-grey hair was slicked away from his high forehead, and as he lowered his sunglasses and scanned the crowd, Kat's blood ran slow and thick. This man had to be Pablo's powerful father, and instinct told Kat he wasn't here by mistake.

He was looking for her. He knew.

Don García didn't look at Kat directly. He swept his eyes across the scene, taking in everything with the disdain of someone used to power and far removed from the mundanity of everyday life. She felt the moment his gaze swept over her, paused, then moved on like a bird of prey waiting to strike. He must have been there for less than two minutes before he nodded to the driver and slid back into the car, but it had felt like an eternity to Kat, and even though the sun was hot and high she felt chilled to the bone.

When she next met Pablo he confirmed her fears, saying angrily that somebody had told his father he was still seeing the English girl from the guesthouse. It didn't matter who had betrayed him, Pablo said bitterly, because he'd always known he couldn't trust anyone in the family home; they were spies, not staff. There had been a blazing row, Pablo standing his ground and refusing to do as he was told while his father shouted and his mother wept. Don García had stormed out, yelling that his son needed to come to his senses before he made him do so, before returning to Madrid.

When Pablo retold these events he was white-lipped with fury, and his voice shook: "He reminded me of my duty to the family. He reminded me who I am and what is expected of a García."

That incident had shaken Kat, but once Don García had safely returned to the mainland, she did her best to put it from her mind and focus on living for the moment. This wasn't the Middle Ages, and parents didn't control their children's marriages. Don García didn't have the power of the Inquisition behind him or any means to do her harm; although he was clearly a bully, Kat refused to be cowed by him. So she put him out of her mind as much as she could, although his return lurked on the fringes of her peace like a looming visit to the dentist: deeply unpleasant, looming up in the future and best put out of mind until it happened.

But now Don García was back, and sounded twice as determined to enforce his will. Kat, despite her fighting talk, felt wobbled.

Pablo's arms were crossed and his eyes dark as storm clouds.

"He insists I join him in Madrid. He says there will be no arguments. *Nada*. It's my duty to obey my father."

"And if you don't?" Kat's voice was shaky. She took a steadying breath, determined not to be frightened. "What then?"

"I have no idea. No one argues with my father. Not if they are wise."

"He's a bully, Pablo."

"Yes. I suppose he is. He's certainly used to being obeyed." He paused, and when he turned to her his beautiful eyes were sad and troubled. "He has people, Kat."

She was confused. "People?"

"*Sí*. People. Men in his employ to watch and do his bidding. You understand he's more than just a businessman, Kat? He has connections. Franco listens to him. Really listens. Father's spent years working his way into the inner circle, and he'll do anything to keep that influence. He wants me to follow in his path and raise our profile even more. I'm supposed to head the family business and then continue our rise into the highest level of politics. His son must marry well and cement influence. Say the right thing. Circulate with the right people." Pablo took her hand, his thumb caressing her palm. "Your family are Republicans. They fled, and to my father and his friends they're the enemy, Kat. *You're* the enemy."

"That's crazy, Pablo! It was all before I was even born."

He shrugged. "That doesn't matter, Haystack Girl. You know it doesn't. My father is right in one respect; you don't belong in our world."

These words stung, even though Kat knew what Pablo was trying to say. She also knew in her heart that her grandparents wouldn't have been thrilled by her association with him.

"But I don't belong to *either* world," he continued quietly. "That's what he doesn't see. Or perhaps it's what he refuses to see. I'm not that person, and I never will be. The only world I want to be in is the one I share with you."

Kat's eyes filled. "The same," she whispered.

He squeezed her fingers. "I'm worried I'm putting you at risk, just by holding your hand."

"Do you think he's having us watched now?"

She felt a cold trail of iced water slither down her spine. Suddenly she was acutely aware of the elderly fisherman mending his nets, the two men tinkering with a sailing boat's rigging, the smart woman sipping coffee at the café opposite. Were they really who they seemed?

"Honestly? Yes. I'm sure of it."

Her skin prickled. "And he'll be watching me? Even when we're apart?"

Pablo hesitated. "I think so. He wouldn't hurt you. Not directly. He doesn't need to, and he's more subtle than that. He has political power. A call to your landlady. A visit to your parents, and a warning. A cancelled visa. A false accusation of crime. He's certainly capable of that."

Kat felt the cold breath of fear on the back of her neck. Their love was everything to her, but suddenly it was dangerous too. The thought of her sweet and totally innocent parents having a knock at their door from Don García's thugs made her want to throw up. They would be so frightened for her, and utterly bewildered too.

She loved Pablo – but that love, Kat realised, had powerful enemies with suits and names and influence.

"What can we do?" she whispered.

"You know what we have to do," said Pablo, and she heard the cracking in his voice which echoed that in her heart. He raised her fingers to his lips and kissed them, as though she was an icon in the church and he a supplicant. "We have to say goodbye. I won't put you in danger, Kat, or your family."

He pulled her against him and buried his lips in her hair. She felt his tears, and their release gave hers permission to fall.

"I love you too much for that," Pablo whispered. "Far too much."

Tears fell now, and they said no more, for there were no words that could mend this situation or comfort them. Pablo wiped her tears away tenderly with his thumb and kissed her trembling mouth. His dark lashes were spiky and he leaned his forehead against hers.

"Oh, Katalina. I'm so sorry. I should have stayed away from you. I knew this from the start, but I couldn't. I could no more have done that than I could stop the tide."

"I don't regret a minute," she said fiercely. "Not a single moment. Whatever comes next, Pablo, it's all been worth it, do you hear me? One day with you is better than a thousand of never knowing you."

They held each other and sat watching the boats rise and fall, saying little because there was no need. Everything had already been said in the beautiful weeks they had spent wrapped in each other, on beaches, drowsing on rugs spread beneath olive trees, on moonlit walks up to La Colina. Their time had always been running away from them, but now it was sprinting and pulling them towards a destination they never wanted to reach.

"Meet me tonight," Pablo said quietly. "One last time? At La Colina."

She smiled, her vision wobbled with more tears. They seemed endless.

"Of course."

Kat returned to the San Estella, and if Maria and Francisco saw her red eyes, they were too tactful to comment. Or were they Don García's spies too? Was Lina? Esteban? Even Clara? Kat was starting to wonder who to trust.

That thought made her laugh, a small glimmer of mirth in the darkest moment she had ever known. Clara wouldn't be bought by anyone, for she had influence too, and hers was the kind that couldn't be purchased. Still, it was horrible to suddenly feel suspicious of everyone and to re-run all her conversations over and over to try and puzzle out what she might have said and done that had given her away.

She packed her basket: some candles, a thick blanket, some peaches, a bottle of wine. This was going to be a special night; a night Kat already knew she would treasure for the rest of her life and keep in her heart until her very last moments.

She dabbed the last of her jasmine perfume behind her ears, in the hollow of her throat and the place on her wrists where the blood was a blue whisper, before slipping into a peacock-hued silk kaftan Clara had given her, saying it was too short for her. But for Kat it was exotic and swirled like a silken waterfall, and made her feel confident and bold and in control, as though a little of its previous owner's magic was bestowed on whoever wore it next. Her hair tumbled down her back in dark waves, and when she looked in the glass the girl peering back looked Spanish and proud and confident. Good. Kat wanted Pablo to remember her as brave and beautiful, to think of her whenever he caught the sweet notes of jasmine or the flash of bluey-green fabric.

She wanted him to carry her in his heart forever, too.

The walk up the hill to La Colina seemed to pass in a daze. The sky turned to pale gold, the sea was powder-blue, and a slice of chalk-white moon floated above Dragonera, looking a little out of place as though too early for an appointment. For once Kat didn't notice the view; she was gazing inwards and reliving the times she had made this journey before, sometimes with Pablo and sometimes alone, yet always with a light heart filled with hope. But this evening that floating happiness was absent, and the walk, with all its associations, was already tinged with nostalgia. Kat knew this was their last time together. She wanted to fight it – but how could she fight a man as powerful as Pablo's father? And even if she wanted to, she knew Pablo wouldn't let her. He would protect her above all, even if in doing so he broke both their hearts. She turned away from the view and its beauty, knowing that to look meant to colour it forever with melancholy.

The tower of La Colina rose like a ghost as she rounded the last curve in the rough road. Its crumbled walls held the memory of every stolen afternoon they had spent there. La Colina was their friend and their sanctuary. It would be woven forever into the story of her life. She brushed her hand against the stone, still warm from the sun, as though caressing a beloved pet, and it seemed to her that the old house sighed too as the sea breeze whispered through the neglected olive trees in the forgotten garden.

Pablo was waiting in the kitchen. He was placing candles in the empty window and setting a taper and matches beside them like a ritual – a spell cast, perhaps, to make this night last forever. Kat abandoned her basket and crossed the room to him. They held each other without speaking, clinging as though afraid that letting go would shatter the fragile glass of their time, before they walked through the old house hand in hand, revisiting all the rooms where they had spun sugar-fragile dreams of a future. As the sun melted into the sea, they trailed through the garden with the scents of rosemary, lemon and thyme following them.

"This will always be ours," Pablo said, as they stepped back into the kitchen.

Kat nodded, unable to speak. Her throat ached.

Pablo lit the candles on the window ledge, one by one, striking the match and shielding each flame with a cupped hand. The first flickered, then caught, casting a soft amber glow across the wall. When the second and third joined it, the shadows danced and the whole house seemed to breathe.

Kat spread the blanket in the place they loved, beneath the gap in the roof where the stars poured through at night like celestial rain. Moths drifted to the flames and the cicadas sang. Below them the sea inhaled and exhaled as it always had and always would, while in the town the lights flickered on as evening cast its shawl across the island.

Pablo turned to Kat. "I am the luckiest man alive to share this moment with you."

Her tears came then. Just a few, bittersweet and the first of the many that she knew would follow later on.

But she had told herself sternly that she would not blight what time remained with tears. She wanted to savour every moment. So she blinked them away, and when Pablo kissed her it was as though a touch paper had been ignited. She wound her fingers into his curls to deepen the kiss and pull him closer. Her meaning was clear, and this time he answered her longing with his own, equally urgent, equally savage in its elemental need.

"Are you sure?" Pablo's breathing was ragged as they broke apart.

Kat nodded. She could not speak, and instead reached for him again, her heart floating free like an untethered paper lantern.

They slowed then, their movements shy and reverent. They slipped from their clothes with gasps, wide eyes and trembling fingers. When Kat's peacock-coloured kaftan fell and pooled around her bare feet, Pablo stepped back with a soft cry. His eyes shone with awe, as though he were gazing at a work of art come to life, and he shook his head.

"Eres hermosa," he whispered. "You're beautiful."

The words were like music, and Kat knew they were already written in her heart before they even fell from Pablo's lips. With him she felt beautiful. Was beautiful. And more than that, she was herself and still he loved her.

He was beautiful too. Skin soft and tanned. Stomach flat. Arms strong. A perfect statue made flesh. The boy she knew and loved was now transfigured by something ancient and all-consuming. Something as old as time, yet forever green and endlessly powerful.

With my body I thee worship.

The words of the marriage service, words Kat had heard so many times yet never truly listened to as the ceremony galloped to its conclusion and the kissing of the bride, came to mind. The recognition was like a blow: she wanted to worship Pablo with her body, and he wanted to do the same for her. This love was holy. It was sacred. It was beautiful. It was a sacrament. And it was utterly right.

The world drifted away. Time narrowed. There was only this moment and this place. There was nothing beyond La Colina, this room, this night, and their whispers. It was all that Kat needed.

When they lay down on the blanket, it was not like the stories in books or the whispered talk at school. There was no awkwardness, no rush, no borrowed lines. Only trust and tenderness. This was love transposed into the poetry of touch and sensation. It was the soft brush of his lips on her neck and the hollows of her collarbone. It was Kat's fingers tracing love letters on the curve of his spine. Fingers twined with fingers. Dark curls tangled with dark curls. Skin against skin. Their breathing rose and fell together, the wild racing of two heartbeats matching until it was impossible to tell where one ended and the other began.

La Colina held them in its huddled stones, a shield against the breeze and the gathering storm of family, politics and reality. Afterwards, they lay curled together on the blanket, drowsy and dizzy. Pablo held Kat against his heart, her head tucked beneath his chin. The candles had burned low, wax pooling on the window ledge. The ruin was dim, and above them the velvet sky was a starry canopy. It was as though they were sailing alone through a magical night, one where nothing but this moment and their love mattered.

"I'll always remember this," Kat whispered, not wanting to break the spell but needing to tell him. "Always."

"So will I," Pablo said.

Kat believed him. No matter what lay ahead, and no matter how powerful Pablo's father might be, this was theirs. She knew they would carry it always, like a candle shining in a dark window long after the world beyond had been snuffed out.

Nothing else mattered.

CHAPTER 20

KAT - THEN

Kat woke with a start. Sunlight slanted across the warm stone, gilding Pablo's arm, still holding her close, to deepest honey. The blanket lay tangled beneath them, and beyond the stubby candles the sky was the colour of new linen. For a perfect moment everything was still, and she listened to the distant chug of a fishing boat leaving the port and the cries of gulls dancing above.

Pablo's steady breath fluted against her shoulder. She lay in the curve of him, his chest warm against her back, their legs as tangled as the roots of the old olive trees. Her world could consist of nothing more, she thought, and she would be content. Pablo's heartbeat, his lingering kisses on her lips, the quiet intimacy between two people who had shared the deepest secrets of their hearts without words. This was enough.

Pablo stirred as sunlight brushed his cheek. His eyelids fluttered, and he blinked against the brightness. Seeing Kat watching him, he gave a sleepy smile.

"Wilt thou be gone? It is not yet day," she murmured.

"I'm not going," he replied.

"You have to." Kat nestled against him, breathing him in, longing to melt into his very bones. The night had passed in a heartbeat, and though she wanted to stretch it out, it was impossible. "I have to work, and you have to see your father."

Her throat tightened and her nose tingled. If the anticipation of losing him hurt this much, what would the reality feel like?

"I'm not going to Madrid." He tucked a curl behind her ear. "How could I? I'll stay here, Haystack Girl. Let him do his worst. I choose you."

She propped herself on an elbow, frowning. "Pablo. You can't."

"I can, Kat. What can he really do? Yes, he could make life difficult, cut me off, disinherit me, play with visas, but so what? We can deal with that. If we're together. If ..." he paused, then pulled her on top of him. "If we're married."

Kat laughed, though her heart thudded against her ribs with excitement. Did he mean it?

"I'm serious," Pablo said. "It's not the proposal I imagined, but I love you, my Katalina. How could I ever leave you? Will you marry me? Do you love me enough to even consider it?"

His dark eyes were alight with sunshine and emotion, a nervous tremor in his voice. Kat stared, unable to find words for the ocean of love inside her. Love bloomed in her chest like the yellow wildflowers on the hillside; bright, fierce and uncontainable.

"Yes. Yes," she whispered, leaning in for a slow, deep kiss that said everything.

The sun climbed higher, and they moved the blanket into the shade. As morning crept toward afternoon, they followed the shadows around the ruin, unable to tear themselves apart. Maria and Francisco would serve breakfast and lunch without her, Kat thought, a surge of guilt rising. She hoped they would forgive her when she told them she was engaged to Pablo de la Vega García. They would be shocked, and maybe even excited. Lina would find it romantic. Clara would make a cynical comment, then throw a huge party. And Pablo's father? That was more worrisome, but Pablo insisted he would have no choice but to accept defeat.

Late afternoon, Pablo dropped Kat at the guesthouse. They were dusty and drunk on love, planning their future with the giddy excitement of children at play. He would work on a fishing boat; she would continue at the guesthouse. Perhaps, once married, they would move to Oxford, or buy and rebuild La Colina. They would bake bread and grow vegetables. Pablo had wound a frond of rosemary around Kat's wedding-ring finger until he could slide a diamond there, and she could not stop marvelling at it. *Señora García! My husband, Pablo García! Mrs García! How wonderful to meet you!*

The town was paused for siesta, shutters closed, only the occasional dog wandering in the heat. It looked the same, but to Kat everything had changed.

"I'll meet you by the boat this evening," he said, kissing her. "Wish me luck with my father."

Kat was suddenly afraid for him. "Will you be all right? He wouldn't hurt you, would he?"

Pablo grimaced. "He'll erupt like Mount Etna. He'll threaten me, but he can't beat me now because I'm too big. He might try, though. If I have a black eye later, I hope you'll still love me."

He tried to lighten the situation, but Kat saw his fear. "I'll always love you," she promised.

Kat stepped from the Land Rover onto the dusty street. Gravity yanked her hand from his; the empty inches between their fingertips were agonising. Everything inside her begged her to stay. As she watched the car disappear around a corner, her heart plummeted into a deep canyon of fear. What if the Garcías forced Pablo away? What if she never saw him again?

"Trust me," he had murmured against her temple under La Colina's pines. "I'll come for you, Katalina. No matter what, no matter how long it takes, we'll end our days together. I swear it."

"What do you swear on?" Kat had asked. "Romeo swore on the moon, but Juliet didn't like that. It changes too often. She wanted him to just marry her."

He laughed. "Women! Sensible as ever. I'll swear on La Colina, on these stones, on the sea! Whatever you wish! I promise I will love you until I die."

It was a vow as sacred as any church ceremony. They had lost themselves in each other again. She smiled, remembering those feverish hours, knowing that had it not been for the rosemary band or the glow of her whole body, she would have thought it a mad dream.

By luck, Kat slipped into the guesthouse unseen. She took a tepid bath, dressed in a plain T-shirt and navy culottes, pulled her hair into a tidy bun, and ventured out to find Maria and apologise.

It would be awkward, coming up with a reason for her absence, but Maria took one glance at her sparkling eyes and swollen lips and rolled her eyes.

"I don't need to hear it," she said, holding up a hand. "I've seen this many, many times. Just don't let us down again. You may be good at keeping the English happy, but if you're unreliable, I'll send you home."

"I promise I won't let you down again. I'm sorry, Maria. Truly, but this is different."

"It's always different," Maria scoffed. "Many a silly girl comes to Andratx for the summer, falls for a handsome local boy, and leaves with more than she'd arrived with. I hope you were careful."

Kat flushed. 'Careful' hadn't even crossed her mind. All the warnings her mother issued had vanished the moment Pablo's lips strayed below her collarbone. She suspected it was the same for every woman in love.

"Holy Mother!" Maria wailed, spotting Kat's guilty blush rising like the tide.

"We're engaged!" Kat blurted.

"*¡Madre de Dios!* You stupid girl! That's the oldest line there is."

"It's *not* a line! It's true!" Kat held up her left hand, the rosemary ring flaking. "Pablo and I are engaged. He's gone to tell the Garcías himself."

Maria paled. "The Garcías? Don Álvaro de la Vega García? Tell me it's not his son you've been sneaking off with?"

"We're not sneaking. We're being careful, because they won't approve," Kat protested.

Maria sank into a chair. "*Dios,* Katalina! Of *course* they won't approve! The Garcías are powerful, close to the Generalissimo. They see and hear everything. You haven't been talking?"

Kat frowned. "We talk all the time."

"No! About politics. I know your family were Republicans. The war seems long ago, but the risk is real. Especially with the Garcías."

Kat felt icy from the ends of her hair to the tips of her toes. The dark car, Pablo's fear, vanished uncles, her grandmother's anguish – it all came back. Could her love survive these shadows?

"I promise we never talk about politics or Franco."

"Shh!" Maria's eyes darted to the door. "Even so, you must understand what's at stake. They'll want a good

Catholic girl who's loyal to the leader. He'll never marry you."

"He loves me," Kat insisted. What did politics matter?

Maria shook her head. "You're in a fool's paradise if you think he's free to marry you. It's not like England here. Tradition runs deep, and Franco has power still."

Kat shivered. The name cast a long shadow.

"You must step away. It's dangerous."

"It's the seventies. Times have changed."

"Not as much as you think. I blame that German woman. She's been putting ideas in your head. Your mother will blame me. I should've kept an eye on you."

"I'm an adult! And you don't even know my mother."

"You're under my roof! I must apologise to her."

"There's no need! I'm happy, really, happy! Pablo and I are engaged, and nothing else matters. He loves me. I know he does."

Maria studied her sadly. "He probably thinks he does. You're beautiful and he's a young man doing what young men do. Ah, what's done is done. I hope you're right, Katalina. I hope he comes for you."

"He will," Kat said. Nothing could keep them apart.

Maria returned to her sweeping. The conversation ended and Kat did her best to sweep it away with the dust in her pan. She floated on air all day. She tried to read, but the words stuck. She lay on her bed, recalling the press of Pablo's skin, the weight of him, the wild rise and fall of her heart, the way he looked into her eyes, said her name. She locked the memory in her heart, drifting to sleep with a smile on her love-bruised lips.

She was first at the boat. Pablo would come after sunset, and each second was agony. She wore a simple white sundress and Grecian sandals, her hair pinned up loosely, jasmine dabbed behind her ears. She knew she would never smell that fragrance again without remembering that night at La Colina.

Kat longed for Pablo. Her skin still hummed from his touch. Where was he? The sun had set; twilight settled over the port. Sailing boats glided from berths, fishing boats lumbered in, people laughed, dogs barked. Life went on, but Kat was suspended in time, waiting.

At last, she saw her new fiancé emerging from a side street and her heart expanded with joy. She had started to fear she might never see him again, for Pablo had been honest about his father's power. She would have understood, too, if he couldn't defy him. But he hadn't failed. He had chosen her.

She waved and smiled, and Pablo waved back, but as he grew closer, Kat realised something was wrong. He was walking without his usual energy, his shoulders hunched as though he were braced against a gale, and his face was tight. He seemed to have aged a decade in just one afternoon.

He stopped a few paces away, staring at Kat as though memorising her, and her stomach did a slow swoop, for his eyes were red-rimmed. The confrontation with his parents must have been awful.

"*Hola,*" he said softly.

"*Hola,*" Kat replied. "You're late. I was afraid you'd changed your mind about me."

"Never," Pablo said fiercely. His voice was hoarse, as though he'd been shouting or crying. He stepped forward and took her hands, holding them tightly and pulling her against him. "I'd never do that."

"What did your father say?" she asked.

"I never saw my father. When I arrived home, my mother was waiting for me. She said she needed to talk."

"She already knew?"

"*Si* – but that wasn't what she wanted to talk about. Not

directly, at least." He passed a hand over his face and swallowed. "There's no easy way to say this. She's got cancer, Kat, and she's very sick. She told me this afternoon."

Kat was horrified. "I'm so sorry. That's awful."

"It's like a bad dream. My poor mama."

She felt his pain, and selfishly knew at once that the world had tilted. This news ambushed their plans and changed everything. How could it not? Kat felt it already, the new distance which had opened between them. Although just a hairline crack now, it would yawn into a chasm she couldn't cross.

"She's frightened, Kat, really frightened. I'd never seen her like this before," Pablo whispered, and his eyes shimmered with tears. "My mother is usually so strong and so in control. She defers to my father, but she is the person he leans on. Today she was so afraid. She said she can't face the treatment without her family by her side. She needs us close for whatever time she has. She needs me, Kat."

"Of course she does," Kat whispered. Although he was still holding her hands tightly, she could already feel him slipping away. She pushed aside her own fears and said firmly, "She has to come first, Pablo. Our plans can wait. I understand."

He kissed one hand and then the other. She felt his tears on her skin, and when he spoke again, his words were laced together with sorrow.

"I told her about you. It was the first thing I said when she asked me to come to her study. I assumed Father had spoken to her and tasked her with lecturing me with the usual guilt trip about duty and family and all the rest of it. I didn't give her time to speak, because I know how determined my parents can be. I said I'd chosen you rather than the life in Madrid they'd planned, and that there was nothing they could say or do that would change my mind. I said I loved you and wanted to be with you. Mama listened while I poured my heart out, and she never once interrupted. She held herself together for all my speech, and then said she had news of her own."

Kat had only seen Pablo's mother once, and then for the briefest flicker of time, but she recalled that haughty, beautiful face, and the chilly gaze that had swept over her. There had been steel in those eyes, too. Kat shivered. Señora García was as strong and as fearsome as her husband. What a powerful couple they made!

"I told Mama I loved you," Pablo continued. He squeezed her hands. "I said I wanted to marry you and that we were planning a future. I said I didn't want the life they'd planned for me. That was when she told me she has cancer."

It was a bomb. The one word that blew all worlds apart.

"At first, I thought she was exaggerating, God forgive me, I even suspected she was trying to scare me into leaving you. Yes, I knew she'd been feeling tired and had seen the doctor. Last week she flew back to Madrid, but I had no idea why. Now she tells me it's cancer, and it's so advanced they need to operate soon. She said she may not have long."

"That's awful," whispered Kat.

"She said it was up to me what I did with the time she had left. She said Father will not stop me being with you, but if I make that choice he'll disown me and I'll be cut off. She will have to obey him, and she knows that means she'll have to die without me there. Mama would go to her grave knowing I'd chosen to leave her when she needed me the most, and I'd have to live with that. God help me. If I stay with you my mother will die without me – and what kind of son would that make me? What person does that?"

He sagged against her, and Kat held him as he wept, his whole body shaking with sobs. Eventually his breathing steadied, and he pulled away, wiping his eyes with the heels of his hands.

"If you stay with me it will poison us," Kat said quietly.

He reached for her, then wrapped her in his arms. "I don't want this, Katalina – but what choice do I have? If I am to be with my mother, Father insists I swear on her soul that I will walk away from you to marry the girl he has selected."

Kat nodded. Her throat burned with grief. Don García was beyond cruel. He was fiendishly manipulative. It was a dead end for them. Kat knew Pablo was right; if he forsook his mother for her, it would lead to guilt. Resentment and bitterness would grow from that seed, and then everything beautiful would be sullied by his choice.

At that moment she understood that their romance was over. If it was not ended now, it would only die years down the line, once guilt corroded his love for her. As much as Kat longed to hold onto Pablo and beg him to stay, to let his mother deal with her treatment alone, she knew she had to let him go.

"There is no choice," she said softly.

He cupped her face. His tears fell onto her cheeks. "I want to stay with you, Kat. So, so much. But she is ill and afraid. I am her only son. I would carry that guilt forever."

"You must choose her, Pablo. If you don't, it will destroy you. It will destroy us. There is no choice. You love me, don't you?"

He stared at her as though the thought she might doubt this was breaking him. "More than anything in the world. Did I not tell you before that if I loved you properly, it would kill me to leave you? That is how it feels now, Kat. Like *I'm* dying."

"I know," Kat sobbed. "I feel it too."

They held each other and cried; two figures lost in the gathering dusk as shadows darkened the water. Somewhere a church bell rang. In the port, a boat horn sounded, low and mournful. The breeze lifted Kat's hair and offered her the tang of the sea, a scent she knew would always be tinged with melancholy from now on.

He didn't ask Kat to wait for him, and she didn't offer. They both knew that something was ending tonight. A path they had embarked upon, hand in hand and with such hope, had bifurcated. Their hands would fall away, and they would choose opposite directions, each footstep carrying them into a future further and further away from one another. She could no more promise to wait than he could promise to return.

Life was not a romantic novel. It was not a fairy tale. It wasn't even *Romeo and Juliet*. It was sad and cruel and relentless in its need to surge onward. Kat understood that Pablo would return to his family and the path planned for him since birth. He would be the dutiful son. He would care for his mother, marry the girl they had earmarked for him, and carry the García name into the future. He had never stood a chance of doing otherwise; his fate had been decided long ago.

And what would she do? Return home when the summer was over, and miss him for the rest of her life, that was what. She would find the job her parents were hoping for, settle down to life in the suburbs, and maybe marry a man who would overlook the fact that she was in love with another. Maybe that man would never know? Or maybe she would live alone? Whatever the future held, a part of her heart would be forever Pablo's.

"I'll love you always," Pablo said. He held Kat tightly as though she was all that stopped him from falling into the sea. "I'll always love you. Even if I never see you again. Even if you forget me. When you move on. You're in my heart. You're a part of me, Don García Girl."

"I'll remember everything," she said, her voice trembling.

"Even the things we never got to do or say. Those dreams. I'll always have them, and that night at La Colina will stay with me always."

"And me," he said, and his voice broke. "I will remember that night forever. A part of me will always be in that place now."

He was still in her arms – but Pablo had already left. Or maybe it was that the future they had dreamed of, a future which had sparkled so brightly only hours ago, had already gone. Hope and joy had left his eyes.

"You can think of me whenever you come back to Mallorca, Pablo. When you look up at La Colina, think of me sometimes."

Tears ran down her face now. The sea, Pablo, the world. It was all a blur.

"I don't know if I can ever come back to this place," he said. "Not without you. I don't think I could. It'd be painful. It'll always remind me of what I've lost."

When Kat thought of the ruined house with its starry ceiling and rosemary breezes, her heart lifted. To her, La Colina would always be a happy place filled with memories as precious and as fragile as spun glass. It was doubly precious now.

"Be happy when you think of me," she sobbed. "If this is goodbye, please know that you have made me so happy, Pablo, and I don't regret a second."

He kissed her then, as though it was the last time and the first, and all the other kisses they should have shared, wrapped into one last embrace. It wasn't soft or slow or longing, but desperate and aching and angry. It was tears and trembles and half-choked sobs. Kat tasted salt and wondered if they were his tears or hers. Maybe both.

When they broke apart, she clung to his shirt as though

this might keep him there. Then he stepped back, and her hands fell away. This time Kat knew she had to let him go. It would take all her strength and his, but there was no other course of action. He had given his word to his mother.

"I love you," he said. "Remember that, Katalina. No matter what happens, no matter how many years pass, I will always love you, Haystack Girl."

He turned and walked away, his tread soft on the boards of the jetty, which rose and fell beneath Kat like a sigh. She didn't follow, but watched him melt into the darkness until he was no more than a whisper of white shirt. Then he was the past. Once he was gone, her knees buckled, and she dropped to the wooden boards, her knuckles rammed into her mouth to stifle the raw sobs of pain rising like the tide from a place of unbearable anguish, threatening to drown her.

She could still feel Pablo's mouth on hers. She could still feel his trembling hands. She could still feel his grief and fear and love. All of it was still there, like the last sunlight on the horizon, impossible to hold but impossible to ignore.

Kat stayed on the jetty until darkness blanketed the port. The distant lights of the harbour shivered on the water like faint embers, and somewhere a bell rang, calling the faithful to a church service. A fishing boat rumbled in the distance, its horn low and melancholy.

She whispered, "I'll always remember you, Pablo. Always."

Then Kat turned and walked back into the town that was quiet now and as empty as she felt. She wasn't sure how she would live the rest of her life without Pablo García.

Or even if she wanted to.

CHAPTER 21

LILY - NOW

Kat hadn't been herself since Lily had mentioned inviting Rafe for supper. Lily couldn't quite put her finger on what the problem was – it was more a feeling than anything concrete – but something had clearly cast a shadow over her employer. Kat hadn't said anything to discourage Lily's friendship with Rafe, nor had she objected to Lily having friends over. In fact, she'd been as encouraging as ever. But she seemed sad and withdrawn, and all shared confidences about the past had ceased.

Lily hoped she hadn't overstepped the line between employer and hired help. Perhaps Kat regretted opening up, or was worried Lily might be gossiping about her with Jenny and José. Nothing could be further from the truth; Lily had been deeply moved by Kat's stories of the past, and it had been fascinating to catch a glimpse of life in Andratx in the 1970s. She could vividly picture her employer meeting Pablo in secret, stealing out to sea or dreaming about him as she went about her work at the guesthouse, and couldn't help drawing parallels with her own relationship. Thank goodness that, unlike Kat, she and Rafe didn't have to hide away. No one cared now if a young woman had supper with a young man or went out to sea alone with him. Times had changed, and Lily was grateful for that.

Several times since their last conversation, she'd felt that Kat was on the brink of telling her more about Pablo. Lily had listened intently, ready to hear more, but each time Kat seemed to pull back. Maybe it was too painful? Or perhaps she'd thought better of growing too close to a member of staff. Lily felt sad if this was the case; Kat was far more than an employer to her. The older woman reminded Lily of Clara, always there to listen, and so wise. Kat never judged, and she understood. She might be older than Lily – but age didn't seem to matter at all, for Kat was, Lily knew without a doubt, her friend.

Jenny and José said nothing about Kat's past. Lily had pieced together that Kat had returned to Mallorca in the early 1980s with her husband David, and that they had bought La Colina as a ruin and renovated the property together. Pablo's name never came up again, and Lily kept it guarded, afraid to mention it in case she revealed something Kat wanted to keep hidden.

One afternoon, Lily walked into town and imagined Andratx as it had been. Little had really changed, and it could still have been 1970 as the fishing boats rolled in and the gulls squabbled on the quayside. Although the bakery was long gone and the guesthouse was a holiday let, the cool narrow back streets were the same as they'd been for centuries. She imagined Kat and Pablo exploring them together, whispering secrets, wandering through the alleyways. It warmed her heart to think her employer had known a deep and true love twice, and it gave her hope too.

Jenny and José often said how much the Señora had loved her husband.

"He was a wonderful man," Jenny had remarked once while mopping the hallway. "So kind to us. Without him, we couldn't have afforded to stay in Andratx. He even helped with furniture for our first apartment. Such a generous man. They were a happy family. Those were such wonderful times."

Lily loved hearing this. La Colina was filled with photos of David Beauchamp – bright, sunny prints from the days long past, the colours saturated like film trying to keep up with the vividness of life. David in trunks by the barbecue. David and Kat, arms wrapped around each other, laughing. David holding two little girls in frilled bathing suits and Fanta-orange armbands. Grandchildren splashing in the pool. Clara, young and stylish, laughing into the camera. Everywhere, photos of joy. Even a wedding picture at the top of the stairs: Kat and David in full 1970s floppy hat and flared-suit glory. But where did Pablo García fit into this narrative? Why had he disappeared? What had gone wrong? She itched to Google him, but it felt wrong somehow, akin to spying. So far, she had resisted, thinking how much she would hate it and feel violated if Kat started snooping around Harrison's Facebook page.

Lily, now consumed by her own summer romance and spending every spare moment with Rafe, longed for Kat to have a happy ending too. She couldn't bear the thought of their love fizzling out when Kat returned to England, all grey skies and wet pavements. As for where her relationship with Rafe was going, Lily had no idea – but she'd fallen hard for him and couldn't imagine a world where she let him walk away.

This felt a lot to Lily like love – but Hannah, ever the sceptic, had weighed in via text:

You don't know anything about him, Lil!

I know enough to know I like him.

That afternoon, Lily was heading to the small supermarket to buy supplies for the evening's dinner.

"Always happy to have a free feed," Hannah had said. "And it'll be good to check out this paragon of virtue and make sure he's all he seems. If he has some fit friends, tell him to invite them as well!"

Lily had run the extra invite past Kat. Although Kat was generous with La Colina, extending use of the pool and the gardens to Lily and even her friends, Lily never wanted to presume. Kat seemed sad lately, too. Maybe she wasn't well? If so, it wouldn't do to have people about the place making noise.

"Of course, of course," Kat agreed vaguely when asked, and Lily frowned. Kat was barely present.

"I'd love you to join us too," Lily said.

Kat waved her hand. "No, no. You young people don't want me around. You'll have much more fun without an old fossil. Besides, I'm going into town to meet somebody."

Lily's ears were on elastic. "Pablo?" she asked, a little too eagerly.

Kat shot her an arch look. "Are you still thinking about my stories?"

"I am," Lily admitted.

"Well, I'm sorry to disappoint," said Kat, "but it isn't Pablo. In fact, you may as well know the truth. It didn't work out, and we broke up at the end of that summer. He married the girl his parents chose, inherited the family business, and lived happily ever after."

The delivery was so blunt, it felt like a punch to Lily's romantic heart. Where had all the joy gone? The passion? The secret meetings? When Kat had spoken of Pablo, their love had felt so alive. They'd been crazy about one another. How could it have ended so abruptly?

She didn't believe that Kat's brief version of events was all there was, but she didn't like to push. They were in the kitchen. Kat was sitting at the island, making a list on a spiral pad. Lily couldn't quite see what it said, but she spotted a letter from Tomás López at Kat's elbow, and her heart squeezed. Was Kat thinking of selling? Was it the developer she was meeting?

"You married David and were very happy," Lily said carefully, sliding onto the stool beside her.

Kat casually pushed the papers aside. The letter she turned face down.

"Yes, I did," she replied. "David was my best friend and a wonderful husband. I never regretted anything that led to our marriage. You need to understand that, Lily. As you get older, you realise life is not straightforward, and feelings are complicated. They're a reflection of who we are in the moment, who our parents made us, and who Fate decides we shall be. Pablo was my first love, and he'll always be special, but David was also my love. You need to know that he wasn't second-best. Far from it. He was everything to me. First love is powerful and stays so vivid because it's new and we have nothing to compare it to. That doesn't mean it's best."

"Did you stay in touch with Pablo?"

Kat set down her pen and folded her hands.

"I did not."

Lily said nothing, sensing Kat wanted to say more.

"We broke up, as young people do," she said after a beat. "It was very painful. For a while, I thought I would die from sadness."

Lily nodded. She'd felt the same way after Harrison. Then

she'd met Rafe. Maybe David had been Kat's Rafe? Oh dear, it was scary how she saw everything in terms of him these days

"I stopped working at the guesthouse at the end of that summer. My association with Pablo did me no favours, as it turned out. His father was associated with Franco, and people were afraid I'd drawn attention to them. That may seem strange to you now, but back then people were terrified of the Generalissimo. Pablo's father had links to the secret police. For a while, people here were even afraid to speak in their own tongue, and they didn't want to bring trouble to their door."

"Where did you go after you left the guesthouse?" Lily asked, ultra-gently. She was afraid of spooking Kat and not hearing any more.

"I thought about staying with Lina, but she was preparing for her wedding, and her parents were also afraid of the Garcías," Kat said, her eyes distant, focused on the misty shoulder of the mountains. "In the end, I went to Clara's. She was a good friend to me."

There was weight in those words. Lily imagined Clara had been a nurse, confessor, boot camp sergeant, and best friend all rolled into one. The kind of person who kicked you back into life when you thought you couldn't go on. That was the Clara she had known. It seemed that Hannah was very much like her great-aunt.

"While I was staying at Clara's, David came to visit. I knew him from England, of course. I'd done some typing for his department and he had helped me find Clara, and work here on the island. It was nice to see him out of context – and funny too! He wore shorts and sandals instead of his academic gown." Kat smiled at the memory. "He was surprisingly handsome once he'd got a tan and lost his earnest look. Not that I noticed at the time. I was far too heartbroken over Pablo.

Anyway, David and I became good friends that autumn. He hired a little car, and we explored the island together. He listened as I told him about Pablo. In turn he told me about how he'd once been desperately in love with Clara and was utterly broken every time she found someone new."

"I wish I'd known her back then."

"Oh, she was wonderful fun. The party was always where she was. In fairness to Clara," Kat added with a wry smile, "she never led him on. Or not too much. If they ever shared more than a kiss or two, they never told me."

Lily laughed. "Sometimes best friends do keep secrets."

"Do you think?" Kat raised a brow.

"Oh yes. If I'd told Hannah half of what my ex got up to, she'd have throttled him!"

"Shame she didn't," Kat said. "Now, dear, the sun's over the yardarm, I'd say. Could you fetch me a glass of wine?"

Lily did as she was asked. By the time she'd retrieved the bottle of Whispering Angel and poured a glass, Kat had collected herself.

"Pablo's mother had breast cancer. That's why he had to return to Madrid in a hurry. We wanted to be together, but sometimes life gets in the way. Even though we were young, we understood that if he chose me over her, it would ruin everything."

"He gave you up?" Lily was shocked. Books and films all said people were meant to fight for love. Her diary was full of such musings, at least in earlier entries when she had longed to win Harrison back.

"He made a very hard choice," Kat said gently. She sipped her drink and her hands shook. A drop of rose-pink wine splashed onto the marble. Kat traced it with a forefinger, watching the liquid part and run in opposing directions, once a whole, now forever divided.

"It wasn't easy," she went on, almost to herself, "but it was the right thing. It was honourable. Duty and responsibility come before the self. Or they ought to. Maybe that's where modern society is falling apart."

"I'm sorry," Lily said, feeling ticked off. "I got carried away with the romance of it all."

"Don't apologise. I shouldn't still feel this emotional. It was a lifetime ago, and I was just a girl." Kat took another sip and placed her hand gently over Lily's. "All you need to know is that he did what he thought was right, for me, for my family, and for his family. He married a suitable girl, took over the family business, and I believe he nursed his mother to the end. She lived for several more years after we parted company. I believe he had a daughter, maybe more children too, but I never tried to find out. We'd agreed to leave our relationship firmly in the past."

"Were you never tempted?" After leaving Harrison, Lily had been forced to sit on her hands several times to stop herself from digitally stalking him.

Kat grinned. "Oh, goodness, yes. I was tempted. But it would've been like opening Pandora's box. Besides, if the past was so good, it wouldn't be the past. Best we all moved forwards."

"So, what happened after that autumn?"

"I returned home. Found a job typing at the university. David asked me out that Christmas, and I said yes." Her eyes misted. "He was the kindest, most wonderful man, and I truly loved him. He never worried about the past, and only cared about what made me happy. He found this place when it came up for sale. He knew I loved it, and he bought it for me as a surprise."

"Wow," said Lily, a little jealous. She wondered what it would be like to have a man so enthralled with her that he bought her a house like La Colina. She'd have to tell Rafe to up his game! Cappuccinos no longer cut it.

"I'd told him why La Colina was special, because it was where Pablo and I had spent time, but David didn't care. He wasn't a jealous man, and he loved the place too. He said the past made me who I was, and he loved that part of me, because he loved all of me. We renovated it and spent so many happy years here with our friends and family. The rest you know."

Lily was too moved to speak. She wished she had her own glass of wine.

"So many happy years," Kat murmured. "How lucky am I to have known true, life-changing love not once, but twice. But now, I think it's time to say goodbye to La Colina – and, in a way, to Pablo."

"You're meeting Señor López tonight?" Lily asked, nodding at the down-facing letter. Kat had received several of these. Tomás López was clearly not a man who gave up easily.

"Yes," Kat replied simply. "His enormous boat has moored up, so it's time to strike while the iron's hot."

Through the drizzle-spritzed window they could see the vast hull of López's superyacht. Hannah would know the crew who moored it and did the tycoon's bidding. Rafe too. There was something almost sinister about its sleek and stealthy beauty, thought Lily, and she shivered.

"I've sent word to him I'll be at my favourite backstreet fish restaurant at half past seven. He's written to me so many times, trying to buy this house, so maybe it's time to put him out of his misery."

There was silence. It felt as though La Colina itself was listening. Then a clatter came from upstairs – José dropping a broom – followed by a rapid flurry of Spanish invective from his wife.

"What if López wants to destroy the house?" Lily asked.

She knew this worried Kat, and Jenny and José often fretted about it.

Kat sighed. "It's a risk I have to take, whoever I sell to. I must be realistic, Lily. I must think about my daughters, and if López is prepared to pay what he claims to be offering, it'll set them up for life, and my grandchildren too. That's what David would have wanted. And perhaps La Colina wants to do that, after all these years. This house has looked after me, and maybe it's time I let it look after us all for the future. I'm not young, Lily. My heart's not strong, and I'm finding it harder to travel out here. It's time to let this life go."

"And Pablo?"

"Pablo will always have a special place in my heart, but I let him go long before deciding to sell this place. La Colina needs a new owner. It's the right thing to do."

"It feels so sad. So final."

"Or maybe," Kat suggested gently, "it's the start of something new. New people here. New love stories. New happy homes. Life must move forward, Lily, otherwise we become fossilised."

The rain was clearing. The sun elbowed its way through the mist and bruised cloud in a burst of lemon-yellow determination.

"You'd better do your shopping before it gets too hot," Kat said. "I'll have a siesta in the garden room, I think, and read my book. Will you book me a taxi for half past six? I'm going to eat first. I can't meet the famous Tomás López on an empty stomach."

The conversation was over, and Lily left Kat in peace. It wasn't her place to try and change the older woman's mind, no matter how uneasy she felt at the idea of a developer buying La Colina. Unless she won the EuroMillions or found a few million down the back of the sofa, there wasn't much she could do. La Colina's future was in the hands of the gods, or the modern-day equivalent – a multi-millionaire with an open chequebook and a superyacht.

Lily booked Kat's taxi, slipped on her sandals and a sundress, and headed to town. She would meet Hannah first for a drink, then visit the supermarket. José had agreed to fetch her and Hannah later, and Jenny would stay later than usual, to help her cook.

"I wouldn't go anyway – I want to see this boy," Jenny teased when Lily thanked her. "We need to make sure he's good enough!"

It was one of those afternoons when the sky seemed too perfectly blue to be real. La Colina dozed, its shutters drawn against the light and just cracked open to the breeze. Lily stood on the terrace in a floaty turquoise dress and surveyed the yellow table, set for dinner. It was laid simply with plain white plates, candles in empty wine bottles, and lots of tea lights in jars scattered about. Perfect. Her hands were dusted with flour from helping Jenny, and her hair was pinned up on the crown of her head with a clip.

"You look like a goddess who's been baking," Rafe murmured behind her.

She turned, and her heart did a quiet flutter. He was dressed casually in linen trousers and a white shirt, sleeves rolled up, collar open, so effortlessly handsome, and just that little bit too good to be real. She could hardly believe he was here with her. He was armed with a bouquet of roses, for Kat he said, and a bottle of chilled Sancerre, and was clearly nervous at being inside La Colina, a house he said he had always admired. Jenny swooned as soon as she clocked him, and quickly press-ganged him into helping her plate up food and open wine, while José rolled his eyes at Lily, a look which said it hadn't escaped his notice that Hannah hadn't received the same treatment, being banished to relax by the pool with a drink and a bowl of olives.

"I grant I never saw a goddess go; my mistress, when she walks, treads on the ground," Lily quoted at Rafe, who laughed and kissed the nape of her neck.

"You're too clever for me. Brains and beauty."

Whenever his lips touched her neck, Lily was always reduced to tattered ribbons of desire. The whole meal could have gone to hell in a handcart while she fell into his arms.

But she forced herself to step away, and smiled. "Hardly, but I have learned how to make some new dishes, so at least we won't starve."

"Well, good," said Rafe. "I can't wait. I've not eaten since breakfast, and that was just leftovers."

"Do you want a drink? Wine? A beer?"

"I'll stick to water, thanks. I'm nervous enough without drinking and making a fool of myself."

It was sweet that he said he was nervous, too. Lily hadn't seen Rafe like this before. He was a little on edge and almost awkward. She imagined it was being at La Colina, one of the grandest houses in Andratx, and that he felt intimidated. She wished Kat had stayed to chat and put him at his ease. She was a wonderful hostess, and Rafe would have relaxed within seconds.

She went to the kitchen to fetch him a glass of iced water. Jenny, straightening up from checking the oven, beamed at her.

"He's *muy* handsome! You are a lucky girl! Now, the food's done, and José and I will leave you in peace. Señora won't be back until late, she said. Lock the front door, *por favor*. She has a key."

Lily thanked Jenny and carried the drinks to the pool where Hannah and Rafe were chatting. Her heart missed a beat. Her best friend and the man she knew she was falling in love with. Would they like one another? Would Hannah approve of Rafe? It was quite frightening how much this mattered.

Hannah was stretched out on a sun lounger under a cream parasol, sunglasses perched on top of her head, thick blonde mane artfully arranged in a messy updo. Her pink mini-dress had ridden up to reveal long tanned legs, and she was sipping her drink and regarding Rafe with a curious expression. Oh dear. Lily really hoped she wasn't giving him the third degree. She hurried to join them, thinking what an awkward number three was, and wishing Kat hadn't cried off.

"One *agua*," Lily said to Rafe.

"*Gracias*."

They chinked glasses and he raised his to the two women. "Here's to a wonderful evening in a beautiful spot. I feel very honoured to be here."

"Me too," said Hannah. "It beats crew quarters, doesn't it, Rafe?"

He nodded. "*Sí*."

"So," Hannah continued, lifting a brow. "How do you guys know each other, again?"

"We met in the port," said Rafe. "Lily threw herself at me!"

She elbowed him in the ribs, and he laughed. "Okay! She fell over some ropes on the quay, and I happened to be nearby."

"Ah, yes. Your berth's there," said Hannah, deliberately casual. "Which boat is it? One of the big gin palaces? I saw Bezos's the other day. It's unbelievable. Bigger even than that beauty out there."

She pointed at Tomás López's huge boat, dominating the mouth of the harbour and glinting in the setting sunshine.

"Rafe's is called *Esperanza*," said Lily. She knew that now.

Rafe leaned back into a chair and sipped his water. "She's a nice Med cruiser. Small enough to still be near the water and to nip about on without needing a big crew."

Hannah frowned. "Who owns *Esperanza*? Wait, it must be Tomás López? I saw you on his superyacht when I arrived. On the deck. Talking to his skipper."

"*Sí.*," said Rafe easily. "I was checking details."

López owned the boat Rafe crewed? This was news to Lily. She tried to remember if they had ever had a conversation about who he worked for, or if she had mentioned Tomás López in relation to La Colina. She didn't think so. She would certainly have remembered it if she had.

"You never told me you worked for him," she said, a little puzzled. "And I would have loved to wave to you from here when you were on the big yacht."

"*Lo siento,*" said Rafe, "but I was only there for a short while."

"Nice life if you can get it," said Hannah, swilling her wine with a lazy flick of the wrist. "Weird I haven't bumped into you before. I know most of Tomás's guys. They always come to Tim's after docking."

"I'm mostly on maintenance," Rafe explained. "Engine work and below deck. Dirty and not very glamorous. I don't drink much either, so I'm very antisocial."

"Fair enough," said Hannah. "Who's López's chief engineer these days? Is it still Alessandro?"

Rafe shrugged. "Maybe. Señor López has a high turnover on the big ship. He's a demanding boss."

"I've heard he's demanding in business too," said Lily. She thought of Kat meeting up with the tycoon and attempting to do a deal with him. The idea was alarming. Kat was a force of nature, but a man as powerful as Tomás López would be a formidable negotiator.

"He's demanding in *every* area of his life," said Rafe with a note of bitterness Lily hadn't heard in his voice before. "Or so I hear. I don't see much of him."

There was a strange tightness to his words, as though he was personally offended by the behaviour of his boss. Lily sipped her drink and tried not to feel unsettled by the peculiar undercurrent to his conversation. Something lurked beneath the surface with Tomás López – she felt certain of it now she looked more closely. There was a seam of bitterness underneath Rafe's jokes about men with flash cars and watches that cost more than houses. It seemed almost personal.

"He sounds a right barrel of laughs," said Hannah.

"I love that expression!" Rafe grinned, his crinkle-eyed, heart-stopping grin, and Hannah smiled back, but the smile didn't reach her eyes.

"We don't know this guy. Maybe he's okay," Lily protested. She sounded like an utter drip, but she was hoping that López wasn't all bad, for Kat's sake and for the future of La Colina.

"I do – and trust me. He is all those things. He's single-minded. Brilliant. Ruthless. Charming. And totally narcissistic," Rafe said. "He's every cliché of a wealthy bully."

Rafe had made scathing comments about the super-rich before, people whose boats were wasted on them since they didn't appreciate the water or know how to drive them. Lily recalled him commenting that true wealth lay in things that couldn't be bought, such as the gleam of first light on molten silver water, the laughter of a child, and the touch of her skin on his …

Wait! There was something here. She knew there was. A tangle of thought was unknotting in her mind, but Lily was too close to focus on seeing which threads were freed and where they led. Where had she heard this before?

"Sounds like you know him really well," remarked Hannah.

"I can't say I know the couple I crew for at all, at least not beyond what they like to drink and that they're tight with tips."

Knowing Hannah well, Lily recognised her friend was on the defensive. There was a thoughtful smile playing on her lips and her blue eyes were wary.

"Better than I wish I did," said Rafe. "Luckily, I don't see him much. He's always on the big boat."

"He's rich enough to pay for people to sit around in case he wants to go out to sea, I guess," said Hannah. "Maybe he's looking for wife number three?"

"Four," corrected Rafe. "And trust me, you wouldn't want to be his wife."

"It suits me he never needs you," Lily said. "It means we can snatch some time together."

Rafe smiled up at her and it was as though the sun shone full beam. "And *that's* the best perk of the job!"

"Maybe I should come and work for him?" Hannah said slowly. "My boss is hell. You'll never guess what happened the last time he was on board. It involved cleaning the heads, and it was gross."

Rafe seemed his usual self again, and he laughed as Hannah regaled them with stories and anecdotes. She finished with one about a wild party in the marina where several people ended up falling overboard and a tender sank.

"It's strange you weren't there," she said, eyes narrowing. "I'm sure the López boats were in the port. Alessandro was there. I think I might have snogged him."

Rafe spread his hands. "I may have been there."

"It's strange I haven't clocked you before. You've got one of those faces. Hard to forget."

Lily knew for a fact that if Hannah had seen Rafe first, she would have done her best to gobble him up. It was a little odd.

Rafe laughed. "Maybe you're just distracted. Crew life is busy, right?"

Hannah laughed too, but a beat too slow. "Yeah. Maybe."

She let the topic go, but Lily knew her friend was troubled – and, if she was honest, she too was disconcerted. She had never known Rafe to be evasive before, but this evening there was a quicksilver nature to his answers which made her nerves jangle. Maybe he had experienced the wrath of Tomás López first-hand? Or perhaps he'd been made to sign an NDA as part of the terms of his employment? That wouldn't be unusual, and even Samantha had mooted the idea. Lily decided to ask him when she next had the opportunity.

The conversation turned to other topics, and Lily relaxed. Drinks finished, they walked up to the terrace and sat at the yellow table beneath the vine-draped balcony, and tucked into the food Jenny and Lily had prepared. Simple rustic bread with tomatoes soaked in garlic oil, pasta with prawns and chilli, and cool lemon sorbet made from the fruit Lily had picked that morning. Rafe helped Lily carry it out, and made sure the glasses were topped up. Cicadas chattered in the background like gossiping women, the breeze lifted napkins and cooled sun-warmed skin. There was something dreamlike in the way the evening unfurled, as though they were characters in a film set in this beautiful house high in the hills.

Hannah told stories as she always did, about the famous folk who had chartered the exclusive boats she crewed. Each tale was more fantastic than the last. The time she danced with One Direction. The Arab prince who'd tried to buy a night with her by offering her anything she wanted from Asprey's. The supermodel who snorted coke all night and was flown to hospital by helicopter. Rafe listened with real attention, laughing in all the right places, while his hand sought Lily's beneath the table and squeezed gently. All was well, Lily thought, squeezing back. She'd been overreacting, and Hannah was just protective. The evening was a success.

Later, when Rafe was clearing the table outside and Lily making coffee in the kitchen, Hannah appeared in the doorway, leaning one shoulder against the frame and looking troubled.

"Lil," she said, her voice low. "You're going to think I'm being paranoid, but ..."

Lily looked up. She felt a fleeting jab of irritation. Couldn't Hannah let her be happy for once?

"But what?"

Hannah sighed, watching Rafe from the window. The dancing candlelight lit the terrace like a stage set and made his shadow loom like Nosferatu.

"There's something off. I don't think he's crew. Not Tomás López's anyway."

Lily gave a small, nervous laugh. "Hannah. Don't be daft. Of course he is. I've been on *Esperanza*."

"I'm serious. I know the crews here. I've never seen him, and I know Alessandro. He left two months ago. You remember, we had drinks at Tim's the night he said goodbye. You had too much Malibu and threw up in the bin."

Lily's stomach churned at the memory. In fairness, it had been an eighties night, and Malibu and pineapple hardly tasted that alcoholic. Now the faintest whiff of coconut made her nauseous.

"So maybe he's new? Or temporary? He did say he's below deck. Maybe he's just a lowly, lowly cook?"

But for once Hannah didn't laugh at the old joke. "Babes, he talks like a man who's used to being listened to. Not like someone who gets bossed around by Tomás López and his cronies. Something doesn't add up. Like López keeping a crew on full standby. I know the guy's rich, but that's madness. And anyway, I made it up. He doesn't own that boat."

Lily swallowed. The dinner was suddenly churning in her stomach. "He's a nice guy, Han. I know he is. Don't make problems where there aren't any."

"I'm not saying he isn't. Just … be careful, Lils. There's something you don't know. I can feel it. He's not what he seems."

Rafe stepped into the kitchen, lamplight catching his smile, as ready and genuine as ever. "Need a hand with the coffee?"

Lily pasted on her brightest expression. She'd learned to do this when she was with Harrison, and she hated that she was now doing the same with Rafe. "Perfect timing. I was just finishing loading the tray."

Rafe came over and lifted the tray. His muscles swelled beneath the thin fabric of his shirt, and he smelled delicious, of lime and basil and pepper and him. As always, Lily melted a little and yearned to touch him, but this time she didn't; something in her chest had shifted. A tiny tilt, a little like the floor beneath her had moved, and the evening didn't feel quite so magical anymore. Something felt off.

"I can see why you love it here," Rafe said later, when the stars had crept out for a look at the harbour and they were alone on the terrace, Hannah insisting on taking a cab back to the marina and Kat still out.

The night was soft with pale moonlight and edged the scent of wild thyme. Rafe held her hand and Lily finally relaxed. Her best friend was being paranoid, that was all. After Harrison, who could blame her for being protective? She would do the same for Hannah.

"It's a beautiful spot," she said simply.

"Will you show me the garden? The places Kat and Pablo knew?"

Lily was jolted. Had she told Rafe that Kat and Pablo had met here? They had spoken about so much in the intense weeks they'd known one another, frantic to cram as much into the snatched minutes as possible, and she had mentioned that Kat once loved a local boy. Rafe had been so moved by the story that his eyes had shimmered with tears, and she'd teased him, saying it was a long time ago. Had she ever mentioned Pablo by name? She supposed she must have done.

"What does time matter if you love someone? Love is forever," he'd replied, and then kissed her so long and so deeply that Lily hadn't thought of much else for some time. Did Rafe mean that he loved her? she'd wondered afterwards, as she lay in his arms with dewed skin and a racing heart. Was he saying that he would love her forever? Was that why the story of Kat and Pablo's long-lost love had moved him? Did Rafe love her? Lily feared that Hannah was right to say Rafe was keeping a part of himself hidden.

She thought of his warring parents. His old grandfather. The half-sisters he didn't know. The odd upbringing which had seen him passed from parent to parent to finally the old man he adored. The answer was suddenly heartbreakingly clear: Rafe wanted a home. A calm harbour. A place to moor that was always his.

Kat had found that in Pablo; and this was what had moved Rafe so much, for he had found this with Lily – and she felt the same. It was the sense of peace and tranquillity she found in his company that she loved, as well as the passion. There was a balance. A completeness.

She recalled that remark now as they walked hand in hand through the moonlit garden, past the statues Kat had collected, past beds of wild geraniums and lavender and across the spiky Spanish grass that Kat and Pablo once imagined might become vegetable gardens or olive groves. Rafe seemed to inhale the place, and when they reached the lowest terrace, the precipice where the land fell away to rough scrub and rock and boiling sea, he sighed deeply and turned to her.

"Oh, Lily. What a magical place. I always knew it would be beautiful, but I had no idea."

She leaned her head against his shoulder. "I don't want this place to ever change. I don't want it turned into some soulless resort for people who don't care about what it is and what it means.'

"No. Of course not. Why would that happen?"

"Kat wants to sell it. She's been in a terrible state. Your boss, Tomás López, has made her several offers. It's so much money she can't refuse, but it breaks her heart to know he'll bulldoze it."

Rafe's face was unreadable. Then he looked away, jaw tightening ever so slightly.

"What?" she asked. "Don't you think that's what he'll do?"

"I suppose so."

"Kat's sad, but she knows whoever buys it they'll do the same. They'd make it some bland, millionaire's hideaway."

"Not everyone," said Rafe. "I wouldn't. I would keep it like this forever. Places like this are rare, and it's easy to ruin something beautiful when you try to make it perfect."

Lily reached for his hand again. She pushed her questions and doubts aside. "So don't try. Just enjoy them as they are."

And then she led him back to the house, up the balcony steps and into her room where, as the moon sailed high and the curtains drifted in the night air, they lost themselves in a moment so perfect it would never need to be any different. Another magical night of love and stars, and their sighs mingling with those of the dark sea below.

CHAPTER 22

KAT - NOW

Kat adored the small fish restaurant hidden away in the back streets of the port. At first glance, it wasn't the most glamorous of settings, squeezed into one of the cobbled alleys between the harbour and the residential area, but she had yet to find anywhere that served better seafood. Over the decades she and David had visited it countless times, celebrating everything from birthdays and graduations to engagements and special anniversaries. So many of their family's milestones had taken place here, so it seemed to Kat the fitting location for a meeting she believed would bring her time on the island to an end.

The taxi dropped her at the top of the pedestrianised street, its drunken cobbles now covered by tables and chairs spilling from a wealth of restaurants, the days when you could drive through long gone. Kat could never walk along this street without remembering how she and Pablo had trundled along in his battered truck in those Lucozade-tinted, Polaroid-framed days of the seventies, dodging the odd dog or waving at the old men sitting outside the bars playing dominoes. Now, this area was reserved exclusively for foot traffic and the wealthy. The old tobacconists and shabby grocery stores of those days had been replaced by boutiques and upmarket estate agencies, their windows gleaming portals to holiday worlds of sea, sunshine and dream homes.

Kat fumbled in her purse, pressed a ten-euro note into the driver's hand and told him to keep the change. As always, she noticed the flicker of surprise on his face at how perfectly this Englishwoman spoke Spanish. That feeling of never quite belonging had never left her, the cast-adriftness of being neither fully Spanish nor truly English. Brexit had made her feel like a foreigner in her birth country, unwanted and other, and so very sad – but she didn't wholly fit in here, either. La Colina was the only place Kat really felt herself. The old house knew her, and she knew it. They had seen one another at their very lowest ebb and still loved what they'd found. They had rubbed along happily for decades, ageing and crumbling at a similar rate, content in each other's company.

Perhaps she would never feel at home anywhere except La Colina. Her Mallorcan hideaway was the only place Kat could be herself. Her love for the house wasn't because of a man or a first romance, though both had played roles in its story, but rather about a place that had sung to her heart and soothed her soul. Kat's love for the property had always been pure and untouched by anything other than the sense that she had found her place.

It would break her heart to part with it.

The restaurant owner greeted Kat with her usual blend of warm familiarity and the deference due to a loyal customer of many decades. The woman who kissed her cheek and smiled was the daughter of the original proprietor, and Kat's heart twisted to see that she too was now grey-haired and slightly stooped. Time took no prisoners. They exchanged pleasantries and family updates before Kat was shown to one of the best pavement tables, close enough for attentive service, far enough away to enjoy watching the evening's parade of diners.

And what a parade it was. Locals and tourists wandered past in designer clothes, children in immaculate outfits trailed behind strutting mothers, and impossibly tiny dogs in diamond-studded collars were paraded like fashion accessories. Lovers draped themselves over one another. Parents pushed children in buggies. British holidaymakers with pink noses and peeling shoulders peered at the menu, read it aloud slowly, then plumped for the safety of the pizzeria further along the street. Above them all, unseen and perched on a tiny balcony hemmed with elaborate wrought iron, a beautiful girl with ink-dark hair and vine-leaf tattoos curling up her legs sat on a plastic chair, one foot resting on the balustrade as she painted her toenails scarlet.

All life was here, thought Kat. As Byron said, *Is it not life? Is it not the thing?*

David had loved the theatre of Andratx in the evening. People-watching had been one of his great joys. He and Kat would sit outside the restaurant with a bottle of wine, inventing stories about the passers-by. She wondered now what stories might be imagined about her, this elderly woman with long white hair pinned up with tortoiseshell slides, sitting alone, nursing a glass of Rioja and holding a menu she didn't bother to read. Nothing as wild as the truth, of this she was certain.

Eventually Kat ordered *padrón* peppers and calamari, knowing that once these would have been mere starters before an enormous paella arrived, pink prawns spiked into saffron rice glistening with jet squid ink. Kat couldn't imagine ordering that now. Her appetite had vanished around the same time she had lost David, knocked out by shock and shrivelled by grief. Now, she was one of those annoying old women who pecked at food, dabbed at sauces and claimed to be full after a few mouthfuls. Her younger self, forever chasing a few lost pounds, would never have believed it. *Be careful what you wish for.*

Some bread, aïoli and plump green olives arrived – on the house for Señora Beauchamp. Kat thanked the waiter, a local boy she had watched grow up, and now in his forties, and nibbled on the crusty bread, not wanting to look ungrateful. Her mouth watered at the tang of garlic mayonnaise. Poor Tomás López, she thought. He'd be knocked flat by her breath, if he showed up at all. Kat had sent a message to his ridiculous boat via José's cousin, who worked for the harbour commissioner, but she hadn't heard back. The note might have gone astray, or López might simply have chosen to ignore it. All Kat could do was wait. Time, like hearts and minds, could not be forced. Another lesson learned over a long life.

Her food arrived, hot and perfectly cooked. The waiter spread a snowy napkin over her lap and topped up her glass. Kat took a bite of the peppers, and the taste sent her hurtling back through the years, through anniversaries and reunions and celebrations filled with the same sweet, salty flavour. Around her, tables filled with lovers, families and friends. Laughter rose and fell like the waves beneath La Colina.

She felt dreadfully alone, and the food was hard to swallow. How she missed those days that she'd thought would never end. A blink of an eye and they had finished before she'd time to savour them. How she wished she had known then just how wonderful and fleeting those noisy, happy evenings had been.

A handsome young man had set up a guitar and amp nearby. Kat glanced up and caught the tilt of his head, the sweep of his lashes, and for a heartbeat her heart jolted then soared.

Pablo!

But no. She blinked and the mirage melted. The boy here was shorter. His hair less curly. His cheeks plumper. Her Pablo was long gone. He would be an old man now if he was still alive, and the boy he had been was as much a ghost as the girl who had loved him.

The guitar notes flowed, soft and melancholic. The young man's voice was sweet and honeyed, his singing enchanting the diners, who clapped and cheered their appreciation after each song. Kat wondered who he was, and if he was singing to anyone special. Was there a girl in the crowd with eyes only for him? Did he sing these ballads for her and melt her heart? Did they long for the evening to be over, the coins tipped from his hat and safely stored, so they could slip away into the darkness? Oh, to be young and in love, yearning for the night to fall and dreading the approach of dawn. Youth truly did slip through one's fingers.

Young love made Kat's thoughts turn to Lily, who was quite clearly head over heels with her young man. It was lovely to see how she had blossomed since arriving at La Colina. The nervous energy had melted away, and Lily seemed to grow more confident by the day. The house had worked its magic on her.

Kat had only met Rafe once, when he had called at the house, but it was enough to know she liked him. She had been relieved, for those handsome boys who worked as crew and strode across the pontoons as if they owned the world could be dangerous for young hearts. Her own daughters had had their pick of the summer visitors, and Kat recalled Aimée breaking her heart one year over one of them, and Mia following her example several years later. They were their mother's daughters. But Rafe, although as handsome as any of the Don Juans of the past, had been different. He seemed shy and a little in awe of La Colina, and when he looked at Lily there was an unspoken accord that reminded Kat almost painfully of what she had shared with Pablo. Not to diminish David – never that, for they had had years of deep understanding – but Kat knew that what she and Pablo had experienced had been instantaneous and unstoppable. Neither better nor worse. Just different.

There was something about Rafe that reminded her of Pablo. His gentle manner, perhaps. Or the tilt of his chin, the set of his nose. Or was it simply the way he seemed to live for Lily, casting aside other distractions? His single-mindedness and quiet intensity stirred memories. Or maybe it was all her imagination, projecting a long-lost love onto young strangers. For all she knew, Rafe might be obsessed with fast cars and nights out with friends. *Sentimental nonsense*, Kat told herself sharply as she bit into an olive. The resemblance was superficial at best. She hadn't seen Pablo since she was younger than Lily. He had walked away from her, down the jetty and into a future where she didn't feature, and that had been that.

Actually, it wasn't quite true that Kat had never seen Pablo again. Nor was it the case that she hadn't been tempted to look for him. If the internet had existed in the seventies, Kat suspected she might have driven herself mad. The truth, as is so often the way, was a curious shade of grey rather than the crisp black-and-white certainty Kat liked to pretend it had been.

It had happened almost two years later. Two years after Pablo had kissed her and walked away. By then, she had a diamond ring on her finger and wedding plans in motion. David had put a deposit down on a smart little maisonette in town, and life was unfolding exactly as her parents had always hoped. Whether or not it was the path Kat had dreamed of was another question, one she hadn't wanted to answer.

Kat loved David. He was kind and sweet, and he loved her. He was her friend, and she knew he would be a tender lover, an exciting one too, for he had hidden depths of passion beneath the mild exterior. Yes, David Beauchamp would be a good husband, and if life gave her the chance he would be a wonderful father. The past was behind her. And no good ever came from longing after something as insubstantial as the morning mist that curled across the Isis in September.

Kat hadn't intended ever to return to Mallorca. It would have been too painful, too much like reopening a wound that had only just begun to scab, but when Clara called to say she had broken her arm and needed help, Kat had known she was fated to return. She couldn't refuse Clara, not after her friend had stood by her and been Kat's greatest support at the darkest time of her life. Clara was packing up Casa Cielo Azul, sold to fund the purchase of a house in Puglia, and Kat rationalised with herself that after Clara moved there would be no need to return to Andratx. This would be her final visit.

The town had changed a little. Kat, however, had changed a great deal. This time she kept herself busy by helping Clara with the practicalities of washing and dressing, sorting her belongings, and wrapping up a life. The days blurred with heat and dust and wine. She visited Lina and Esteban and held their new baby, her heart and arms aching, and visited Maria and Francisco, who greeted her like a long-lost daughter. She and Clara drank coffee at the harbour and watched the boats ride the tide. Pablo's boat, of course, was long gone, and although Kat felt a ripple of sadness, she thought she hid it well. Clara knew, anyway. Clara knew everything – she knew every painful detail – and she also knew never to mention what had taken place during that dark time after Pablo had left. It sat between them, sad and unsaid, but this was the only way Kat could deal with it, for Pablo hadn't been all she had lost that summer …

Now at the restaurant the old sadness swept over her, as potent as it had been over half a century ago, and Kat was glad of the sad music, for it would explain the tears in her eyes. Funny where the ungoverned mind could take you. She sipped her wine and let her thoughts drift back to that last stay at Casa Cielo Azul. To the last time she had seen Pablo de la Vega García.

That stay had been a patchwork of emotions: melancholy stitched with nostalgia, hemmed with fondness. A door was closing on one part of her life and another was about to open to a new world of marriage and houses – and, she hoped, motherhood. Clara had a new lover, an Italian count, no less, and was moving to Puglia to paint and sculpt – and, as she'd laughed, 'have lots and lots of sex'. Kat, who was waiting until her wedding night, had smiled, but felt wistful. And, unbidden, a memory surfaced: Pablo's eyes holding hers as they danced beneath the stars. His beautiful face, shadowed by moonlight. His mouth on hers …

Even after all that had happened, Kat couldn't regret a single moment she'd spent with Pablo. She had even visited La Colina again, driving up the old road in Clara's battered 2CV and jumping over the low wall as she used to. As soon as she arrived at La Colina, the house had felt as though it welcomed her back. *There you are,* it seemed to say. *I've missed you.*

She ran her hand across the stonework, stroking the wall like a beloved pet and whispering that she wished she could have stayed. The wind whispered back through the pine tree, and Kat could have sworn it was the house replying. La Colina was telling her she would be back and that it was waiting for her. This was still her place.

Strangely, being there hadn't made her sad. Nor had it made her long for Pablo. Instead, it had made her happy, because she remembered the carefree girl she had been then. It was also impossible to be sad with that view spread out before her like a feast for the senses. La Colina was linked to Pablo, but she didn't love it because of him. Kat loved La Colina because it felt as though this was where she belonged. The house was holding her close and telling her she was part of its fabric, just as much as the listing beams and sagging walls. She would miss it terribly, and driving away from it had felt like parting from an old and beloved friend.

The last of Clara's belongings to be disposed of, apart from her beloved potter's wheel, which was being shipped to Italy at great expense ("The count's problem, not mine," Clara had said with a careless flick of her ponytail), was her car. It was sold to Lena and Esteban, who were thrilled and drove off beaming, their plump baby reclining on the back seat, dangerously close to bouncing out of the open sunroof.

The next day the door of Casa Cielo Azul was locked for the last time, and Kat said a silent farewell to the house, the magical place where she'd first kissed Pablo. So many stories were here. So many versions of her left behind. She cried – unlike Clara, who was champing at the bit to begin her next adventure – and she wished she could be more like her friend.

Clara and Kat took a taxi to the airport together at first light. Clara's flight was at midday, Kat's not until late in the evening. As the taxi drove through the old town, Kat turned and watched as the sea and the port receded, consigned to memory now and placed in the past. It felt like another loss.

She truly loved it here, and the life she had started to make. She was excited about the future, but how she wished she could have had just a little more time to discover the woman she might have been.

The friends kissed goodbye at the airport, promising to stay in touch and visit, but Kat knew it would be a long time before she saw her friend again. Clara was a butterfly, always on to the next flower, and she would soon make a new life and collect a host of new friends. Kat was glad for her. It must be a lighter way to live. Not wanting to spend the day sweltering at Palma Airport, Kat asked the taxi driver to go back into the city. She lost a few hours wandering through the cool hush of the cathedral and explored the winding side streets, admiring beautiful shops filled with treasures she could never afford. By lunchtime, she was hungry, and ready for a glass of wine.

Kat found a restaurant with a jaunty striped awning casting delicious shade over tables scattered at the edge of a leafy square. She chose one where she could pretend to read while watching the world go by. Across from her was an art gallery with bold banners announcing a new exhibition, and every now and then people would climb the steps and vanish inside. It made her think of Clara. How her friend would have loved to stage an exhibition here!

As she sipped her cold white wine and nibbled olives, a sleek black car pulled up at the foot of the gallery steps. The door opened slowly, and it was as if memory had come to life.

A chauffeur stepped out and opened the door for a man. Tall, slim-hipped and dressed in a dark suit and bright white open-necked shirt, he slid from the car and held out his hand to the woman who followed him. She was petite, dark-haired and beautiful. Dressed in couture from head to heel, she held onto his arm as she tottered over the uneven cobbles in sky-high sandals. This couple was wealthy, polished and untouchable.

Kat knew the man instantly. She knew the shape of his head, the sweep of his eyelashes, the scent that used to linger between his shoulder blades. She knew the satin smoothness of his skin. She knew he hated expensive wine. Laughed at the Goons. Loved peaches. She knew him the way you know yourself. She *knew* him. Oh God. She would always know him anywhere.

And then, as if sensing her, he looked up and their eyes met across the square. The world fell away as a single moment stretched to infinity. Eternity was folded into a held breath.

Pablo.

The language of longing flowed between them in that look. It said everything: *I remember. I ache for you. I loved you. I love you still.*

Kat saw the sun glint off her engagement ring. She saw Pablo notice the sparkle, and he smiled. It was a sad, wistful smile, and one that said he was glad for her, as much as seeing it sliced his own heart.

The woman at his side spoke. She tugged the sleeve of his jacket and he turned away from Kat and climbed the steps with her, disappearing into the gallery without looking back.

Kat never saw Pablo again. But on that flight home she cried, and when she fell asleep back in her childhood bed she dreamed of him. In her heart, she was certain, wherever he was, Pablo dreamed of her too …

"Señora Beauchamp?"

The voice at her elbow startled her. Her wine slopped onto the linen tablecloth like blood.

"*Desculpe*, I've made you jump."

Kat peeled herself away from her reverie. A tall man stood opposite. Early fifties, perhaps. Dark hair swept back from a high forehead. His white teeth flashed, shark-like, too bright. Grey streaked his temples, and dark stubble framed a strong jaw. He wore a white shirt, dark jeans and a navy jacket, casual, but the quality screamed money. A heavy gold watch – a Rolex, of course – gleamed on his wrist, and his belt bore the emblem of an eye-wateringly expensive designer brand.

Tomás López had arrived.

CHAPTER 23

KAT - NOW

"Señor López," Kat said, starting to rise to her feet.

Tomás López raised a chivalrous hand to stop her struggling up from the low chair. Lamplight caught his watch.

"Please, Señora, do not disturb yourself on my account. I apologise for not replying to your message before we met this evening. If I had received it sooner, I would have been here on time."

His tone was sincere, and despite everything she knew about him – the wealth, the ruthlessness, the brutal destruction of Clara's beautiful *finca* for yet another glass monstrosity – Kat didn't bristle as she'd expected. Instead, she felt mollified and even a little charmed.

Careful, she thought. Tomás López had a certain dangerous appeal. He was silver-tongued. Handsome. Dangerous. Smooth. She needed to have her wits about her.

"May I?" He gestured to the empty seat.

"Of course," said Kat. She signalled to the waiter, who appeared instantly, the restaurant's owner hard on his heels, menu in hand and wreathed in smiles. Everyone knew Tomás López, it seemed. Except Kat, apparently.

"Good evening and welcome, Señor López," the proprietor gushed, practically genuflecting. "What a pleasure to see you again. How are you? And how is your wife?"

"I'm fine, and I am told she is very well, thank you," he replied coolly. Kat wondered if he was trying to decide which wife the restaurant owner was referring to. Rumour had it, he was on number three, soon to move on to number four, and each woman was younger than the last. Or so she had gleaned from Jenny's gossip. At least being on her way to eighty meant she was safe!

"What can I get you? We have a very fine sole tonight, freshly caught, lightly cooked in butter—"

"No food for me," López cut in, his voice sharp with the single-mindedness of a man whose time was constantly monetised. "A bottle of your 1997 Burgundy, if you have it. And perhaps some olives. Black, not green. And sea salted."

"A good choice, Señor," the owner beamed. Kat suspected she was singing hallelujahs inside at the markup on the wine.

"Thank you for coming," Kat said to López, once the olives were delivered and they were alone.

"I was intrigued by your note," he replied. "Surprised, too. Of course I had to come."

"Surprised that I've given in at last?"

His brows pulled together. "I'm sorry, Señora Beauchamp. I don't understand."

Kat switched to Spanish and repeated her remark, and López laughed.

"Forgive me. I didn't mean I don't understand English. I often speak English for business matters. The British don't tend to do so well if I speak Spanish! I meant I don't understand what you mean by 'giving in'. How have you given in,

Señora Beauchamp? We have not met before. If we had, I would have remembered. I never forget a beautiful face."

Kat frowned. His silvered tongue wouldn't work on her. Whatever game Tomás López was playing, she wasn't prepared to join in. She was about to launch into an angry explanation – after all, he'd been pestering her to sell La Colina for months – when the waiter returned with the wine. An elaborate performance followed: opening, pouring, sniffing, tasting. López insisted she share the bottle. Fine, thought Kat. If his time was precious, hers was finite too. She wasn't about to waste another minute on games, but she would enjoy good wine.

"This Burgundy is excellent," López said, sipping deeply and then rolling it over his tongue. "Notes of seafood and marzipan. Maybe earth."

Time hiccupped. This pretentious comment and lengthy tasting ritual reminded Kat of Pablo, parodying wine tasting with a rough red she'd brought to La Colina from the guesthouse. "Wealthy people nonsense," he'd said, convinced even his father couldn't tell the difference between plonk and vintage. They had laughed and laughed, making up ever more ridiculous comments to describe the wine. Kat wasn't so sure about López. He seemed as sharp as the filleting knives behind the counter. She suspected he could identify this wine blindfold if challenged.

"Let's cut to the chase," she said, not bothering to try hers. "You win, Señor. I'm finally prepared to sell. For the price you named. Not a cent less."

López regarded her over the rim of his glass. "And what exactly are you selling me?"

Was this his idea of a joke?

"La Colina, of course. My house."

His brows shot upwards – or rather, they tried to. Too

much Botox, Kat realised. The small vanity somehow humanised him, and she felt a touch more powerful.

"La Colina? That is a spectacular property, Señora. Such history. The tower! The gardens. The olive grove below. People would kill to possess that property. It has the best views in Andratx. It's development heaven."

"You don't need to tell me why you want it so badly. I'm not a fool."

"Oh, I can see you're far from that, Señora."

They eyed one another over the table like opponents in the boxing ring. Who would throw the first punch? And who would end up on the ropes?

"I'm realistic," Kat said finally when he remained silent, dark eyes regarding her quizzically over his glass. "I know La Colina could be developed very successfully. You could easily build four houses there. Quadruple your money. I accept that. Any sale would be without conditions too."

López took a sip of wine. "*Sí*. Development would be a very good reason to buy it. And yes, I'd be interested if it were for sale. But I'm confused. Have you advertised it? Had it valued?"

"For goodness' sake!" Kat exploded. "Stop playing games. You know I haven't! You've been pestering me to sell it to you. You've been writing letters all summer. Offering more and more money. What are we at now? €3.4 million. It's practically harassment. Is this how you conduct business? Or do you enjoy bullying people too old to fight back?"

She wanted to overturn the table. Her twenty-one-year-old self was yelling *Run! Tell him to get lost!* But these days Kat would barely make it to the corner of the street. Besides, she had to sell. She knew this in her heart, and she owed it to David to make sure their family was safe. He had already slipped his moorings, and Kat knew her own were a little looser every day.

But far from seeming jubilant, Tomás López appeared genuinely upset by her outburst.

"Forgive me, Señora. I don't wish to upset you, but truly I have no idea what you're talking about. Yes, I've admired your house for many years. Who has not? It's prime real estate, and of course I'd be interested if it were for sale, but I have never written to you. I swear on my mother's life. On the holy virgin. On anything you like. I have never contacted you."

His voice rang with sincerity, and Kat's anger guttered and was extinguished. She could see his confusion wasn't feigned.

"But I've had letters from you. At least five this summer. In the last one you offered €3.4 million."

"Did I?" he said. "*Dios*. You should take it."

"I know!" she snapped. "That's why I'm here! To tell you I accept. Can we stop playing games?"

He reached across the table and placed a gentle hand on hers. "Señora, I am sorry. I do not mean to tease, and I am not playing games. The offer didn't come from me."

Kat stared at him. Her head was spinning. "That's impossible. Of course it did."

"Señora. I have never once thought about offering to buy your property. People come to me when they are ready to sell. I do not need to hustle."

"Your name is on the letterhead. It is an offer from you!"

"May I see these letters, Señora?"

She sighed. "I confess I tore most of them up because I was angry at your persistence. I truly believed it was you writing. I felt pestered."

"I don't blame you for tearing them up, then."

Kat was rummaging in her bag. "I kept the latest, though, once I'd decided to sell. Here."

She handed it to him. López smoothed the letter flat on the table, pulled spectacles from his breast pocket, and studied it intently. Then he exhaled and steepled his index fingers together.

"Ah. I see."

"What do you see?"

"Many things, Señora. And I am afraid to tell you that this letter is not from me."

"But it's written on your headed paper. López. And the family crest. See? How can it not be from you?"

"It is our crest," he agreed. "Our company paper too. However, that letter was not written by me. Somebody else has made the offer."

"Then it's a fraud?"

López looked up sharply. "No. It's a very real offer. Just not one from me."

Kat wrapped her hand around the wine glass. The ruby red liquid trembled. "I don't understand."

He pushed the letter across the table and stabbed his finger at the bottom. "Look closely at the signature."

Kat squinted. Letters blurred and danced. *Tomás Raphael de Cruz López.*

"I see your name."

"No. It isn't my name."

"I don't understand."

López's eyes were filled with an emotion she couldn't quite pin down. If pressed, Kat would have said it was pain.

"I'm Tomás Ferdinand López."

"Who the *hell* is Tomás Raphael de Cruz López, then?" Kat almost shrieked.

A muscle tightened in his cheek and he drained his glass. "My son."

"Your *son?*" echoed Kat. She was confused. "The man who wants to buy La Colina is your son?"

"*Sí*."

"And he hasn't run this by you?" Kat was staggered. Aimée and Mia had pulled some stunts in their time, but this was something else.

López exhaled wearily and spread his hands. "We are estranged, Señora. My son is an adult, a man, and he can do as he pleases. He does not work for me or answer to me."

Kat stared at him. This made no sense. Unless the son wanted to compete with his father and buy La Colina from under his nose to spite him? But Tomás López was quite clear that he had not been intending to approach her. La Colina had never been in his line of sight.

What was going on here?

"Your son didn't tell you about making an offer?"

"We have little contact. He has lived with his grandfather, my former father-in-law, for many years, and I am afraid to say he has a very low opinion of me. Maybe it's deserved? I was not always kind to his mother. I regret that now, but in my defence Isabella was not always easy to love."

Kat said nothing. She could see Tomás wanted to explain but was struggling to articulate his story. Pride or pain, she imagined, held him back; then as a parent she realised it must be the latter. Just the thought of being estranged from her girls made Kat's heart hurt. The reality must be excruciating.

López took a long sip of wine. His fingers tapped once on the stem of the glass. A tic, perhaps, or nerves. He was poised to bare his soul, and Kat felt as though she was a priest in the confessional.

"I like beautiful things, Señora. Houses. Art. Horses. Cars. Women most of all. Women are my weakness. I am sure you have heard the stories about me."

Kat flushed, and he smiled ruefully.

"I can see you have. Ah, *Dios*. They are mostly true."

"You've been married three times, haven't you?"

"Yes," he said. "Three times. Once for status. Once for power. And once because I thought I would change."

"And because you loved her?"

He raised an eyebrow. "You are a romantic, Señora."

"I believe in love," said Kat staunchly. Pablo and David had taught her that true love was unselfish, kind and gentle. Status and power, and using a person to elicit change, were not in love's remit. Hearts were not trophies to be collected. She suddenly pitied Tomás López. The man had everything, yet he had nothing.

López sighed wearily. "Perhaps I loved Isabella. If I did it was not enough. Now I try not to repeat expensive mistakes. I will be honest with you, Señora, I was not a good husband to my first wife, and I regret that bitterly. We parted very badly, and my boy took his mother's side. He was seven when Isabella died, and he blamed me. Maybe rightly." He swallowed. "She overdosed."

Kat's hand flew to her mouth. "I'm so sorry."

He closed his eyes. "The inquest said it was a tragic accident. Too many sleeping pills and too much wine. She had been at a party, and everyone said that outwardly she was happy. There was no note and no indication that she meant to ..." He passed a hand over his face. "Anyway, my boy blamed me. I had left his mother for Antonia, and in his mind that was why she was so unhappy. The truth is maybe more complicated. Maybe not? His grandfather blamed me for a while, but even he has accepted that her death was a terrible accident. But Raphael never did. He blames me still."

Raphael.

Something shimmered in the darkness of Kat's subconscious. She wanted to tug at it, unknot the tangled wool of thought, but López was still talking, and she knew he needed her to listen. This was a man who rarely spoke about the things which drove him to pour his soul into making money. She wished she could make him see that all the money and success in the world were nothing compared to losing his son, but only time would allow Tomás López to understand this.

"I never cut him off, but we have little contact. He turned his back on my business and me. He wants nothing to do with it, which is why this letter surprises me."

"So, what does he do if he isn't involved in the business?"

"He has a boat he charters. It belongs to his grandfather. It's far smaller than my boat, *Ultimo*. You have seen her? She is moored outside the port." He glowed at the thought of his superyacht.

"I have," said Kat. She wasn't impressed. When would men realise that size really wasn't important?

"He has some investments from his mother. He also expressed an interest in ecological developments, after reading Environmental Science, and at one point I hoped he might join me to develop that aspect of our company, but no. He wants to make it alone, as did I. He's idealistic and impulsive, but he is honest. This deception is not like him. I don't understand."

"If he's honest, why is he using your name to make an offer on my house?" Kat shook her head.

"Well," López said, mouth tightening, "he is a López. And his mother's inheritance alone left him a wealthy man. His grandfather is a man of means, too."

"But why would your son want La Colina? A house he's never seen?"

"I have no idea, Señora. Perhaps he has fallen in love with it? Perhaps he wishes to make an ecological development?

Perhaps his grandfather liked it? He knew the island in his youth, I believe. Maybe my son thought you would take an offer from the López name seriously?"

There was truth in the suggestion. Tomás López was wealthy. La Colina was small change to him, and this was why Kat had considered the offer: his name carried weight. She had been approached in the past by many smaller realtors and ignored every single one.

"He is also my son," continued Tomás. "Raphael knows a good proposition when he sees it. He is bright." She noticed a note of pride when he mentioned his son's instinct for making money. "His grandfather will have raised him to love history, and I know he brought Isabella here a lot when she was a child. She loved Mallorca. Perhaps this place reminds my boy of his mother. His grandfather will encourage him, no doubt."

Kat let the words settle. There was something here that resonated deep within her, like the note from a sound bowl that shivered in the air long after the metal was struck.

"What does his grandfather have to do with this?"

López shrugged. "Ah, maybe nothing. Maybe everything. The man is stubborn, and a member of the last of the old Spanish dynasties. The kind of man who believes honour is currency. Who loves the past more than the future. He would adore La Colina with its tower and history. He's a powerful man, but he's unwell and reclusive now. I hear he gives most of his money away."

The tone of López's voice made her skin prickle. "You don't like him."

"He doesn't like me. He never wanted me to marry his daughter. He told me I couldn't love her, not if I loved money more than people." He shrugged. "Maybe he was right, but money has never let me down. I respect him, Señora – but no, I don't like him."

Because he sees through you, thought Kat. She felt a chord of sympathy with this wise father-in-law. How hard it was to watch your children make mistakes and place their hearts, the precious hearts you had held close to yours from the first moment you knew they existed, in careless hands.

"I admit I showed off in those early days. I wanted to impress. I was young. Brash. New money. Ambitious. A show-off. He lectured me, some nonsense about wealth being a quirk of Fate not a mark of worth. Love is wealth. And so on." López drained his glass and set it down with a thud. "Easy words when spoken by a man who never had to make his way in the world. I clawed my way up, Señora. I made every penny myself, so I know what wealth is. 'Wealth is not a badge of worth. Love is true wealth.' Pah! Patronising old fool."

A bolt of electricity zipped through Kat. A fish-scale flicker in the deep green water of a memory pond, before reeds tangled clarity and the water grew cloudy. There was something here …

Wealth is a gift of Fate, Katalina, not a badge of worth. It should fill the heart with gratitude not pride. Love is real wealth.

Her head was spinning. Kat gripped the edge of the table to prevent herself sliding beneath. Her heart was skittering in her chest, and she struggled to breathe. Was it the wine making time and place kaleidoscope? Sometimes Kat couldn't recall what she'd eaten for breakfast, yet she could recollect conversations from decades ago with perfect clarity. It was a sunset-of-life paradox.

"Señora? Are you unwell? Do you need a glass of water?"

Kat's mind was blurring things, that was all. She needed to focus on the present and the reason she had met this man. She needed to sell La Colina.

She inhaled sharply and caught her breath. Her heart rate slowed. "Goodness. The wine is strong," she improvised. "Anyway, you say your son, the son who wants to buy my house, adores his grandfather?"

López's mouth twitched down. "Yes."

"You say that as though it's a fault in him."

"I say it like it's a fact." He poured another glass of wine. Kat covered hers with a hand. "My boy grew up in luxury, in a beautiful villa in Madrid. He had everything on a plate. Education. Toys. Holidays. My name. I would have given him the world, but he chose to side with his mother when we divorced. Ah, I cannot blame him. Maybe Isabella was right? Maybe I cannot make anyone happy?"

The words surprised her. They sounded almost like regret. But with a man like López, who knew? He had the air of someone who collected regrets like others collected wines: rare, expensive, and stored deep away from sunlight. He would move on from it, back to the serious business of making money.

"But none of that explains why he wants my house," Kat said.

López leaned forward, his voice softening. "My boy is no fool. La Colina is a gem. Not just the view, though that's enough to make architects weep. It's the history. The old tower. The bones of it. The acres of wild olive groves. I've sailed past it for years, dreaming what I'd do with it. It's a developer's fantasy."

"Let me guess," Kat said, voice cool. "You'd flatten it and put up something boxy and glass-fronted."

He placed a hand on his heart. "I'm wounded. Even I know some houses are sacred. Forget my son, Señora. I will buy it if you wish to sell. I swear I will cherish it. You can remain at La Colina as my honoured guest for as long as you wish. Sell to me. I will give you €4 million. More. Name your price."

She believed him. The money was tempting and would

give her girls security for life and provide comfort in her old age – and yet something still curled in her stomach. López might preserve La Colina, but it would be on his terms, with his signature carved into its walls. And how could she be a guest in her own home? It would be beyond painful.

"What about your son? Would you outbid him? Steal the property he wants?"

López didn't answer at first. He turned the wine glass slowly between his palms, watching the ruby liquid catch the fairy lights strung overhead.

"No," he said quietly. "Of course not. If Rafe wants to buy La Colina, I won't stand in his way."

Kat stared at him. There was a rushing in her ears, as though the sea had swept inland and was racing towards her.

"Who?"

"Rafe," he said patiently. "My son. His name is on your letter. Tomás Raphael de Cruz López. Rafe. No, Señora, if Rafe wants to buy La Colina, I won't fight him. Nor do I want to upset his grandfather any more than I already have in one lifetime. If Pablo García's behind this offer, I won't stand in his way."

And with these words the tide rushed in, knocking Kat from her feet and sweeping her away. Her heart pounded at the shock of hearing the name she had carried inside it for a lifetime, and although she tried to reply the words her tongue summoned refused to come to heel. The glass slipped from her hand, the world receded, and the last thing Kat heard was Tomás López crying out for help.

And then the world turned black.

CHAPTER 24

LILY - NOW

Rafe didn't stay the night with Lily. Neither of them felt it was right for him to do so without asking Kat first, but knowing they were doing the right thing didn't make parting any easier.

Even so, first light was turning the sea to silver as Rafe left. In the height of summer the sun rose early – too early – but the world outside was still hushed, and the warmth of the previous day lingered in the air when he opened the balcony doors. The muslin drapes stirred sleepily in the jasmine-scented breeze and the waves sighed below.

The whole world was as replete and drowsy as Lily felt. She lay tangled in the white cotton sheet, her skin still humming from his touch, and watched Rafe dress. He moved quietly, shirt unbuttoned, curls tousled, and barefoot on the dark floorboards as he gathered his clothes. He smiled at Lily, but didn't speak. The early morning stillness was a reminder of the night's magic.

She sighed. "I wish you could stay."

Lily felt sure Kat wouldn't mind. She couldn't imagine her

employer being shocked to see Rafe appear in the kitchen. Kat's stories of Pablo de la Vega García suggested she would understand entirely. Approve, even.

He glanced over, tugging up his jeans and almost toppling back onto the bed. "If I don't show up I won't be popular. The skipper will throw me overboard."

"I thought *you* were the skipper?"

Lily couldn't help herself; Hannah's doubts had seeped into her mind like raindrops running into well-worn tracks. Used to Harrison's lies and evasions, she feared she was susceptible to doubt, and this thought made her sad. Would her past always colour her future? She wished Hannah hadn't said anything. Now Rafe would think she didn't trust him.

And Lily did trust him.

Didn't she?

"I'm more of a hobby sailor who got lucky," Rafe said. He pushed his feet into his deck shoes before crossing to the bed and kissing her. "I seem to be getting even luckier lately."

Lily laughed and her doubts vanished. This was Rafe, not Harrison. Sweet, funny and honest Rafe.

"I bet you say that to all the girls."

"No," he said. "I don't."

He kissed her again. "Shall we meet up tonight?"

"It depends on what Kat's got planned. I should finish at six, but I might see if I can cook for her," said Lily. "She's not been quite herself. Something's troubling her."

"She must have come home quite late," said Rafe.

Lily nodded. "She's often up by now too. She makes a coffee and then carries it back to the garden room. It's not like her to sleep in."

They both paused, listening for the chink of a mug and the hiss of the coffee machine. There was no sound from the kitchen below, and the garden room door was closed and the curtains drawn. Caught up in the tangle of one another, they hadn't heard a taxi engine as a passenger was dropped off or the thump of the heavy front door. Kat must be fast asleep by now, and neither Rafe nor Lily wanted to disturb her. Even La Colina seemed to hold its breath.

"I'll use the balcony steps," Rafe whispered.

Lily nodded. "Turn left at the bottom. The gate unlocks from the inside, and there's no alarm. I'll fasten it later."

La Colina had high walls and good security these days. There would be no hopping over walls as in Kat and Pablo's time. Lily felt like Juliet as Rafe stepped onto the balcony. He turned once more, as if memorising her as she was at that moment – flushed from lovemaking, her hair a wild tangle against the pillows – and a look passed between them that made her shiver. It was full of longing and promises.

Then he was gone.

Lily lay in the stillness. She heard the click of the gate, and moments later the engine of the Defender coughed awake. She hoped it didn't disturb Kat, but there was still no movement from the garden room. The morning was unfolding around her, soft and beautiful, and she sank back into bed, reliving the night and unable to stop smiling.

Lily felt sure that if Kat had bumped into Rafe as she made her way to the kitchen, she wouldn't have thought badly of her. The older woman would have understood. There was something ageless about Kat Beauchamp; she was generous and insightful, and she didn't judge. She'd seemed to like Rafe, too, when she'd met him. Maybe he could visit again, and this time stay the night with Kat's blessing? The idea made her smile, and she imagined Kat teasing her over a glass of wine. She was being daft to have doubts. Everything was fine.

Hannah, though, would be harder to convince. Although they had all laughed last night, sharing wine and stories on the terrace until late, Lily sensed Hannah was holding back. She caught her friend watching Rafe closely when she thought nobody noticed, and several times she had asked questions about people they might have in common in the marine world. It was subtle, and hopefully Rafe hadn't noticed, but Lily knew her friend far too well to miss this scrutiny. Hannah had misgivings.

It was this which made her uneasy. Hannah didn't often get things wrong. Her instincts were sharp, annoyingly so sometimes, and she had never warmed to Harrison. Kat had said Hannah sounded like Clara, and recalling how Clara once warned Kat about Pablo breaking her heart made Lily shiver. Was history repeating itself?

Hannah had been right to say something was off about Harrison, and Lily wished she had listened, but his time her best friend was wrong. Rafe was different. He was nothing like her smooth-talking ex with his polished manners, charming smile and empty words. Rafe Cruz was warm. He was kind. He had a wonderful sense of humour. He was easy to talk to and not afraid to show his feelings. He also possessed a melancholic, vulnerable side that melted her heart, and they had shared things with one another that both admitted to never speaking of with anyone.

Lily had been moved when Rafe confided, during a conversation held on their ledge which turned to having children (Rafe wanted at least five, Lily settled on two) that his mother had died when he was a child. It was an accidental overdose, he said, but for years he had blamed himself for not knowing how unhappy she was.

"I should have stopped her," he said. "I should have realised how sad Mama was."

"Rafe, you were *seven*." Lily was horrified to think of a child growing up with this burden. "It wasn't your job to look after your mum or know what was going on in her life. You were a child."

He turned away, fixing his gaze on Dragonera. The *churros* in his hand snowed sad icing sugar onto the rocky ledge. "Maybe, but I still knew she was unhappy. Whenever my father left it was like the sun had gone out for her. She adored him, even though they fought."

Lily said nothing, although she knew he was describing a toxic marriage. She let him speak, and the past poured from Rafe in a torrent. He told her how it had been for him growing up with a distant father he feared and disliked, a string of stepmothers and potential stepmothers who found him a bother, and how it felt to carry the burden that he should have stopped his mother from overdosing. Guilt had shadowed his life ever since. Her heart breaking for him, she listened as he described life with his beloved grandfather, the man who raised him and who Rafe said had shown him what it really meant to be a man.

"Grandpa has been a true father to me," Rafe said, his voice hoarse. "He's a wonderful man, Lily. So kind and so true. He doesn't care about money or status, he says love is true wealth, and he would give his last euro away if somebody needed it. If I can be half as good as he is, I'll be proud. You'd love him. Everyone does."

"Maybe I'll meet him one day?" Lily said.

"I hope so, but he isn't a well man now, and he's getting old, even though he doesn't think so. He says he's twenty-five in his head."

"He sounds like Kat," Lily said, and for some reason the hairs on her forearms rippled. "She told me she wants to get a tattoo!"

How she and Kat had laughed about this. Kat had said, why

not? It wasn't as though she would have to live with it for years if she hated it!

Lily gave him a little nudge. "Hey, maybe we should set them up?"

But Rafe didn't laugh. The mention of Kat had seemed to upset him even more.

"Grandpa's in remission from cancer – for now, at least, they say – and he needs to slow down. To rest and be somewhere he loves."

"I'm so sorry." Now Lily understood the nature of Rafe's underlying seam of melancholy.

He swallowed. "It's gone for now, but it's taken its toll. I thought I would lose him, and I didn't know what I would do. He's all I have. I'd do anything for him. Anything. I want you to know that, Lily. Whatever I've done, whatever I may do, it's all for him."

This made no sense, but Lily guessed he was talking about all the events of his life. There was nothing Rafe had to explain to her.

"You need to know that," he repeated. "He has done so much for me, and I'll repay him no matter what I have to do. Oh God, Lily. What if the cancer comes back? I can't imagine life without him."

He wept then. Lily had held him until the tears subsided, and he sagged against her, wrecked by the storm of emotion.

"God, sorry," he'd said, wiping his eyes on his T-shirt. "I didn't mean to dump all that on you."

Lily hugged him. "I'm glad you did. I'm glad you can talk to me. No secrets, Rafe."

"*Sí,*" he said.

But he hadn't repeated her sentiment or really agreed, and Lily had been left with the uneasy sense that there was more to this story. Rafe Cruz was damaged by the past, and inside him was the seven-year-old boy he had once been, still grieving and angry and afraid. She hoped his beloved grandfather would live for many more years. Rafe was clearly devoted to the elderly man.

So. Lily *did* know Rafe. He'd bared his soul to her and shown a vulnerability that caught her off guard. She knew him. She did. She felt it down to her very bones. This time Hannah was wrong.

She drowsed until the sun was a little higher, peeking in through the curtains and tapping her on the shoulder. Time to get up and walk into town, to meet Hannah for breakfast – and, she secretly hoped, catch another glimpse of Rafe at the marina. She took a shower, loving the way the jets needled her skin, and struck by the contrast of her tanned limbs against the white tiles, before dressing in a loose sundress that fluttered around her legs as she wandered through La Colina.

The house was still, washed with early light, and she padded into the kitchen. The coffee pot was cold – Kat really *was* having a lie-in – and Lily filled it and perched on a stool while the pot spluttered and hissed. The rich scent of coffee filled the air and drifted out onto the terrace with Lily, but even this was not enough to wake Kat. She must have had a late night.

The sea was turquoise silk and the sky shell pink. Lily stood on the terrace, sipping slowly, and watching the port come to life below. It was hard to believe that just a few months ago she'd been trudging through grey days and a grey life, wondering if life would ever change. Really change. And now she was here. Living in this place. Spending blissful nights with a wonderful man …

It was like a dream. Almost too good to be true. La Colina was a dream house; the cascading bougainvillea, the blue-tiled pool glinting in the sun and vanishing into the even bluer sea which melted into the curve of the dragon island. The pool rippled in the soft breeze, and she was tempted to slip off her dress and dive in. Only knowing that Jenny and José were due to arrive and wouldn't appreciate seeing her splashing about in her underwear stopped her. That, and knowing she was going to meet Hannah soon. Arriving dripping wet would not be a good look.

She took another sip of coffee and let her gaze drift to the garden room. Kat's curtains were still drawn. The house was silent. Lily decided to leave her employer to sleep in. Jenny and José would be here before long to open the shutters, make more coffee and prepare breakfast. Until then, let Kat enjoy a lie-in.

Her coffee finished, Lily picked up her bag and slipped on her faithful DM sandals. She left La Colina by the gate Rafe had used earlier, and locked it behind her. The world was still, and the only sounds were the slap of her soles on pavement and the distant cry of gulls circling over a trawler.

She loved the walk down into the town, the steep road winding between terracotta walls and wild fig trees, pavement swapping sides at random intervals, and sea flashes flickering through the trees and framed by elaborate gates. The world was beautiful, and Lily couldn't stop smiling. She knew why, and it was time to admit it.

She was in love with Rafe Cruz.

There. She'd allowed herself to think it. The words danced through her mind, bright and unapologetic. She hadn't known him long, but what did that matter? She had known Harrison all her life, and what did that count for in the end? Kat had known Pablo for only a matter of days, but had known she loved him. What did time matter? Rafe Cruz had found his way into her heart, and Lily knew he was there to stay. It was crazy, but somehow inevitable, and she loved this because it felt organic. It was serendipity. It was real. Rafe made her happy, and she hugged the joy close as she descended into town.

The port was coming to life around her. Shutters were open. The smell of bread drifted from the bakery. A cat sitting in a doorway washed its paws and watched her pass with utter disdain. The world was sunlit and unhurried, and as she strolled along the harbour road, Lily raised her face to the light and smiled.

She was meeting Hannah at a small café on the waterfront, close to the boats. The only barrier between the tables and the green water was a sun-bleached rope strung between weathered posts. Wicker chairs with patterned cushions filled the terrace, and most of the tables sat empty, save for a few locals sipping coffee and scrolling on their phones, and some giggling female tourists waiting for the hire-boat boys to arrive.

Lily settled at a table on the water's edge and ordered a *café con leche*. Boats nodded at their moorings, and the hills opposite shimmered in the morning haze. Casa del Mar squatted beside Club Vela, and she shuddered to think of the poor au pair slaving for Samantha within those bright walls. Thank goodness she had tripped up that day. She felt sure her godmother had been watching out for her. Maybe Clara had even stuck out a platform-soled foot and sent her flying? The notion made her feel warm inside, and loved.

While she waited for Hannah she pulled her diary from her bag. The feel of it in her hands was comforting, and although dog-eared and soft at the corners, it was her dear friend. The pages fluttered like her thoughts as the breeze ruffled them, as though eager to see her scribble lines of fledgling poetry.

Lily tucked her curls behind her ears and picked up her pen. Her coffee arrived, rich and hot, and she took a slow sip as she poured her thoughts onto the page. Writing was a magical process, and Lily was always surprised at how it seemed she had been writing for mere minutes, only to discover hours had passed. She never minded waiting when she had her diary. As Oscar Wilde had said, one should always have something sensational to read. Her cheeks flushed as she scanned what she had written about the previous evening. She must make sure nobody ever read that, especially Rafe. He would be quite swollen-headed!

"Sorry I'm late," Hannah said, sliding into the chair opposite. She pushed her Maui Jim into her hair and dropped a canvas tote onto the floor. "I had to run back to the boat. I'd left my phone charging in the galley again."

Lily closed her diary. Reading upside down was one of Hannah's many skills. "It's fine. I was enjoying the quiet. Isn't it a beautiful morning?"

"Oh God," groaned Hannah. "You've got it bad."

"Is it obvious?"

"You're practically floating. You had your wicked way with that poor boy, didn't you?"

Lily couldn't stop the smile tugging her mouth upwards. "No comment."

"None needed," said Hannah.

The waiter appeared, and they ordered orange juice and a croissant for Lily; espresso and *tostadas* with tomato and *jamón* for Hannah, who looked as though she hadn't slept much.

"All okay?" Lily asked as her friend yawned widely.

"Fine. Lots of wine at yours, and then I bumped into Enrique. He's an old friend from Ibiza. We were catching up until dawn," Hannah said with a wink. "Anyway, how's Kat this morning? Did she have a good evening?"

"I haven't seen her. She was still asleep when I left. She must have come in late."

"Maybe she had a wild night too. Must be something in the air."

Lily laughed. "I'll ask her for you, shall I? Mrs Nosey Parker!"

But Hannah wasn't laughing any more. She looked troubled. She tipped sugar into her coffee and stirred it vigorously. "Can I ask you something? About Rafe?"

Oh no, thought Lily. *Here we go.*

"I've been thinking about him," Hannah was saying, carefully, "and as nice as your new man seems to be, something doesn't add up. I've crewed around the Med for three years. I know most of the people who pass through the marinas, especially if they're regulars or good. And I've never heard of him."

Lily bit back a flare of irritation, because Hannah was looking out for her. She was being a good friend.

"Like he said, he works for Tomás López on his small boat. Not the big one. That's more low-profile, right?"

"True," Hannah admitted. "But here's the thing. Enrique crews for López on the big boat. He says they're short-handed and desperate for someone before they sail to Barcelona. You'd think Rafe would hop across. That's standard practice."

Lily's smile faltered. "Maybe he prefers the smaller boat?"

"Maybe. Or maybe he's not crew at all. He agreed when I said the boat he works on belongs to Tomás López?"

Lily nodded.

"Well, it doesn't. I was testing him. It belongs to someone else. I checked."

And there it was. The first crack in her new-found happiness.

"Who?"

"I can't remember," Hannah admitted. "Cut me some slack, I'd been drinking. But that's not the point. Enrique also says *Esperanza* isn't López's boat."

Lily looked down at her plate. The sunlight still danced on the water, the scent of coffee and pastry still lingered in the air, but something began to feel sour.

"Enrique might be wrong."

"Babe, he works for López. He's the chief engineer. He'd know what boats his boss owns."

Lily stared at her croissant. She felt sick.

"I don't mean to ruin anything," Hannah said gently. "I know you like him. I can see it. But I've seen girls fall for stories before. It's a small world out here, and when someone shows up with a face like his, no history, no ties, and just the right words … I get suspicious."

Lily met her eyes. "You think I'm being stupid."

"No," Hannah said patiently. "I think you're being hopeful, which is lovely. I don't want to see you hurt again."

Lily tried to reach for hope. "I don't think he's lying. I think he's just private. That's part of what I like about him."

Hannah didn't argue. She sipped her coffee and shrugged. "Okay. Just keep your eyes open. That's all I'm saying."

"No. I want to settle this," said Lily. "And since you want to give it, I'll need your help."

Hannah raised an eyebrow. "How?"

"You said you know all of Tomás's crew, right?"

"Yeah," Hannah said carefully.

Lily pulled out her phone and scrolled through the gallery. She paused on one of Rafe and nodded. That would do. No shades. His beautiful smile. Rafe laughing at something she had said, just before he reached for her and all thoughts of photos were forgotten.

"Then help me find somebody who knows Rafe."

Hannah nodded. "Okay."

"And when you do, and they say he's who he said he was, will you leave it? Eat some humble pie?"

"For every meal," her best friend promised.

They paid their bill and headed onto the pontoon. It was busier now, and the marina was alive with people. Tourists queued to book hire vessels to put-put around the bay. The charter boys in their smart polo shirts and chinos were helping customers onto gleaming boats. Fishermen wound green trawls onto net drums. Busiest of all were the crew tending the boats of the wealthy, expected to have everything ready at the drop of a text.

It was a circle of these people, dressed in navy shorts, white trainers and turquoise polo shirts emblazoned with a scarlet emblem Lily recognised from sales boards and vans across the island, that Hannah headed for.

"Hey!" she called.

A man looked up. He had a deep tan and a lion's mane, and his mirrored shades reflected Hannah and Lily in miniature. A grin stretched his stubbled cheeks. "Couldn't stay away, hey?"

"If you're lucky you may be invited back one day to see if you improve," Hannah replied with a toss of her ponytail.

The man's friends laughed, and he did too. "*Dios*, Hannah. Marry me?" he said.

Hannah ignored him. She turned to Lily. "This is Enrique. He's an old friend."

Enrique put a hand on his heart. "Friend?"

"Acquaintance, then. Or casual shag?"

He turned to Lily, mock-stricken. "Is she always this cruel?"

"Afraid so," said Lily.

"Listen, we need a bit of help. Lily's trying to trace a guy who says he crews for López on *Esperanza*. I know López doesn't own that boat, but this guy is adamant." Bored with the banter, Hannah held out Lily's phone, shading the screen with her hand. "You crew for López. Do you recognise him?"

Enrique leaned forward and squinted.

"*¡Madre de Dios!*"

"You recognise him?" Lily's heart was racing.

"*Sí*. Of course!"

"So, he *is* crew."

Lily wanted to cheer, but Enrique was shaking his head: "No, he's not crew."

"Who is he, then?" Hannah demanded.

He frowned. "Seriously? You don't know?"

"No," said Hannah. She glanced at Lily. "So, help us out, yeah?"

"That," Enrique said slowly and in the manner of Simon Cowell announcing an X Factor successful, "is the young boss."

Lily was confused. "I don't understand."

"He's Rafe López. Tomás López's son. The heir to the López millions."

Lily's breath caught. The pontoon dipped and rolled.

"Rafe's Tomás López's *son*?" Hannah echoed.

"*Sí*. You didn't know?"

"No," Lily whispered.

The world tilted. Rafe was a López. He was the heir to a fortune. Tomás López's son. Rafe stood for everything he claimed he hated. Every word he had spoken had been a cover for the truth of who he was. He was a stranger. The man she had fallen for had lied about who he was.

Why?

Her heart slammed against her ribs. The deception was huge. Rafe was related to the man who was trying to steal La Colina from Kat. He was a López. Wealthy beyond imagination. The boy in faded shorts and deck shoes didn't exist. He was a dream.

Was she part of a bigger plan? Had Rafe deliberately targeted her to get close to the house? To report back to his father and subtly see if he could change Kat's mind?

A thousand ugly scenarios tore through Lily's imagination. Her blood drained from her limbs and her head swam. What game was Rafe López playing? She stared at his image, still smiling up from the phone, and knew she had been played.

Rafe's beautiful smile had hidden everything.

CHAPTER 25

KAT - NOW, THEN, THE FUTURE

It was the rhythmic hiss and sigh of an artificial tide that Kat noticed first, followed by the pungent odour of disinfectant instead of rosemary and jasmine. The bed she lay on was hard and narrow, and she was on her back, pinned in by a tight sheet. What was happening?

When she managed to open her heavy eyelids just a fraction, Kat discovered she was staring up at sterile white tiles rather than dark beams. A cannula tugged at the back of her hand and wires snaked from every free patch of skin. Something beeped insistently each time she breathed out. Or in. She couldn't tell.

A hospital. She was in a hospital.

Her eyes fluttered fully open but closed almost immediately. The light was intense, and so bright it hurt. Everything was white, too, and although the blind was drawn it was a bright square.

What was she doing in hospital? And how had she got here? Kat tried to recall where she had last been, but her memory refused to oblige, and all she could picture was sitting on the terrace at La Colina.

She had been at home. Until …?

She had been at home, and then …?

The previous day was wiped from Kat's recollection. What had happened? Had she caught her sandal on the edge of the terrace, tripped and banged her head (highly likely; she had done this before), or perhaps been to a party on one of the big boats and taken lots of mind-altering drugs? (An exciting scenario, but unlikely.) Or had she had another of the heart episodes that had frightened her so much last time, and which had been why her daughters had fretted about her travelling to Mallorca? Oh dear. She really must be more organised with her pills.

Kat really hoped it was the mind-altering drugs that had landed her in the hospital. Anything else, and she would never hear the end of it from her girls. They'd have her in sheltered housing before you could say 'old-age pensioner'. If only they could spend ten minutes in her shoes. Then Aimée and Mia would understand that Kat was no different to them in her mind and soul. It was just the chassis letting her down.

She swallowed. Her mouth was dry, so dry she couldn't call out for a nurse. Kat couldn't even whisper. All she could do was lie here and drift in and out, her awareness rising and falling in time with the gentle sighing of the machines.

As she swam in and out of consciousness, she became aware that she wasn't alone; there was somebody else in the room. Kat wasn't sure how long they had been there or how long she had been asleep, but she realised she was no longer alone. Maybe it was a nurse keeping watch? Somebody who could explain what she was doing here, call her daughters, and fetch her some water. Kat longed for a drink. Her mouth felt dry and scratchy.

She turned her head, expecting to see a nurse checking a monitor, and was surprised to see a man sitting at the side of her bed. He was slumped in a chair too small for his broad frame, and his head was tilted awkwardly as he snored gently. His white shirt was loosened at the throat and crumpled, and his jaw was stubbled with dark shadow. He must have been here all night.

A memory lightning strike. A name. Tomás López.

The restaurant in town. Their meeting. His denial that he had ever approached her about La Colina. The memories started to bubble. Kat let them rise without prodding. She didn't want any to pop before she had seen them clearly. She had collapsed while with him then, and he had stayed with her. Kat was touched. He hadn't needed to do that. That was kind of him.

Maybe there was more to this man than she had thought? In repose he was nothing like the dangerous businessman the papers loved to vilify. He looked younger with hair no longer oiled back but falling over his face, and she was moved to see that his hand rested on the sheet beside hers. Yes, there was kindness beneath the ruthless businessman veneer.

Kindness. Kindness was so important. López wouldn't buy La Colina because of …

The bubble popped. Kat focused on the next flash of memory. She had been at the fish restaurant with Tomás López. They had been discussing La Colina. She had met him there believing that the infamous developer who had been circling her house like a shark was ready to make good his offer. Then there had been a shock. A big one. It hadn't been him who wanted to buy La Colina, but his son Rafe. Rafe, whom Lily was seeing. Rafe, who had never mentioned anything about wanting the house or being wealthy beyond most people's wildest dreams.

Rafe, who had no links to La Colina and no idea what the place meant – unless somebody had told him.

Somebody like Pablo García.

Kat hadn't imagined that name. Absolutely not.

Pablo. No longer young, but a beloved grandfather. Rafe's grandfather.

Kat's eyelids fluttered closed. She felt woozy with whatever drugs were slipping from the IV bag into her system, and the memories began to shimmer at the edges of her mind. Not of Tomás. Not of the seafood restaurant. Not of the agonised hours of sitting on the terrace of La Colina knowing that she would soon be handing it to another. Instead, Kat thought of a boy with a laugh that made everyone happy. The taste of ripe peaches. The deck of a boat hard against her spine and the softest of kisses on her lips. Warm sand between her toes and cold water on hot skin.

Pablo.

La Colina had been theirs. They had promised to always love it, and she had kept that promise. How had he known that La Colina would come onto the market? Jenny must have said something, to a friend maybe or perhaps while at the shops, and the rumour had started about La Colina. Maybe the Garcías still had influence on the island, even though their house had been sold many years ago. She knew without having to ask that Pablo would never willingly let La Colina slip into the wrong hands. Did he think to step in and protect it as a shrine to what they had once shared and been?

It was possible – but then why was his grandson involved? Why would Rafe pretend to be his father? It made no sense. If Pablo wanted the house, and wanted to keep the promise he'd made to his parents all those years ago, he could have instructed a realtor to act for him. He wouldn't have needed to contact Kat, and she would never have needed to know who the purchaser was. The deal could have been concluded through lawyers and trusts.

There was one other explanation. Was it possible Pablo had no idea what Rafe was trying to do? Had Pablo's grandson grown up hearing stories of Mallorca and La Colina? Did Rafe know who Kat was all along? Knowing what La Colina meant to his grandfather, had Rafe decided to buy the property to keep it safe for Pablo? Was love the motivation?

As Tomás's only son, Rafe de Cruz López was a very wealthy young man. The purchase was easily within his reach. That was not in question. Yet Kat was uneasy. Had Rafe used Lily to ingratiate himself with Kat to facilitate a deal? She thought not. Kat had only met Rafe once, and he had never mentioned buying property, or casually asked if she wanted to sell La Colina. Besides, it was clear he was smitten with Lily. Kat wondered if Rafe López had found himself in what her beloved David would have called a pickle, and kept his identity secret because he was falling in love with Lily. He must have been so torn between following his head and his heart.

If this was so, how like his grandfather this young man was! Full of fire and passion and honour, all wonderful qualities individually, but collectively ones which Kat knew only too well could prove destructive when combined. Lily would be hurt, and the trust between them shattered. Oh, why did youngsters make life so complicated for themselves? What a shame it took until this age to realise that the truth was by far the best way, even if it felt so much harder.

A lifetime later Kat's past was tugging her back into her story like the relentless tide. Nothing was truly lost. Nothing was really forgotten. Kat had never forgotten Pablo. The pain had lessened, and when she thought of him now there were smiles rather than tears; the boy she had loved that first summer here had always stayed dear to her. She had often wondered whether he cherished her memory too. Did he think of her? Had she mattered to him like he had to her?

Now Kat had her answer, and although she was tired and her chest ached, she was strangely happy and peaceful. She closed her eyes and let the machine watch over her and allow the memories unfold as the hiss and sigh and the regular rhythm of Tomás's breathing lulled her to sleep. She drifted back through the years.

This time her dreams were not of Pablo and that first summer, but of the life that had followed. Her love for David wasn't the all-consuming passion she'd known with Pablo, but it was no less real, and it was love. David made her feel steady and safe and loved for who she was. He had been the bedrock of her life. Her dear friend. Her confidant. Most of all he'd made her feel hopeful, and taught her that life was a gift to be enjoyed rather than a challenge to endure.

Her wedding day spooled before her vision. It had rained in the morning, soft and steady, but by the time they walked into the ancient chapel just off Magdalen Street, the clouds had cleared. A shaft of sunlight angled through the high stained-glass window, painting the aisle in blue and rose and gold, and Kat had felt it was a message that she was forgiven for all that had happened.

She stood very still in the porch, her fingers tightening slightly around the small bouquet of wildflowers Clara had tied with a blue silk ribbon. Nothing showy. Daisies. Lavender. Thyme. The flowers that grew in the cracks of the old stone walls at La Colina. Her something old? An old life perhaps.

Her dress was simple, an ivory column, bought second-hand in Jericho and altered by her mother. She wore no veil, just a floppy hat, and plain court shoes. Waiting by the altar in his best flared navy suit was David. Upright and bookish and elegant. He smiled when he saw her, and she smiled back because she knew he was saying *I see all of you. And I choose you still.*

Afterwards, they walked through the time-smoothed streets of Oxford to a tiny pub by the river, where the wedding breakfast was held. A roast was served on mismatched plates, and Mozart played on a crackling record player. Clara gave a wildly inappropriate toast while her count got horribly drunk and passed out in the cake. Kat's had mother cried and thanked the Holy Mother her daughter was no longer on the shelf, and David's father kissed Kat and said she was a lovely new daughter. David reached for her hand under the table and Kat thought, not for the first time, that love didn't always need to burn. Sometimes it could simply warm.

The scene shifted. It was a spring morning in Oxford, and Kat was a young mother. She had just put Mia down for her nap, arms flung wide like a starfish in the cot, one dimpled hand still clutching the corner of her teddy. David was downstairs, pottering about in the kitchen as he made lunch. She heard the phone ring, and moments later the rise and fall of her husband's voice. He sounded happy, but that was David Beauchamp. He was always good-natured.

Kat stood at the sitting room window, her teacup cradled in her hands, watching the pale green leaves tremble on the cherry tree in the small patch of garden. She loved this doll's house of a home, and the life they'd made inside it: the quiet rhythms, the cosy clutter of books and toys and the constant stream of students in and out for tutorials. Still, some days she missed the sun and that other cerulean sky. Sometimes she ached for Mallorca, where the colours were so bright and every day was drenched with warmth. Oxford was beautiful, but it could feel claustrophobic and grey.

David appeared in the doorway. "Sit down a moment, my love," he said. "I've something to tell you."

Kat was always happy to put her feet up. Aimée and Mia were her world, but small children meant hard work and little time to rest. David perched on the arm of the settee and pulled an envelope from the breast pocket of his tweed jacket.

"I've done something without running it by you first. I hope you won't mind, but I wanted it to be a surprise."

Kat's mind was racing. Her husband wasn't big on change or spontaneity. She hoped he hadn't accepted a chair at the other end of the country. She really needed her mother's help with the girls.

"What?"

"This."

He passed the envelope across. Kat opened it and pulled out a piece of paper. It was folded, but thick and stamped with an official seal. She scanned the details, and her eyes widened. "You've bought La Colina?"

He nodded. "It came up for sale. Clara heard, and tipped me off."

Tears filled her eyes. "David! It's just a ruin! Why would you do that?"

He reached for her hand. "Because I know what it means to you. I thought we could make it our place now. For us and the girls. For the summers. For friends, and lazy lunches, and naps in the heat. Joy from a ruin. It seemed fitting, my love."

Kat's throat ached with the rush of memory: dusty olive groves, hot stone beneath bare feet, laughter in the wind, the stars bright in a cobalt sky. Pablo. His loss was softer now, and he was a thread in the tapestry rather than the whole design.

"You bought it for me?" she whispered, beyond moved. David was the best of men and the most wonderful husband. How had she been this lucky?

"For you and for all of us," he said, hugging her. "Hey, it's not an unselfish gesture. I remember how breathtaking that view is. It's a great investment. Seemed the right thing to do with what father left me."

"The girls will love it! We can build a pool. They can plant flowers and play in the garden!" Kat could already see them, their plump little limbs toasted golden and their hair sunshine light.

David laughed. "Slow down, love. It's a wreck, and we'll have to do the work as and when we can afford it, but it's ours and we can do all those things. I know it's special to you, and that makes it special to me too."

"There are memories there of before," she said carefully, wanting to acknowledge the past and Pablo.

"And you will always keep those," David said gently. "But you can make new ones too. La Colina deserves that, and so do you."

They sat quietly, hand in hand, the stillness broken only by the muffled sounds of Mia stirring upstairs, and the spring breeze rustling the curtain. *A new chapter* thought Kat with growing excitement, and the continuation of her story. She couldn't wait to return to La Colina with her family and start to bring the house back to life. She was certain that if Pablo knew he would be pleased. Maybe he would see the renovations from his boat and smile to know that part of their dream had come true.

The memories leapt forward. It was a decade later. The yellow table was on the terrace, listing because the stone paving was uneven, but a beloved and treasured find. Plates were loaded with olives, grilled peppers, hunks of fresh bread and bowls of aïoli. Aimée had written a menu in crayon and taped it to a wine bottle. It was the perfect setting for a lunch party. The pool sparkled beyond, and each time she saw it Kat thought of her late parents, who had never seen this place but whose legacy had paid for so much work to be done. The new kitchen. The French doors leading to the terrace. The garden room, which had finally been given a beamed roof over the spot where she and Pablo had once held one another and gazed up at the stars.

Kat stood in the doorway, watching her friends and family laughing on the terrace. Clara, visiting for a few weeks, wearing a pink kaftan and gesticulating wildly with her hands as she told a story. David in his sunhat, laughing at her, and their new neighbours, the Santiagos, utterly captivated and hanging on her every word.

Mia, ten now, was in the pool with the Santiago twins, splashing and shrieking as she dive-bombed into the deep end. Her daughters' faces were tanned and their eyes shone with sun-warmed happiness. La Colina was filled with joy and friends, just as she had always imagined. The walls were still crumbling in places, the tiles patched with mismatched colours and the old pine tree lopsided, but it was alive once more.

She stepped out onto the terrace and David looked up and smiled at her like he had at the altar all those years ago. Kat smiled back, her heart overflowing with love. She still thought of Pablo, not with pain now but with gentle gratitude. She had loved him wildly, and part of her always would, but this was the life she had built with David, and the view, like that from the terrace, was more beautiful than anything she could have hoped for.

She called her guests and the girls to the table for lunch.

Once they were settled, Clara raised her glass. "To Kat! The Queen of La Colina!"

Everyone echoed the toast and clinked glasses. Kat blushed and took her seat beside her husband, resting her hand on his thigh and letting the warmth of the moment sink into her bones. Their dream had come true.

The memory skipped forwards. It was evening and the light was low, pouring over the terrace like syrup. A yacht slipped into the port like a hand into a glove. The cicadas chirruped softly, and the day's heat rose from the terrace.

Kat sat on the wicker sofa by the French doors with a book open on her lap. Her hair was threaded with silver and there were lines around her eyes. David, emerging from the kitchen with two coffee cups, wore reading glasses and his hair was thin over a pink scalp. For some reason this always made her heart squeeze with love and tenderness.

"One shot," he said, passing her a cup. "The pot's on the blink again."

"It always sulks when the grandkids go."

He chuckled. "Not the cheap beans, then."

"Maybe," she said. "Oh dear, the place seems so quiet without them all."

Aimée and her children had left that morning. The flotsam of jelly shoes, books and empty cups strewn throughout the house, and which Jenny spent hours scooping up, was gone. The house was too silent without their shrieking and squabbling. Kat missed the laughter and the busyness. She missed being a mum with a lively, growing family.

"Do you remember the first time we came here once it was ours?" Kat asked, as they watched the last of the daylight caress the hillside.

David nodded. He smiled into the dusk. "You were clinging

to the girls as though you thought they might tumble down the hill."

"And you pretended you weren't horrified at the state of the place."

"I didn't fool you?"

"No. I had eyes too!"

They laughed. Decades had passed since they had arrived at La Colina, excited and daunted by the adventure that lay ahead.

Kat reached for his hand. "I still can't believe you bought it for me."

David turned to her. His eyes, dimmed now, still twinkled. "Glad I did?"

"Always."

"Glad about it all? No regrets?"

She knew what he was asking, and she squeezed his hand. "Yes, my love. I really am. I don't regret a thing."

The memory jumped forward, the way her old record player used to, skipping words and time but still holding meaning. Now Kat was alone at La Colina. She stood outside by the big front door David had insisted they buy from a reclamation yard, and struggled to turn the key in the lock. It was swollen by salt air and lack of use, José and Jenny insisting on using the back door.

It creaked open and the scent hit her, familiar and filled with nostalgia: dust, polish, sun-warmed wood and time. As she stepped inside, lugging her suitcase behind her, Kat thought how quiet the house was. Although it was still full of them, of him, and the many years they had spent here, it was still. José and Jenny kept the place clean and maintained, but the heart had left La Colina. The clock in the hall had stopped. The cardigan she had worn the previous year was still draped over the chair in the sitting room. The dried husks of last summer's wildflowers, gathered by her granddaughters, drifted petals onto the mantelpiece like tears. La Colina, unvisited for so long, felt as sad as Kat did to arrive here alone.

David had died the previous autumn. Peacefully, with her hand in his and the family close. At his funeral Aimée had read a poem about trees and roots. Mia had played her guitar and sung a song that Clara, long gone, had taught her. They had celebrated David that day, and everyone who comforted Kat said what a wonderful man he had been. The best husband, father, grandpa, teacher. Professor Beauchamp was a man much loved, and he would be missed.

There was a flurry of activity. A time when Kat was so busy she couldn't think straight, let alone mourn, and when the phone had rung constantly. Then everyone else had returned to everyday life and the phone had fallen silent. Kat was left alone, and it had been so hard to wake up every day. She pretended she was fine. Nobody wanted to hear that her grief was so deep and so consuming that sometimes her heart sank when she opened her eyes in the morning. There was a disconnect now between who she really was and the person others saw, which made her feel even more lonely.

There was only one place she could go where she could be herself, a place that had seen her broken-hearted before, and the only place Kat could allow herself to be broken without putting on a brave face. La Colina. Kat knew it was here that she could mourn David and the life she had lost without imposing her heartache on her friends and family. Here she could revisit the past in a way that was comforting and healing. La Colina had healed her before, and she knew it would do so again.

Kat was slower now, and her heart stuttered if she climbed

too fast. She knew that walking up from Andratx would be a struggle. Her hands ached in the mornings. But she had wanted, needed, to see the house again. La Colina was a part of her.

She walked through the house slowly, her fingers trailing over the plaster, the cool marble of the kitchen island, running over bookshelves stuffed with novels, old boarding passes and birthday cards wedged between cracked spines.

She paused by the French doors, looking out over the garden and down towards the olive trees, and thought of her husband standing here while he waited for the kettle to boil, and of Pablo, who had kissed her in the shade of that wise old pine tree.

Two men. Two loves. She had carried them both in her heart for all those years, separate yet entwined. One was fire and one was water. Both were elemental. She was so lucky to have known them.

The memory faded. The bright light against her eyelids was changing. Kat wasn't sure when. The light had been white and the room shielded from the sun by the lowered blinds, but now it seemed golden and she felt as though she was bathed in sunlight. The stillness in the room felt deep, like a lake, and Kat realised she could no longer hear the hiss and sigh of the machine or Tomás's soft snores. Her eyelids fluttered open, and she was curiously unsurprised to see David standing by the foot of her bed. He was never far.

She looked at him, her heart soothed to see the familiar tilt of his head and the soft crinkling of his eyes. He was wearing his tweed sports jacket, slightly too big for him as always, and she smiled.

"Hello, my love," he said.

"Am I dreaming you?" Kat whispered. She wasn't sure if she spoke out loud. It didn't matter. David heard.

"Maybe?" His smile widened. "Or maybe not?"

Kat struggled to sit up, but she couldn't move. "I miss you," her heart said.

"I know," he replied gently. "But I'm still here, Kat. Just in a different way. Love is never far."

He was at her side without moving. She felt him take her hand, or perhaps it was the memory of that hand's comfort she could still feel.

"Is it my time?" she asked. It was odd, but she didn't mind. To follow him now would feel as easy as a hand slipping from a glove.

He shook his head. "No, my love. Not yet."

"But I miss you. It's so hard to be without you."

"Darling, you still have so much to do. The girls still need you. The grandchildren. La Colina. They need you." His gaze was as loving as always, even if the words he was saying weren't what Kat wanted to hear. "There's also a story that hasn't ended. There's someone else who loves you. Who has always loved you."

Kat was confused. "I don't understand."

"You will. And love doesn't end, Kat. It isn't finite. The more we give the more there is. It never ends. Life is bigger than grudges. It's bigger than the past. You've seen that."

The memory flooded. Kat understood. "I'm so thankful for you," she said.

"And I for you." Was that a kiss on her forehead? Kat felt sure it was.

The golden light began to fade. The sound of the machines returned. Rubber-soled footsteps squeaked on lino. A chair creaked.

"I'll be here for you," David said. "Always."

Then he was gone. The light was cool again, the daylight muted by blinds and the bustle of a morning in hospital. Kat opened her eyes and there was a figure beside the bed, but it wasn't David. It was Tomás López.

He rubbed his eyes. "*Hola,* Señora."

"*Hola,*" Kat croaked.

"You're awake."

"So are you," she teased, and he smiled.

"I didn't mean to fall asleep. I was meant to be keeping an eye on you."

"That was kind. You didn't have to."

He looked bashful. "It's going to harm my reputation as a heartless businessman, no?"

"Afraid so," she agreed.

Kat saw Tomás properly now. There was a tenderness underneath the ruthless exterior he looked to present to the world. He was a man who would sit at the bedside of a woman he didn't know. A man who would pass water to her, and hold it while she sipped.

"You came in the ambulance with me," she recalled.

Tomás replaced the glass. "*Sí.* I didn't want you to be alone. I felt responsible."

Kat was quiet for a moment. The monitor bleeped. "Your son wants my house."

Tomás nodded. "Yes. But it isn't for him."

"No," said Kat. "It's for Pablo. You married Pablo de la Vega García's daughter. Isabella de Cruz García. Pablo's the grandfather Rafe adores."

He bowed his head. "I have messed it all up, Kat. My marriages. My relationships with Rafe and my daughters."

Kat told him what David had said. "Life is too short for grudges. It's never too late to say sorry."

Tomás nodded. "I understand, I think. You're the woman Pablo always loved. The one he never got over. Isabella always knew about you, and her mother certainly did."

Kat felt terrible. "Did that make her unhappy?"

"I doubt it. Isabella's parents divorced when she was very young, which caused a scandal, but her mother married again and very happily. She adored her stepfather." He paused. "I need to tell you, Señora, that Pablo García never married again. As far as I know he never had another relationship. He never loved anyone but you."

A tear slipped down Kat's cheek. "That is so sad."

"It's beautiful," corrected Tomás.

"Since when were you such a romantic?"

"Maybe always? Or maybe since last night, when I realised what that stubborn and difficult old man's whole life has been about," Tomás offered. He passed a hand over his eyes and smiled. "It pains me to admire him at times, but Pablo García is a man of strong passion, and he keeps his word. He has 'honour' engraved in his heart – next to your name, I suspect, because you're the love of his life, Señora. You are the woman he never got over, and the one he loves still. I'm certain that Rafe is hoping to buy La Colina on Pablo's behalf and with his own inheritance."

"Could he do that?"

"*Sí*. Isabella was a wealthy woman in her own right, and that inheritance went to my son. I very much doubt Don Pablo knows Rafe has tried to do this for him. He would be furious, despite Rafe's good intentions."

"Pablo never contacted me," Kat said, half to herself. "Not even when his parents died."

"No, Señora. That would not be his way. A vow once made is one he will keep. As I say, a stubborn man."

"An honourable one," Kat flared. She would never hear ill of Pablo.

Tomás inclined his head. "*Lo siento*. He will keep his word to the grave, which may not be far away now."

Kat frowned, and Tomás looked down at his shiny shoes.

"What does that mean?" she whispered, suddenly icicle cold.

"He is not the young man you knew, Señora. Pablo García is old, and he has been very sick."

"I'm not the girl he knew, either," Kat parried.

"He's had cancer," Tomás said quietly. "I cannot say how well he is now, but I think my son wants to help him make his peace …"

His words tailed off. The machines bleeped and hissed in agreement, and Kat closed her eyes as a wave of grief crashed over her. The words of a poem studied a lifetime ago whispered to her: *Had we but world enough and time, this coyness, Lady, were no crime.* At her age the time for being reticent was over, thought Kat wearily. She wondered if Pablo would ever come to understand this, or if the vow he had made to his parents would always stand in his way.

"Oh, Tomás, I'm so sad to hear that," she said. "But don't you see? Neither of us are well, or young, any more, and life set us on different paths – but we're the same inside. That never changes."

Despite the long years apart, Kat yearned to see Pablo García again, if only once more. Even changed as they were, she knew that his heart, like hers, was the same, and she supposed that meant she still loved him. There was something Kat needed to tell him too, something he had to know and something she should have told him over fifty years ago. It would take courage, and Pablo might be angry – or, even worse, not care – but Kat owed him the truth. Maybe she owed it to them both?

Exhausted suddenly, Kat closed her eyes, and the last thought she had before she slipped into sleep was that Rafe was the only buyer worthy of La Colina. He was the one person she would trust with her beloved home. Yes. She would sell to Rafe López, but there would be very exacting conditions to the sale, for La Colina was Pablo's place as much as hers. His memories dwelt there too.

The time had come for Pablo García to return to La Colina and become its guardian.

CHAPTER 26

LILY - NOW

Rafe had lied.

He wasn't who he said he was. The person she thought she knew didn't exist. The man she had fallen in love with and allowed into her heart was no more than an illusion. Was anything Rafe López told her true?

"I don't understand," Enrique was saying to Hannah. "Why wouldn't you want a *chica* to know how much money you're worth? Especially if you're worth the millions and millions Rafe López is worth?" He grinned a slow, wolfish grin that lit up his pale eyes, making him look even more lupine. "I'd be telling all the girls. If they thought I was as rich as him I'd be fighting them off with a stick!"

"And that," Hannah said to Lily, "might explain it."

Lily could accept this, for Rafe had often made comments about true wealth lying in love and friendship. He'd talked at length about his parents' unhappy marriage, his father leaving to marry a very wealthy woman, and how money was his father's god. She also recalled how Rafe had wept when he spoke of his mother's overdose and how he adored his grandfather, who told him true wealth lay in a person's heart. Her heart, however bruised it felt now, still ached for this side of him. But it was one thing to choose not to disclose how rich you were, perhaps to make sure the girl you were seeing was genuine; it was another altogether to lie about your true motives.

Had she been a way for the Lópezes to buy La Colina? Had Rafe and his father hatched a plan to win Kat's confidence by having her, Lily, on side? Were they laughing at the silly English girl who had fallen so easily for the charms of a handsome Spanish boy? And were the nights she had spent with Rafe, nights which had been so special to her, no more than a means to an end for him? The thought made her stomach roil.

"I need to talk to him," Lily said. Her temper was rising to boiling point. "I need to find out what the hell's been going on. He's been playing games, Hannah."

Her best friend hesitated. "I'm not sticking up for him, babes, but I can understand why he might be nervous about telling anyone his real name. He's worth squillions. That kind of money attracts gold diggers."

"I know," said Lily, "but he's also lied to Kat. I think it's all been about Tomás López getting his hands on La Colina. Maybe Rafe never liked me at all. Maybe he just used me."

"No, Lils. I was suspicious of him because I knew something didn't add up, but he's smitten with you. That I've never doubted."

Lily wanted to believe her friend, but all she could think about now was how much Tomás López wanted to buy Kat's house. Everyone knew he was ruthless and would stop at nothing.

"His father's been trying to buy La Colina for ages. Kat's been under so much pressure to sell to him. It's a strange coincidence, don't you think, that I just so happened to bump into his son?"

"But I don't understand how that would work. You don't own La Colina. And he didn't know where you lived when he met you."

"Once I was in the taxi he did." Lily's temper was as hot as the summer's heat. "He was going to ingratiate himself into Kat's confidence and persuade her to sell. God, he must've been laughing at me. What an idiot!"

But Hannah looked doubtful. "Maybe you should ask him what's been going on."

"I fully intend to, don't you worry," said Lily.

She strode down the pontoon towards the gleaming white hull of *Esperanza*, the boat that belonged to goodness knows who. Rafe himself, probably.

"Maybe calm down first, babe," Hannah called, but Lily wasn't listening. She wasn't about to calm down. She was just getting started.

Rafe was sitting on the deck, a hatch open and a coffee steaming gently while he spliced a line. He looked up and, seeing Lily, broke into a delighted smile, but when he saw how angry she was his expression faltered. "What's wrong?" he asked, abandoning the lines and crossing the deck in several easy strides. "What's happened?"

For a moment Lily was lost for words. How was it possible that she could be so angry and yet still love him? Her heart didn't seem to understand that it should turn those feelings off. How could he look the same? Smiling mouth, twinkling happy eyes, those floppy curls? So good-natured, merry, and kind?

"You tell me, Señor López," she spat.

Rafe recoiled. His face paled. "Lily, I can explain."

"Oh, you don't need to," Lily said. She wanted to be furious, and she *was* furious, but tears were already tightening her throat and burning her eyes. Why did she always cry when she was angry? It was so frustrating. "You used me to get close to Kat. How could you, Rafe? I thought you were genuine."

"Lily, I swear that I never used you. Everything I feel for you is real."

She screwed her hands into fists. "Don't lie! I'm not stupid, I know I was your ticket into La Colina. I confided in you how much Kat was struggling and how her daughters wanted her to sell." Her voice congealed with misery. "It was never about me at all."

"No! That isn't true! I was shocked when I realised you lived at La Colina. I've grown up hearing about the place. I've seen it many times from boats, but I never got involved with you because you worked there. I was crazy about you before you even got in the taxi. You had me as soon as you fell over that rope. You must believe me. In fact, it made things so much more difficult to know you lived there. I almost didn't see you again."

"I don't believe you," Lily said flatly. "Your father's company's been pestering Kat to sell all summer."

"There was a reason for that. Please, I need to explain—"

Lily's phone vibrated in her pocket, shrilling 'La Bamba' at full volume. She slid it out. *Jenny*, the screen read. She ignored the call. Whatever Jenny needed would have to wait.

"There's nothing more to say, Rafe. It's over. I don't know who you are."

"I'm *me*, Lily. I'm still Rafe."

Lily's heart felt like it was shattering. She'd been so foolish to believe this was real. Rafe was no better than Harrison. In fact he was worse, because Rafe had pretended what they had was real. Maybe Harrison had pretended towards the end, but when they were teenagers they had been close. There had been love once. But Rafe had used her to try and find a way in. His family firm wanted La Colina, and from what Lily knew of the López company, they wouldn't stop at anything.

He stepped forward. "Lily, please!"

"Leave her alone!" flared Hannah. "Haven't you done enough?"

The phone vibrated again. *Jenny* was flashing on the screen like a shout. Lily wanted to ignore it and continue to nurse this flame of anger, but it wasn't like Jenny to call. Jenny hated phones and barely ever used them. Lily had never received a call from her, even when she was in town and Jenny urgently needed a certain spice or some milk.

"I'd better take this," Lily said. To Rafe she added, "You and I are over. Don't contact me again."

She spun on her heel and stalked back down the pontoon, fighting back tears, to take the call. As soon as she did, she had to hold it away from her ear as Jenny, panic-stricken, was shouting down the phone. It was a torrent of English and Spanish, mingled and incoherent, and Lily had to strain her ears to listen.

Something about Señora being taken ill in the town. Something about the hospital and her heart.

A wave of dread drenched Lily. "Calm down, Jenny. I can't understand you. Please, slow down."

But Jenny couldn't. Her words tsunamied down the line, becoming more fragmented the more distressed she became. She slipped fully into Spanish, and although Lily could speak a little, she couldn't keep up with the rapid-fire stream of distress. All she could glean was that Kat hadn't come home and was in hospital.

Panic spread through her like wildfire. Why hadn't she knocked on Kat's door? The answer was that she'd been so wrapped up in Rafe and her own night that she hadn't even thought of doing so. Oh God. She'd neglected Kat. She'd left her, perhaps lying on the floor—

"I don't understand you," she gasped. "Please, more slowly."

Rafe was at her side. He placed a hand on her arm. "Give me the phone, Lily. Now. It doesn't matter that you're angry with me. Let me talk to Jenny."

He had followed her, Hannah close behind, and had heard enough to know something was very wrong. He was right; this was not the time to argue. Silently, she passed him the phone.

"Hola, Jenny, soy Rafe. ¿Qué pasa?"

Instantly Jenny began pouring out a long, frantic speech in Spanish. Rafe interjected now and again, nodding and frowning. *"Sí ... sí ..."*

Lily tried to listen and glean some meaning, but she was lost. A few minutes later Rafe ended the call and handed the phone back. "Kat's in hospital. In Palma."

Lily felt as though all the air had been sucked out of her. How many shocks could there be today?

"According to Jenny, she collapsed last night at a restaurant in town. A suspected heart attack. They think she's stable now," Rafe said.

"Jenny had no idea?"

"She only found out when she went to clean the garden room this morning and Kat wasn't there. Apparently my father called the ambulance."

Lily stared at him. "Your *father*?"

Rafe looked as confused as she felt. "It seems she was dining with him last night. Perhaps thinking he wished to buy the house."

"He does," Lily said. "I've seen the letters. He really wants it."

"No," said Rafe. "My father has no idea about La Colina.

That was me. I wrote those letters."

"*You* did? No, that's nuts. I saw them. They were from Tomás López."

"*Sí*. That's me. I'm Tomás Raphael López. My friends and my grandpa call me Rafe. No way do I want *his* name."

"I'm confused," said Lily. "Why would you want Kat's house?"

"There isn't time to explain now," said Rafe. "We need to get to the hospital. Kat could be in a bad way. I can explain everything on the way to Palma."

"What do you mean, *we*? I'm not going with you."

"Yes. You are. It's quickest that way."

"I'd rather walk," Lily snapped.

"For goodness' sake!" said Hannah, stepping between them. "Whatever's been going on with Rafe can wait, Lil. Kat must come first. You need to put it all aside and get to the hospital. You're the closest thing she has to family."

Lily's mouth closed. Hannah was right. Her anger with Rafe and his deception paled in comparison to Kat's health.

"Jenny's already on her way," said Rafe. "We'll take my car. Let's go."

Lily didn't argue, and within minutes she was in the front seat of Rafe's Defender, rattling towards Palma. She chewed the skin around her thumbnail, frantic with worry. She realised now just how much Kat meant to her. Kat was her mentor. She was a friend and felt like family. Lily couldn't bear to lose her.

Rafe was focused on the road, threading through the fast-moving morning traffic, but Lily could feel the words building in his chest. She stared out of the window, though everything in her still ached to touch him. He looked the same. He smelled the same. He still felt like the same boy who had held her against his heart and whispered to her the night before.

But he wasn't the same, because he wasn't just Rafe Cruz the deckhand. He was Rafe López, the son of one of the richest men in the country, and he had a whole life she knew nothing about.

"Why didn't you tell me who you are?" she blurted. They still had nearly half an hour. Might as well use the time as a confessional. After today, she was resolved never to see him again, so she might as well leave with answers.

Rafe swallowed. "I hate being Rafe López. You've no idea what comes with that name. The expectations people have when they hear it. They think they know who you are, what you care about, and what you can do for them." His dark eyes darted to her, then back to the road.

"People are hard to trust, Lily. When you're born into wealth like I was, how do you know who genuinely likes you? Who really wants to be your friend? How can you tell them from the ones who only want you for your money or your name?"

It was a fair point.

"I understand," Lily said softly. "But you led me to believe you were working on a boat that belonged to somebody rich. That you lived with your grandfather."

"Both those things are true. *Esperanza* is technically my grandfather's boat, and I use it in the summer. And yes, I live with my grandfather. He's old and quite poorly. He raised me, Lily. I absolutely adore him. So did Kat once."

"Who is he?" she asked, but something inside her was already whispering the answer.

"Pablo de la Vega García," Rafe said quietly.

The final piece clicked into place. Pablo was Rafe's grandfather. Of course.

"My grandfather knew La Colina when it was a ruin," Rafe explained. "He fell in love with a girl there and he has such fond memories of it. He's talked about that house my whole life. When I was younger, and Mama was still alive, we'd holiday in Sant Elm at Pablo's house. It's long gone now, but I loved staying there and being out on the water. My grandpa would point up at La Colina and tell me that was where he spent the happiest times of his life."

Lily nodded. Kat had said something similar.

Rafe's voice grew quieter. "His parents didn't approve of the girl he loved, and his own mother was sick. He married my grandmother instead; family expectations were high, and my grandmother was from an old family who supported Franco. Back then, Lily, it was a huge deal whether or not your family had supported his regime. Grandpa and my grandmother divorced only a few years later, and caused a big scandal. After that, he became reclusive. He was rich, very rich, but he was sad. Grandpa always says wealth is measured by what's in our hearts, not our wallets. He said love was the most precious thing of all."

Lily's mind was racing. Kat had repeated this too.

"My grandfather never held grudges, and he never resented his parents," Rafe continued. "And my grandmother was well looked after with her divorce settlement. She died many years ago, a happily married woman. But now my grandfather's very ill, and I don't know how long he has left. What I *do* know is how much La Colina meant to him, so when I heard in the town that the owner was thinking of selling, I decided I'd try to buy it."

"But why doesn't *he* buy it?" Lily asked.

"Grandpa always said he'd made a vow to his parents that he would never contact that girl again. I did ask him once why he kept that promise even though they were long dead, and he looked so disappointed that I'd even needed to ask. A man's word is holy, he said, and if you cannot trust it, then he possesses nothing of value. He also said that he loved that girl so much that he'd let her go to live her life. He knew she was happily married and although he never found love again, he was so happy for her."

Rafe flicked his eyes to the rear-view mirror, overtook a Mini, and pulled back in. Then he said quietly, "Lily, my grandfather was in love with Kat. That is why he would never dream of contacting anyone to buy La Colina."

"Pablo García," she said. "Kat told me about him."

"I only met Señora Beauchamp when I came up to La Colina to find you, and I knew then why my grandfather loved her," Rafe said sadly. "She is everything he always told me she was. I didn't know she was widowed until then, but even so I knew Grandpa would never approach her. He's old-fashioned and if he promised never to contact Kat, that's what he would do. So, I decided to buy the house for him. I wanted him to be able to return, and I knew he would be broken-hearted if a developer bought it. I hoped too, I think, that he might meet Kat again and put that part of his life to rest."

It all made sense to Lily, apart from one detail. "But why pretend to be your father?"

"Technically I am also Tomás López."

"That's a cop-out, Rafe."

"*Sí*. The truth is that my father is powerful. People listen to him. I knew if a López made an offer, it would be taken seriously. Without it, I was just another person. Rafe Cruz is nobody."

"That's not true," Lily said softly.

He gave a humourless laugh. "I spend most of my life trying not to be Tomás López, but the one time I tried to be him, that name destroyed the most precious thing I've ever found."

Lily stared out at the road, blinking back tears. They were

getting closer to Palma. She could see shop signs, the glint of building in the distance, *apartamentos* clustered like Lego bricks beside supermarkets.

"I never wanted to be Tomás López the Second," Rafe said, his voice low. "My father and I haven't spoken in years. He made my mother so unhappy. I've had little to do with him."

"So, Pablo means the world to you."

He nodded. "He is my true father. The money? It's been a curse."

"Wealth doesn't define us," Lily murmured. "But what we do with it does."

"That's what my grandfather says."

Lily's head was spinning. Rafe had wanted to do something for his grandfather, that was all. Something important before Pablo grew too sick to appreciate it. He'd lied because he'd been afraid. He was as torn and confused as she was, and simply trying to figure out the right course of action.

As everyone was.

"I'm truly sorry, Lily," he said. "I would never have lied to you if I didn't feel I had to. I know it'll be hard for you to believe me now, but everything I said to you, and everything I feel for you, is real. I'd give up all my money in a heartbeat to have back what I had this morning. When I kissed you goodbye, I was the richest man in the universe. Without you? I have nada."

His voice was hoarse with misery. Lily knew he meant every word, for Rafe's sadness was so palpable it filled the car.

"I wish you'd told me who you are," she said sadly. It would be hard to get over this.

"Would it have made a difference?"

There was a heartbeat's silence.

"That's my answer, then," he said wearily. "Of course it would."

He was right; it would have made a difference. Lily had been bruised by her encounters with wealthy people like Samantha. She'd seen how the rich played hard, and rode roughshod over others. She'd watched wealthy young men like Rafe take their pick of beautiful, leggy blondes, and knew they didn't choose girls like her. Lily would never have approached him or let herself believe he could be different.

And that was when it hit her; she would have stereotyped him. She would have judged Rafe as just another vacuous, supercar-driving rich boy, just like all the others who loved their fast boats and colonised the bars. She wouldn't have given Rafe López a chance to show her he was any different. But when she glimpsed it from his perspective, the world turned inside out.

"I'm still me," he said quietly. "I'm the same person."

She didn't reply. There was so much to absorb.

They turned off at the next exit. Rafe guided the car through the busy morning traffic, following signs to the hospital. The sun glinted from the cars snaking in front of them, and he reached for his shades.

"I'm the same person, Lily," he said hoarsely. "I'm the same Rafe who loves to swim, and fish, and kiss you, and watch the sun go down while eating *churros*. That's who I am. You know me, and you're the only one apart from my grandfather who ever has. I love you, Lily. That hasn't changed. I am like my grandfather; I love deeply, and nothing changes my heart."

He sounded broken, and there was a deep loneliness in his voice. It was the isolation that huge wealth brought: the shifting sands of never knowing who to trust, and of being left with nannies and staff paid to care for him but not to love him. She heard the deep sadness in his words, and it cut her too. Only Pablo had loved him, until Rafe had allowed himself to let her in.

Lily closed her eyes. She loved him too. Could they move past this?

"I'm sorry I was so angry," she said. "I was hurt. I felt like I couldn't trust you."

"I'm sorry I lied," he replied. "After what you'd been through with your ex, I knew I'd messed up. I just didn't know how to get out of it."

"I bet," said Lily. "You'd have to have come up with something good. That massive superyacht outside the harbour takes some explaining."

He gave her a small, lopsided smile. "Maybe I'd have pretended I won the lottery."

"And were just humble crew because you gave all your money to the poor?" Lily raised an eyebrow.

"La Colina would've taken every penny of my inheritance anyway. Once I'd bought that house for Pablo, I would've just been Rafe with the boat."

"I really liked Rafe with the boat," Lily whispered. She drew a deep breath, poised to dive, and placed her hand on his knee. The relief of touching him made her giddy. "But do you know what? I think I like Rafe who would do anything for his grandfather even more."

Rafe's hand moved from the wheel to hers, and he raised it to his lips.

"Once we've finished here, I want to tell you everything," he said as they pulled up outside the hospital where ambulances waited and medics hurried by. The real world beckoned them.

Lily slipped her fingers from his. She knew this would have to wait.

"I'll listen," she promised. "But for now, let's find Kat."

CHAPTER 27

LILY - NOW

The glass doors swished open in front of her. Lily froze, her stomach twisting into a knot that held her back from crossing the threshold. The doors sighed shut, then opened again as two medics strode through, clipboards in hand, their purposeful conversation carrying them past without hesitation. Lily envied them their certainty. She felt utterly lost.

Out here in the sunshine, everything was still the same. Kat was alive, well, smiling at La Colina. Jenny would be setting the yellow table for lunch, José trimming the olive trees beneath his battered straw hat. Lizards would dart across the terrace while gulls swooped to drink from the pool. The world would turn as it always had, so long as Lily stayed outside. But the moment she walked through those doors, everything could change.

She wanted to keep the summer exactly as it was.

"What if it's bad news?" she fretted.

Rafe took her hand, and she didn't pull away. He didn't try

to tell her it would be fine; he didn't offer hollow comfort. Lily knew he understood she was fighting her own fear.

"What would Kat do?" he asked quietly.

Lily didn't need to take time to consider. *Kat faces everything head on.* She stared down fear, made impossible choices, and never wallowed. She hadn't shied away from meeting Tomás López; she had confronted it, even while grappling with her own mortality and the heartbreak of leaving La Colina. Kat was no victim. She met life with strength and grace, and Lily admired her more than she could ever say.

"She'd walk in with her chin up, ask to see a doctor, and demand the truth even if it was the worst news."

The sunlight caught in the waves of Rafe's dark hair as he pushed them back, his eyes steady on hers. "So, are you ready to do the same for her?"

Lily lifted her chin and squared her shoulders. It was a poor imitation of Kat's poise, but she was determined to honour her friend. No tears. Not in public.

"*Vamos*," she said.

The hospital lobby was a swirl of hushed voices, brisk footsteps and antiseptic air. The smell alone tugged her back to the days of her godmother's illness, and she almost turned and fled. Only knowing that Kat needed her made Lily stay. Jenny and José were family, yes, but they weren't here yet, and Kat's daughters were far away. Clara would tell Lily to buck up and she would be right. Lily sent her godmother a quiet promise that she wouldn't leave her dear friend alone.

Rafe made a quiet enquiry at reception, the raven-haired clerk lighting up under his gaze. He thanked her politely, then turned to Lily. "Room 353. Second floor. Cardiology. She's allowed visitors."

"That has to be a good sign," Lily said hopefully.

"I hope so," Rafe murmured, his tone far less certain.

The lift crawled upward. Lily's heart thudded louder with every floor and with every step they took towards Kat's room.

As they reached it a tall man turned from the window opposite. "*Hola,* Rafe."

He was in his mid-fifties, maybe older, but age had only burnished his Mediterranean features. His expensive linen shirt was rumpled, his greying hair tousled, and shadows beneath his eyes betrayed a sleepless night. There was a powerful presence about him, and he possessed the same commanding bearing, the same firm jaw and the same dark intensity as Rafe.

Lily knew before anyone said it. *Tomás López.* Rafe's estranged father. For a long, brittle moment, neither moved. The silence thickened.

"Father," Rafe said at last.

They shook hands stiffly, as though strangers, before Rafe turned to Lily, his jaw tight.

"This is my father, Tomás López. Father, this is Lily Wilson. She works for Señora Beauchamp."

Tomás inclined his head, his dark eyes tired, yet striking. Then, unexpectedly, he smiled, and the sudden warmth was like lightning breaking through a storm. "*Encantada,* Lily. Delighted to meet you."

Lily blinked, dazzled.

"Señora Beauchamp has spoken of you," Tomás added.

"She's been talking?" Lily gasped.

Tomás's smile softened. "Awake, demanding tea. Very English. And furious at not being discharged. She insists she has things to do, and no time for lying in bed."

Relief swept through Lily so fiercely she almost hugged Tomás.

Only Rafe's tense expression held her back. "What

happened?" he snapped. "I know you were with her at the restaurant. Don't pretend otherwise."

Lily flinched. She had never heard that edge in his voice.

Tomás only shook his head, then launched into rapid Spanish. The tone wasn't angry, more frustrated, tinged with resignation, but respectful. When at last he stopped, Rafe translated.

"He says Kat collapsed after their discussion. He called the ambulance. He thought it was a heart attack."

Tomás nodded gravely. "It looked like one. Very distressing. But the doctors say it was a severe attack of angina. Painful, frightening, but not fatal."

Lily pressed a hand to the wall. "Thank God."

"*Sí*," Rafe agreed.

Tomás's smile was weary. "But a warning. She must take it seriously, or next time …" He let the thought trail.

Lily's knees weakened. The fear she had carried crashed over her. Kat *would* recover. That was all that mattered. Everything else could wait.

"She hadn't been taking her medication," Tomás went on. "The doctor said a collapse was inevitable sooner or later. It wasn't meeting me that made her sick, no matter what the rumours say."

Lily almost smiled when he mocked himself, but Rafe's scowl deepened. "It wouldn't have helped."

"She was anxious about meeting me," Tomás admitted. "For some strange reason she thought I was there to buy her house. I had no idea what she meant – unlike you, Raphael."

"That misunderstanding is my fault," Rafe said quietly. "I made the offer because—"

Tomás lifted a hand. "No need. Kat and I pieced it together. But what struck me most was not the business. It was when I mentioned your grandfather. That truly shocked her, and she collapsed."

Rafe groaned. "Pablo's name, after all these years, must have been too much."

Tomás spread his hands. "They were once lovers, yes?"

"*Sí*. He's loved her all his life. And kept his word never to contact her again. Even though it broke them both."

Tomás grimaced. "That man. So proud. So stubborn. So bloody-minded."

"Don't insult him!" Rafe flared. "Grandfather is the most honourable man I know."

"I agree. But pride and stubbornness are still his, and ours." Tomás studied him intently. "You tried to buy La Colina for him, didn't you? To give him back his heaven. And you used our name because yours alone wasn't enough."

Rafe's shoulders sagged. "*Sí*. He's very sick. I thought if he could spend his last days there …" His voice cracked. "I only wanted to help. Instead, I've made everything worse."

Lily's heart ached. His grief for what hadn't yet happened was raw, familiar. She knew too well how death looming on the horizon clouded judgement.

Tomás looked away. "Sometimes our best intentions carve the deepest wounds. What we hope for twists and misfires, and we destroy what we most love. To be the architect of your own heartbreak is an exquisite punishment."

The quiet between father and son throbbed with unspoken things: regret, compassion, recognition.

Rafe turned to Lily. "I'm so sorry I hurt you. That was never my intention."

"I know," she said softly.

Before she could say more, a nurse bustled out of Kat's room. "Señora Beauchamp is doing well," she said in brisk Spanish.

"*Gracias*," Tomás replied, and the relief lit his face, startling Lily with how much he suddenly resembled his son.

"*You* need rest, yourself," the nurse scolded. "Up all night! You'll be no good to your mother if you collapse."

Rafe blinked. "Your mother?"

Tomás coughed. "It was the only way they'd let me stay. I couldn't leave her alone."

The nurse smiled warmly. "He's been a wonderful son. He wouldn't leave her side."

"Please," he said. "People will think I have a heart. Terrible for business."

"But good elsewhere," Rafe said quietly.

The nurse tapped her clipboard. "One visitor only. No excitement, no agitation. She needs calm."

"I'll go to her," Lily said quickly, before either López could make things worse for Kat. "You two can go and get coffee."

Tomás raised an eyebrow but inclined his head. "Shall we, Rafe?"

It was more than an offer of coffee, and Lily held her breath until Rafe, after a pause, nodded. "Sounds like a plan."

He turned to her, his expression hopeful. "Later, please let me explain further. I want to make this up to you."

Lily saw the honesty in Rafe, and she knew he wasn't Harrison. Unlike her ex, Rafe meant it.

"Yes," she said. "After this, we'll talk."

Lily wasn't sure she could promise more than this. Trust was hard to build and easy to shatter, and whether she would ever feel able to trust Rafe López again was a question she still couldn't answer.

CHAPTER 28

LILY - NOW

Lily stepped into the darkened room and was alarmed to find Kat propped up in a hospital bed surrounded by an array of monitors. Although she was pale and looked dreadfully fragile amid the wires and the drip, she beamed at Lily.

"Look at me, causing all this excitement!"

"Is that what you call it?" Lily scolded, taking a seat at the bedside. She was relieved to find Kat in good spirits after what must have been a terrifying ordeal. "Poor Jenny's practically having her own heart attack, and so is José, since she's making him drive through the rush hour traffic to Palma."

Kat grimaced. "Oh dear. They'll probably end up in A & E. He's a dreadful driver these days. They didn't need to worry. I don't need all this fuss. I do hope they haven't called my girls?"

"Kat! Of course they have. You collapsed and you're in hospital. We're all worried sick! We thought …" Her voice caught.

"Oh darling, don't look at me like that. I'm not about to

shuffle off yet," Kat said, her voice a little weaker than usual but still laced with its usual determination. "It wasn't the big finale, just a spot of angina. Apparently, my heart fancied being dramatic, just like the rest of you, it seems." She reached out, her fingers trembling as they curled around Lily's hand. "It looked far worse than it was. Poor Tomás López is way more shaken than I am. I've told him that if he invites a woman out for dinner, he should expect some excitement."

"He's still here. He travelled here with you in the ambulance!"

"Yes. He sat with me all night, it seems. Extraordinary, don't you think? He's not the man I thought he was."

"It's a family trait," said Lily darkly.

"Ah," said Kat. "You know, then."

"Yes." Lily swallowed, suddenly close to tears. "I found out this morning that Rafe is Tomás López's son. The person I knew, the deckhand who loved to be on the water, was nothing more than a fiction."

Kat looked sad. "Oh, my dear. I'm sure that's not true."

But it was true. Lily was overwhelmed by a surge of loss for the Rafe Cruz she thought she'd known. She'd fallen for the merry sailor with salt in his hair and the ocean in his soul. The wealthy heir to a property empire was a stranger. Rafe might say that she knew him, insist he was still the same person who kissed *churros* sugar from her lips and floated beside her in empty coves, but to Lily it felt as though she had lost that perfect boy, if he'd ever existed.

"He was never that person, Kat. Rafe Cruz didn't exist. But Tomás Raphael de Cruz López does, and he kept his identity a secret. We all thought it was Tomás pressuring you to sell La Colina, but we were wrong. Rafe was hoping to buy La Colina for his grandfather."

"Pablo," Kat said quietly, her expression unreadable. "After all this time."

"You know?"

"Tomás and I put the pieces together over a very good bottle of red. I think he was even more confused than I was at first, until it became apparent what had happened. He looked so upset, the poor man, and this morning he said he feels utterly responsible for my welfare. I told him not to be. None of this is his fault or Rafe's."

"It *is* Rafe's fault." Lily protested. "He's lied to all of us."

"Oh darling, is that how you see it? That must be unbearably painful."

Lily blinked away hot tears. The hurt of the deception stung like seawater on rock-grazed knees. "Rafe lied to you and to me. When you found out, you collapsed."

"No, Lily!" Kat's voice was firm. "I collapsed because I haven't taken my medicine properly and managed my health. I sunk half a bottle of Burgundy on just a few olives and some calamari rings, and with the shock of hearing Pablo's name uttered out loud after so long, it's not surprising it was all too much." She squeezed Lily's hand gently. "I'm not angry at all with Rafe, and neither should you be."

"You're really not?"

"No, darling. I'm touched. Imagine, after all these years, that Pablo remembers me and our time at La Colina. That he told his grandson stories about it and pointed out the house from their yacht. That Rafe cared enough to try and bring something back for him isn't business or a calculated deception: it's *love*." Her gaze softened. "Rafe sounds as thoughtful, as loving and as romantic as his grandfather." She gave Lily's hand another squeeze. "You're a lucky girl. Don't throw a chance of happiness with a man like that away because of one mistake, or because of pride."

"But he lied. Like my ex did!"

There. The real issue was uttered and acknowledged.

Kat leaned forward, tugging wires and tutting at the tangles. "Rafe is not your ex-fiancé. He hasn't cheated on you or told you countless lies or deliberately chosen to do so. That dear boy must have been so torn. He had a plan, a kind one, and a mission to do something for a man he regards as a father. It was all going so well until love was thrown into the mix and everything was turned upside down. The poor lad! What could he say to you without giving himself away?"

"He could have asked Pablo to approach you." Lily wasn't prepared to let Rafe off the hook so easily. Kat could go all misty-eyed if she wanted to. *She* wasn't the one whose world had been upended.

"Ah, but he couldn't, said Kat. "You see, Pablo swore he would walk away from me and marry the girl his father had chosen. So that was what he did."

"But his parents died years ago!" Lily didn't understand, and was frustrated by what she saw as inertia on Pablo's part. This business of 'walking away' was semantics, at least as far as she could see. "If he was divorced and his parents dead, surely any vow was null and void?"

But Kat thought very differently, and was shaking her head: "It was a political alliance, and the families were linked for years afterwards. Honour is something old families hold dear, and Pablo kept his word to his father, even after death and divorce. He accepted that he had made his choice. He would never dream of approaching me."

"His marriage didn't work out!" Lily cried. It seemed such a waste to her. "Maybe he wanted you to find him?"

"But *my* marriage did work out," Kat reminded her sharply. "Of course I never sought Pablo out. I loved David. Pablo kept his vow, which probably sounds old-fashioned, but speaks volumes about him and why I loved him so very much. He's honest and true to his word. He would never dream of approaching me. He walked away, as he'd said he would."

"But *you* could have contacted *him*," Lily said slowly. "That wouldn't have meant breaking the vow. *He* married the girl they chose, and *he* walked away from you. That would mean that he never broke his word. He never promised you wouldn't find him."

The older woman laughed. "You sound like a lawyer!"

"It's technically true."

"Yes, I guess so. Technically at least," agreed Kat. "But I was very happily married, and I had no need to seek Pablo out. I thought of him sometimes and wondered, but I had made a wonderful new life with David. I know now that Pablo was divorced not long after his daughter was born. He never remarried, and from what Tomás tells me, he's been alone ever since. He could have broken his word, I suppose, once the Garcías were dead, and attempted to rekindle our love affair – but wouldn't that have been selfish? And changed who he was?"

Lily nodded reluctantly. "I guess so."

"True love meant leaving me to be happy, even if that happiness came at the expense of his own. Love meant being there for his mother. Respecting the choices he had made. Putting himself last. Love isn't black and white, my dear. It isn't simple. Or always pretty. It's painful. Cruel at times. And it's bloody messy!" Kat paused. "It's putting yourself last."

Lily had a lump in her throat. Kat was right; love wasn't always about grand gestures. Harrison had been great at those. He loved making a show of what a devoted boyfriend he was. In the end, that had been meaningless.

Love was to be found in the small things. A bag of sugar-dusted *churros*. Coffee made just right. A hug when you felt sad. Love was found in gestures that went uncelebrated. She looked down at the white counterpane. Her sense of hurt remained, but her anger was faltering.

"Okay, I get that Rafe wanted to do that for his grandpa. But would Pablo want La Colina after all this time?"

Kat smiled. "Some places don't let go of you. They're part of you and your story. You see, La Colina was where Pablo and I dreamed of the life we wanted to lead. It was where we were alone. Where we went to make love."

"Kat!" Lily was taken aback, and Kat laughed.

"You youngsters, did you think you invented sex?" she teased. "Pour me some water, dear. I feel as hot and bothered as you look!"

Lily did as she was asked. Kat sipped quietly for a moment before placing the glass on her tray and settled back against the pillows. Seeing Lily was recovered, she continued with her story.

"So, La Colina. That place holds so many memories. Sad ones, yes, but so much joy too. Maybe Rafe wanted to give those back to his grandfather, and for his grandfather to end his days in a place he loves."

Lily nodded. These were questions which only Rafe could answer.

Kat smiled sadly. "I can't imagine Pablo would want me now, or hope to rekindle our love affair. We were over a long time ago, and our story is told. You can't recapture the past, no matter how much you might want to – but Rafe hasn't learned that yet."

This was true. Rafe wouldn't be able to recapture what they had shared, either. If Lily continued to see him, they would be starting again and from somewhere new. Their blank piece of paper was now ink-spotted and curling around the edges.

"He *used* me."

"Oh, do buck up, Lily. You don't really think that's true, and neither do I. Not for a second. That young man cares for you. I saw the way he looked at you. That said it all." Kat shook her head. "Rafe may have borrowed his mother's surname, but his feelings were his own. Can't you find it in you to forgive him?"

"It hurts, Kat." Lily could still feel the sting of his betrayal. "I can't believe Rafe didn't tell me. Or even you. You might have sold to him if you'd known the truth."

"Rafe couldn't tell you. He couldn't tell me either. Don't you see? Pablo had sworn, all those years ago, that he'd walk away. Rafe was trying to honour a promise his grandfather had made in a very different world." Kat paused, trying desperately to reach for the right words. "It wasn't a lie. It was a kindness, however clumsy and ill thought through. He must have been torn. He wanted to do this for Pablo, a man he loves dearly, even though he knew it could cost him the girl he loves. He kept his grandfather's vow for him. He's loyal and true, Lily, so you make sure you hold onto him. Men like Rafe are rare treasures."

Lily sat in silence. The low hum of hospital machines filled the space between them. Her fingers were laced tightly in her lap, but her shoulders had dropped. Her outrage dissolved a little more with every word Kat said.

"I don't want to be angry," she said eventually. "Not really, but he let me fall for him. And I have, Kat. I'm in love with Rafe. Properly in love. The kind of love that makes everything feel possible. He made me realise I'd never been in love or loved before." She gave a resigned laugh. "When it all came out, I felt like the ground had shifted under me."

Kat reached out, brushing Lily's hand with her fingertips. "That feeling means it mattered. And it means it still matters."

"You think?"

The older woman regarded her with utter certainty. "Rafe didn't lie to trick you. He lied because he didn't know how to tell the truth without breaking something sacred. That conflict he felt? You think it makes him weak, but it doesn't. It makes him like Pablo."

Lily looked up, surprised. "Really?"

Kat's eyes were cloudy with memories. "Pablo loved me enough to walk away and leave me to be happy with David. That was the shape his love took, and it cost him his own chance of happiness. Rafe wanted to find a way back to what his grandfather had lost before it's too late. He's torn, yes. He's made mistakes too. But he's not false. Neither man is."

Lily exhaled. She was wrung out. "Then I was wrong. He wasn't using me. He just didn't know how to choose both things."

"And he doesn't have to," Kat said gently. "Tell him you know what he was trying to do, and why. Tell him you understand and still love him. The rest will come. Trust me." She passed Lily a tissue.

Lily blotted her eyes and sniffed. "When did you get so wise?"

"I'm not wise. I'm all in a dither since I heard Pablo's name. I might be almost eighty, but I'm still the same girl inside. There's a piece of wisdom for you; the outside changes, but we remain the same underneath."

Lily considered this. It made sense, since she still felt sixteen. "Do you still love Pablo?"

"I think part of me will always love him. He was my first love, and we didn't part because we wanted to, so our story never finished. We never had the chance to see where it might end."

"Would you have left David for Pablo if he'd come back for you?"

Kat frowned, her hand pleating the sheet. "I hope not – but who knows? I loved Pablo with everything I was."

"I know you loved David," Lily said carefully. "And you seemed happy. Were you?"

"Very happy. But it was a different kind of happiness. And a different kind of love."

Lily was quiet. She knew Kat wanted to say more and she waited.

"I've never told anyone this," Kat continued quietly, "except for Clara and, later on, David –but that summer changed me in every way. I never told Pablo, either. If I had, it would've changed the course of both our lives. He would have married me – but it might have felt as though I'd forced his hand, and I was afraid he would've ended up resenting me. I couldn't have lived with that."

Lily leaned forward. Parts of the puzzle were clicking into place. "I think I can guess."

"I'm sure," said Kat. "You see, by the time Pablo left I'd found I was pregnant. He went back to Barcelona to care for his mother. She was very ill. He loved me, but things were complicated. His family had strong ties to Franco, and there were whispers even then and dangers."

"Did you think about going after him?"

"Every day. But I didn't. I couldn't. Not with his family's people watching me.. I couldn't go home either. In the early seventies an unmarried mother would have caused a scandal, and I didn't know how to weather that."

"It wasn't really that long ago – but it was so different," Lily reflected.

"It really was," Kat agreed. "I did know one thing, though. I wanted that baby. I loved it with all my heart. I wanted it. I loved it as fiercely and completely as I loved Pablo."

Lily reached out and took Kat's hand. The skin was thin, and the plaster securing the cannula puckered it like tissue paper caught by Sellotape.

"I told Clara first," Kat said. "I borrowed Francisco's scooter and went to find her. I was terrified, but Clara was magnificent. She didn't flinch. Just poured me a brandy and said, 'Well then, if you're determined to keep it, let's work out what to do.' She said I could live with her for as long as I wanted, and she would help. We made plans. I was going to raise the baby, find work, be a mother. I didn't care what people thought. I was determined to do it."

She stopped. Her voice caught.

"But one day I lost control of the scooter. A sharp corner. Gravel. I wasn't even going fast. But I fell." She placed her palm gently against her hip, as if she could still feel the bruises. "I sprained my wrist, and I thought that was all, but later that night I began bleeding."

Lily let out a small gasp.

"I lost the baby," Kat said sadly. "And something inside me broke. I don't remember much of the weeks that followed. Clara said I didn't speak for days. I couldn't face the guesthouse, so I moved in with Clara. Maria and Francisco were already uneasy because of Pablo's family, and if they suspected what was wrong with me that was shameful to them – a girl under their care getting into trouble – that would have been unacceptable to them. The summer ended, and the autumn arrived, and then winter approached and I was still at Clara's house. I couldn't bear to leave Mallorca, because I had lost everything. How could I go home? I wasn't the same girl. I thought my life was over."

"It must have been awful." Lily thought this put her anger with Rafe into context.

Kat stared at the drawn blind; her face unreadable. "Yes. And this was when David came."

"David Beauchamp? Your husband?"

Kat smiled. "Yes, my darling husband. Clara and he were old friends, and he was having a sabbatical to work on his thesis. He'd helped me get the job here in the first place. I knew him back in Oxford when I was a typist. He was a kind, shy academic. Polite to a fault. He came to Casa Cielo Azul and stayed in the guest room with the sloping ceiling, next to mine. He must have heard me crying, but he never asked questions."

"And he helped you?"

"He became my friend," Kat said simply. "He sat with me while I cried. He brought me notebooks and pens and said, 'Write it all down.' He thought it would help."

Lily nodded. She understood how pouring words onto the page soothed the soul. She'd be writing reams about Rafe.

"He'd drive me into town and read the paper while I drank coffee. We'd sit in silence on Clara's terrace. I cried, and he let me. I told him everything and he didn't judge. Gradually I felt myself mending. I was like a vase, Lily. I was repaired, but the damage would stay there, and anyone who looked closely would see cracks. I knew I was damaged goods, but David didn't see me that way. He thought I was more precious for the mending, and he didn't care about the cracks. He said they made me who I was. He loved even the damaged and flawed parts of me. That, my dear, is what love is."

"Wow," said Lily. She had often wondered about the man who smiled out of so many photographs at La Colina. He had looked kind, and now she knew just how warm-hearted he had been. "He was out of time for the seventies."

"David was out of time wherever he went," smiled Kat. "He was the most generous and kindest of men. Not a pushover, mind, but never one to judge. He was easy to love, even though it took me a while to recognise that it was love I felt for him."

There was a long pause. Lily waited.

"It wasn't like it was with Pablo," Kat said finally. "Not fire and lightning. It was more like sunlight coming through shutters. I'd never expected to feel love again, but I did. I went back to Oxford and took a job in his department, typing papers and helping with admin. The job my mother had dreamed of for me. David and I were engaged the next Easter, and two years later we were married."

"And you were happy?"

Kat nodded. "Oh yes. David loved me with his whole heart. There was no part held back, and I loved him dearly in return. He bought me La Colina because he knew I loved it, and he never once asked me to forget Pablo. He understood. That's what made him extraordinary."

She fixed Lily with a steely look. "Don't turn love away through pride. If your Rafe is as wonderful as Pablo, hold onto him. He will love you until his final breath."

"He lied about who he was."

"No," said Kat firmly. "He's himself. Rafe is the man you know. He's still that man, and Rafe López too. We are all many people, my dear, and many versions of ourselves. He's Pablo's grandson. Hold him close, Lily, for men like them are rare, and they don't come along twice in a lifetime."

Lily nodded. Kat was right about men like Pablo being rare. She was right, too, about Rafe; he had been caught up in events he couldn't have foreseen or explained without breaking a promise made over half a century before – but she was wrong about something else: it seemed that a man like Pablo García *could* come into Kat Beauchamp's life more than once.

If Rafe did buy La Colina, maybe this time Pablo García wouldn't have to leave.

CHAPTER 29

LILY - NOW

The solicitor's office was cool and quiet, worlds away from the sun-bleached bustle of Palma's streets. Here the air didn't smell of hot pavements and fumes, but hung almost heavy enough to see, weighted with the aroma of aged documents, beeswax polish and decades of deep thought. An ornate wood-and-brass ceiling fan clicked and circled in an endless rhythm. A stately clock ticked a steady heartbeat from the far wall. A pen scratched on paper. Even the shrill of a phone from the office next door was muffled by heavy panelling. It felt to Lily as though the entire room was designed for waiting with breath held while important matters were concluded, and although the air conditioning was arctic, perspiration glued her dress to her skin.

It was hard to imagine what could be more important than what was happening here today. In just a matter of hours, the future and the past would hold hands. Old wrongs would be righted. Past sadnesses soothed. Grudges and estrangements healed. Lily was beyond glad that the process was almost completed. For a while, she had wondered whether it would be, and everything had felt as though it was precarious, the future dancing on the head of a pin as the past overtook the present to shape it into a new form.

Pablo and Kat hadn't seen one another for over fifty years, but as soon as this paperwork was concluded and the legal process signed and sealed, they would inevitably meet again at La Colina. Neither had instigated contact yet, but this would change once Rafe became the owner of Kat's beloved home. What happened next would be down to them, but Lily hoped they would choose to see one another once more, if not as lovers, then as long-lost friends who shared a bond so deep that not even half a century could dim their memories of that time together.

Kat's and Pablo's hearts had been broken decades ago. As the years passed, those wounds had inevitably healed, but faint scars remained. Kat and Pablo had thought their story written long ago, with the final chapter penned, the last page turned, the narrative concluded and *The End* scrawled beneath it.

Maybe this would have been the case if Rafe hadn't decided there was to be an epilogue. If Kat had been shocked to learn it was Pablo's grandson who wished to buy La Colina, Pablo himself had been utterly floored by the news. Rafe told Lily that Pablo couldn't even speak, and for a moment, Rafe had been afraid that his grandfather was angry.

"I thought I'd made a big mistake," he said to Lily. "Grandpa stared at me, and I did my best to explain why I wanted to buy the house. I said I knew what it meant to him, and that I'd met Señora Beauchamp. He had to sit down, and when he recovered, he asked so many questions about her. He was like a drowning man gasping for air."

Lily's throat tightened. "He still loves her."

"*Si*," Rafe agreed. "He's loved her all his life."

The shocked Pablo had no idea that his grandson had

listened so attentively to all his stories about La Colina. Nor had he realised that a love story left behind in the seventies had touched Rafe's heart so deeply and shaped the man he wanted to become – a man, Pablo had said, that he was so proud of. When Rafe explained how buying La Colina would preserve it from developers like his own father, and added that Kat agreed, and supported the sale, Pablo had buried his face in his hands.

"She forgives me?"

"She was never angry with you," Rafe assured him. "She said she's never blamed you for what happened then. Not once. She would love you to return to La Colina, if you feel you can and are strong enough to travel. She wants to show you how she cared for it and made the dream come true. The circle, she says, can't be completed until you do."

Pablo wept then, and through his tears had told Rafe to buy the house with his blessing.

The López family had access to some of the best property lawyers on the island, and Tomás had helped Rafe navigate the mechanics of the sale. Father and son still circled one another warily, but there was communication between them now, and respect.

Lily saw the similarities in them: both were determined, stubborn and passionate. She suspected these traits meant they were destined to lock horns from time to time. But she noticed, too, how Rafe listened to Tomás, took on board his experience and advice, then added his own opinions to ensure that his voice was heard and that Tomás respected his input. Something was softening and changing between them, and when Tomás joked that Rafe would soon be ready to take over the business Rafe had laughed too, but had not dismissed the idea.

Like his father, Rafe had made mistakes, and Lily knew he

could see how doing the right thing could lead a man to make choices that rippled outwards and stirred all areas of his life. She had forgiven him and understood why he had hidden his identity, but it had taken a huge effort on her part, and a leap of faith too. Trust was fragile, and rebuilding it would take time. Rafe understood that Lily was hurt. She hadn't pushed him away, though. She knew she was still in love with him, and her time in Mallorca had taught her that when love came you cherished it. That didn't mean giving it a hall pass, as her ex had believed, but it did come hand in hand with accepting that you loved a human being as flawed and fallible as yourself, and that listening and forgiving were just as important as attraction and moonlight kisses.

Wow. Lily was so glad she had met Kat Beauchamp. This summer – the first, she hoped, of many here – had taught her so much. Most of all, it had taught her about herself. It had shown her the strength she possessed and her capacity to love, and it had given her the confidence to respect herself. Whether or not she and Rafe had a future together was unwritten, and she was looking forward to finding out – but it wasn't just him that Lily had fallen in love with this summer: it was herself as well.

Lily felt sure that Clara would have approved.

There was another benefit to her being able to move past her own injured feelings; Rafe seemed to have a little more compassion for his father. Rafe had said that if Lily could forgive him for having hurt her so badly, he knew he could find it in his heart to begin to forgive Tomás. Mistakes, he realised, were easy to make and hard to correct.

"He's messed up, but he's human. And there's another thing. My grandfather doesn't blame him for what happened to my mother, so it's time I did the same," he said one evening when they were lying on the deck of *Esperanza* and watching the stars create a join-the-dots picture in the inky sky.

Lily hadn't said anything. She reached across and held his hand as the boat rocked them gently. She knew how much it had cost Rafe to say this, for the narrative of Isabella García being driven to take her own life by Tomás' absence had underpinned Rafe's entire worldview. Having spoken to Tomás more in the past few weeks than in a lifetime, Rafe had learned that the marriage hadn't been easy. Tomás admitted he had made mistakes – and Rafe recalled his mother leaving several times to set up home with a new lover, leaving him with Pablo while Tomás was away working. Rows had followed, followed by making up, then more rows. Isabella would party and drink, and Tomás would walk out. Then the cycle would begin again. It had been unbearable for all of them. Nothing was black and white. The cliché about shades of grey was often apt; people are flawed and narratives subjective.

"Not that I'm letting my father off completely," Rafe remarked. "He's already told me that if I change my mind about setting up a trust for La Colina, he has a wonderful development opportunity for the site that will quadruple my investment! Never turn your back on my Tomás López."

"Leopards and spots," Lily said.

Rafe kissed her. "Another English saying. I will know so many by the time I visit the UK. Ducks to water. Raining *perros y gatos*! You like animals, as a nation!"

"You're coming to see me in the UK?" It was terrifying how happy this thought made her.

"Try to keep me away," he said.

When Kat was home from hospital, Lily confided that she still believed there could be a future with Rafe. Kat was pleased: "I see Pablo in him," she remarked, which was high praise indeed. "He was a wonderful man."

"But what about David? You loved him too. Wasn't he wonderful too?"

"Of course! He was my other great love. How lucky I've been, to find great love twice! I can never, ever regret my wonderful marriage to David. That was the bedrock of my life, and we built a beautiful family together that we adored and treasured. Events had occurred that brought him to me. I couldn't understand them at the time, my dear, but perhaps we're not meant to understand. I was so very happy with David."

She could, though, Kat said, now grieve for the baby she had lost and the others that could have followed, and grieve for the years with Pablo that had been stolen, and for the lost life that might have been.

"Who is to know if we would have been happy? Life is full of possibilities and sliding-door moments into other lives – as you can testify, my dear!"

Kat leaned her elbows on the yellow table, her eyes trained on the constant movement of the port and the shifting hues of the sea. Tomás López's vast yacht was still moored in the deep waters of the outer bay, and Lily needed to pinch herself frequently to believe she had eaten dinner there several times now. Hannah had laughed very hard when she heard that Enrique had arrived to fetch Lily for a drinks party; Rafe, however, was unimpressed. There were too many people on a ship this size, he whispered into Lily's neck as they stood on the deck and looked across the dark water jewelled with lights from the decks to the slumbering hump of Dragonera. He preferred a boat where they could be alone. As he kissed her and she trembled like reflected lights on waves, Lily had agreed.

So yes, life was wonderful. It was filled with adventures and love. She knew now that it spun on one in a million million possibilities: catching her foot in a rope, coming home too early, a lost child in a crowd, a scooter losing purchase on a gravelly road, an art class attended at random by her grandmother … all these things had led to this point, and spotting the gleaming white square of Samantha's house squatting above the yacht club, Lily shivered. How incredible that these apparently unconnected events could change a life so much.

"Maybe our relationship would have ended naturally?" Kat mused.

"Or maybe you would still be married now, and sitting here together, sipping wine and squabbling contentedly while your grandchildren splash in the pool." Lily could picture a universe where that had happened too. But then – no Rafe. No being here right now. If she thought too hard about it all it made her head ache.

"The tragedy was that Pablo and I never had the chance to find out. It's the wondering that hurts and the feeling that something's missing," Kat explained. "There was also the danger that when life is tough, you start to yearn for the maybes of the past. But Lily, you're blessed because you and Rafe *do* have that chance. You can discover if you'll be together for a season or for a lifetime. That's a gift from the gods, not to be taken lightly."

And Lily agreed; it was. She would see where life took her and Rafe, because they were lucky. They had a chance to find out. The summer was ending now, and the time to move forward was close. This was no longer a thought that filled her with sadness, for endings could lead to wonderful new beginnings. They weren't always sad. Sometimes they were right and necessary.

That was another lesson Lily had learned from Kat. There had been so many that she hardly recognised herself these days. She liked the person she was becoming: a woman who knew her own worth, who valued herself, who wouldn't be bullied by people like Samantha or accept second-best, counterfeit love from men like her ex. A woman willing to give her heart but without giving herself away. A woman who could listen, understand and forgive – for love was, as Kat had said, messy.

It was messy and complicated and utterly wonderful …

"You're miles away," said Rafe. "Admiring the ocean?"

He and Lily were standing beside the barred window at the far end of the solicitor's office, staring out at the tiled rooftops and towards the glittering sea. She knew he ached to be on that water and heading towards the horizon, the wind snatching his hair as *Esperanza* sliced through the waves. He longed to be free to be himself again. Not Rafe López or even Rafe Cruz. Just Rafe. A man who loved the water, sugary *churros* and her.

"Thinking about heading out to the horizon," she offered.

He nodded. "Maybe we will, once this is over."

A leather folder sat unopened on the partner's desk. It bore Rafe's full name. The solicitor, a slender Mallorquín woman with horn-rimmed glasses and the quiet authority of a professional who had seen generations squabble over property, adjusted her chair and opened the folder.

"Shall we begin?" she said, gesturing to the pair of seats set out to face the desk. "Only a couple of signatures, and we'll be there."

Rafe turned to Lily. The look on his face was one of relief. "At last," he said.

They crossed the room to sit opposite the solicitor, and Lily tried hard to keep her legs from jiggling. This was partly excitement and partly nerves. So much rested on what happened next.

"This document," the solicitor said, glancing between Rafe and Lily, "finalises the transfer of ownership of the property known as La Colina, located in Andratx, from Mrs Katalina Beauchamp to Mr Tomás Raphael de Cruz López." Her accent wrapped the names in a musical elegance, but the eyes behind the glasses were sharp. She continued to explain the legal terms: the transfer of deeds, the precision of boundaries and registries, the clauses placed into the legal work on Rafe's instruction, and their implications.

Rafe sat still, only the tightening of his jaw betraying his nerves. This purchase had cost him every cent of his inheritance from his mother, but Lily knew it was about far more than money. It was about safeguarding a memory and thanking a beloved grandfather. Most of all it was about setting the past free.

She listened, struggling at times because the solicitor spoke in Spanish, and although her own grasp of the language was improving, there was no way it was good enough to keep up with legalese.

Rafe reached for her hand and held it tightly. "If we could continue in English, please?"

"Of course." The solicitor swapped languages with an ease that Lily envied. One day she vowed she would be able to do the same. She wouldn't be a Samantha, shouting and complaining if menus weren't translated.

More explanations followed of how the transaction would proceed. Clause after clause followed, and even though they were now explained in English, Lily still felt lost.

"Clause 17," the solicitor read, her tone softening. "The vendor, Señora Beauchamp, shall retain the right to reside at La Colina at any time, for any duration, for the remainder of her life. The property shall remain her home, in spirit and in function. No changes may be made to its structure or significant interior without her written consent. Are you happy to proceed with that clause, Señor López? It is highly irregular."

Rafe cleared his throat. "That clause stays exactly as it is. It's non-negotiable. That's the only part I ever cared about."

The solicitor nodded, satisfied. "It will be binding, as you wish."

Outside, the faint rumble of traffic bounced against the stone buildings. Rafe's grip on Lily's fingers was vice-tight. She knew how much he wanted this part done. It would free him.

The solicitor turned to the final page, her finger running down the margin and resting at the halfway point. "There is one more clause I wish to clarify," she said. "Clause 18."

"Ah, yes," said Rafe. "That's very important."

The solicitor read the clause aloud.

"It is the express wish of Señora Beauchamp that Señor Pablo de la Vega García, grandfather to Señor Tomás Raphael de Cruz López, be permitted full access to La Colina for the remainder of his life. He may visit, reside, or stay for any duration, without condition or restriction. The house is only sold to Señor López on that proviso. La Colina is not only a property, but a memory held in stone. Señora Beauchamp insists it will always belong to them both, even when they are long gone."

The words spun in the air like dust dancing in a ray of sunlight. They were beautiful and magical. Lily closed her eyes and hoped she wouldn't cry.

The solicitor continued. "And finally, upon the death of Señor Pablo García, La Colina will be held in a private trust for the López family in perpetuity. It shall never be sold. Its purpose is preservation. It is, and will remain, a protected home. A part of Mallorca's heritage."

Silence followed.

Lily's throat tightened. Her hand, clasped by Rafe's, was numb in his grip. "Not just a house, but a past forgiven and a love story enshrined," she said.

"*Sí*," he said. "Finally Grandpa can make his peace with the past."

The papers were signed with quiet ceremony: first Rafe, then Lily as witness, and finally the solicitor. Now all they needed was for Kat and her supporters to do the same. By midday, said the solicitor, the contract would be completed.

Rafe and Lily thanked her and headed outside. The sun was climbing to full strength, casting shadows across the venerable stone of the courtyard, and light bounced painfully from white stone and bright awnings. Palma buzzed around them, mopeds whining in the distance, the clink of cutlery from a café terrace and the shout from a street vendor.

Lily tilted her face to the light, her eyes closed. "I still can't quite believe you're about to be the owner of La Colina."

Rafe gave a soft laugh. "Only on paper. I'm just a broke guy with a boat and a house I can't ever sell."

She looked at him. There was no hint of laughter and she realised that Rafe wasn't teasing. "You gave your inheritance up for La Colina."

"I didn't want my mother's money. I wanted *her*. I never wanted any of the family baggage."

"And is your father okay with that?"

Rafe shrugged. "We've said what needed saying. We'll never be close, but we're not fighting any more. That's enough. One day I'll have to think about the rest. Not today, though."

"The company is your inheritance. You're a López." Lily was worried. This was a world she knew nothing about. It was filled with power players in suits who flew to meetings in private planes or were chauffeured about in sleek cars. This was the world Rafe had been born into, but it wasn't her world, and it never would be. His father's yacht was impressive, and the luxury that accompanied the López family was seductive, but it wasn't a life she aspired to. It felt suffocating, and she knew she wouldn't fit in. Would Rafe resent this? And would she, in turn, feel as though she were a burden?

Rafe turned to her, brushing her hair gently back from her face. "If I had to choose between being a López or being the man on the quay that you fell in love with when you tripped over a rope, I'd choose that man. Every time. Without thinking."

Lily swallowed hard. "You're sure?"

"Lily, I'm never more myself than when I'm with you. When we're together I'm me. In the sun. On the water. In that office out here. When I'm with you, I'm who I want to be."

She wound her arms round his waist and rested her head against his chest. They held each other, still in the bustle and oblivious to the noise and heat. His heart beat steadily beneath her cheek, and she knew they were going to be fine.

Then a thought occurred. Lily stepped back and placed her hands on her hips. "Hold on! Who says I fell in love with you when I tripped up?"

Rafe grinned, that slow and slightly lopsided grin that melted her and made her smile too. "Come on, Lily. It's true. That was how it was for me. Was it not the same for you?"

What was the point of pretending? "Yes," she admitted, as they linked hands and strolled towards the car. "Of course it was."

They drove home, chatting about how they had met and making plans for what might come next. The road from Palma to Andratx curled through the hills, olive groves blurring in the golden light, and the land, terracotta-hued, darkened to deep green where pines began. Summer was beginning to loosen its grip. There were fewer tourists now, and a hint of coolness in the early evenings. Lily leaned her head against the window, watching the landscape roll by while Rafe drove, one hand on the wheel, the other resting gently in hers.

By the time they reached the port the sun had turned the water to diamonds. Fishing boats steamed in, pleasure boats bobbed in their berths, and a few visitors sat beneath striped awnings sipping cocktails. The rhythm of the town was slowing for siesta.

They walked the familiar path along the harbour, hand in hand, past shuttered shops and restless boats. Then down onto the dock, where Rafe's boat waited. He helped her aboard with a smile and untied the ropes, and within minutes they were sliding out into open sea. The wind caught her hair, and Lily laughed for pure joy at the freedom of heading out into open water.

Behind them, the coastline stretched out like an invitation to reach for new adventures. Above it, perched on the headland, stood La Colina. Its apricot walls glowed in the light, the blue shutters thrown open to the sea, and the old tower stood guard as though corsairs might come marauding in at any time.

Rafe glanced down at his phone, then back up at the house. As if reading his mind, a text message buzzed.

"Noon," said Lily. That solicitor was good. "La Colina is yours now."

"No," Rafe replied. "It's theirs. It always was, I think. David Beauchamp and I are its guardians, but La Colina is Kat and Pablo's."

"Yes." Lily knew he was right. The circle was completed.

He turned to her, serious now. "I know summer's ending,

and everything's changing. Kat will go home. Jenny and José will take the rest they've earned. The tourists will leave. And I'm not staying, either."

She looked at him, puzzled. "You don't want to spend time with your grandfather? Be at La Colina with him?"

"No. This is *his* time." He swallowed, suddenly looking nervous. "Lily, I want a La Colina of our own, and I want to sail away and find it with you beside me. Will you sail away with me, Lily Wilson? If you will, I don't need houses or inheritances. I'll be the richest man alive."

For a moment, the world stood still. The sea, the boat on the waves, even Lily's breath was motionless. The answer she gave would determine the course of her life, change her future, and lead her away from everything she had known before. Was she brave enough?

Then Lily realised she already knew her reply. She had known from the moment she tumbled into this man's life that she would sail over the horizon into a new future with him.

"I will," she whispered. "I'll sail away with you, Rafe López."

As they sealed this promise with a soft kiss, La Colina watched over the boat as it danced towards the horizon. Keeper of the past and guardian of the future, it would hold their story in its walls. Lily glanced up at it, the windows twinkling like smiling eyes, and the walls glowing, and knew the old house was sending its blessing as they made promises to sail towards something that would be forever their own.

CHAPTER 30

KAT AND LILY - NOW, THE FUTURE

Kat sat on the terrace as the sun began its slow descent, encasing the hillside in amber, and making La Colina's walls glow. The autumn breeze stirred the olive branches, soft and familiar, and the old pine sighed longingly. Kat echoed its yearning, and her heart was fluttering with a nervousness that made her wonder whether she had somehow slipped back into her twenty-one-year-old self. She had dabbed jasmine perfume behind her ears and on her wrists, shrugged on Clara's peacock kaftan, kept carefully all these years, and let her silver hair spill over her shoulders. The scene was set. She was ready.

Kat did not rise when she heard voices – Jenny and José welcoming the new arrival – and the footsteps on the paving did not cause her to turn around. She didn't need to, for she knew who it was. She had known he was here before the old door knocker had sounded, for every cell in her body had rejoiced at his closeness.

Kat was almost afraid to look up, now that the long-awaited moment had arrived. Had it come too late? Would he recoil at the sight of this older woman, with her lines and white hair and stooped gait? Or would he see the girl he had loved? Twenty-one-year-old Kat? The fiery twenty-one-year-old Kat who was yelling at her to jump up and greet him: *You've been waiting for him your whole life! What are you waiting for? This is it!*

She was right: this was it, but now that the moment had arrived, she was afraid. This meeting was the distillation of everything she had felt. It was the overdue conclusion to something that had been ended too soon. It was an ending which had scarcely enjoyed a beginning.

Pablo was returning to La Colina.

And maybe to her.

He hadn't broken his promise to his parents. It was the other way about. Rafe had given Pablo's email address to Kat, and knowing how conflicted he would be she'd written first, a short but warm message which conveyed her delight at being in touch, hinted at her sadness at the twist of Fate that had kept them apart, and thanked him for his greatest act of love – allowing her to live a full and happy life with another man.

Her letter had opened the floodgates. Calls. A flurry of emails. Cards from him, and flowers too. His words conveyed his deep affection and a promise that La Colina would always be hers, no matter whose name was written on the deeds.

'It's yours, Haystack Girl. La Colina knew you straight away,' he wrote.

''It's ours,' Kat had typed back, knowing David would understand and approve. 'We found it together, remember?'

'I remember,' Pablo had replied almost instantly.

Kat's heart soared higher than the gulls when she read the rest: 'I remember everything, Haystack Girl. Maybe not what I had for breakfast or where my glasses are, but I remember and cherish every moment we spent together. They were the happiest of my life.'

He had glasses. He was forgetful. More evidence that they were not the same people as before. Their emails grew longer and more detailed until Kat could tell him everything. She confessed the truth about the baby and its loss, and the guilt she still carried for riding the scooter, and she asked for his forgiveness.

When Pablo's reply arrived, her stomach knotted. Would he be angry? Bitter? As she opened the email, her hands shook.

'My dearest Katalina,

My heart broke to hear what you endured, and that you had to bear it alone. You carried that worry and grief for me, and I wish I could turn back time, so you never had to suffer. I wish I could have held you and grieved with you for our little star who never got to shine, but I know is the brightest in all the heavens.'

As she read on, the screen blurred. Kat wept – loud, wrenching sobs that brought Jenny running. But Kat could not explain herself, or tell Jenny that these tears were almost sixty years overdue. All she could do was cry for the baby she had lost, the future she had imagined, and the boy who had been forced to walk away. They had been so young, so malleable. She understood how Pablo's father had manipulated him through his mother's illness, and now she understood, too, how vulnerable all of them had been under the weight of family and culture and society's expectations. Franco's regime had cast a long shadow; it was impossible to explain just how afraid people had been.

She wiped her eyes with the tissues Jenny handed her.

"I've been in touch with Señor García," Kat said, her voice hoarse. "He wants to come and visit."

Jenny looked alarmed. "And you don't want him to, Señora?"

"No," sniffed Kat. "Quite the opposite."

"*¿Que?*"

"I want him to come very much," Kat said, suddenly realising the depth of her longing for him. "I've been waiting far too long."

And now he was here, at La Colina once more. Kat felt him arrive before she heard him. It was a frisson in the air, and a soul recognition as instinctive as breathing.

Pablo de la Vega García.

She turned, knowing this moment had been written a lifetime ago. He had always been meant to return. His curls were silver now, and time had curved his back, but his eyes remained the same – steady, sherry warm and deep as the sea beyond. They might have dimmed, but to Kat they were the eyes of the boy who had once made her feel like the world was turning just for her.

Pablo approached slowly, leaning on a cane. His hands were bruised and his once strong frame was frail, but to her he was still beautiful.

He was still Pablo.

"I didn't leap the wall, Haystack Girl, but if it was the only way I could have seen you today I would have tried," he said with the same warm humour and sweet smile that had melted her heart all those years ago.

She rose, and they embraced gently, both feeling the relief of arriving home after a long journey. He was still Pablo, and she was still Kat. Their wrappings had changed, but the essence of who they were remained.

"You look exactly as I remember," he said, his voice warm despite its wear. "You're so beautiful, Katalina."

Kat laughed. They both knew she had changed. Yet, oddly,

he looked the same to her too. Her heart recognised him. It would always recognise him.

"You always were too kind to me."

"Never," said Pablo fiercely. "I wasn't kind enough. I should have fought harder. I should have--"

"No shoulds or coulds," she said. "That's the past. Let's enjoy *now*. It's all we really have. Come and enjoy the view. Is it as good as you remember?"

"No," he said, looking at her. "It's even better."

They sat together on the terrace, side by side on a rattan sofa, with their old ease. The years that had kept them apart seemed to fold in on themselves, and the voices that had railed against their parting fell quiet at last. Maybe this was closure, though Kat. An ending after an ending.

"I love this place. It always feels like home, even though I've lived in Barcelona for many years now," Pablo said softly, watching the water.

"I never thought of you in a town," Kat said, surprised. "I always imagined you as living by the water."

"My house is by the water. It's quite beautiful. You must visit one day."

She nodded. "Maybe. If I can travel there and back without causing havoc."

"Come and don't leave," he said simply.

She laughed. "What, forever?"

"That doesn't sound long enough." Pablo reached for her hand, and Kat felt tears of joy rise at the sweet familiarity. His skin was thinner and the back of his hand bruised, but the sense of rightness was the same as it had always been. Their fingers knitted together with a memory all of their own.

"I believed our time had come and gone," he said. "I never dared hope I might see you again, let alone touch you. It's like a dream."

"Maybe Rafe has brought it back?"

"*Sí*," Pablo agreed. "Maybe so." He stared out to Dragonera, slumbering in the deep water as though waiting to see what events came to pass. "I regret many things, my Katalina, but I can never regret that circumstances brought me Rafe."

Kat squeezed his hand. "I understand. I could never regret my family either."

They sat quietly, looking over the water, powder-blue in the liminal time between day and sunset. Kat knew Pablo was remembering Andratx as it had been – fewer houses, no cranes, no sugar cubes where Casa Cielo Azul once stood – but that town existed only in their memories.

"It is just as we dreamed, isn't it?" Pablo said eventually. "The town has changed, but La Colina is timeless."

"Yes."

"Did you make a garden?"

"I did. I never made bread, though."

"Neither did I."

"Never too late," Kat said. "This is your house now. Bake, dig, plant things. Do as you wish."

But Pablo sighed. "Time isn't on my side."

She nodded. Rafe had told her the bare facts of his grandfather's illness, and Pablo had confided the details. It made her ache with the anticipation of loss. Those bruises and the thinner frame were not all down to age, but these things only made him all the dearer to her. More precious. Life had worn parts of him away, honed others until he shone more brightly and tempered him into steel. Kat had loved the boy so dearly, but she already knew she loved the man just as much.

"Me too. It goes with the territory. You should see the pills I'm on. I practically rattle."

But Pablo looked sad. "I'm not the man I was back then."

"I know," she agreed gently. It was true; although she still saw the boy she had loved in the man beside her, Pablo was also a man who had buried his only child, raised his grandson, and loved her enough to set her free to be happy. "But, Pablo, don't you see? You are so much *more* now than he was then. You have lived a life."

"Could you love a man like that?"

She smiled into his eyes. "I never stopped."

They sat together peacefully as the light deepened into soft oranges and dusky violets. They spoke of that first and last summer, of dream gardens and seventies music, of people they'd loved and lost. He adored the house, and admired the way she and David had transformed it. And there was no bitterness or sadness, only peace.

Later, Kat would show him around the property his grandson now owned. She would explain how their fledging dreams had eventually merged with hers and David's, but there was no rush. She could see Pablo was very tired, and understood he was content just to sit with her and watch the lights of Andratx star the hillside.

"Would it be too forward," Pablo asked finally, his voice barely above a whisper, "if I asked to stay in the garden room with you tonight, my Haystack Girl? Just to hold you once more, sleep with you in my arms and imagine we're young again beneath the stars?"

Kat reached out and they linked hands, their fingers fitting together as though almost six decades had never passed. The lost time made her ache, as did the weariness in his voice. Whatever time remained to them now was a precious gift; Kat would not squander it with quibbles about what was suitable or right.

"Of course you may," she said softly. "Tonight, and always, Pablo."

Far below, Rafe's boat slipped out from the port into open

water. Lily stood at the wheel beside him, her hair blowing in the breeze and her gaze trained on the horizon. They were leaving for a voyage of their own making, Lily to write while Rafe searched for the place that would be their La Colina; while an old love was finding peace at last in a safe and much-loved harbour, new love was setting sail for new adventures.

As *Esperanza* sailed towards the sunset, Mallorca fell away, its cliffs softening in the gathering dusk and the lights of the town growing distant. High on the terrace of La Colina, Pablo held Kat's hand as they watched the boat slip into memory. Another chapter was beginning, just as another closed.

Her last summer and Lily's first, thought Kat, were meeting in the most wonderful way, and carrying them both towards the undiscovered realm that was the future. Who would have ever guessed when Lily and Kat had met, that this random encounter would lead her back to Pablo? Maybe Clara had a hand in it all? Kat liked to think she had been watching over them and was smiling now, pleased to see her kaftan worn once again, her dear friend happy, and her god-daughter loved by a young man who was the best of them all.

The pattern was complete, and it was wonderful. *Life* was wonderful, even when it was tinged with melancholy, and Kat was so thankful for all that she had learned and everyone she had loved between her first and last summer here. Whatever followed next, she felt truly blessed to have this moment. After all, *now* was all anyone ever really had.

Jenny had left champagne cooling in an ice bucket, and Kat and Pablo toasted Rafe and Lily, wishing them luck and happiness. Then they raised a thankful glass to David and to Clara, and a quieter one to other friends and loved ones they'd known, and lost, along the way.

"And to meeting you then and now," Kat said to Pablo finally.

As they chinked glasses, La Colina wrapped the night around them and the years tumbled away. The walls crumbled, bold weeds pushed through the terrace and the roof above the garden room melted until the stars blazed down. The sun slipped into the sea and the day was done; the sun was setting over La Colina too, just as Kat knew it would one day for her and for Pablo. But not yet! There was still so much living to do. So many new adventures to be had. Maybe even love would bloom again this first and last summer …

She smiled at Pablo. Then, hand in hand and without speaking, they made their way to the garden room, to hold one another once again as the stars smiled down at their reunion. As Kat glanced across the water to the glittering town her heart sang, for all her summers at La Colina had shown her that even in the deepest darkness there was, and always would be, light.

THE END

THE END

RUTH SABERTON NEWSLETTER

WELCOME TO MY NEWSLETTER AND POLWENNA BAY

I hope that you enjoyed my Balearic adventure in The First and Last Summer

If you haven't joined already, please feel free to sign up for my newsletter.

You'll get updates on my writing, details of upcoming new releases, exclusive content, and competitions.

Just click the link below
sign up to my newsletter

You will also receive a free download of Polwenna Bay 1, **RUNAWAY SUMMER** and Polwenna Bay 2, ***A TIME FOR LIVING.***

POLWENNA BAY NOVELS

ESCAPE TO CORNWALL WITH THIS FEEL GOOD AND MULTIGENERATIONAL SERIES

🩶 **Polwenna Bay** – open the first page a stranger, turn the last as a friend 🩶

Runaway Summer
A Time For Living
Winter Wishes
Treasure Of The Heart
Recipe For Love
Rhythm Of The Tide
Catching Hearts
Christmas By Candlelight *
Journey's End
The Gift

POLWENNA NOVELLAS

Cornwall For Christmas *
Polwenna Day Trips

The Polwenna Bay books are a joy to write because they bring together many of my favourite novel ingredients – a beautiful Cornish setting, second chance love, conflict and a multi-generational narrative.

If you enjoyed these aspects of my novels, you may also enjoy my Rosecraddick Chronicles, three books which take place between 1914 and the present and are set in Cornwall.

THE ROSECRADDICK CHRONICLES

TRAVEL BACK IN TIME TO AN AGE OF GREAT HOUSES AND DARK SECRETS

Set in Cornwall between the First World War and the present, prepare to lose yourself in a lost world of class boundaries, war and forbidden love.

The Letter
The Locket
Oyster Shore

The Lost Angel (a companion novella)*

PENCALLYN - CORNWALL AT WAR

Set between WW2 and the present, the Pencallyn novels explore the 'friendly invasion' of American GIs to Cornwall and the impact, emotionally and socially, on the local people as well as the aftermath seventy years on. Secrets, forbidden love and betrayal leave a legacy that will last decades...

THE ROSECRADDICK CHRONICLES

OTHER NOVELS SET IN CORNWALL

The Island Legacy
Hobb's Cottage (a novella)

ROMANTIC COMEDIES

Katy Carter Wants A Hero
Ellie Andrews has Second Thoughts
Amber Scott is Starting Over
Dead Romantic
Escape For The Summer
Escape For Christmas *

CHRISTMAS BOOKS

The Season For Second Chances
Christmas on the Creek
Plus all books marked *

Pen Name Books

Writing as Jessica Fox
THE ONE THAT GOT AWAY
EASTERN PROMISE
HARD TO GET
UNLUCKY IN LOVE
ALWAYS THE BRIDE

WRITING AS HOLLY CAVENDISH

LOOKING FOR FIREWORKS

Writing as Georgie Carter

THE PERFECT CHRISTMAS *

For a complete list of my books, click here to visit the My Books page of my website

REVIEWS

I REALLY HOPE THAT YOU HAVE ENJOYED READING THIS BOOK

If you did, please pop a review on Amazon or Goodreads.

Not only does this let the writer know that you enjoyed their work, but it also helps other readers to discover and enjoy the books.

Thank you

ABOUT THE AUTHOR

Ruth Saberton is the bestselling author of *The Letter, Katy Carter Wants a Hero* and *Escape for the Summer*. She has also written a wealth of commercial fiction for major publishing houses under her own name and various pen names including Jessica Fox, Georgie Carter and Holly Cavendish.

Born in London, Ruth now lives in beautiful Cornwall. She has travelled to many places, but nothing compares to the rugged beauty of the Cornish coast which never fails to provide her with inspiration for her writing. For the latest on Ruth and her writing you can also follow her on social media.

Facebook: Ruth Saberton Author
Instagram:Ruth Saberton Instagram
Web: www.ruthsaberton.com

Printed in Dunstable, United Kingdom

72219659R00227